A Fractured Legacy

Book Two

Cristen J. Faulkenberry

DragonNook
PUBLISHING LLC

A FRACTURED LEGACY

THE LENOIR LEGACY TRILOGY - BOOK TWO

Written by Cristen J. Faulkenberry.

Published by DragonNook Publishing LLC.

ISBN: PB: 979-8-9851800-4-6

Cover by Stefanie Saw; Edited by Karen Robinson; Map by Jared Faulkenberry; Chapter Icons by Josh Kaul.

Also By
Cristen J. Faulkenberry

The LeNoir Legacy Trilogy

The LeNoir Legacy

Published March 11, 2022

A Fractured Legacy

Published September 9, 2022

The Remnants of a Legacy

Coming Summer 2023

LeNoir Legacy Stories

The Crown's Inheritance

Published September 2021

The Twin Blades

Coming Spring 2023

Future Stories

Ode to the Lone Soul

Coming Summer 2023

*To my current and future readers, thank you for
joining this journey!*

Hoelia
Alkaan
Algatha
Volante
Jearnia
Andalexa
Lycene
Violet Grove
Hazad
Dasca
Orda'an
Vandyl
Camadad
Delphi
Izari
Tenoa
N
E
S
W
50 miles

PRESSURE

CHAPTER ONE

"Lower your weapon."

Rosealyn's whisper echoed in the large cavern the ancient Magna had once occupied. Water dripped around them, a slow and steady nuisance Rosealyn refused to let distract her from the murderer on whose chest her sword rested. Not that it mattered, not if what Xannan claimed was true. She kept her breathing shallow, believing if her chest moved, Xannan's murky cold blade would pierce her skin. Shivers crawled down her shaking arms. One major event after another had prevented proper rest. She'd had little time to process or to decide what to do.

"I die, you die." Xannan's voice was flat and low.

Rosealyn ground her teeth together at his apathy. He had threatened everyone she cared about: her home, her family, her people. A slight uptick of his lips preempted the lowering of his weapon.

"I'd like to test that theory." Rosealyn willed her arms to stop shaking so she could control her movements. A quick shove was all it would take. It wouldn't be the first time she'd claimed another's life. Of them all, he deserved death the most. After all the lives he'd taken, all those she'd been trained to protect, and now she was stuck in a cave with *him*. None would witness it. The cave would remain empty until Synda returned. If she chose to return.

Her muscles trembled, so Rosealyn gripped the hilt tighter. The sword shimmered, its white crystalline hue fading into the nicks and divots of an overused metal sword. Her father's sword. Her sword. Futurae, Celena had called it. A once-mythical twin blade, designed and forged by the elves, then blessed by the ancient Magna's flame, it held a power none would ever comprehend. An invisible pressure rested on her chest, a ghost of Xannan's sword, where she held the tip of her sword against his chest. Right above his heart, though she doubted he truly had one.

The faint sensation made her force her shoulders back to stand tall, refusing to concede. "What did you do to my home?"

His face was void of emotion, spiking her anger. The tip of his sword digging into the dirt, he rested both hands atop the pommel and met her gaze. "It was not my decision. What happened to Vandyl. Eilon ch—"

"You were part of it." Rosealyn applied a modicum of weight to the blade on his chest.

"You won't apply more pressure," he murmured, his tone even more disarming than when she had first awoken in the cave. Her grip faltered in clammy hands.

Xannan smirked and stepped forward. Her sword shifted backward from an invisible force and clattered to the dirt floor. Her wrist spasmed. Hissing through her teeth, she glared at him and shook her hand to alleviate the tingling. His rising chuckle was cut off by Rosealyn's punch to his face. It hurt worse than the sudden movement of the sword. The man's face was like a rock.

"Feel better now?"

Her punch hadn't moved him. Nor had she felt it land on her own face. *Could the connection be fading? If so . . .*

Fierce anger welled up and she shoved, both hands meeting his shoulders. He stepped backward, his sword clattering to the damp cavern floor next to hers. But she wasn't done. Once he returned to his full height, Rosealyn kicked him square in the chest. Xannan shuffled back several steps, rubbing a hand where her foot had landed. His head tilted, green eyes too similar to her father's in more than just appearance meeting hers.

He spread his arms as though to placate her. "What will this accomplish?"

Rosealyn feinted a punch to his chest and swept her leg into his knees. This time he fell to the cave floor. She smiled and dug her bootheel into his chest, wondering if she could knock him unconscious without harming herself. She paused at an odd realization. The punches, the kicks, inflicting pain on another—none of it alleviated the whirlwind cascading inside her, none of it soothed the rising panic, none of it could bring any of those he'd killed back to the land of the living.

"You've killed." She pressed down with her heel, finding his lack of a pained grunt infuriating. "Murdered. Destroyed." He grasped her boot to push it away from his neck. "You've taken loved ones from families, from friends. You have hurt so—so many."

She lifted her foot, clenching her hands into fists. Tears were forming, and the lump of sobs to accompany those streams was not far behind. Rosealyn refused to let those rivers flow, even as waves of emotions threatened to force her to her knees. Instead, she concentrated on the steady dripping from the cave's ceiling and the metallic, though stagnant, scent.

Xannan stood, brushed off his pants, and retrieved his blade from the cave's damp floor, sheathing it with a fluidity she momentarily envied. "I highly doubt that is the last time you will want to hit me, but it is the last time I will let you succeed."

Her glare slid to him. After a quick appraisal that made Rosealyn want to punch him again, Xannan turned to stand at the cavern's edge where it overlooked a thriving land Rosealyn had viewed just once before . . . before all had turned to madness and insanity.

Grinding her teeth, Rosealyn grasped her sword and stared at his back. Time had passed since the sword had split back into two, and a malicious part of her wanted to slash her sword through his neck. Careful cautious steps, a raised arm, a soft intake of breath, and. . .

His sword blocked hers. "The blades yearn for one another, call to each other. Especially now they've finally been reunited." Xannan turned, pushing his blade into hers. No emotion coated his voice or appeared on his face. "If you wish to succeed in a surprise attack to kill me—which won't work—it will not be with that sword."

Rosealyn opened and closed her jaw, opened then closed again. "It's wrong," she muttered. "Everything. Everything is so, so wrong."

Framed by stark blond hair, a face which looked younger than her own tilted to the side again, the skin of his forehead wrinkling. "What, precisely, is wrong, Princess?"

"Why should I tell you?" She pressed her blade against his. "I'll put up with you for as long as it takes to find a proper way to be rid of you for good."

"We both know you don't have the guts to kill me yourself; otherwise, you would have continued kicking when you knocked me down." His smirk was beyond infuriating, but she could not rebut his stupid logic. "So go ahead and tell me. It appears I'll be close enough to learn anyway."

Rosealyn's head jerked. "Is that still true? The swords are no longer connected?" Their blades remained between them, neither willing to be the first to pull away. She gestured at the swords. "How could you kill Father with that sword, but not me?"

He lifted a shoulder but didn't move.

A low growl crept from her throat. "Obviously we cannot kill the other, at least not with these weapons, but . . ." She tried to hold his stare and cursed silently when she was the first to look away. "You could stay here?"

"Would you prefer that?" His abrupt laugh sounded more haunting than amused. "Save yourself the pain of *killing*?"

Their swords remained pressed against each other, and a soft hum emanated from each in an odd rhythm. Her chest lifted and fell in shallow motions.

Rosealyn wanted to pull away, needed to remove her sword from pressing against his, but it wouldn't budge. They were frozen in a moment in time while the rhythm of the swords' humming synchronized and crescendoed. She tried to step forward, to move, to do anything besides stand and stare as images formed in tendrils of smoke around them.

Small creatures whose vicious teeth dripped with dark liquid ran toward her, disappearing as they reached the now-glowing swords. Visions. That was what Gailin called them in his journals. For him the visions were rare, though he claimed Xannan could relive moments as though he were there, living through them once more. A quick glance at Xannan confirmed he could see them too. Once emotionless, his eyes held a twinge of fear, flinching each time another creature appeared in the mist surrounding them. *If he fears these, after taking down Eilon . . .*

Rosealyn strained against the invisible force, only to be bombarded with a new image. There had to be a way to break the connection, to make sure this murderer got his due end. The mist maintained the image a moment longer, its rendition of their personas uncanny and infuriating. Nothing in this world would make her choose to work alongside him. *Blaze take me, I will not be some training ground dummy for him again.*

The glow faded and the humming diminished until only the sounds of their breaths echoed off the cave walls. Neither spoke for several agonizing moments, nor did they move, swords crossed as though they would begin to spar. The cavern's walls seemed to shrink in.

The shock on Xannan's face mirrored her own. Rosealyn worked moisture back into her mouth while Xannan's gaze remained fixed on the place where the last strange-looking creature had dissipated into nothing.

"What were those?" Even at a whisper, her voice created a booming echo. "What did those visions mean?"

She should have anticipated the ferocity in his gaze, which made her step back.

"Those—" His voice broke and he swallowed. "Those were droki." Xannan glanced around the cave, whispering, "I thought Magna eliminated them."

"How do you propose we understand"—Rosealyn waved her free hand where the faint images had appeared—"whatever that was?"

Xannan shrugged and sheathed his sword, tilting his head from side to side and rubbing the back of his neck. For a time he roamed the cave, as though hunting for something specific, until he paused at the opening's precipice. "How many generations?"

The question was soft, almost a plea. It would be easy to send him tumbling down the cliffside, considering the opening was wide enough for a dragon to enter. But a surprise attack had already failed once, so Rosealyn sheathed her weapon, aching for its continuously soothing touch. Wearing it around her waist helped, but holding the blade helped alleviate the tension in her muscles. When she remained silent, Xannan turned. His hesitant movements made her wonder if he had actually not been unscathed by the battle with Eilon, if the magic of the swords did pull from them both when combined.

"How many generations are between you and Gailin?" Xannan reiterated.

"Why would that matter?" Rosealyn crossed her arms and resisted the urge to stretch her neck.

"Tell me," he growled. "Five? Thirty? I know it's been at least a century since my brother was on the throne, but . . . how many?"

A thought of her father brought the too-fresh pain in her left side and weaker aches as she thought of her ancestors' fatal wounds. A sting in her chest above the heart, an overwhelming sensation of cold, then heat bubbling her skin. Thoughts of Gailin, whose stories and writings she'd studied relentlessly throughout her youth, brought a quietness, as though life released him into death rather than plunged him into it.

After a calming breath to wash away the invisible pains, she said, "Five. Now tell me why."

"Not useless, misunderstood," he mumbled.

Rosealyn inhaled sharply. "Tell me why it matters," she gritted out. He'd been right earlier—she definitely wanted to punch him in the face again. Repeatedly. Since she had no desire to be on the receiving end of such a blow, or bruise her knuckles, she kept her arms crossed in front of her while confusion became rampant.

"You haven't tried to leave this cave, which means you're worried you can't leave me behind and you're afraid to find out."

She opened her mouth to speak, but he held up a hand. There was that void again, the absence of emotion from his features while his tone held an aggravating arrogance, as though he ruled over her.

"Based on what I *can* recall, once the swords combine then the wielders are irrevocably connected."

"Irrevocably?" Rosealyn tensed and glared at him. "As in forever?"

She closed her eyes and counted her breaths, inhaling slowly through her nostrils and breathing even more slowly out through her mouth. The exercise created a low whistle, and she continued for several more breaths until the bubbling pot of her stomach calmed.

"I had no plans to be stuck with you either," Xannan murmured, shattering the calm her breathing exercise had brought. "This was supposed to happen with Gailin, but he always refused. He feared what would happen when the swords connected." He tugged his blond hair loose from its simple string and leaned against the cave wall, continuing to speak without looking at her. "I think you've misunderstood how long the connection lasted. Most of the time, I felt nothing, true. Then I, too, lost consciousness."

"Good, serves you right for how much you ransacked my body with your carelessness."

"It's a limitation," he explained with a heavy sigh she had not anticipated. "One I'm not sure these weapons were designed to have."

Rosealyn shuffled on her feet and shifted her attention to the bright blue sky visible from the cave's entrance. "Synda made the invisible wound's pain of the Passing go away." She gathered her skirts in each hand. "It was not until some time after her touch I even noticed the hum alongside the need to follow a certain path."

"It would have been useful to converse with Magna." He frowned as his gaze bounced around the cave, halting on a rock near the center. "I'm positive I never met her." The frown deepened along with his voice. "But Eilon planted falsehoods amidst reality."

CHAPTER TWO

Synda glided far above the clouds; she had no wish to encounter the other dragons of her home. Not yet. Many would hold her responsible for Magna's death, and some would harbor jealousy of her inheritance. Not would but did, Synda recalled as she tried to suppress the ever-present ball of flame heating the far reaches of her throat. She shook her head in an attempt to alleviate the pulsing. Between finding her flame and gaining such vast stores of magic as Magna once held, Synda found control difficult.

The wind lifted her slightly, and she beat her wings languidly, debating the worth of dipping below the clouds to see the expansive landscape of her home. As Magna's progeny, she had been kept in that cave with the ancient dragon more often than not. Head dipping below the clouds, the ball of flame flared inside her.

A hard swallow which felt like consuming a thousand bones at once eased the flare. Pockets of decay were forming in her home. Only pockets, not widespread destruction like she had seen in her brief glimpses of Orda'an's fields. But they were there nonetheless.

Head and neck shimmying, her flame grew again. Unstoppable this time. Synda lifted her head above the clouds, bracing for the onslaught that would singe the innards of her neck, heat the roof of her mouth, and coat her nostrils with the stench of burns. Gaining her flame had not been as exciting as she once believed it should be. A small pocket of fire released, Synda continued her glide above the clouds, turning west, away from her home to search the other lands.

Moments which felt like hours passed as she beat her wings against the wind. Early winter storms were sometimes entertaining, but not now, not when she needed to know. It seemed too dangerous for all of her to fly below the clouds, so she poked her head through them at intervals. First came the uniform plantations surrounding the sprawling Jearnian castle. The stupid orb of flame quickened its pulsing again as she wondered if those few sections were supposed to be darker than the rest. Next came the dilapidated fields of Orda'an before she turned her attention north. Those lands always remained colder, always found it more difficult to grow crops, but even there Synda found pockets of decay. And more.

A small pack of droki, relatives of the dragons but with no sentience. Their bite or scratch was as deadly as a beheading. One small pack was more than enough for Synda's flame to pulse with a new intensity as Magna's vast store of magic called to her. She pushed it away for fear she would use it wrong again. Celena, and those two who might never get along, would need to know: the land was off-balance.

Blinding red swirled with orange and heated to an intense bright white, forcing Rosealyn to shield her eyes from the onslaught. It spiraled above them, not singeing their hair nor skin nor clothes. Rosealyn held her breath, as though that would aid in protecting her from the swarm, and dared to open her eyes. Flames caressed the walls, dancing around her and dissipating into the open cavern.

A comforting heat lingered as the blinding blaze dissipated, reminding Rosealyn of home, of the warm fireplace in her room. With a quick release of held breath, Rosealyn's gaze found Synda sitting on her haunches near the cave's ledge. Behind the dragon lay lush open land, and Rosealyn swore she could see the moving dots of other flying beasts. But the white dragon, her flame pulsing at the base of her long neck, drew Rosealyn's attention. The dragon appeared larger than before. Soft cloud-like ripples of feathers gave way to leathery scales at the tips of her wings. Paws which no longer appeared too big for her body hid the nubs of her claws until they kneaded the ground in time with her pulsing orange orb. Rosealyn followed the sinews of Synda's neck until she reached eyes of deep violet.

A blink and those same eyes were white. Even without closing her eyes, Rosealyn witnessed a singular image accompanied by a brief piercing pain radiating through her head.

She and Xannan, side by side, weapons poised to meet. Not striking at each other, not attacking, but working together. A frustrated muffled screech clawed at her throat. She stepped back from the cave's ledge, glowering at the dragon and rubbing her temples to alleviate the oncoming headache. Such an image was not what she wished to see, nor did it answer her unspoken question. Sword hilt in her hand, the pain of the image dulled.

"Magic," she mumbled, lifting her face to the tall ceiling of the cavern and tightening her grip on the hilt until the onslaught of the image turned into a distant memory. Inhaling deeply, she studied the calm dragon. Synda nestled her snout into her front paws, violet eyes darting from Rosealyn to Xannan with what could only be described as a scowl. Rosealyn shook her head and whispered, "I have so much to learn about how these weapons work."

"We both do." Xannan moved from his precarious stance. He barely glanced at Synda, as though her arrival neither shocked nor interested him.

At the cave's entrance, Synda stopped kneading the ground.

"I was wondering if the weapon would separate here." Celena's voice came from the dark tunnel behind them. "It was made here, though it appears our dear Lost Prince does not remember this."

"I was there?" Xannan asked too quickly.

Questions roaming through her mind, Rosealyn turned toward him, noting the slight slump of his shoulders, the crossed arms. Something unknown rested behind his arrogant facade. But looking at him made her anger spike. Trapped with a man who no longer knew what he was, trapped with a man she'd planned to destroy. With effort, she resisted pulling her sword on him—again—and shifted the belt around her waist. Muscles groaned with the effort of standing tall and tossing her shoulders back. Aches could be ignored for a display of strength.

"Yes." Celena walked in a straight line to stand by Synda. She rested a loving hand on the dragon's leg, and a softer rumble emanated from Synda. "You, Gailin, your parents. Myself, Arjun, and Arjun's father, Eonar. Along with Magna and Eilon. They created the weapon as a gift, but it was truly forged amidst a battle of wills. Whatever they did unlocked my ability to communicate more directly with the dragons. In a way, I can see their thoughts. Not the images they share with you, but what they think, what they want to say. When Eilon tried to take Magna's magic, she trapped his. The sword was not supposed to split in two, but there was no other way to contain Eilon's magic."

Celena stroked the dragon as Synda continued her appreciative rumble, orange orb ebbing and flowing with the sound.

Rosealyn's hands clenched into fists at her side. She straightened her fingers and crossed her arms, dropping them to her sides to create fists again. Inside her throat, another scream threatened to escape. She swallowed it down and closed her eyes. Rather than scream, or yell, or question, she counted. And smiled. The counting would always remind her of Charles. The thought brought calm and a slight flush to her cheeks when she remembered their hands intertwined, and so close to. . .

"I don't remember that," Xannan proclaimed, disrupting her pleasant daydreaming. "I met no dragon before Eilon. I would remember this cave, I would—"

Rosealyn tilted her head and studied the man standing before her. Green eyes flashed toward her, and her curiosity recoiled into rising rage again.

"What do you remember, dear ancient lost prince?" Celena asked with a knowing smile.

In the few weeks she'd known the elf, Rosealyn had yet to see much emotion. So far it had been simple statements of fact with that cool, blank, unmarred facade.

"Father's bedchambers," he mumbled. "Then darkness. Slivers of light from time to time, memories crowded by tendrils of smoke tainting them." Xannan motioned with his arm at the cavern. "I would remember this place! I would remember my first meeting of a beast the size of Eilon or of Magna!"

"With time, the memories will mend," Celena said. The matter-of-fact tone was gone, replaced with a soothing almost matronly tone that made Rosealyn's jaw drop. The elf-woman *pitied* Xannan; Celena was offering him *sympathy*. "Soon you will know what you did of your own volition and what was by Eilon's command."

Uncertainty tickled at Rosealyn's mind again like a thousand tiny bugs crawling down her neck and into her dress. She could not stop the shudder but tried to turn it into a slight shake of her arms.

"How do we separate the blades properly? So we aren't connected?" Rosealyn asked, gaze darting between Xannan and Celena. He looked . . . distraught.

Celena met her gaze, which made Rosealyn's insides drop before the words left the elf's lips. "I don't think you can."

Rosealyn nearly screamed, vision blurring once more. No matter the sky was a perfect blue, no matter a stark white dragon sat mere feet before her. "There has to be a way!"

"You saw what happened when Gailin asked," Celena reminded her and glanced around the cave with a small frown. "Come, you may rest in Andalova again, though they may not be as kind to offer mounts a second time when their first have not yet been returned."

Rosealyn grunted, adjusting the too-large belt, belly aching at the thought of consuming delicious elven food. She wore the simple pale dress Celena had gifted her in Violet Grove. Similar in color to her favorite beige dress, it enunciated the darker hue of her skin even in the dimming light of the cave.

"Hard to return a borrowed horse when you have no idea how you got to the cave in the mountains," Rosealyn muttered.

The elf-woman smiled, the red irises of her eyes twinkling in the sunset. "True."

All looked to Synda, who puffed smoke through both nostrils and met Celena's gaze.

After a moment's silence, Celena said, "But it was not Synda who brought you both here."

"You really can communicate with her?" Rosealyn asked, trying to think of something to do with her fists besides clenching them at her sides. Angrily punching those around her would not be the best way to get answers.

Celena nodded, staring into Synda's purple eyes, the twinkle of her smile slowly fading into a frown. "Like I said, you may rest at Andalova. Synda will meet us at a field tomorrow. She and I both have ideas which may assist. Somehow, someway, the magic Eilon lost and the magic Magna trapped should be able to be released. But I do not know how, nor do I know what it may do."

Without additional explanation, the elf reentered the dark tunnel. Rosealyn followed after a moment's hesitation, accompanied by a silent Xannan. In the overbearing darkness, Rosealyn wondered how she was to understand a magical entity which wasn't supposed to exist in the first place. More importantly, she wanted to know how to get rid of Xannan for good and survive.

CHAPTER THREE

Pen gripped in one hand, Charles stared at another blank sheet of paper. He thought sitting in Phillippe's study, in the late king's seat, might help him think. Instead, Charles felt guilty.

A chilling wind brushed through the open window behind him, scattering the half dozen crumpled papers littering the broad pale wooden desk which occupied most of the room. He didn't want to send a message with incorrect words or phrases. He needed to be both forward enough Duchess Adela and Dukes Theo and Alan understood his request, but cryptic enough in case the letters found their way to the wrong hands. Charles grunted and shook his head. The dragon which once threatened them lay dead atop a cliff next to the matriarch he'd believed invincible.

Rubbing a hand along his thigh, he massaged the tender skin where Eilon's wing had sliced through and nearly broken his leg. Arjun had remained at Vandyl to aid with healing the wounded during the two days after the strangest battle Charles had ever fought. Small drops of a simple liquid, and wounds knit closed almost as if they'd never been there. The gash in Charles's leg had taken longer to knit back together, the space between the torn skin much wider than what a dagger would leave.

With effort, he avoided rubbing a finger against the scar along his side. A parting gift from his father during the trial which had earned Charles the title of king of Jearnia. A title which meant he needed to return to Volante. Even though he wanted to remain at Vandyl and assist with the repairs, he had other responsibilities. He focused on the blank paper, wrote Duchess Adela's name, and paused.

Steady beats of mallets against stone echoed down the hallways and through the open door of the study. Several sections of the castle needed to be rebuilt. The library, the royal family's quarters, almost half the castle had been lost to flame. Charles listened, grateful the grunts of effort and strain were for a good cause. Moss's voice rose above them, shouting for aid. Azeiah would be proud of how well Moss, young and quick to action, had protected the Orda'anian soldiers in the midst of Xannan and Eilon's attack. Azeiah's death was another reason to find, and annihilate, the Lost Prince, wherever he'd gone.

That thought knocked loose several others as he debated what piece of information to write down first. Xannan and Rosealyn connected. Synda protecting them. Eilon dead. Magna dead. The battle. His wound. The Twin Blades. He had started and scrapped half a dozen messages, crumpling one paper after another. Fragments with scribbled and crossed out lines, none with any vital information, littered the desk and floor, and a few had landed on the nearby shelves.

He leaned forward to write, but someone knocked on the doorframe. The door itself was gone.

Moss stood in a half-bow half-salute, and Charles almost laughed at the sight but winced instead. Though Moss's burns had faded from their angry reds, they would leave the light-brown-haired man scarred in a way that would always age him.

"Aren't you leading the repairs, General?"

Moss straightened. "Aren't you supposed to return home, Your Majesty?"

Charles laid the pen down and buried his face in his hands while resting his elbows on the desk. "I need to." He peeked through his fingers at the blank paper. "First I need to send these messages to

Duchess Adela and Dukes Theo and Alan. I'm just not sure how to explain what all transpired."

Moss shrugged. "General Azeiah always told us to tell the truth, Your Majesty." He snatched a crumpled ball of paper from the floor. As he read the few attempted lines, Moss's lips thinned as laughter danced across his marred face. "And you always instructed me to be direct with my words." An almost indiscernible smirk made his lips quirk up, causing him to wince. "Ironic," Moss murmured low enough he likely thought Charles hadn't heard.

"I'm not sure I've processed the truth myself." Charles lowered his arms atop the table, holding his hands and tilting his head to the side. "I'll tell them of your new appointment as general and how repairs here have begun. Your diagram outlining the new structure was thorough. Subtle changes, but smart. Once finished, there will be fewer points of weakness with the rounded walls."

Moss bowed his head, and Charles twirled the pen between his fingers. "They'll want to know where Rose is, but all I can tell them is I believe she's alive. Where, how. . ." Charles shrugged, and the pen's movement halted. He stared at the silver ring on the first finger of his right hand. A bold flame prominent in its center marked it as his signet ring, though a slightly different model than the one his father had worn, the one which had given him the scar along his chin. "I'll include my full name." He twisted the ring with his thumb. "And title."

"The Dukes and Duchess will appreciate your honesty, Your Majesty."

"Did you need another set of hands for the repairs?"

Moss's gaze flickered between the strewn papers and down, as though he could see Charles's leg through the solid wooden desk.

"It's mostly healed." He massaged his thumb along the tender skin and stood. After a quick glance out the window behind him, Charles suppressed a sigh. He'd sat down when the sun was at its peak, and its rays now coated the horizon in a warm glow. "I should leave tomorrow, unless you need me to stay?"

Though he hoped he didn't sound too eager, Charles knew he did. Returning home meant resuming the mantle of king he'd thought he would avoid. One month had turned into one year and before he knew it, a decade had passed while under Phillippe's protection. He now understood the impact of those years. A twinge of guilt hit him, knowing his people had suffered in his absence. But he would change that. It had to have been part of Phillippe's plan all along. He'd learned to have patience, to think through his decisions, to trust none here would try to sink a dagger into his heart as many Jearnian nobles likely wanted to.

Charles tossed the pen onto the desk, watching it roll to a stop as he shifted his brown hair off his forehead. "Perhaps a stroll will help knock loose the right phrasing, and then they're each getting the exact same message." He skirted around the desk. "Join me?"

Moss crouched to gather the few crumpled papers which had landed on the floor and set them in a pile on the desk. He inclined his head as answer to Charles's question, pausing when they entered the hallway. Several paces to their left, the hallway disappeared, a gaping hole of singed stone in its place. Hallways he'd walked daily for years, all while constantly berating himself for thinking of Rosealyn in any way except his charge to protect her as requested. They turned right, toward the sound of amicable shouts and steady hammering.

"I grew up on a farm before joining the army." Moss paused at the entrance to the garden balcony, frowning at the withered plants. Winter would take hold soon, halting what little growth the foliage still managed. "Almost every day was spent repairing one fence or another." He tapped his sword hilt, surprisingly pensive. "Until it all burned, most of my family with it. My little brother refused to follow me, said he heard of a different army to join, one that would pay better."

Though the revelation seemed out of place, Charles didn't tell Moss to stop. Days of intense emotions and life-threatening dangers dredged up memories. Almost as one, they entered the stairwell leading to what was once the training yards. The ringing of hammers and shouts echoed through the stairwell, increasing in volume until they were in its midst. When Moss halted at the base of the stairs, Charles studied the young soldier, realizing that though he felt he had made friends, he'd always kept them at arm's length. Even after knowing the general for two years, he hadn't known Moss had lost so much.

"For all I know, he's been burned to ash, too." Moss's hand strayed toward the burned skin covering the left side of his face, pausing before making contact. "Seems to be my family's destiny." He gripped the hilt of his sword, swallowing and clearing his throat. "All that to say, I can help others push through the pain of loss, understand how to help heal their wounds. If I may speak openly, Your Majesty?"

Charles chuckled. "You already are, Flynn." Calling the man he had insisted become the general of the Orda'anian army by his first name felt odd, but also necessary. "What more do you have to tell me?"

Moss's flash of a smile changed to a wince. Though Arjun had applied the same healing liquid to Moss's burns as he had to Charles's leg, the damage had already been done. As Arjun had explained, each wound reacted differently, and while he could lessen the damage, burns were always the hardest to heal.

"You have the look of one who's avoiding what needs done, a silent war between what you desire and what is being asked of you. I used to see it on my brother's face when he didn't want to help around the farm." He shifted his weight to one leg and leaned against the door frame while watching the gathered men and women. "I'll make sure the messages get into the appropriate hands, Your Majesty."

"As I was hoping you would." Charles rubbed his chin, wincing at the uncharacteristic stubble prickling his skin. He walked into the courtyard, offering subtle nods to those who paused in their work to offer bows or curtsies. Hammers pounded chisels into stone; several groups of workers rebuilt barracks, and others carried baskets of linens or meager amounts of food. Everyone, including the soldiers who'd traveled with him from Volante, were busy with a specific task. He continued walking, holding himself as he always had during his years at Vandyl, one hand gripping the sword hilt—which no longer needed its leather strips to disguise the Jearnian insignia—the other hand loose at his side. "My offer to help was me hoping for a distraction."

Moss's sharp inhale made Charles lift a brow and turn to the general, who spoke in a soft whisper. "The Jearnian soldiers, though they've been helpful, make many of us nervous, Your Majesty."

Charles pressed his lips together and surveyed those hard at work again. It was easy to locate his soldiers, most of whom wore red-tinged coats several shades darker than his own, and whose skin was a shade paler than the Orda'anians, just like his. "If any of my men do anything out of line, tell me. And hopefully Ashtar hasn't found the alcohol." The former statement earned a firm nod, the latter a slight chuckle. "I plan to leave by midday tomorrow. So put them to good use today, General."

They stood before the empty space where the general's command center once resided. The stone cylinder leading to Vandyl's rarely used dungeons had remained perfectly intact. Several men who had joined Xannan's mercenary army were down there, awaiting whatever punishment their currently absent monarch might give.

As he stared at the stone cylinder, listening to the bustling sounds of a castle at work, Charles said another silent wish for Rose to be alive, for her safe return home. Sadly, the fervent request did not lead to her sudden appearance beside him.

Chapter Four

The journey down the mountainside took almost an entire day and allowed time to think. Too much time, Xannan decided. Try as he might, the memories were just out of reach while he was concentrating on not falling off the narrow path. The elves of the village were kind enough and, unlike the naïve princess, did not glare at him nor threaten to kill him every time he spoke. Since they were not prone to guests, the elves offered one room. Two separate beds awaited, and Rosealyn was quick to claim the one near the entrance.

While the two women whispered by the door, Xannan sank into the bed flush against the opposite wall, lying prone atop the blankets and staring at the ceiling. Decorative vines etched into the wood greeted him, and his mind strayed. He'd seen these vines before. Not a similar design, but. . . he covered his eyes with an arm, trying to shut out the princess's rising aura of anger and worry as Celena continued to speak with her. From what Xannan overheard, they'd been unconscious for two days after he killed Eilon. The journey to Andalova added another day, which was more clarity than how the days beneath Eilon's control had melded together.

Eyes closed, he sought the evenness of sleep, pushing away the idle worry of how he could survive without Eilon's magic. Every memory he dredged up was colored by a black haze, masked by Eilon's desire changing his own. Rosealyn's and Celena's voices continued back and forth—an argument, one the princess wouldn't win. Not that night.

He tried to shut down his senses, to ignore the surrounding room with its soft lighting, its wooden earthy smell; its comforting presence was reminiscent of a life ripped from him before he could understand.

While hunting for sleep, he located dark recesses of his mind, hidden corners where memories lay deep and forgotten, as though someone had pushed them to the brink of existence but could not shatter them completely.

Soon he viewed the same cave where the swords had split, where the young white dragon had found them, and where the elf-woman had questioned his memories only to receive his aggravated scowl. Shorter spirals grew toward those growing from the cave's floor, accompanied by a steady annoying drip.

She was right; all those she had said were there. Eonar and his son who had brought crystals to the fight with Eilon. Xannan grimaced, wondering how it was possible for him to have lived more than a century.

Out of instinct, he reached for the sword hilt but paused. The weapon had changed him. He could see it now, how Eilon's overbearing magic suppressed the past he should have lived. Hints, blurred images showed what should have been rather than what had happened.

It was a vision like the ones he'd seen before, but clearer. No awkward haze at the edge. A sharp clarity. Seeing through the eyes of his younger self, he surveyed the cave with an insatiable curiosity.

He stood opposite the three elves, beside his brother, just behind their parents. Between the two groups was a singular crystalline blade. Crafted by Celena and Arjun before Eonar had provided the finishing touches to the weapon's smooth edges, it shimmered and sparkled, resting atop a cloth patch-worked in black and white squares—the colors his father had chosen for the LeNoir line, for their newly founded country of Orda'an. This weapon, this sword, would be a gift for the peace his father had brought to the vast majority of the continent. Praesidio, a bodiless voice intoned. In solidarity with the elves, and to show their thanks as well, the dragons had agreed to bless the weapon.

Those dragons, those massive beasts whose bodies stole whatever words he could use to describe them from his mind, sat on their haunches to either side of the cave. Eonar had called the white one Magna, explaining she was the matriarch of her kind beyond these mountains. A body like pillows, the ones with tiny feathers inside that made him drift into dreams with ease—unlike the one on which his head currently rested, as apparently the elves did not consider comfort a priority.

Magna's feathers covered leathery skinned wings, and her scales formed a pattern which begged to be followed. Her light blue eyes occasionally turned a pure white, and she stood towering over him and his family.

Opposite her was Eilon, once a patriarch but now the last. No feathers adorned him, his presence neither soft nor comforting. Black leathery wings attached to a body covered in uniform ebony scales. Young Xannan feared the beast, but now he smiled. He had killed that beast, and he would kill him again to be free of any who tried to control him.

The memory beckoned him to the past, so he ignored the heated conversation between Rosealyn and Celena. Answers they both needed might be found in this memory, so he sank deeper into this vision than he had into any other. Unlike those Eilon had once showed him, this vision caused fewer aches and throbs. Fulfillment. Contentment. This process was *right*.

While Eonar began the ceremony, Xannan watched the crystalline weapon. The longer Eonar spoke, the higher and faster the pristine blade moved until it froze at its peak, centered between the two great dragons. Other memories threatened to invade, the image of Gailin's despair of losing their mother clear . . . no, he refused to let those thoughts coalesce. There had to be a way to remove the connection between himself and Rosealyn. Since killing her had already proved impossible, searching his memories was all he could think to do next.

After generations attached to another, he had no desire to be anyone's punching bag or lackey. He was a prince, destined to become a ruler, to continue leading Orda'an in his father's footsteps. A bright pleasant future, a future torn from him by another's lust for power.

Murmured words floated from Eonar's lips, making Xannan wish he could understand what the elf was saying. Perhaps the words would provide a clue, but all Xannan could make out was the low drone of a voice. He watched with horrified wonder as the pulsing orbs at the base of each dragon's neck brightened until they beat in time with one another—the same as the hum of those two blades before they merged.

A warning or command must have been given because Xannan covered his eyes with an arm but shifted it to squint through his fingers at the blinding flames encasing the sword. Curiosity convinced him to continue watching, eager to see what would happen to the pristine weapon Eonar and the elves had created.

Heat, overwhelming and cumbersome, made him and his family stumble backward. Wind, no, a blast of something much stronger, knocked him onto his back. He struggled, trying and failing to lift his head, to look, to learn. Above, the cavern's ceiling warred between bouts of flame. Red, to white, to black, to orange, each with a new level of intense heat. Is that what a dragon's battle looks like? Feels like?

While the invisible air kept him flat on the ground, Xannan tried to reach toward . . . something? Someone? More bursts of flame continued to spew from both dragons, each greater than the last, each with more heat, more force, more. . . Magic, Xannan realized. This is what magic could feel like, what it could do. As the acknowledgment settled, Xannan struggled against the wind to no avail. Frozen in place, unable to stop whatever happened above. A battle of wills raged on while the two sources of flame intertwined, growing in their intensity until Xannan shut his eyes tightly. Arms pinned to his side, he couldn't block the light seeping through.

The longer the battle of the dragon's flame lasted, the quicker his breaths became. Gailin and his parents had to be close by, but he couldn't see them, couldn't make sure they lived. Something formed in the far reaches of his mind, beckoning him, soothing him.

The unmovable wind dissipated, no different from slowly easing oneself into the chilled waters of the Vadamon Sea. Xannan inhaled and sat up, gaze locking onto the blade he now knew so well. It yearned for him, begged him to reach out and hold it. So he did. He wrapped his hand around the hilt, the new entity in his mind blossoming further, beckoning to be understood and used. He looked up, wondering what emotions he might read on the dragon's awe-inspiring features. Eilon had disappeared without a trace. Magna lay on her belly, sprawled out as though exhausted beyond reason, her once-white scales streaked with striations of brown.

A movement in his periphery, to his left. Gailin, a crystalline blade in his hand, sat with a dull expression. The twin brothers met each other's gaze, quizzical.

"It's like it——" Gailin began.

"Molded to you," Xannan finished.

Gailin shook his head. "Called to me," he corrected.

A hum sounded from both weapons, pulsing almost in rhythm with one another. They stood, surveying the scene. Everyone else lay unconscious. While Gailin rushed to their mother, Xannan stared at the weapon in his hand. The blade was definitely molding to him, regardless of what his brother had said. It was not a calling. The sword was becoming a part of him.

"She's waking," Gailin shouted over his shoulder, setting the weapon aside to help her sit up. Their father sat up on his own, wide-eyed.

"What happened?" his father demanded, eyes narrowing at the sword in Xannan's hand. "What is that?"

Xannan approached the others, gripping his new sword. Celena and Arjun stood, slowly and carefully. Between them, Eonar remained seated with eyes closed. Magna lay behind them, more brown streaks coloring her once-pristine scales, and the orange glow of flame at the base of her neck was much paler than before.

"Be careful with those," Celena whispered, glancing between each weapon, a question in her eyes, and looking back to Magna. "Such power inside one. And if they touch. . ."

The young elf shuddered, as though she did not wish to know what would happen. Eonar stood and moved closer to Magna, resting a hand on the dragon's side.

"What happens if they touch, Celena?" Arjun asked.

Celena closed her eyes, scrunched her lips together, and shook her head.

"What happens if they touch, Celena?" Arjun repeated, a tad more forcefully.

"Magna trapped Eilon's power in one of those weapons, and whoever is connected to them when they combine will be able to wield Eilon's power. But such a joining comes at a price for one wielder, and for both. Once a connection is forged between the wielders, it can only be undone through death. Of one or both, I do not know. Nor does Magna," she blurted out, clasping her hands over her mouth and glowering at Arjun.

"*Whoever is connected to them?*" *Seth asked, pushing himself to standing and helping his wife. "How could one be connected to a dragon-blessed weapon? That's preposterous."*

All eyes looked to Celena, but she kept a hand clasped over her mouth, gaze darting between each person surrounding her and toward the tired dragon.

"Until now," Eonar murmured, stroking Magna's side and earning a deep, appreciative rumble in response.

Xannan lifted the weapon that had beckoned to him, his brother picking up the other half from the cave's floor. He walked toward his brother, ready to raise his new sword and see what happened. But Gailin shifted away, shaking his head with wide eyes.

"It feels . . . wrong," Gailin whispered. "I can't tell you why, but it does."

"Until now, Father?" Arjun asked, moving to stand amid the others. "What does that mean?"

Eonar's eyes bulged. "The LeNoir twins have received the gift of the dragon's magic, though it is likely tethered to these weapons they now hold."

"There's more." Celena approached the tired matriarch of a dragon, hovering both hands above Magna's snout as she tilted her head. "I can hear. . ."

A shudder racked through Celena's body, and she closed her eyes. "Eilon only agreed to come in hopes of capturing Magna's magic and using it to reform his own race. The droki." Celena glanced behind her at the dragon whose sad eyes faded to a dull white, and Celena's voice turned hoarse. "He considers the droki his children, his creation. They hunt magic because it is their missing piece. The droki require magic to survive."

Xannan opened his eyes to see Rosealyn sitting on her bed, hands gripping the edge. "Answers?" she grumbled at him with a glance at the closed door.

"Only one which may appease you." He rubbed his head and paused. No lingering ache, no piercing pain, no need to grip the sword's hilt. Revisiting that memory had been so unlike every time Eilon had shared a vision with him. Unfortunately, this one had been almost as cryptic as those Eilon often shared. "We can sever the connection. But one of us will have to die to do so. Or both. It's unclear."

"I know many who would be happy to kill you for me," came the grating grumble of hers that told him how much she loathed his existence.

"I'd rather find a method to extricate ourselves from one another besides continuously threatening death." He studied the sword lying next to him and frowned. He was younger than he remembered when given that weapon.

"I have no qualms with you disappearing for good," she said. "Having you around will cause nothing but trouble."

"Having *Eilon* around caused nothing but trouble." Xannan tried not to hiss the words through his teeth. The constant threats were grating on his nerves. "He's dead, and if neither of us wishes to die, we will have to learn to work together."

"Why should you live?" Her arms tensed when she gripped the edge of the bed. "I have a country to fight for, people to protect and lead, and . . . people who care about me. Some would give their life to protect mine. Who have *already* given their life to protect me! And some of them *you* killed!"

She pushed to standing, arms crossing as soon as she began pacing. He sat there, waiting.

"Tell me again," she spat down at him. "How many did you kill in Vandyl?"

He stared, unspeaking, unblinking; he had not counted how many got in his way.

"Even one was too many." She stopped in front of him to use the full difference of her standing height. "I refuse to work with you."

"For now, you have no choice." Head tilted enough to meet the ferocity of her light brown eyes, he smiled.

"Why is staying alive so important to you? Anyone and everything you once cared to protect is long gone."

"Are you going to continue the tirade or allow me to speak?"

The glower creasing her brown-tinted skin deepened, but the pacing stopped and her lips tightened.

"Because *our* country is in turmoil," he reminded her. "Or did you forget I, too, am of the LeNoir line and an heir to a currently unprotected crown?"

Chapter Five

"*Our* country?" Rosealyn screeched at him. "*Ours?!* You have no right to *my* throne or any other aspect of Orda'an. Not after you attacked and allowed Eilon to destroy it."

She paused, reminding herself how remaining calm could help. "All that death, all that destruction, and for what?"

"Again, Eilon—"

"Is not the sole entity responsible for this—this!" She threw her hands up in the air. Whatever *this* was, it was not pleasant. "Blighted fields, a mercenary army, a treasonous mother, then you . . . my father . . . Charles—"

"The soldier turned royal?" Xannan's brow lifted. "I did nothing to him."

Rosealyn's eyes narrowed; she found it difficult to believe Xannan would leave anyone she cared about alone.

"Well, no, but. . ." Words were lost to her. *Why did I mention Charles? Because . . . I miss him?*

Xannan's low, subtle, smirk-ridden laugh made Rosealyn want to threaten his life again, but she forced herself not to let the growing growl of aggravation make a sound, gritting her teeth instead. He stood, dusting his dark pants and straightening the strange brown vest that left more than she wished of the man's chest visible. As he shifted the sword belt, loosening the blade in its sheath, she frowned.

"How do you know Charles is royalty?"

"You were truly out of it for that fight, weren't you?" Xannan's voice softened, as though he might have a modicum of feelings or perhaps sympathy toward another. When she nodded, he explained, "Charles helped me kill Eilon. And then punched me, more than once. Drew blood, too."

The last was a tone of both surprise and approval that made Rosealyn roll her eyes again.

"Good," she said.

Xannan barked a laugh in response. "You felt his punch, not I," he said through the chuckles.

She pressed her lips together. "Enough," she whispered through the grimace. "As much as I do not wish to see the destruction *you*—"

"Eilon, again, Eilon," Xannan interrupted.

She glowered at him. "The destruction Eilon *and* you caused, I must return to Vandyl." Rosealyn surveyed the decorative woodwork surrounding them. It would be logical to remain here and find a way to break the connection. The elven city was comforting, peaceful, if *he* weren't there. But she had to leave. The Gift was pulling her toward home, though her heart tugged elsewhere.

"Vandyl," he agreed, bringing her focus back to him as an aggravating smirk tugged at his lips and he spoke with a tone of teasing her. "Though it seems Charles may be important?"

"My people must come first." Rosealyn crossed her arms and turned away from his smug face.

"But Charles has a weapon blessed by a dragon," Xannan mused aloud.

Despite her frustrations, she looked over her shoulder at him, brows furrowing.

"A weapon blessed by a dragon not connected to another? Another weapon we could study, perhaps use to break the connection of the Twin Blades?"

At the suggestion, she turned, heart soaring and beating impossibly fast as her brain clicked Xannan's idea into place. "You want to visit Charles? And do what? Fight him?" Her heart flopped. "Kill him?"

"Not unless he gives me reason to." Xannan smirked when her breath hitched at his statement. He tapped the pommel of his sword. "It may only take a simple touch of the weapons. There is magic in his blade, I know that much." Xannan grimaced. "It is, after all, not far from here."

He sat back on the bed, facial expression turning more smug than before. He was right. Again. She thought back over the past few weeks, about all the knowledge learned and everything they did not yet understand. Dragon-blessed weapons, *the* Twin Blades—the greatest magic history claimed could exist—in their hands. Compared to such power, her desire to reunite with Charles seemed trivial. Yet it could also be vital. And for Xannan, of all people, to offer her a way to see Charles. . . She plopped onto her bed. A logical theory, to see what happened when other dragon-blessed blades interacted with their own.

"Once he knows he can kill you without harming me, he will," Rosealyn said, resting her head and back against the wall.

"He may try," Xannan agreed. "But I would not let him succeed."

"Then we are not going there." Rosealyn's shoulders tensed. Her Gift and heart remained torn. "I will not put anyone else in danger of having your sword shoved through them."

"So you wish to hide here?" he retorted in that menacing tone she remembered. He stood and stepped closer with each question he asked. "You think you can control me? Think you can command me? Do you think I never hurt? That I never experience pain or loss?" His hands curled into fists, arms shaking. "It was *my* pain and loss Eilon used for his own gain. It was my need for revenge he fueled, planting false memories so I could conform to *his* plan to retrieve *his* magic from this weapon."

Her insides recoiled with each additional word. The closer he walked, the further she tried to press herself into the wall. Legs tucked in close with arms wrapped around them, Rosealyn had no retort.

Xannan paused, pulling out the dark blade and sneering at it as though it disgusted him. Its crystalline shell harbored a river of black clouds circling and tumbling within, no longer the sable blade once used to kill. "I was convinced this weapon was a gift from the dragons, a blessing. Now I understand why Gailin wanted to be rid of it. It's nothing more than a curse. If I can find a way to be free of this curse and live, that is where I wish to go."

Despite trying to convince her muscles to relax, they didn't. His sword, though no longer solid black, haunted her dreams. The Passing of her family Gift allowed her to witness, and feel, her father's death. What Xannan said was not wrong; the swords were more a curse than a gift. She remembered Celena's favorite phrase, and the pull to go home returned.

Dragon-blessed weapons were not common, and the one Charles received had been blessed by Magna with intention. Its creation was not an accident, not like these. She studied a vine carving up the wall until it met the ceiling, slithering along the edge and dipping back down to meet another carving. A visit to Volante could release their connection and reunite her with Charles. And if the blades were disconnected, Charles could help her get rid of Xannan for good.

"It is logical." Rosealyn released her grip on her legs. "Volante, to see if other dragon-enhanced blades can make any difference. But then I—" She closed her eyes and breathed deeply, acknowledging the reality of their future if nothing changed with the weapons. "We. We must return to Vandyl."

After a moment's silence, he asked, "Will you let me in if the connection is broken?" His voice was further away, so she opened her eyes again, grateful the murderous sword was hidden away. It rested against the bed upon which Xannan lay, thankfully not looking at her.

"I— We will see what happens tomorrow. Celena did tell us Synda had an idea."

A grunt was the only answer he deigned to give before rolling away from her. Rosealyn relaxed, head sinking into the soft pillow. When was the last time she had slept in a bed? It, too, had been in an elven city. And in that city, she had killed her mother's cousin. All because she possessed a magical blade which others now knew existed. What she and Xannan had done would not go quietly into the night. Many lives had been lost to Eilon's flame, though both King Nathaniel of Alkaan and the Honorable Jordan of Hoclia had survived. They had returned home, likely eager to claim what she had offered in exchange for their aid.

Rosealyn shut her eyes tight against the tears. So many of her actions had led others to their deaths. Once settled in Vandyl, she would need to send proper condolences to both Jordan and Nathaniel, perhaps with additional offerings of land. If the priests agreed.

Xannan's even breathing and occasional snoring was a comfort only because it meant he wouldn't speak. While he had been reliving the day the blades were made, Celena had returned what Rosealyn once refused to read. The letter from her birth mother sat on a small table next to her bed. She ached to read it, desperate to know why her true mother had left. At the same time, she was afraid of what would be within. Was it her fault? Even in her youth, had Rosealyn done something to prevent her real mother from being able to stay? The greatest question of all was why her natural mother was anyone but the woman her father had wed. She doubted he would break a vow, but this letter was evidence there was a lot about her father she had never learned.

Rosealyn rolled onto her side to grasp the letter and tucked her legs beneath her with a silent prayer for the letter to be more thorough than the final message from her father.

Chapter Six

The handwriting of the thick letter was long and flowing, page darkened occasionally with small circular blobs. Tears, Rosealyn realized, scanning the pages and settling back against the wall. Fingers shaking, she gave the room a cursory glance to confirm Xannan remained asleep and read.

My dearest Jaida,

At the time I write this, you are sleeping next to me. So young, so beautiful, so perfect in every way. I believe your father when he says you will make us proud, though I now know I cannot stay and watch you grow.

We tried, we really did, but people talk. The best way to protect your future, my sister's, and especially Phillippe's, is to leave. Remove the suspicious piece and the rest will fall into place. I understand, I do, but a part of my heart and soul will remain here. The marriage arrangement was not with me and, according to the Tenoan council, could not be any other way. I begged, I cried, I argued, and all I got was one answer: no.

Those on the council are fools. Roseanne and I are of the same lineage. It should not matter who was born first. What your father and I have is something he and Roseanne will never have. They may learn to care for one another, maybe like each other, but I doubt he will ever grow to love her. Or she him. A pity how politics are so quick to guide one's life. Mine, Roseanne's, Phillippe's. Even yours before three years old.

I hope you'll remember me. At least fleetingly. Though there is something you will not recall unless I tell you explicitly, which is why I must write you this letter. I fear it may never reach your hands, but I would be a fool not to write it. There is more about me which others fear. It is why neither the council nor the Orda'anian priests would ever consider me instead of Roseanne. I possess something she does not, something greatly feared. More than fear, there is a worry of how naturally inherited magic may combine with the LeNoir Gift. I find it ironic, though, that my ability is feared while the Gift is revered as that which determines Orda'an's true monarch.

The gardens around the Tenoan council, those here in Vandyl—I created them. Built them by infusing them with magic. My magic. Most are unaware, but the Tenoan council knew, helped keep it a secret since my father was on the council. I was allowed only to aid the plants' growth around the council building. But here your father let me grow plants from nothing. The green-tinged black roses were the first I ever made on my own. Not what I intended, of course, but Phillippe adores them. Says they remind him of the name I chose for you. The green hue is like a jewel amid darkness, just like you.

Magic is beautiful, Jaida. Precious and fulfilling. My ability stagnated while I carried you inside me, which I'm led to believe means you will have magic of your own aside from the LeNoir Gift. I do not know what your ability may be. Perhaps you will have the same affinity to nature as I, or something different entirely. Whatever it is, I believe you will treasure it as you do all things. You care so much for those around you. It is what I adore most about you, my precious little Jaida. Though your feisty nature is likely to cause my sister many a headache in the years to come.

This is my last night with you. Your place is here, and I know Phillippe will do all he can to protect and prepare you. Remember his teachings, but do not forget the importance of learning.

By the time you receive this letter, if you ever receive it, you may know much, but not all. Trust the elves as I do. It is why I am leaving this letter with them before I leave the continent. I must put distance between myself and Phillippe, otherwise I fear I cannot stay away regardless of the consequences. The elves tell me of an island sanctuary for those who have natural born magic. A place where I can be at peace with what I can do.

He doesn't know I plan to leave. Neither does Roseanne. It hurts. All I want to do is hold you in my arms, never to let you go. The downfall of the truth, that the honorable and upright King Phillippe had a child with me rather than the woman he married? It would be madness and create more chaos than already ensues. Between Jearnia's constant attacks, their petty attempts to claim this land as theirs even though it never has been, and the growing unrest in Hoclia and Alkaan, the country needs to be unified. Such drama in the castle as this truth would create would not assist.

I lied to the elves when they asked if you would have magic of your own, though I'm sure Phillippe will probably figure it out.

If it is ever safe to do so, or necessary, I will find you. I'm sorry I won't be here to watch you grow and learn. Please remember, Jaida, the beauty of nature, of life itself.

All my love,

Your Mother, Catarina

Rosealyn read the letter a second time and a third. It helped place pieces of her childhood, how she appeared so similar to Roseanne but could never quite connect with the woman. Was the resentment of the woman who raised her of her own making or of Roseanne's? A rift caused simply because Rosealyn existed? She chewed on her tongue, tracing the loops and whirls of her birth mother's handwriting, understanding now why her mother and father always appeared at odds with one another.

But there the logic ended. The only magical thing about her was the Gift, and she barely understood how it worked. Rosealyn's instructors had never explained anything about magic. They didn't even know everything about the LeNoir Gift except that it was attached to her bloodline, passed from one generation to the next.

Rosealyn pressed the crinkled papers atop her chest. She had fleeting memories of Catarina. All in the gardens. It was no wonder her father had spent so much time there. Perhaps it was why she enjoyed spending time there as well; the gardens were often the only place she could get a decent night's sleep. So she imagined she was back there, sitting on the bench in front of the black roses she now knew her birth mother had made.

When the question of whether the roses had survived Eilon's flame arose, she shoved it away. Instead, she pretended her father was alive and she was sitting next to him, head resting on his chest, his arm wrapped around her shoulders. Then she pretended Catarina, her birth mother, sat to her other side. A proper family, an image she could never recreate for real. Life now was not beautiful. It was exhausting, overwhelming, and aggravating.

She folded the letter, tucking it back into the envelope, and set it on the table. She moved the blanket so it covered her. *Blaze help me, tell me what to do now. Please.*

CHAPTER SEVEN

Adela perused the document again, head swaying with the motion of the servant brushing her long sandy-blond hair. The tale was interesting. The miserable story of the Lost Prince was true. A dragon had destroyed Vandyl, and her brother had been sheltering a Jearnian. She'd suspected the last, but the others were difficult to accept. The servant finished the brush's long stroke and intertwined the strands of hair into one long braid. For a time, Adela had harbored jealousy of the more unique braids worn by both her sister-in-law and niece, until she realized she could do just as much good for the people as her brother did as king by staying in Cantadad as their duchess. Her older brothers—Theo and Alan—did likewise as the dukes of the northern regions.

She preferred Cantadad. This castle was much more pleasant than Vandyl's. With Cantadad closer to the desert, the weather was less prone to mood swings as well. While Vandyl spent several months with sodden snow-covered ground, Adela could visit a sandy white beach by taking a walk outside. But the comparison made her frown. The message from the king of Jearnia claimed destruction of more than the castle. An entire city, not just its fields, engulfed in a dragon's flame.

Her gaze lingered on the letter's salutation; Charles was the Jearnian boy her brother had insisted on sheltering despite her, Alan, and Theo demanding he do otherwise. But Phillippe had been persistent, and it was hard to say no to a king who had a sense for what the future could hold.

"So much he knew but never shared," Adela whispered as her maid placed pins to hold the loose hairs away from Adela's face. When the maid reached for the face powders—which neither the princess nor their queen had partaken in during Adela's last visit, likely because of Phillippe's funeral—Adela murmured, "Not today, Daphne."

After folding the letter into smaller squares, Adela tucked it inside a small pocket she had asked to be sewn into the bodice of every dress. She would need to compare her message to what her brothers received. For the first time since Phillippe's funeral, they would be in the same room. Adela appreciated their haste in response to her latest message.

Entering the hallway, she left the fresh salt-scented air which wafted in through her balcony doors. The Vadamon Sea, a mesmerizing, enormous body of water whose soft whooshes and crashes lulled her to sleep every night, was the best part of Cantadad. Many hallways were open to the surrounding air but not those where she had taken her rooms. She had searched for the one with the best view, and a closed hallway was a small price to pay for walking onto that balcony and basking in the beauty of the wide open sea every morning. So freeing after being cooped inside from birth to adulthood.

Twists and turns led to a pair of grand stairs she knew were more for awe and flamboyance than functionality, and then she was in the foyer, her smile broadening at the sight of her two older brothers despite their grim countenances.

"Come now," she said in the most encouraging voice she could muster. "We are here and together. It's been much too long."

Theo grunted and rested a hand atop his sword hilt like all men did when nerves got to them, but Alan remained pensive. Where Theo would often get confused for Phillippe, Alan was the spitting image of their father. Neither had the green eyes Theo and Phillippe shared, nor did she. Her sandy-brown hair and light brown eyes were a common appearance among Orda'anians. If she chose, she could walk the city streets with her hair loose and few would recognize her as their duchess.

"I'd rather we not need to meet under the circumstances outlined in this," Alan said, waving a crumpled paper in his hand. "Half of it is too ridiculous to be true, but the other half adds logic to make the illogical part true!"

"I know." Adela smoothed the wide skirts of her dress and clasped her hands before her. "Phillippe told us things would change. And when Roseanne sent us away—"

"My contact at Delphi claims Roseanne is there." Theo's hand remained on the sword hilt, one finger tapping impatiently. "But Rosealyn is missing, according to this Charles's letter." He crossed his arms, brows furrowing. "Why is the king of Jearnia communicating with us?"

"I think we should be grateful one familiar to those at Vandyl could help initiate the rebuilding process." Adela gestured toward the open door to her right and guided them inside to a lengthy oval table where the food was already set. This room showed the flamboyant nature of Cantadad. A dozen brightly flaring torches glimmered against golden walls, and a chandelier centered above the table made an impressive visual. The lackluster food dotting the dark plates before them ruined the image. Adela forced herself not to grimace. The castle cooks could barely provide enough for their own families.

"Killed a dragon?" Alan guffawed, nudging the withered chunks of fruit with a fork. "A dragon!"

"So he claims," Theo muttered, piercing a small chunk of fruit and wincing as he chewed.

"You'd think, given the length of this famine, you two would stop making such ridiculous faces while eating." Adela tsked and shook her head as she inspected the fruit on her fork. "I'd like to read the letters you received, for comparison."

"A dragon took Rosealyn, Charles returned to Jearnia and won his challenge for the throne, and then he helped the elves, Rosealyn, and Xannan kill Eilon," Alan said in a quick tumble of words. "Oh, and Roseanne went missing; Vandyl was destroyed." Alan turned to Theo, eyebrows raised. "Yours?"

"Mine said much the same," said the eldest brother. "Like Alan said, there is logic in this illogical sequence of events."

"As did mine," Adela murmured, pulling the parchment from its hidden pocket and reading aloud. "'I hope you will consider the events I am about to outline as the truth and not a means to fool you into a trap. I—'"

"He wrote the same message to each of us," Theo said. "Do we believe him?"

"Phillippe trusted him." Adela sipped her water. "I see no reason not to believe his words, regardless of how insane they may sound. You recall the strange nature of our dear brother's death."

Her brothers nodded in solemn agreement.

"Now what do we do?" Alan asked, grimacing as he swallowed another bite of food.

"We stabilize the monarchy," Theo announced, failing to hide his own glower as he inspected the food on his plate. "There are methods by which we can stabilize Orda'an without searching every corner of this continent for Rosealyn."

"But Theo, the Gift, the Passing, she went through it!" Alan set his cutlery on the table to either side of the plate he had hardly touched and leveled a stare at his older brother. "Or are you still jealous of who earned the Gift?"

"Please—" Adela began, but Theo halted her with a raised hand, and she pinned him with a sharper stare than Alan's.

"Jacin could assume the throne," Theo announced. "He's of age, several years older than Rosealyn, well trained, intelligent, and a LeNoir—"

"Who did not inherit the LeNoir Gift!" Alan said. "That's not how it works here, Theo."

"And why shouldn't it? It's how every other country would handle this situation. There's no reason we couldn't be a proper monarchy. I have been . . . thinking about it for some time," Theo said. His cutlery also rested beside his plate.

Adela briefly closed her eyes with a deep sigh. *Brothers!*

"Why not you then? Or I? Or Adela?" Alan retorted, gesturing with a hand toward each of them and thumping his chest when referring to himself.

"You realize we should be grateful the newly crowned king of Jearnia did not already claim our lands, yes? The last thing we need is for our own family to fight for Orda'an's throne," Adela said, standing and pinning them with her iciest stare.

She had always been closer to Phillippe. Barely two years younger than Phillippe, she had visited him more often, had more conversations with him after he experienced the Passing.

"We three can work together as stewards of the throne until we find Rosealyn," she said, sitting down slowly and deliberately. "Perhaps Jacin can help find his cousin?"

Theo crossed his arms and leaned back in his seat, eyes more studious than before. "The priests would not be happy with such a stewardship for long, and there's no way to know if Rosealyn is alive. Even Charles's message expressed doubt, based on her own words." He pulled out his copy of the letter, hunting for the lines. "'She claimed she wasn't positive we would see each other again, but then we did at the Cliff of Lycene, before I helped Xannan kill Eilon. She was in too much pain . . . and by the time I could get back to her, she had disappeared. I want to believe I'll see her again, and I believe she can take care of herself, but I do not know where she is.'"

Theo folded the letter, tucking it away for later. "He says she disappeared. So until we *know* she is alive, we should proceed with nominating a new heir to the throne."

"Have any other LeNoirs experienced the Passing?" Adela glared at each brother. Heat rose to her cheeks and chest, and her palms were sweating. Did tradition mean *nothing* to Theo anymore? Her brothers shook their heads. "Then we protect the throne for Rosealyn's return."

"We have to go to Vandyl," Alan added. "For one, we must show our support to those who have suffered such great losses. And we must learn which of the priests survived. If none survived, we can revisit the conversation of protecting the throne for Rosealyn or nominating a new heir. Regardless of what the priests tell us, Jacin should search for Rosealyn. Agreed?"

Adela's eyes widened slightly, surprised at Alan's logical mediation to the growing tension, especially since he was often the source of unease between the siblings. "To Vandyl, to learn who survived," she agreed. "Theo?"

"It is the best course of action to take." Theo rubbed his trimmed gray-streaked blond beard. "Another matter, however, is how to respond to the king of Jearnia? And we have received requests for plots of land from both Hoclia and Alkaan—do either of you know anything about these requests?"

Adela and Alan shook their heads.

"I can delay the issue between Hoclia and Alkaan until the matter of succession is settled." Theo poked at his remaining food. "And in response to the king of Jearnia?"

Adela inhaled to speak but paused. It felt wrong to send a note of thanks to the country they had fought against for so long, and a part of her harbored the idea Charles could be to blame for Vandyl's destruction and Rosealyn's disappearance. He had, after all, been assigned as her bodyguard. But so were others who should have also watched over her. So instead, Adela frowned and smacked her lips shut.

"Odd for you to be silent, dear sister." Alan chuckled at her side. "Do we offer him thanks for the information, or do we question him on future intentions? There was no offer of mending the rift between our lands, simply information."

"Both," Theo said in answer to Alan's question. "As Adela said, Phillippe trusted Charles enough to shelter him for a decade."

"He trusted Charles more than he trusted Roseanne," Adela muttered, her gaze over the room growing distant as she remembered their last conversation. "He said the Jearnian's future would guide the continent to a 'type of peace.' I wish Phillippe had mentioned Charles's heritage, though. Or at least what agreement he'd made with the man."

Alan rested a gentle hand atop hers, squeezing it. "A message of thanks and cooperation to the king of Jearnia, and then"—Alan lifted his glass—"to Vandyl."

Chapter Eight

Charles waited atop his mare for the large gates of Volante's castle, now his home, to open. Beside him sat General Ashtar, who showed a modicum of respect, though the man's viewpoint on certain matters grated on Charles. He fought the urge to look behind him. Since repairs were well underway and the messages had been sent, Charles had no other reason to stay at Vandyl. By returning to Volante to truly accept the responsibility of Jearnia's monarch, he was honoring the agreement.

A low creak followed by a thud announced the gates were wide enough. Before Charles could nudge his mount forward, Ashtar held out a hand to stop him. Charles frowned at the aging man who reminded him too much of his father. The grizzled face, the beady dark eyes, the permanent scowl of disappointment, and the gray streaks in his short hair were all attributes which gave Charles pause when speaking to the man.

"You should have let me leave soldiers at Vandyl, my King," the general said in his low, gruff voice.

"Our goal was not to take Orda'an but to help them get rid of a threat," Charles reminded him. "We aided in killing Eilon and assisted in rebuilding Vandyl until my leg healed so I could travel, but I did not wish for Duchess Adela nor Dukes Theo and Alan to consider us a threat. I sent them each a message, updating them on the situation."

"The situation, Sire?" Ashtar emitted a grunt which could have been a laugh. "And how did you explain this situation?"

"With the truth." Charles nudged his mount forward a few paces and dismounted with caution. He paused, testing the weight on his leg, even though it was fully healed. Satisfied he could walk without pain, he handed the reins to a young squire standing in the vast open courtyard which led to the castle grounds.

When he had returned home nearly a month ago, he had not taken the time to appreciate the familiarity of the place. Memories had surfaced, causing him to reminisce and mourn brothers he had not been able to protect from themselves. Where Vandyl's castle was built for efficiency, Volante's was meant to impress. Towering stone walls were broken by occasional parapets with gilded staircases to reach them. And everywhere there was stone. But not the dragonstone of Vandyl, which had unbelievably *melted*. This stone was a mixture of soft grays and dull whites. It covered the castle proper, sprawling out into finger-like wings of hallways.

Charles tugged on the sleeves of his bright red and golden orange coat, though he didn't need to, and turned to the men crowding into the courtyard. The barracks and training grounds were outside the castle walls, though the men kept their mounts stabled inside the gates.

"Rest." Charles studied the men who were dismounting and relinquishing their horses to the dozens of nervous squires awaiting them. "I'm not sure what comes next, so rest while you have the time."

After Ashtar's simple nod, Charles turned back to the sprawling castle. Inside was his mother who should be recovered from the attempted poisoning. At first, he'd assumed she was poisoned by his father's dagger when she attempted to stop the trial, but the dagger did not have the telltale signs of poison. It was one of the many thoughts which festered in the late night, preventing sleep. Perhaps his brother, who had never showed in Vandyl or at the Cliff, would be home and have insight into how their mother was being poisoned. *If I can trust him.*

He walked through the maze of the castle's hallways, distracted by the many paintings and images adorning their walls. Phillippe had removed such decoration from Vandyl, but Charles had been with Rosealyn when she found the stack of tapestries which once covered her home. She had chosen one to display in her rooms, a bright-colored mess that . . . was gone. Never again would he study a bold-colored rug while hoping she hadn't noticed the heat rising to his cheeks. Never again would he admonish her for neglecting to care for herself before others. Never again would he see her tucked into one of those odd-shaped chairs she'd collected, reading.

A mouse-like squeak pulled him from his thoughts. In front of him, bowed at the waist and shivering from head to toe, was a young golden-haired girl who could not be more than twelve years old. He closed his eyes and sighed, assuming the softest tone he could muster.

"It's okay, you can stand up." He almost stepped closer but decided against it when her shaking increased at the sound of his voice, which served to make him sigh again. "Is my mother in her rooms?"

The young girl nodded without lifting from her bow.

"What is your name?" As he stepped forward, his sword hilt clanged against his belt, and the girl flinched. With a shake of his head, he muttered, "I forgot what it felt like to be in my father's domain."

He held the hilt of his sword so it wouldn't make another sound and gently pulled her up by her shoulder. She followed the motion, silent tears streaming down her face. "You have seen what my father would do?" Charles asked her, and she nodded, sniffling. "Loved ones lost?"

The young girl nodded again, and his heart fell. His father had been so careless with the value of life. "I'm sure this will not be the last time I say these words." He crouched to her level. "I am not the man my father was."

The young girl's eyes went wide, and she sniffled again, running an arm against her nose, but her shoulders relaxed.

"Let others know." He paused, remembering she had not answered his earlier question. "Your name?"

"Marigold, Your Majesty," she said in a soft whisper he had to strain to hear.

"Marigold." He smiled, hoping it portrayed kindness and no hint of animosity. "Let the others know what I told you. There is no reason for a castle, for a kingdom, to live in fear of their leader."

Marigold curtsied and squeaked out a high-pitched "Your Majesty," before racing off down the hallway.

He listened to her fading footsteps, studying a portrait on the wall. It was of himself before he left, before he tried and failed to kill King Phillippe as his father had ordered, before he learned respect could be earned in much kinder ways than threatening a dagger slice to the neck. He frowned at his image, contemplating whether to tear it down and rip it to shreds. *Memories? Is that why Phillippe had those tapestries hidden?*

Fearful of what other versions of his past adorned the dark walls, Charles focused on the path to his mother's quarters.

He rounded the corner into the next hallway and stopped short, more memories flooding. It wasn't the last place he had seen Rosealyn, but something had changed between them there, something that made him desperate to see her again. She had been right about needing his sword, a simple-looking weapon enchanted by a dragon's breath, and wrong about seeing her again. Rather than recall the pain etched across her face from the weapons connecting, Charles longed to press his palm against her cheek. With an absentminded hand, he tugged at the collar of his coat, topmost button undone, and tugged at each sleeve. *She can take care of herself. And then, if she wants to . . . or should I look for her?*

"Ah, King Charles, you've returned." Eonar's pleasant accent sounded beside him. "So, I imagine the beast of a dragon is dead?"

Charles nodded, staring down the hallway. He remembered their foreheads touching, his desire to follow the braids adorning her head from each temple mingling with his memory of being so close to kissing her. His mother's admonishment to "leave nothing unsaid" was exactly what he'd needed to hear, though he worried it had been years too late. He tugged at his sleeves again, straightening.

"Queen Nerida's condition has improved." Eonar gestured toward the queen's door with a frail, withered hand. "Though I expected a quicker recovery, given the medicines I crafted."

Eonar, Arjun's father who had miraculously convinced Charles's father to accept him as the Jearnian castle doctor, stepped toward the door before Charles could hold out a hand to stop him.

"Meaning?" Charles turned from his reminiscing study of the hallway to search the elf's red-irised eyes. "How quickly should she have recovered?"

"As quickly as you did, Your Majesty." Eonar shrugged apologetically. "The dagger was not poisoned."

"But Mae *was* poisoned?"

"Aye, and for some time too, Your Majesty." Eonar lowered his voice. "I have controlled her intake as best I can, but the poison continues to infiltrate her system. The medicines I make assist, yes, but I must find the source to help her make a full recovery."

"Thank you for informing me." Charles surveyed the dark stone floor. He had forgotten how few torches lit the hallways, and how few windows dotted the walls compared to Vandyl's. "Have you told anyone else your suspicions?"

"No, Your Majesty." Eonar clasped his hands behind his back. "I have been treating her for it regularly, but she continues to dismiss my concerns."

Charles nodded again, lost in thought. His mother was the one good thing about his past in Volante, the one person who had almost convinced him to return home long before Phillippe told him to; however, his agreement with Phillippe covered much more than his own livelihood. *Sacrifices*, Phillippe had once told him. *All monarchs make sacrifices, either of their morality or of their relationships.*

He forced his spine straight. "Why would anyone want to poison Mae?"

Eonar shrugged and opened the door. Voices murmured amicably inside. Charles followed, surprised to find both Christopher and his Aunt Marsha speaking with his mother. A shawl wrapped around her shoulders, his mother appeared healthier than when he had left. Eonar's words repeated in his mind: she wasn't recovering quickly enough, and he couldn't locate the source of the poison.

Chapter Nine

When the door opened to his mother's rooms, Christopher leaned back in his seat and attempted to appear casual. "Decided to return, I see."

He knew what his brother would ask about first. The Orda'anian princess had told him to leave, so he did. As soon as he returned home, Marsha had put him to work speaking with the wealthy landowners of the country, planting seeds of trust or distrust.

Charles said nothing as he stared at their mother. At his entrance, she set aside the plain white cloth and bold red thread, finally pausing in her seemingly incessant motion of pulling string. Christopher never understood how she could continuously move that needle up and down, nor how such images would grow and appear from the cloth's center to outer edges, nor why it always seemed to be an image all in red. Always red.

"The mountains must have cursed me with broody sons," his mother murmured, shifting the shawl resting on her shoulders. "I'm glad you're home, and well. And Eilon?"

"Dead." Charles spoke the word as though killing a dragon had been easy.

But when Christopher glanced over at their mother, he found a slight twinkle of approval that so rarely graced her features for him. Christopher stood, brushing off his pants to distract himself from grinding his teeth.

His brother added a somber "as is Magna."

Silence lingered between them, none truly looking at the other. Christopher crossed his arms and resumed his seat. The clinks and taps of glass as the doctor prepared medicine were like peals of thunder. A whisper of a thank you followed Eonar handing over the small bowl of broth.

"Better." Eonar glanced at Charles. "But what I said before holds true, Your Majesty."

A curt nod accompanied Charles's frown, but he spoke with weariness. "Thank you, Eonar."

The doctor bowed his head and left, leaving the four of them to avoid each other's gaze. Their mother's soft slurps reverberated in the silence, accompanied by her knowing smile peeking above the rim of the bowl every time she tipped it.

"So," their mother finally began, pausing at a slight cough. "What happened after Eilon's demise?"

Christopher followed his mother's intense stare over to his brother, who rubbed a hand over his face and shifted the hair off his forehead. It was strange to see Charles in the proper attire, complete with a thin gold crown on his head. Not the crown their father had worn, though. Charles had destroyed that one.

"I wanted to ensure Vandyl was well cared for before leaving." Charles took the empty bowl from their mother. "And Eonar's son, Arjun, insisted I rest a few extra days to properly heal."

"Heal?" their mother asked with that overbearing protective tone only a parent who truly cared could muster.

All Charles did was nod, squinting. He was assessing their mother, Christopher realized, as though he didn't trust the doctor's statement.

"The proper messages were sent for the events in Orda'an." Charles added the bowl to the growing pile of items on the small table Eonar had added to their mother's room. He leaned against the wall, arms folded. Whatever injury he'd had was definitely well healed; Christopher couldn't determine what wound his elder brother might have suffered. "Now to begin the work here."

"The landowning families have been arriving." Marsha's announcement rang out. She inhaled to speak again, but whatever words waited dissipated.

"I know I wasn't here long before leaving, but I am aware there is much I will want to change," Charles explained. "Starting with the plantations."

Their aunt pursed her lips but gave a silent nod of agreement.

"Who did you bring to the castle in my absence?" Charles added. "I'm sure there are many, all of whom should stay in preparation for the ceremony."

Despite himself, Christopher chuckled. "Keeping some traditions while breaking others?"

"Certain traditions deserve to be broken." Charles lifted from the wall and shrugged. "While others must be kept. A proper ceremony will be the first sign to this country of their new leader."

This time Marsha released a soft guffaw. "If you think of yourself as a leader, and not a ruler, you will not get far here."

Trust, seeds of trust.

"He will if we support him." Christopher almost surprised himself with how sincere it sounded. He let their glares roll off his shoulders; he had endured worse looks than they could muster.

"The ceremony should be in no less than a week," their mother said, softly, as though to not aggravate her throat and induce more of those coughing fits which lingered regardless of what the inane doctor offered. "You've already pushed that tradition to its limit by not agreeing to it before leaving the first time."

"I know," Charles said, shoulders falling with a soft sigh.

"Would you like—" Marsha's voice halted when Charles looked at her in a way that made Christopher wonder if something had already happened between the two. Their aunt had been the first to recognize Charles as the new king, which their uncle had not yet done. And neither had he. *Does that make him trust her more or less?*

"All of the spokespeople for the lands they own should be here," Charles said to Marsha. "Send those messages immediately. We will meet tomorrow to address the specifics of the changes I would like to make."

"As you wish." Marsha approached the door, meeting Christopher's gaze as she opened it. His jaw clenched, wondering what his aunt wished to tell him later.

Once the door shut, their mother stood and took several shaky steps. Both Charles and Christopher moved to assist, but she waved them off. Standing before the table, she poured a glass of water. "If you two wish to argue, you can do so elsewhere."

"There's nothing to argue about," Christopher grumbled before Charles could speak. He knew what questions his brother would have, understood his brother might be angry, and hoped his lackluster explanation would suffice. "Princess Rosealyn did not need anyone there as her protector. She did fine on her own. Though not unscathed."

Charles lifted a brow, and Christopher forced himself not to roll his eyes.

"The Tenoan Praetor wanted her sword and tried to kill her to take it." Christopher leaned back in his seat and rested his ankle on his opposite knee. "So kind during the meeting only to sneak into her room that night to attack. By the time I got there, she had a dagger buried in her leg while her sword was buried in his stomach. So when she told me to leave, I saw no reason to stay, considering she's much better at killing than I am."

Charles's brows knitted together, and the already travel-worn man's shoulders dropped further as he combed a hand through his hair.

"She used what I taught her." Charles let his hand drop to his side. "I—"

Christopher waited, expecting more from his brother, but the breath fell into nothing. A weak squeeze came from his left, from his mother's too frail form. She wore one of her knowing sympathetic smiles, of understanding exactly what emotions were roiling through any of her children.

"I suggest you help Marsha send those messages," she whispered, with a tilt of her head toward the door.

He bit his tongue to force down the retort lingering on it as he glared at his brother. It was like looking into his future. They had the same subtle curl to their hair, the same soft blue eyes, similar strong jaws, and their mother's subtle cheekbones. Until that scraggly scar along Charles's jawline. Though that memory was vague, Christopher had been there when it happened; he had been fortunate to not receive any similar injuries courtesy of their father.

Charles murmured his agreement. It was useless to argue. Fingers clamped around the thin metal handle, Christopher tempered his movements to prevent slamming the door as he heard his mother's words to her prized son. The phrase "king we need," floated from her as the door shut. Christopher stared absently into the dark hallway.

Marsha's rooms were close to his mother's, and he found her sitting at the small table most of their rooms housed, drafting one message after another and sealing them. Each was simple: "Your presence is requested at Volante. Arrive with haste."

Christopher watched Marsha seal each message with her husband's family ring. "Not your signet?"

"Did you come to help or stare?"

In answer, Christopher grabbed paper and pen, writing messages similar to Marsha's. Folding each in preparation for the seal, he reiterated his question.

"Few were at the trial." She whispered as though they weren't alone. "By using my husband's signet, I make a statement."

"You were the first to acknowledge him as king," Christopher said. "But this is a request under Lionel's name, not yours."

Marsha gave a curt nod, sealing another letter and writing a family name on the outside. "There are more parties at play here than the Tremaine family."

He paused in his writing and grimaced. "Charles forgot some things, but he remembers that ceremony, remembers its importance."

"Lukas will side with whatever majority is present." Marsha's hand moved with an intense ferocity across the page. "The furthest landowners in the north and south will not care, so long as they can maintain their current status of living. A status, I fear, your brother intends to change drastically."

"Would that be so bad?" Christopher blew gently on the paper he had written to dry the ink. "Besides, it's not like you were trying to get on his good side there."

"If he ever trusts anyone here but your mother, it'll be a miracle." Marsha folded the paper he had tossed. "Do you think he trusts you?"

Christopher shrugged, pulling another blank piece of paper toward him and staring at it. One sentence, spoken properly this time rather than as an idle threat, and the crowning ceremony would become much, much different. He had the knowledge, the connections, the training, perhaps even the trust of the country. A smarter man than he would have taken that step long ago. And, he decided silently, that smarter man would already be dead.

Instead, he plastered on a fake smile and gathered the marked papers. "I'll take these to the messengers for delivery." He shuffled a few of the folded letters so they would be less likely to fall. "I suppose whoever gets dismissed by him last is likely the one he trusts the most."

CHAPTER TEN

Charles barely registered the door closing behind him, his attention back on his mother and the phrase she'd hung in the air between them. Her knowing smile faltered when she raised the glass to her lips, skin crinkling as she pursed them together.

"Eonar told me."

His mother's smile disappeared. "Perhaps it is simply my time." She set the glass on the table beside her and pulled her shawl tighter. "Every year at the Harvest Feast, I made a wish. As many do. The same one, each time, since I was old enough to understand my parents' plans for me. For love to overcome the hatred, the prejudices our country holds." She straightened in her seat. "You can create that, Charles."

He tensed, remembering what would have awaited his successful return a decade ago. It wasn't his place to question his parents' relationship, but he could create a future where families would not be tossing young women his way, or his brother's way, vying for gain within the hierarchy their ancestors created.

"It can." His mother's voice strengthened as she wrapped a hand around the winged pendant she always wore. "Love, true love, can do so much."

Her words hit him like a thousand icy rain drops, and he leaned back against the wall, one hand gripping his sword hilt as he shoved aside the memory of using his sword to end his father's life.

"Did you. . ." He swallowed, knowing he might regret having the answer.

"Love can be found." Sharp blue eyes bore into him, reminding him of all she had done to protect him and his brothers. "Especially when you have more than yourself to look after."

He shifted and forced himself to loosen his grip. "You've done more than enough for me, Mae. Let me take care of you now."

That simple knowing smile returned. The shawl fell from her shoulders as she patted the now empty chair beside her, beckoning him closer.

Charles moved to oblige her request, nearly falling into the chair as she said, "Now please tell me you kissed that girl before she left."

At the thud and his shocked expression, his mother laughed. A soft pleasant sound he once believed he would never hear again. He glanced down at his hands, remembering Rose's hands intertwined with his, and an idiotic smile plastered itself onto his face for a moment. His mother's hand reached for his, squeezing it tightly. "I want to hear about your time there. As much or as little as you wish to share."

He returned the squeeze, sifting through the memories and deciding to start near the beginning. She listened with rapt attention, soaking in his every word. Solemn when he spoke of fighting alongside the Orda'anians, laughing with him at Rosealyn's sometimes unpredictable nature, and smirking after the laughter faded.

For hours, despite being tired from the journey home, he talked. Story after story came to mind, and it wasn't until the light from the glass windows in the ceiling above turned dark and a lamp needed to be lit that his mother said, "Rest, Charles. And don't forget to be as kind to your brother as others have been to you."

And there was the hidden reason, he realized as he stood. She must have noticed the tension between them and crafted this idea of a journey down memory lane to make him recognize the impact of another's actions. Mentally, he braced for another argument with Christopher.

With a soft sigh and a shift of his hair out of his eyes, he said, "I know. I'll see you tomorrow, Mae."

The soldiers Ashtar insisted on assigning as a royal guard followed him, which led to a much too pronounced grimace. Protecting others was *his* job. So he told them to stay by his mother's quarters, to report back to him anything and everything they saw. As he continued, alone, he questioned the command. Those men could be spies for Ashtar or Christopher. His expression deepened; his mother did not see Christopher as one not to trust, but Charles wasn't so sure.

His legs ached from the ride. Muscles heavy with exhaustion, he went to his childhood rooms. No one had mentioned the empty king's quarters. Those rooms, Charles decided, would likely remain empty for a long, long time.

He surveyed the room, not surprised to find the spacious area immaculate nor to find a servant standing beside the long table near one of the room's fireplaces. Older than Marigold, the maid stared at her feet, hands clasped in front of her too small frame, bushy curled hair covering each shoulder. Waiting. He shut out the memories again, not wanting to remember what he was like ten years ago.

On the table was a dinner fit for a king. A dinner she had likely carried here herself, awaiting his return to clear the plates and whatever he didn't eat. Charles removed his sword belt, resting the blade against a bed large enough for four.

The wafting smells made his stomach grumble as he pulled on the sleeves of the bright coat that had been dulled by the four-day journey from Vandyl to Volante. He had lost track of time while speaking with his mother, and neither had asked for any food to be brought. After hanging his coat on the back of the chair at the head of the table, he sat down.

"There's too much food for me to eat alone," he said and winced when the servant started shaking. For fear of him or for the simple thought that, as the eldest, he would be most like his father, he wasn't sure. Careful words, careful tone. He could be kind and firm. "Have you had your evening meal yet?"

She didn't look up, but the trembling lessened when she shook her head. Charles made a simple plate, a part of him eager to enjoy the pasta the Orda'anian cooks had thought him insane to ask for once.

"Share the rest with anyone else who has not eaten yet," he said. Her chin jerked up. "No need to waste it," he added and muttered to himself in recognition of what so much food meant. "The famine doesn't extend to here."

The young girl gathered the platters together, stacking them into a basket which allowed her to carry them all at once. He watched silently, thoughtfully. Once every platter was positioned, she chanced another glance up.

"Thank you, Your Majesty," she murmured with a deep bow.

"Thank you for bringing the meal." He twirled his fork in the middle of the plate and decided it was not the time to mention his newfound disdain for titles. A rank was one thing; this was another. He lifted the full fork and added, "Enjoy it."

He wasn't sure her eyes could get wider, but they did.

She hesitated and, at his arched brow, whispered, "The coat needs washed, Your Majesty."

"Right." He swallowed his bite and grabbed the coat from the back of the chair as he stood and walked to her to hand it over. She nearly dropped it but adjusted her tenuous grasp as she bowed again and walked out, leaving him alone in a spacious room.

The meal dredged up other memories, a different path than he had traveled as his mother listened. The memories of a childhood he had chosen to forget. For ten years he had allowed himself to be made new, to be changed into the man he was now. A protector, a leader, not just a ruler. Memories of a time long past continued to pester him as he ate in silence while reflecting on his upbringing.

He went for another bite, only to discover the plate was empty. Exhaustion seeped into his muscles, so he lay down. Memories, however, continued invading as he drifted into sleep.

So particular, his father. No matter if it hadn't been his fault, Charles took the blame. Time and time again. A back-handed slap, blood dripping that he refused to wipe away while harsh words reverberated around him. A quiet tent after a warmly shared fire. And with a twist of his wrist, his fate had been sealed. An agreement crafted and honored.

Clashes and shouts jolted him awake, making him reach for his sword. He nestled back into the bed when he recognized a soft mattress below rather than the uneven hard ground.

He stared above him at the small glass squares adorned in the soft pinks and purples which preceded the rising sun. The pinks and purples turned to a light blue, casting rays of light along the stone floor covered with simple dull colored rugs which offered a path to a bathing chamber and a closet. As he passed the closet, Charles noticed the small room was filled with half a dozen coats of the same shade and cut as the one the servant had taken the previous evening and nothing else. Same with the pants. All black and plain cut.

After splashing cold water on his face, he returned to the closet for another simple white shirt to replace the one he wore and donned another of the bright flame-like coats with a silent hope all of them were brand new. He paused at the final button and smirked. No reason to be even more uncomfortable today.

In the sitting area, the same servant from the previous night waited with a much smaller amount of food for his morning meal. Buckling the sword around his waist, he told her, "I'll take my morning meal in an hour in the main dining room. With Christopher."

She offered a silent bow and replaced the few platters into the basket, this time with much less shaking. He paused near the door, remembering how quickly servants had been rotated before aiding in the fight against Eilon. When he turned toward her, the platters were covered and she stood with head down, staring at her feet like she was inconsequential.

"I'm glad you were comfortable enough to return." He almost rested his hand on the sword hilt before catching himself, knowing such a movement might make her tremble from head to toe again. All of them, every servant, had feared for their lives every second in his father's presence. Charles knew why, had seen it happen firsthand until he felt numb to such quick, unfeeling deaths. One move out of order, one word out of line, one thing out of place and that ruby-hilted dagger appeared.

"I'll inform the kitchens and Prince Christopher's servant, Your Majesty." She bowed deep, head lowered.

"You should look up more often so you can see where you're going," he said. "And if you are to remain the servant in charge of these rooms, I need to know what to call you besides . . . you."

"Viola, Your Majesty," she answered without looking up.

"Well, Viola, if anyone inquires about me, I will be in the training yards." His hand had settled onto his sword hilt despite the effort not to do so. He whispered to himself, "And hopefully there will be a few soldiers not too afraid to spar against me."

CHAPTER ELEVEN

"They've been here a week," Celena reminded Arjun, her centuries-old friend. They stood in the middle of the hallway—her with arms crossed, him with hands shoved into the deep pockets of his billowing robes whose color matched his tawny hair and skin. Because he was expressionless more often than not, she was surprised to see a brief albeit feisty flash of a glare from Arjun when she added, "I've exhausted all options for either severing the connection or forcing the weapon back together."

"Does she know they're here?" Arjun indicated the door behind which rested the wielders of Praeteritum and Futurae. Celena shook her head, and Arjun sighed. "I don't like this idea of yours."

"If we don't take it and hide it, she will instead." Celena tried not to speak through clenched teeth. "She slithered her way into controlling the island meant to contain her. If she knows this—"

"She knows," Arjun interrupted with a faint grimace. "Naomi can wield the power the crystals contain, can use them to obtain information she otherwise would not have."

The movement of his hands caused glass bottles to clink together within the folds of cloth covering him. "If this works, if we can remove Eilon's magic, what will we do with it?"

"Return it to its rightful owner."

"Are we ignoring the fact the rightful owner of said magic is now dead?"

"Magna's magic transferred to Synda." Celena shrugged. "Eilon's would have done something similar if it were not trapped, correct?"

"Then why not try and take it when they killed Eilon?" Arjun retorted.

Celena frowned ever so slightly. "The balance of these abilities must be properly restored, Arjun." Celena gritted her teeth, deciding not to tell Arjun how her previous attempt had failed. Did Naomi even know Eilon had resurfaced? Or that he had been defeated? Those were answers to discover another day, once they knew where Eilon's magic would stay.

"And who are you to decide who receives Eilon's magic? A well as deep, if not deeper, than what Synda inherited?" The robes swayed, followed by the tinkling cascade. "Where is our kind white dragon, anyway?"

"Keeping an eye on the resurging drokos," Celena muttered. "And yes, the one who is able to know the innermost thoughts of the dragons should help decide where their power goes. My connection is often one way. I hear them even when they do not want me to. But I choose when they hear me."

"How can you be so sure?" Arjun's tone shifted, more a demand than a curiosity.

She almost growled at the small tug against her chest, the desire to immediately answer her longtime friend. "If they did, Eilon would certainly have engulfed me in flames long ago."

"And there are no other options left?"

Again, that small tug. She glowered at him and grumbled, "Short of tossing them into a danger legitimate enough for the weapons to warrant combining again, no."

"Sorry," he whispered as she rubbed an open palm against her chest. "I wanted to be sure."

"You would think, after a century, you would trust me." Celena dropped her hand to her side.

"What you are planning—" Arjun shook his head, loosening several strands of long tawny hair from their hold at the nape of his neck. "Questions get answered. That is all. But this?"

She faced the door and nudged Arjun with a sharp elbow. "You are very convincing," she said, opening the door swiftly and quietly.

A twang of guilt surfaced for not offering them separate rooms, solely for this possibility. Surprisingly, only a few death threats had been tossed between the two. In their week-long stay, that was becoming the new normal for the long-lived Xannan and naïve Rosealyn. More surprising had been the knowledge the weapons prevented them from killing one another. That had to have been a byproduct of the weapons' combining, otherwise Xannan could never have killed Phillippe with Praeteritum.

Rosealyn stirred and did not wake, but Xannan lifted to his elbows with a mocking grin. "It won't work." He rolled onto his side, face to the wall.

"What won't?" Arjun inquired with his commanding tone, head tilting to one side with an air of curiosity.

"The magic inside the weapons cannot be moved," Xannan said, his voice muffled, with no indication if Arjun's influence had truly persuaded the Lost Prince of Orda'an or if the man had chosen to reply.

"It will work. It has to," Celena said with a sidelong glance at Arjun.

He pulled a newly formed crystal from the folds of his robes, handing it over and walking between the two beds. When his hand grasped the hilt of Praeteritum, Xannan sat up and grabbed Arjun's wrist.

"It will not work." Xannan enunciated each word, wrenching the weapon from Arjun's grip and setting it on the bed beside him. He turned toward Celena, who was holding the crystal, and muttered, "Idiots."

Celena looked to Arjun, hoping he could read her unspoken question. A slight shake of his head made her frown deepen. Xannan chuckled, the sound which covered his persistent annoyance at Rosealyn's constant death threats.

"Go ahead." He tossed Praeteritum, and Celena caught it with her free hand as he said, "Last I understood, magic has a mind of its own."

Lips tightened, she studied Praeteritum and the empty crystal she'd asked Arjun to retrieve. "Futurae?"

Arjun picked up Futurae, resting a hand on Rosealyn's shoulder to help her settle back into sleep. At Celena's raised brow, Arjun said, "I was curious if it would work, especially since it barely worked on him."

She nodded and knelt to lay one sword atop the other. Resting the crystal Arjun had retrieved atop where the swords crossed, Celena whispered, "A new crystal for an ancient power, a storehouse for the magic, a tether until it can be restored to a proper host."

The crystal shuddered in her hand, reverberating through and around her. Shedding its metallic façade, Futurae flared as bright as Praeteritum. Celena squinted at the crystal humming in her hand. The vibrations started slow and steady. A crack appeared and widened. The new crystal shattered into dust. And even the dust faded into nothing. Celena ground her teeth. "What am I missing?"

Both swords returned to their normal appearance. Celena grasped the weapons and stood, then hissed and dropped them. The clatter made Rosealyn stir in her sleep until Arjun's calming hand rested on her shoulder.

"Like I said," came Xannan's gruff voice as he bent to retrieve the swords. "The magic has a mind of its own."

He glanced askance at Rosealyn, head tilting at Arjun's hand on her shoulder, and looked back to Celena. "Who is Naomi?"

"An elf of Tribe Izari." Celena shrugged at Arjun's raised brow. She saw no reason to withhold the information, especially if it meant the current wielder of such powerful magic might help them. "In her fear of magic going wrong, she hoards it. Stores it in one crystal after another, and now uses it herself."

Another tilt of his head, sharp green eyes unreadable. "For what gain?" Xannan asked, as though assessing a new plot of land to purchase rather than a threat to their livelihood.

"Control." Arjun stepped away from the princess. "Against elves, dragons, and all magic wielders. None could help in her time of need, and that fear drove her to find a way to contain the magic, find a way to use it whenever she needs it. In the last few years, she's perfected the crystals which can harbor magic."

Arjun gestured at Celena, and she added, "That crystal Arjun managed to retrieve had been grown by her. How, he refuses to tell."

"But as power tends to do, it corrupts." Xannan stared at the blade in his hand. It was not a question but a statement of his own experience, which made Celena wonder what Xannan would do if they broke his connection to the blade. Stay and assist his distant relation to rule the country he would have ruled before being kidnapped by a dragon? Or would breaking the connection kill him? For curiosity's sake, Celena would have to follow Xannan closely.

Arjun shoved his hands back inside those obnoxious billowing robes. Celena held her hands as though the weapons remained in her grasp, and Xannan returned to his bed to sit cross-legged.

After a moment's silence, Xannan asked, "Do the elves hold true to their core values?"

"Bound from birth to never kill?" Celena watched the confused and groggy Rosealyn sit up. "Arjun and I are bound, yes, but not all of the Elven Houses hold those same beliefs. I am unaware if Naomi's family did or did not bind their young."

"Then until this Naomi is on the same continent as us, I see no reason to worry about her." Xannan rested his hands atop his knees.

"Besides, I'm sure the princess will be more than happy to send enough death threats her way for the both of us."

"Depends on if they deserve to die," Rosealyn said, gathering the blankets into her chest.

"What excellent peacemakers," Celena muttered. "If only Praesidio had done what Magna, Eonar, and Seth intended."

Understanding lit up the princess's eyes a second before they furrowed at Arjun's closeness. "What did you do to me?"

"And that answers if she would know." Arjun wrapped one hand around his chin and looked down at the princess. "How do you feel?"

"Extra . . . groggy," she said, peering around Arjun at Xannan, who still stared at the ceiling. "Naomi?"

Celena sighed. "We have exhausted all options here for severing the connection of the weapons. I doubt either Charles's or Christopher's swords will assist."

Celena left the room, followed by Arjun who muttered a soft apology to the princess, as he always did after using his abilities on those he cared about. Closing the door, he turned to Celena and asked, "Will they trust us?"

Celena grunted. "Will they have a choice?"

Chapter Twelve

"The training yards?" Christopher asked Viola again and, at her affirmative nod, shifted in his seat. He'd gone in search of his brother, hoping to learn what Charles's grand plans were for the country. For the past several generations, the fields had been used as punishment. Owners of each plantation often weaseled their way into the castle at one point or another, families hunting for the right match to propel future generations to more prosperity than their own. A similar push had landed their mother in the castle at one point and allowed her to be chosen.

"And morning meal in an hour, in the main dining hall, specifically with me?" Christopher clarified. Viola gave another affirmative nod. He waved a dismissive hand in her direction, only knowing she'd left by hearing the door open and close.

Rather than wait, Christopher decided to visit his brother. He remembered the awe of watching his elder brothers spar, admonished on occasion by various mentors. Too young to join, Christopher memorized their movements, how they flowed around each other. But his lanky limbs weren't meant for graceful weapon showmanship. He wiped his hands on his legs, desperate to annihilate the thoughts that he was inconsequential. An afterthought.

Even his rooms were set apart from the rest, closer to the training yards. Within moments, he was outside and climbing the stairs to the pathway between the parapets. A sheer rocky cliff of the mountainside was an arm's reach away, but Christopher quelled his desire to touch it by hurrying to the training yards. Soon it was evident he wasn't the only one curious how Charles handled a sword.

Soldiers in simple gray slacks and gray shirts surrounded the only occupied ring outside the main castle square. Logically, only one soldier had been willing to enter the ring with their king: Ashtar. They parried back and forth with wooden swords. Charles's movements were as graceful as Christopher remembered; Ashtar's movements were slow in comparison. The general wore his gray uniform, the golden bars on his shoulders marking his rank glinting in the morning sun. Charles, however, had removed his coat, the white shirt clinging to him despite the occasional gusts of chilling winds.

Christopher rested his arms on the stone wall, noting the comfort Charles exhibited within the ring, an ease absent at almost all other times. His movements showed a lack of tension, a fluidity from one swing to the next. Despite Ashtar's bare-teethed growls, Charles was calm. Neck, heart, side, wherever Ashtar left an opening, Charles found it.

Eventually, Ashtar fell to one knee and held up a hand as a request for them to stop. With a simple step back and a firm nod, Charles obliged and rested the tip of the sword on the chaotic swirls of dirt.

"I'm surprised you held back," Christopher shouted down to them and was met with the awestruck faces of the observing soldiers.

A brief smile flashed across Charles's face. "Care to work up an appetite?"

Christopher tilted his head and chuckled, whispering to himself, "I'm sure you would enjoy the chance to 'assess' my abilities." With a mental reminder he needed to earn Charles's trust, he hollered, "It will be much less exciting than what you all just witnessed, I'm sure."

Ashtar grunted as Christopher took the nearest stairs down to the training yard. The general had overseen some of his training but had left most of it to his brothers. After Caedmon's death, no one had taken up his training. Not that he requested it. Fighting in these rings for hours was dull. Stories were better.

Standing before the weapon rack, Christopher chose two wooden daggers. Glancing behind him, Christopher noticed a slight tension reappearing in his brother.

"Dagger versus a sword is always . . . interesting, is it not?" Christopher approached, holding each dagger pointed at the ground.

Charles's white shirt was sticky with sweat, but his breaths were slow and controlled, unlike Ashtar's.

The dirt below them had been sifted by Ashtar's and Charles's movements, which could make footing uneven. Christopher took a long step and slashed upward, only for Charles to step out of the way. Christopher became a flurry of twists and turns, no different from what Caedmon had once taught him, but Charles sidestepped each slash, not even lifting his sword to block a strike. Up, down, around, side, side, up, up, down. Christopher mentally recited his pattern, hoping it would tire Charles before long. Christopher went through his pattern three times. A fourth. A fifth. Each strike, Charles avoided. Their blades met once. Once in the five times Christopher went through the pattern of slashes.

Chest aching for more air, Christopher stepped back, pacing while he worked to breathe evenly. Charles had the same look on his face that their mother so often offered to him. Pity. Definitely pity. Perhaps a hint of shame?

"How was your chat with *Mae*?" Christopher twisted a dagger so it pointed forward and lunged. Charles grabbed Christopher's wrist, halting the movement. No matter how Christopher wriggled it, Charles held him firm.

Behind Christopher, Ashtar cleared his throat and mumbled incoherently under his breath. Soon naught but the frigid mountain wind surrounded them. Christopher was grateful there was no longer an audience, though Charles's grip did not lessen.

"I get it." Charles tossed the wooden sword aside and removed the dagger from Christopher's hand, tossing it to the ground as well. "You're angry. At me. At Father. At Mae. Perhaps even yourself."

Christopher thrust with his other dagger, but Charles moved faster. Smarter. Still holding Christopher's wrist, Charles stepped behind his brother and had Christopher's arm wrapped at a precarious angle that made him bite his tongue to prevent any grunt or scream of pain from escaping.

"I'm angry at *you*." Christopher dared a glance over his shoulder. The pity now resembled worry, and Christopher had the urge to suffer a broken arm to punch his brother in the face. Christopher faced forward, mentally preparing for the pain, but Charles's grip loosened. Christopher feigned a half step forward when Charles released his hold but didn't give his brother the chance to move by stomping on Charles's foot and plunging the lone dagger blindly behind him. It found naught but air, and Christopher gritted his teeth.

"You want me to think you care?" Christopher rotated to face Charles. His brother was weaponless and hadn't made a sound when Christopher's heel slammed into Charles's toes. "Is that it? That you care? Now? When it's too late?"

Christopher didn't wait for an answer, lunging forward with his dagger poised. As he suspected, Charles stopped the arm holding the dagger but didn't see Christopher's punch until fist had met chin. Or chose not to.

"My options were . . . limited." Charles wrinkled his nose as he tugged the second dagger free of Christopher's hand.

"You? Limits?" Christopher scoffed, flexing his hand. The sting of contact was more satisfying than he'd anticipated. "I wasn't aware you could be held to any *limits*."

"What do you mean?" Charles frowned, releasing Christopher's wrist and gathering the discarded weapons. When Christopher did not immediately respond, Charles returned the weapons to the rack, close to the castle wall where his coat also lay. The king's coat.

Christopher crossed his arms, resisting the urge to rub his wrists. "Did you mean what you said? About a compromise?" He slowed his breathing, wondering if his wrists were bruised.

"Not just a compromise," Charles amended as he donned the red coat. He made no move to button it. "A future where we learn to work together toward a common goal. Finding value in the lives of all who surround us, not just those closest to us."

Christopher chuckled. "You and she are made for each other, aren't you?"

Charles raised a brow in question, but Christopher waved a dismissive hand. "She, too, finds value in all life. Or so she said."

"They all do in Orda'an." Charles filled an empty wooden cup with water from a nearby barrel. "It was Phillippe's motto. Protect, defend, but do not provoke an attack."

The opposite of their own, Christopher realized, shoulders stiffening while he replayed their brief sparring match. Charles had stayed on the defensive, had not outright attacked once. All Christopher had done was throw one strike after another.

"*This* was never truly in my future." Christopher gestured sharply at Charles's attire. "And you cannot replace what I had with my brothers. You and *Mae* should both know that." Jaw clenched, Christopher muttered, "Mother stopped letting us call her that. Mae. When you. . ." He swallowed and tugged on the collar of his deep red jacket with dull silver buttons and gold trim.

Christopher approached until he was inches from his brother's face. Charles's unflinching, unfaltering gaze caused Christopher's nostrils to flare. "I have no interest in any type of *compromise* where I'm left to follow in another's shadow."

Perhaps there was a wince, maybe a dark shadow, but Charles remained calm. "I'd like to discuss my plans during the morning meal. Join me?"

Christopher blinked, mouth agape. He'd thought his brother's words no more than talk, an empty promise. It's what his father had always given him. Empty promises followed by demands.

"You want me. . ."

The thought was too foreign; Christopher had trouble finishing it aloud.

"Your advice, your knowledge of the current plantation owners, whatever information you have that could be of use, yes," Charles said with a subtle inclination of his head. He tipped back the remainder of his water. "Unless you'd prefer—"

"No." Christopher grimaced at his hasty speech. "I'll join you. What about Aunt Marsha?"

"We can update her before the meetings with the plantation owners who have already arrived. But note that by the time the official crowning ceremony is complete, the plantations will never be home to slaves again. Paid workers with proper living conditions, yes. Slaves, no."

It was a small offering, no different from the outstretched hand he'd once failed to provide. But it was a shadow. "As you command," Christopher said with a small bow.

Chapter Thirteen

Rosealyn flinched when the door closed behind the elves, rubbing her arms and standing. "What was that about? Who is Naomi?"

"Not our concern." Xannan stood and buckled his sword around his waist. "Let's leave now, before anyone else interrupts our beauty sleep."

Rosealyn scowled. "That's not an answer. Why were Celena and Arjun in here? And why didn't I wake up when they came in?"

"I'm ready to leave." Xannan opened the door. "We've rested, bathed, now it's time to go."

Grumbling, Rosealyn gathered the few supplies Celena had offered the previous night. Several packs of food, which Rosealyn did not plan to share, and her mother's letter. Perhaps, soon, her own magical abilities would manifest. She paused, letter gripped in her hand. What would happen when her magic manifested? Would it be a different way to break the connection of the Twin Blades? But how could she force the magic to work? If she even had any?

Xannan's footsteps sounded down the hall, and something tugged at her chest. *So that's what it feels like when we roam too far.*

A moment later, he reappeared in the doorway, glowering. "Do you want to get rid of this connection or no?"

"If you hurt anyone—"

"Threats are pointless." He turned down the hall again, leaving Rosealyn to grind her teeth. She shoved her mother's letter into the sack, gave the room one last cursory glance, and followed.

"Shouldn't we let Celena and Arjun know we're leaving?" She looped each of her arms into the straps.

"They know."

"Wouldn't you like supplies of your own?"

"You'll share."

Rosealyn considered making a vulgar gesture at his back but resisted the urge. "Horses?"

"It's a two days walk. No need."

She sighed. He had a point, and the elves were annoyed their last borrowed mounts had not yet been returned. Another matter to take care of upon her arrival in Volante. Their, she corrected. Their arrival. Wherever she went, he would have to go as well.

After additional prodding, Xannan stopped by the kitchens and asked for a pack of food, a bedroll, and a map. He studied the map extensively, jaw clenched when he finally tucked it into his pack.

Two days of travel also meant two nights sleeping beneath the sky while trusting each other to remain safe. Once Rosealyn had wondered aloud if either of them dying meant death for the other, the threats had become less frequent. It had not, however, assuaged her constant desire to hit him.

Though it was the middle of the night when Celena and Arjun had interrupted their sleep, it was dawn by the time they left Andalova. The sun's glow was faint, blocked by the impressive height of the Mountains of Ingoria.

"Two days?" They paused at the village's edge. Standing there felt momentous and anticlimactic. Stuck together, forced to work together, to travel together, but what choice did she have?

He offered a grunted affirmative and set a grueling pace, barely glancing behind to see if she was keeping up. Slit skirts were beneficial, but soon the sun warred with the icy wind. Her legs, buffeted by one swift breeze after another, became chilled to the bone while her shoulders and head felt warmer and warmer as the sun climbed higher. The sun passed its zenith, crawling its way down the sky opposite the mountains and making the snow-capped peaks sparkle. In other company, she might have paused to appreciate the beauty of it.

Dusk neared, and her stomach rumbled, so she stopped and removed the pack of supplies, setting the bag on the ground to better rummage. Before she placed her hand in the bag, Xannan grabbed it.

"We have company," he whispered, eyes darting around them. "Food will have to wait."

She opened the bag further, plunging a hand inside to find something to consume lest her stomach eat itself; she should have paused earlier but hadn't wanted to delay the trip any. Xannan tugged her arm away, closing the bag with his other hand.

"This is not pleasant company."

"How would you know? They're people traveling along the road like we are so—"

"Not people."

His tone made her pause and stare at him. How could he know these newcomers were not people? How could he sense them, whatever they were, and she couldn't?

"Not peop—" And then she saw it, much closer than she would have liked it to be considering how recent Xannan's warning had been. She had seen them before. The vision in the cave, the smaller dragon-like creatures, vicious teeth dripping with a dark liquid. That vision had been of a pack. This was just one. Their name escaped her.

Though far enough away to not bring immediate fear, it was close enough for her to see the dark splotchy scales of its wings, the long snake-like tail, the narrow snout, and the wrinkled skin of its chest and belly. It stood on higher ground, lifting to its hind legs while its neck stretched up, uncoiling. Dry, why did her mouth always go dry when encountering the unexpected?

"A drokos," Xannan confirmed, though she hadn't asked. "Fortunately for us, dragon-wrought blades are good at killing the dragon fodder."

She worked moisture back into her mouth and hoped her voice wouldn't crack. "Dragon fodder?" All Xannan did was nod, so she added, "You said Magna eliminated them. That thing shouldn't exist."

"I see it. Do you?" He watched the drokos as it sniffed the air, head maneuvering, hunting.

"Unfortunately," she mumbled. "What now?"

"If we kill it, others will know of the magic in our swords. Droki hunt magic. So we don't use the swords, hide away from it, and it will leave us alone."

A creature able to smell magic was both fascinating and terrifying.

"And if we possess magic other than that found in the swords?"

His gaze whipped to hers, eyes narrowing, surprisingly, with concern. The lifted brow was a demand for an explanation, but the drokos moved and uttered a sound unlike any Rosealyn had ever heard before. One she definitely did not want to hear again. As if at her thought, it quieted. The drokos lowered back to all four feet, lying prone and silent.

"What did you do?" Xannan asked quietly. His hand gripped her wrist, nails digging into her skin.

"Nothing," she mumbled, wrenching free of his grasp. "But shouldn't we gain more distance before it follows us?"

"They are a nuisance to kill, even with this sword." His scrutiny of her made her feel more unlike herself than she had since the weapons had combined. "And I'd rather not deal with the swords combining again, lest I become the punching bag this time."

For too long a moment, he continued studying her, and whatever retort she tried to dream up disappeared from her mind. That tickle of curiosity came again, mingling with barely veiled anger. At that precise moment, all she wanted to do was get away from the drokos.

After a cursory glance at the prone drokos, Xannan turned and walked faster than before. Off the dirt path, inside the trees which grew near the base of the mountains. She dared to look back once, wondering if she would see the drokos following. Its shrill cry rang out when she thought of the creature, causing shivers to run down her skin. *I really hope it stays far, far away.*

Xannan stopped.

Chest heaving, she surveyed their surroundings. A small clearing surrounded by trees of various heights. Stones jutted from the ground at odd angles, an indication of their proximity to the mountain's rocky facade.

"Good as anywhere, I suppose," she said, hoping to avoid any discussion of the strange creature they had encountered.

Xannan grunted, nodded, and began gathering wood. Before long, they sat opposite each other, a blaring blaze between them. As night fell, Rosealyn appreciated the warmth, snacking on the nuts Celena had proffered the previous night.

For a long time, they sat in silence. No threats, no jabs, simple silence.

"Which parent?" Xannan's question jolted her, breaking her daze into the flames.

"What?"

"From which parent did you inherit magic?"

"Oh." Rosealyn dug her toe into the dirt. "My birth mother. Do you have any? Magic of your own, I mean?"

Through the dancing shadows the light of the flame cast on his face, she saw his lips lift on one side.

"Wouldn't you like to know?" he murmured.

If the fire weren't separating them, she would have punched him.

He poked at the flames with a stick, green eyes illuminated by their glow. "How did your magic manifest?"

"It hasn't." Rosealyn rubbed her arms. She should have asked for a cloak in addition to the travel bedding. Night air in the valley by a mountain range was as cold as a winter's night back home.

That earned his common response: a soft grunt.

"Rest," he said. "I'll take the first watch."

"And if the drokos—"

"I can smell them long before they arrive." He prodded at the fire with a branch. "Now I understand why it chose to land." He tossed the branch into the fire. "Besides, they are not stealthy creatures."

Rosealyn nodded, spreading her travel bedding out close to the fire. Once snuggled inside, she found sleep elusive. Every time she closed her eyes, the snake-like neck and beady black eyes dominated her vision.

Chapter Fourteen

Though her brothers had offered to find a carriage, Adela refused. The sooner they could control the situation at Vandyl, the better. So she rolled with the movement, jerking forward and back with the horse's steady pace. Not that she couldn't ride a horse on her own, but the overall length of the journey had almost persuaded her to accept the carriage. Four days. Four days of her thighs rubbing against the saddle, four days of the smell of men surrounding her, four days to mentally prepare for seeing the destruction of her childhood home.

Familiar fields where she once roamed and played as a girl stretched around them. Surrounded by those ever-present soldiers. Like her brothers, they had prepared her for the possibility of the Gift Passing to her, though the priests were adamant a woman would never receive it.

Not all women are created equally. The friends of her youth looked over families of their own, raising children. A blessing Adela would never experience. When her first child had died of illness within days of his birth, Adela prevented future heartache. Losing the one had nearly destroyed her, especially so close to losing her husband in that first battle against Hoclia.

Phillippe had consoled her, and apologized, but Alan made sure the grief didn't consume her. Her thoughts drew further inward, remembering the disapproving glances from Theo. He hadn't understood; he'd lost no one. Not outside their shared losses, that was. Theo's wife trained young women, and their son Jacin had joined the ranks of the Orda'anian army.

The jangle of horses around her stopped as they crested the hill. Dilapidated buildings were dotted with fresh wood, melding into one another and giving way to the castle's stone walls within the city's center. Melancholy citizens ventured through the streets, visages tense and cautious, wary of the new arrivals. Her flitting gaze snapped back to the castle, to the melted stone walls.

"Even the dragonstone," she breathed, and her brothers echoed the sentiment. In a reverent whisper, she added, "May the Blaze of our ancestors carry them home and comfort those who remain."

She nudged her horse into a slow walk, reminding herself to breathe as she surveyed the damage. Grandiose walls which had once protected those inside lay in shambles. Stones had melted, leaving large gaps which would grant anyone access, and distant shouts sounded amid pounding hammers. Repairs. Standing in the center of the singed courtyard was a man too young to be so scarred or to be wearing General Azeiah's uniform. She closed her eyes and said another silent prayer for the fallen general.

"Welcome home, my lords, my lady," Moss said with a bow to each. He approached her mare to hold the reins while she dismounted. The wrinkled skin on the left side of his face momentarily distracted Adela, providing a stark reminder that fire had harmed more than buildings. If the marred skin bothered him, Moss's visage belied it. "Rooms in the repaired area of the castle await, and a meal will be ready within the hour."

"Good." Adela maintained her grip on the pommel after dismounting. They'd ridden for the past several hours, and her legs were not as sturdy as she wished them to be. "And the remaining priests will join us?"

Moss nodded, though a muscle in his jaw twitched when he did. "Yes, my lady. Those who remain."

"It sounds like the repairs are going well." Alan stood beside her, looking as though he hadn't spent the past half a day stuck atop a horse.

"As much as it would be nice for us all to get caught up—apologies, General Moss—we should prepare for this meeting," Theo reminded them.

Adela frowned. "What's left to prepare, Theo? We present the idea of a council until we find Rosealyn."

Her answer came when another group arrived from the opposite direction. Her eyes narrowed as she recognized the younger man. Age had only made Jacin the spitting image of his father. Dressed in deep brown leathers and holding himself like the bona fide soldier he'd become, Jacin dismounted and gave Adela an apologetic glance. Lips pursed, Adela turned her glare to Theo.

"It would be wrong not to present all options," Theo said. "Hoclia and Alkaan have sent many threats against our lands. We cannot last long without a proper ruling body for our country, or those two will take whatever they can get their hands on."

"As Father likes to remind me," Jacin said as he strolled toward their small gathering in the courtyard, continuing in a slightly mocking tone when he reached them. "'Our ancestors gave too much of themselves to let those Northerners take what is now ours.'"

"Always going behind our backs," Adela muttered, glancing between her brother and her nephew.

"I've already been looking for Rosealyn." Jacin didn't flinch when Adela pinned him with a glare. "As soon as Father's contact in Tenoa sent confirmation Queen Roseanne was there, he sent for me. But it is difficult to traverse quickly through the Northern lands. And cold."

In the North? Odd. It took too much effort not to cross her arms and let the glare deepen at each of them. Tradition should mean something. The young general remained wide-eyed between them. And then Alan, the once instigator of sibling chaos, became the voice of reason when hers had disappeared.

He offered one of his broad disarming smiles, clasped their nephew in a bear of a hug, and announced in a jovial tone, "Not only is there much to discuss, I'm sure we each have many stories to tell."

"I'd rather know Theo's angle now," Adela said, the words surprising her when they tumbled out. Her brain was reeling, slowly putting together the pieces of Theo's plan. "Why was Jacin in the Northern lands? All the way to the Northern coasts?"

After a quick glance to his father and a subtle nod from Theo, Jacin explained in a single word that was far from suitable as a proper answer. "Scouting."

"You," Adela snapped at Moss, wincing at the tone of her voice. "Which room are the priests to meet us in?"

"The dining rooms were—"

"Good, we'll meet them there." Adela straightened her arms which had crossed subconsciously in her frustration. She waited for the general to walk several steps away and asked, "Scouting for what purpose?"

"To know what's coming," Theo said. "Jearnia stopped attacking and Tenoa became an ally through the union, but Hoclia took all of his attention. So I decided it would be good to monitor Alkaan by placing someone I trusted within their midst."

"And what, pray tell, did you learn with all this scouting?"

Jacin, who had always been as brash as his father, gave Theo a sidelong glance and looked down. "Most monarchs, given the chance, are as greedy as the next and always want more. More land, more food, more money, more power. Usually for themselves. The young king of Alkaan is no different."

"Few are," Adela agreed, surveying Jacin's odd posture again. "What has your father told you of his plans here?"

"Enough," he said. Another insufficient answer.

"And how do you think Rosealyn would react to this plan?" Adela turned to her brothers. "And you both, what do you think she'll say?"

"Well," Jacin answered first. "I'm sure she would agree to my being here before relinquishing ourselves over to some other kingdom. But, um. . ."

Theo snapped, "But what, Jacin?"

"Rosealyn offered both Hoclia and Alkaan portions of our land in return for their aid in killing a dragon. Few of their men survived, so now they want more retribution than just land."

A stream of curses flew through Adela's mind. "Get rid of one threat only to face others," she gritted out as she walked inside the castle proper. The clanging of metal and creaking of armor followed her, echoing through barren halls of singed stone. No tapestries depicting their history, no portraits showing past monarchs. Each step provided further evidence of Phillippe's presence within this castle and made her skin feel clammy, wishing she could have one more conversation with her kind-hearted brother.

When they arrived at the dining room, Moss stood outside with a lanky, well-dressed man who was taller than any of the priests Adela remembered meeting. His white tunic was tarnished with streaks of dirt hiding the customary gold thread along the cuffs, but the black pants were unmarred. Brown hair held taut with string made the priest's beady eyes stand out, despite the spectacles which magnified his darting pupils.

"This is Maslin," Moss said, nodding at the priest. "The other priests were all about their duties at the time and. . ." Moss rubbed the back of his neck, scarred face turning somber. "Maslin is the last."

A sheen formed against Maslin's skin.

"Who did you train under?" she asked.

Maslin wet his lips and stuttered out, "Elder Matthias."

"So you are familiar with the laws of succession established by King Gailin?"

Maslin offered a bobbing nod in return.

"Excellent." She motioned for them to enter the dining room. "We'll let Theo present his idea first and see how our lonesome priest thinks it fits with the proper laws of succession. General Moss, join us. If only to keep my brother safe from my stares of disapproval."

Alan chuckled, halted mid-sound by the glare she gave him, and they all entered the dining room and sat down. Like the hallways, the dining room walls were bare. A simple table, large enough to seat ten, encompassed most of the space. Glasses of water waited for them, and Adela reminded herself to sip the liquid rather than gulp it, as her mother had always instructed.

"The laws of succession are truly quite simple," Maslin began, as though he were about to lecture them. Adela tightened her grip on the glass but decided the reminder would do Theo a decent amount of good. "All it takes is for one child of the current monarch to experience the Passing, to receive the LeNoir Gift, and the crown is theirs."

"And if a monarch dies with no heir?" Theo asked, avoiding Adela's eyes.

Maslin's jaw worked up and down, gaze roaming over the room. "Well . . . um." He paused, staring at the ceiling in thought.

"As I suspected," Theo said, "We—"

"Can create a plan for such a possibility," Adela said, more harshly than she'd intended.

"Why would it be so wrong to have Jacin assume the throne, Adela?" Theo demanded. He stood behind his chair, hands gripping the top edge as though he would pick it up and throw it across the room. "Why are you so adamant to protect a tradition that may have died with Rosealyn?"

"Because moving on would mean believing she is gone." Adela leaned forward, pressing her hands against the table. "And I refuse to believe that. Rosealyn may be naïve and young, but she is also strong-willed and cares. I realize what we witnessed during our last visit here was worrisome; that was not the Rosealyn we watched our brother raise. A dragon, Theo. Rosealyn helped kill a dragon to protect Orda'an."

"It's barely been a week since they killed Eilon, and Cap—" General Moss cleared his throat. "King Charles is surely looking for her as well."

The soldier's eyes barely widened when all heads swiveled to him, and he tensed. "I doubt they've admitted it to each other yet, but that won't stop them from looking for one another."

"Did he tell you more?" Adela demanded. "Something that wasn't in his letter to each of us?"

Moss withdrew into himself for a moment, his lack of experience as a commander briefly showing, and stood tall again. With a quick rounding of his shoulders, he answered with a firm resolve. "I believe we would all know if Her Majesty were gone; therefore, I believe she can either be found or will soon return to us."

Adela smiled briefly at the general's use of proper honorifics for her niece, but the frown returned at Maslin's droning voice.

"We would need confirmation of her death before allowing another who did not experience the Passing to assume the throne." Maslin spoke like a lecturer. Beads of perspiration were evident along his brow, and his breaths were shallow, but he had said what Adela needed him to say.

"And until we provide such confirmation?" Theo asked, muscles bulging from his tight grip on the chair.

"Our initial plan we agreed upon in Cantadad," Alan said as a half question and half statement. "We three as a council of stewards. Jacin could continue searching for her?"

Moss spoke softly. "I'd start in Jearnia."

Adela squinted at him. "You know more than you've said."

A shake of his head, a visible swallow. "Just a hunch, my lady."

She released a long breath, closing her eyes and inhaling as deeply as she could manage, finding her center, finding calm. When Alan's hand touched hers, she smiled, grateful for how much they had grown together as siblings. He understood her more than the others, for he too had lost his small family. But it was not the time to wallow in her past; she'd grown from it and refused to let it consume her ever again. It was time to find her niece, and this young general seemed to know exactly where she could be found.

"The new king of Jearnia is familiar with you, so, Moss, you will take me to him," she said, before anyone else tried to change her mind.

"Adela," Alan said as a warning while Theo merely grunted and finally sat in his seat.

"I will not change Theo's mind, and based on what I've seen of Maslin here, he will not deny Theo's request." Adela shifted in her seat. A quick look to Theo, with Jacin glancing sidelong at his father, confirmed her suspicions of what he would likely do. "I'm going to have a chat with our new friend in Jearnia while you three make sure Hoclia and Alkaan do not take what is ours. Understood?"

"Understood," Alan and Theo said in unison, with that slight tone of dejection, as though she had admonished them as their mother once did.

"As for—"

"The second Rosealyn comes home, it is hers," Adela proclaimed. It was the least she could do for her niece, to fight for what was rightfully Rosealyn's, even if her brother had formed other ideas.

"I'll come with you," Jacin said.

Eyebrows rose in shock before she could stop them; the cousins had not been close, but they had not been enemies either.

A grunt from Theo proffered additional words from Jacin. "Aunt Adela is right, Father. The crown belongs to Rosealyn, not me."

Thank the Blazes the young man has a head on his shoulders! She offered Jacin a sympathetic smile and was about to say more to Theo when the priest spoke again.

"What about Her Majesty, Queen Roseanne?" Maslin asked, innocence shining through the gleam of those nervous beady eyes. For a moment, Adela pitied him. Pitied all those here, all those who knew the pain of loss.

"What do the laws of succession say?" she asked softly.

"The surviving monarch is overruled by the heir who receives the Gift," he recited.

"My contact states Roseanne is safe and well," Theo said. "Rosealyn can decide if she wishes for her mother to return here. Until then, we have a plan. Alan and I can take care of matters here. Who is your second in command, Moss?"

"Oh, um, we've concentrated so much on the repairs, so I haven't. . ." He cleared his throat at the collective stares. "I'll make sure I outline the ranks before we leave."

Another pause.

"I'd like to visit with the townspeople tomorrow, and then leave the following day," Adela told him. Her stomach grumbled at her, reminding her how long it had been since the morning meal. They hadn't stopped for the typical noon-time meal, too eager to arrive home when they were so close. "For now, I believe it is time to eat."

CHAPTER FIFTEEN

Gailin's Journal-Annotated by Rosealyn

My father is laid to rest, but there is no rest for me. A coronation, a crown that never should have graced my head, a burden that never should have fallen on my shoulders, and an ability that has done more harm than good [*Sounds like the Gift - or more?*]. Because of my urging we went in search of a way to remove the weapon's connection to us. Xannan would not want it removed. It's why we didn't tell him the truth of why we went. Useless elves, claimed nothing could help. So I returned to the mountain cave. I wrote elsewhere about my desire to search the skies, and it's not wrong. One of those dragons is to blame, I'm certain of it. I know there are more than Magna and Eilon, but they've kept scarce since that day in the cave [*Necessity? Told to? What do their deaths mean for the other dragons?*].

An aggravating visit, one which nearly killed me. Magna showed me how future generations will inherit my ability. I'm not sure if that was before or after she tried to remove the connection as I asked. This Gift, this weapon, brings naught but pain and suffering. I do not want to keep it nearby and yet I have little choice. Without it, I feel weak and worn down [*So keep the sword close like Father said*], like I've fought one battle after another with no rest in between.

One touch of Magna's snout against my forehead, and I thought I was drowning. No air, heart racing, one gasp after another until she huffed a simple warm breath over me. No one can understand how precious air is unless you've experienced its absence for even a brief amount of time.

There was a second image I can recall seeing, an end to the torment this connection [*Swords' connection to each other? Or between the LeNoir's and this blade?*] has caused me and my family. It will not occur in my lifetime, which makes little sense based on what I saw [*Is Gailin the key to breaking the connection?*]. I dare not write it down yet [*Not helpful*]. For now, I will stand firm in my belief that everyone's future can change even if it's already been seen. [*Not my experience. Not yet at least.*]

PROTECTION

CHAPTER SIXTEEN

The sprawling castle at Volante towered above Rosealyn and Xannan, casting shadows on their steady climb of the hill on which it rested. As they neared the gates, she wondered how they could convince the guards to allow them entry. Last time, Christopher had led the way. She gripped her dress-skirts, wondering where the younger Jearnian prince had gone after she told him to leave.

Standing before the gates, she searched the wall for soldiers. One or two had to be near. Mouth open, Rosealyn realized she had no idea what to say.

"We need to see King Charles," Xannan called, loud enough to be heard across the valley.

She scowled at him. He shrugged.

Two guards peered over the wall and stared for a moment too long, disappearing behind the stone. A painful amount of time passed before one peered at them through a small window at their level. "Who are you?"

"Rosealyn LeNoir, crown princess of Orda'an," Rosealyn said in her most regal-sounding voice. She stood tall, hand on the hilt of her sword. With a jerk of her head toward Xannan, she added, "He's with me."

An amused grunt came from her left, but the last thing she needed was Charles attacking Xannan before she could speak to him. A second guard joined the first and whispered in the other's ear.

"Take me to King Charles," she said. The title felt strange on her lips.

The two guards exchanged a glance, and one shrugged and opened the door. Once inside the gates, several more guards surrounded her and Xannan with hands on their sword hilts, focus shifting from her to Xannan.

"This brings back memories," Xannan said at her side. "Though I was looking for you."

Rosealyn decided punching him there, in that courtyard, surrounded by Jearnian soldiers, was not the best use of her time.

Regal. Commanding. She knew how to assume the posture. A queen in all ways, except ceremony.

"Lead the way." Rosealyn gestured at the castle. The soldiers whispered fiercely among themselves, eliciting a low chuckle from Xannan.

"We'll need your weap—"

"No." Xannan squinted up at the castle proper and, after a moment, glanced toward her with a smirk. Ignoring the guards' protests, he walked brusquely. His long strides consumed the ground beneath his feet. She waited. It might be better to follow the lead of the soldiers standing beside her. But she couldn't ignore that stupid tug at her entire body, the indication of how close the swords wished to be that day. Rosealyn bit back the scream clawing its way out of her throat. That day was going to end with her head pounding again from how often she clenched her jaw.

Charles studied those seated around him and fought to keep his face neutral. Unfazed at being the only woman present, Marsha guided the conversation more often than he had from her seat to his right. Opposite her was Christopher, who'd observed and listened without consuming a single bite. Several others, whose names he tried to remember, joined them at the table—ruling families of the many plantations which not only surrounded the castle itself but created uniform plots of land stretching throughout the valley. A mansion in the valley often meant a place on this council, a spot in this group of men Marsha labeled his advisers. Men coveted those plots to the point they would kill for them.

Ten men, his aunt, his brother, and him. He sat at the head of the table, wearing the regalia of the Jearnian king. The signet ring, the flame-like coat, and the crown were all pieces that labeled him their king. He twisted the ring around his finger as a lame attempt to focus his thoughts. He'd reminded those seated around him to treat those in their care properly and had to have a more direct conversation than expected to explain exactly what he meant by such a statement. If he was to call Volante home, life in Jearnia would have to change.

He should call Volante home because it had to become his home. But he hadn't heard from her, from Rose. The dukes and duchess of Orda'an returned his message, thanking him and agreeing to cooperate in working to repair the longtime rift of their two countries.

Nothing from Rose. Or Xannan. Nor any message from the elves, though Arjun claimed he would share what he learned.

A gentle hand atop his pulled him from the tumbling depths of wonder and refusal to believe the worst.

"Charles?" Marsha's voice was softer than the disapproval etching lines into her forehead.

"I'm fine." He cleared his throat, straightened in his seat, and glanced at all the pairs of eyes staring back at him. "I was thinking."

A plate filled to the brim sat before him, and like his brother, he had not eaten a single bite.

"We must share our crops with those beyond the hills." He swirled his fork within the sauce-covered noodles and consumed his first bite. It was mouthwatering and delicious but also bland because his people had so much while others had so little.

"We have sent those messages." Marsha leaned back and placed her hands in her lap. "We agreed as a council there will be an exchange; however, we cannot give freely without receiving."

He nodded and swallowed a sip of his wine as he considered those gathered at the table. Some shifted at his stare and looked away, others glanced down, but he caught the quick glint of fear in their eyes. He'd done everything differently than his father would have. No threatening, no weapons flashing. Calm conversation and orders as needed. He was his father's son, though, and he knew their wariness was a worry he could snap like his father often would. It was possible, considering his past.

Soothing his tone, he asked, "Anything else to discuss?"

Marsha proffered a cautious smile, thin strands of dark hair falling across her face as she tilted her head and lifted her glass. "Nothing more, except enjoying the dinner." Her announcement-like voice echoed against the tall ceilings, reverberation dissipating when a guard opened the doors decorated with intricate carvings. Guards entered first, followed by two people Charles recognized well. He shoved his chair back, standing with tense muscle and a heart beating more erratically than he thought possible. *What in the Blazes is he doing here with her? Of all people. . .*

Gripping his sword, Charles stalked toward Xannan. Charles reminded himself *not* to draw the blade, not to give in to the anger smoldering inside him. Not after he had worked so hard to make them see him as someone different from his father.

The murderous man was in his sights, until she stepped between them. It had been years since he'd found Rosealyn's emotions unreadable.

"Don't attack Xannan," she whispered with a firm shake of her head. No soft twinkle graced her deep brown eyes; instead a fury blazed that likely surpassed his own.

"Our council is concluded. Leave us," he said to those seated at the table. He followed Xannan's movements as he heard the cascade of honorifics amid the muffled scrapes of chairs behind him. Charles monitored exactly where Xannan stood, estimating how many steps it would take to attack him.

"Charles?" Marsha said, in a much different intonation than her earlier question. Her voice was closer to him, but he wouldn't look away from Xannan.

"I'll be fine, Marsha," he said. Maintaining a level tone in the past week had become a useful skill, making it easier to speak with others who feared him. His fingers curled around his sword's hilt, watching Xannan lean against a wall and cross his arms with a slight smirk. "You and Christopher are to leave. Now."

"I'd rather stay," Christopher said, his shoulder-length curls invading Charles's periphery.

"It might be ideal," Rosealyn added, looking from Charles to Xannan. "There is a theory we need to test. A possibility of breaking the bond of the Twin Blades."

"Or perhaps," Marsha said in a soft murmur, "we should all leave the young princess and our king to speak alone, as he requested."

Charles's gaze shifted to Rosealyn. After a mere second of hesitation, a soft smile lit her features.

"I figured we'd test the theory now," Xannan said, and the lack of malice momentarily disarmed Charles. After glancing around the room, Xannan met Charles's eyes again and smirked. "Might need more space though."

If not for Rosealyn's intervening, Charles would have punched Xannan, but she moved in front of him each time he stepped in any direction. After the fourth or fifth step, Charles settled back on his heels. "Are you still in that odd connection?"

"No—" Rosealyn said, halting his forward movement with a firm hand on his chest, pushing him away from Xannan. After several steps, she whispered below her breath, "Not fully connected as before, but he could kill you."

"I wouldn't let that happen," he whispered back.

"And I'm making sure there is no possibility of such at this precise moment," she returned. "Because if our idea doesn't work. . ." A mixture of despair and acceptance flitted across her face, and she glanced back at Xannan.

Charles stiffened. "The connection didn't break when it became two weapons, did it?"

She shook her head and removed her hands from his chest with a breathy whispered apology. Charles refused to let her pull too far away, wrapping his arms around her shoulders and pulling her into his chest. In his arms, she relaxed.

He wanted to find comfort in her return, to find comfort in her closeness, but he couldn't. Not while Xannan lived and posed a threat to her livelihood.

After a moment, she shifted away from the embrace and spoke in a soft whisper. "I almost refused to come here." A pause, a faltering smile. "It was his idea. I only agreed because I know that once the connection is truly removed, you'll have no qualms about helping me kill him. For now, we have to stay within a relatively close distance to one another. As much as I'd love to shove him in some hidden corner and leave him, I wouldn't make it far. After a time, we just—" She shrugged. "Can't go any further. Even after the blades split in two. We tried. Synda's magic, her flame, the weapons themselves, we've tried so much already."

Charles attempted to relax his jaw and shoulders. "We can worry about that later." He released his hold of her, wishing they were alone, and clenched his hand into a fist at his side. "How far before. . ."

"The furthest was a few hundred yards," Xannan said from across the room, and Charles winced alongside Rosealyn. "It changes and not even the elves know why."

With a heavy sigh, Charles turned to Christopher. "They'll need rooms in the same wing then. And he will need to be heavily guarded."

Xannan chuckled, loose blond hair swaying with the movement of his head. "I can't kill her myself. Already tried."

Charles ground his teeth together, his forward momentum halted by Rosealyn's hand pressed against his chest. Her touch, her gaze, made his heart race.

"I tried to kill him, too," she murmured as she slowly removed her hand and ran her fingers along a fraying braid while the other gripped her dress-skirts. "He's right. We cannot kill the other without also harming ourselves. Whatever magic connects us through these weapons won't let us truly try to deliver such a blow."

"A few hundred yards," Charles mused aloud. The castle sprawled much further than a few hundred yards in various directions, and his boyhood rooms he'd insisted on keeping were far from the guest wing where visiting nobles lodged. But other rooms near his had been empty for years, rooms his mother would not be pleased he was offering.

"You'll both stay in the same wing as me," he said aloud, his heart sinking at the idea of allowing Xannan to occupy any of those rooms. The man belonged in the dungeons. Or better yet, dead. But they were connected and not only did he selfishly want Rosealyn to survive, her people needed her to assume her role as their queen.

Behind him, Christopher said, "Mother will not approve."

"I know." Charles pinned Xannan with a stare, and the others flinched. "If you try anything outside of what we agree on, I will be more than happy to kill you."

"I'd expect no less." Xannan appeared relaxed, almost bored. "But I have no plans to die. And this time I'm ready for whatever your sword might do when it meets mine."

Charles loosened his sword from its sheath, muscles poised to strike, recalling the concussion of their swords and how it had felt to bury a comrade.

"What happened to later?" Rosealyn lifted a brow, and Charles paused with his sword halfway drawn.

Despite Xannan's amused grunt, Charles slammed the sword back into its sheath and flexed his hands at his sides.

"Fine." Charles couldn't relax, but he reminded himself to lead by example and soothed his tone. "Christopher, organize guards to stay posted in our wing at all times and to follow him. Marsha, thank you for your guidance today. I will see you at our next meeting."

He paused, waiting for Marsha and Christopher to leave while staring at Xannan. The man's relaxed posture and smirk infuriated him. If she hadn't asked him not to, he would've at least knocked the man unconscious.

"Later," he repeated, more for his benefit than for theirs. "Plenty of open fields surround the castle, which would offer the space we will probably need. My personal guards will accompany us there when we're ready."

"No amount of threatening me will change who or what I am." Xannan pushed off from the wall with no sign of fear. "But make your plans, form your schemes. I have experience in foiling those."

Charles gripped the sword's hilt again; it was just the three of them now.

CHAPTER SEVENTEEN

"Blazes." Rosealyn placed a hand on Charles's before he pulled his sword free, but he shifted away. "This was a terrible idea."

The pressure of her hand on his would not dissuade him; she could see his gleam of desire to annihilate Xannan. Neither Charles's nor Xannan's swords had left their sheaths, but both men held those hilts.

"And this is probably a worse idea," she mumbled as she drew her sword first and rested its tip on the stone floor of the glittering, ornate dining room.

"Might as well see what happens when a different dragon-blessed weapon touches one of these." She gestured at her sword and met Charles's gaze. He stiffened, the muscle in his jaw pulsing almost as erratically as her heartbeat. "We already know what happens when the Twin Blades touch. They have yet to combine again. Sometimes images of the past appear, and other times images we assume are pieces of the future." She tilted her head and lifted the blade a smidgen. "Tap your blade against mine. See if you can break the connection here and now."

When Charles flexed both hands at his side, Rosealyn tapped the sword on the stone, causing an echoing ringing sound.

"If it's anything like the last time"—Charles's soft blue eyes darted between her and Xannan, and he grimaced—"then he's right about the space issue."

Tense muscles eased, and she sheathed her sword. "Then as planned. Later, in the nearby fields." After adjusting her belt, she gripped her dress-skirts and chewed on her bottom lip. A quick glance at Xannan almost made her roll her eyes, so she faced Charles. "He won't try anything while the connection exists."

Debating if she should move closer to Charles or reach out for his hand, she added, "Celena thinks this a fool's errand. Though she didn't prevent us from coming here."

She took in more of the dining room. Her stomach grumbled at the rich scent permeating the air, and she almost approached the table. But she wanted to speak with Charles. Alone. His presence was familiar yet different because he wasn't wearing the solid black of an Orda'anian soldier but the flame-like colors of Jearnia. Topmost button undone, the jacket accentuated his strong, tense shoulders.

Rosealyn's palms grew clammy as she scoured his appearance, halting when she met his gaze. Pale blue eyes reminiscent of the sky softened, appearing incredulous she was standing before him. She considered laughing at his expression but chewed on the inside of her cheek, swallowed, and asked, "Rooms?"

After a firm nod and a sharp wave of his arm, Charles led them through winding hallways too quickly for her to observe the many portraits lining the walls. Xannan didn't argue but simply laughed as multiple guards stood beside the door Charles reluctantly opened for him.

It wasn't until the burgundy clad guards took their position before the room Charles had placed Xannan in that he approached a set of doors Rosealyn remembered well. She recalled standing outside them with the nervous servant at her side for several long moments, mustering the courage to demand the truth from him.

He opened a door to the right of his, gesturing inside with darting, cautious glances at each of the posted guards. Rosealyn's chest tightened, and she gripped her dress-skirts. *His people, his castle, his . . . his kingdom.*

"Rest well," he mumbled as he turned away, but her hand on his forearm paused the movement. He tensed at her touch, as though they'd never had that conversation and she was still out of his reach. Rosealyn studied his demeanor, noting the invisible weight of a monarch's responsibility beneath the veil of anger and the pinched aspect of exhaustion. She tugged on her lower lip, her other hand gripping that brightly colored cloth that was much softer than she anticipated.

"We have a conversation to finish." She searched his features to see what else was wrong. *Not leaving, not following. . .*

"I already know about the destruction at Vandyl," she whispered, heart sinking as she said it. She'd asked questions, tried to demand answers, and no matter what verbal tirade she'd tossed at Xannan, he sat there and took it with an emotionless demeanor. That fleeting thought returned, the musing of how much truth there was to his being brainwashed.

Charles gave her an apologetic grimace, whispering, "I should have stayed, I could have helped, I could—"

"Have been killed along with others," she said. It hurt more than she would ever admit that she hadn't been there to help either. She jerked her head toward the room and pulled him along.

Reluctant and stiff, Charles allowed the movement. A quick survey of the room told her it was similar to Charles's and, though it was clean and maintained, showed no signs of regular use. One bed, one tall dresser, and one fireplace whose logs crackled and warmed the space.

"Is Christopher's room in this hallway, too?" she asked, wondering which of Charles's siblings had once occupied this room.

"No," he said. "Christopher resides in the north wing of the castle. An addition made after I left."

This room held no table like in Charles's rooms, nor did a set of chairs linger anywhere. She walked to the bed and rested her sword against the frame. After sinking into the plush mattress, Rosealyn propped herself onto her elbows and studied the ceiling of crisscrossing wooden beams. Between them, windows allowed the deep red of the setting sun to cast a comforting warmth.

Stretching her neck, she pushed herself into a seated position and patted the space beside her. "Like I said, we have a conversation to finish."

"And others to begin," he said, sitting next to her. Stiffly.

"I thought we were over the stiffness now." She frowned at him.

The simple gold band on his head reflected the flickering flames and was bright against his dark hair that seemed longer than she last recalled. Charles shifted his sword but didn't remove it from his waist. He tugged on each sleeve and winced. Rosealyn swore he also blushed, but it was hard to tell if it was his skin flushing or the reflection of that coat against his skin. *Their crest the flame, ours the beast which created it. Whoever decided the LeNoirs. . .*

The thought died, recalling how Xannan had said he too was a LeNoir and had a claim to her throne.

"I'm very glad you're alive." He shifted to face her, and she smiled at him. Before she could respond, he launched into a series of explanations. From helping Moss begin the repairs at Vandyl to the messages to her aunt and uncles and the possibility of his mother being poisoned. All she could do was absorb the information, amazed at everything he had managed in the two weeks she'd spent trying to get rid of Xannan.

"I'm sorry," he said, twisting the ring on his right hand. "I was injured and by the time I managed to get to where you were, you'd disappeared. Arjun provided a vial that helped mend the skin back together. . ."

His repeat explanation trailed off when she intertwined her hand in his.

"Thank you." She leaned closer, inhaling the scent of snow that always lingered around him. He placed his hand on her cheek, guiding her toward him and resting his forehead on hers. The small golden crown he wore slipped from his head and bumped onto hers. She chuckled and set it aside.

"You helped my people while I recovered," she whispered and added a soft, almost playful, "King Charles."

"You do *not* need to call me that," he said with a brief flinch.

"It's who you are now." She stared into his eyes, grateful he didn't pull away. "But I understand."

His hand shifted on her cheek, a small indication of releasing tension.

"Still wearing those braids." He stroked the fraying braid which expressed her station as the princess of Orda'an.

"Are you trying to distract yourself or me?" She grabbed his wrist, halting his movement as his eyes returned to hers. Her breaths shortened, pulse thrumming in her ears.

"What happens if we don't separate the Twin Blades?" He lowered his hand.

Rosealyn leaned away and glowered at him, brows furrowing. "I'm stuck with him until he or I die." All of the inner turmoil she'd fought and accepted resurfaced. "And I'd rather not talk about that right now."

"Leave nothing un—"

"Doesn't apply to this situation at this precise second." She reached for his hand, but he pulled away. "Are you forgetting where our last conversation left off?"

"No, definitely not." He raked his fingers through his hair. "But. . ."

She rested a hand on his cheek, rubbing her thumb over the scar on his chin and waiting for him to face her. "We have titles, yes." His gaze lifted to hers, strengthening her resolve. "We have countries to rule and people to care for." When he inhaled to speak, she placed her finger against his lips. "We have responsibilities. Changes to make and issues to solve. But we also have each other. No matter what comes next, Charles."

His shaky breath was warm against her finger. A level of determination, resolve, and desire she'd never felt before surged through her.

Rosealyn leaned forward and planted her lips on his. He tensed, and her chest and cheeks grew heated as she realized she didn't know what to do next. Then his hand warmed her neck and pulled her closer, his lips pressing against hers with a desire she hadn't expected from the stoic, pensive man. Charles paused, light blue eyes glowing with an eagerness she reciprocated. Despite her chest aching for air, Rosealyn grasped his collar and pulled until their lips were meshed together again.

Words and thoughts fled, replaced by new sensations. His fingers threaded through her hair, and his lips explored hers until he pulled away, breath as heavy, if not heavier, than her own.

"That," she said as their foreheads touched again, "was a proper end to our conversation."

"Agreed." His voice was deeper, scratchier, and his hand still warmed the back of her neck. "Rose, I—"

Her mischievous smile returned. That kiss was much too pleasant not to repeat, and she moved to steal his breath again, halting seconds before their lips met. A low thrum she couldn't attribute to her heartbeat sounded nearby.

"What is it?" Charles asked in the voice of a protector, of the man in charge of her safety. She shook her head, trying to shake the sensation. But that strange tickle of uncertainty surfaced anyway, sending shivers down her spine. When the hum of her sword sang loud and clear, a pit of ice opened deep inside.

"Nothing," she said, knowing it would never convince Charles. "A byproduct of the stupid connection."

He placed his hands on her shoulders, the earlier despair in his eyes replaced with concern. "I've spent enough time with you to know when you're lying. Tell me."

"The sword is humming. Slow, for now, but it was the precursor to creating the dragonsword."

He lifted a brow. "Dragonsword?"

Rosealyn shrugged. "Xannan named it. But I think if the swords want to be combined then they—"

"Sense trouble." Charles ran his hand through his hair, and Rosealyn had the strangest desire to tug on one of the forming curls. Muted voices sounded outside Charles's door.

"That's Christopher," Charles said at the same time Rosealyn recognized the second voice.

"And Xannan," she said, knowing he wore his weapon because she could hear its hum beckoning to be united with hers. She groaned, praying to the Blaze of her ancestors she would be the one inflicting damage the next time the Twin Blades combined.

"And what could be near that the magic of those weapons deems dangerous enough to warrant combining?" Charles asked.

Rosealyn wished the sword would stop humming. They had left the drokos behind.

She had no desire to encounter any of those creatures again.

CHAPTER EIGHTEEN

Charles berated himself for being a fool, lifting his hair from his forehead and trying to focus on something aside from how much he'd enjoyed that kiss. A mixture of soft and fierce, Rosealyn hadn't held back.

He stood and shifted his sword belt. If he remained seated beside her, they might ignore whatever was happening in the hallway. "When else have they hummed?"

"After Synda removed the invisible pain. And before they combined." Rosealyn tilted her head and smoothed several wayward strands. "It was both a hum and a call, as though some block had been removed which allowed the weapons to seek out each other. What is yours doing?"

He considered pacing but didn't. These weren't nerves, just thoughts, questions which needed answers. Charles approached the bed where she sat, propped on one elbow in an enticing lean, auburn hair swaying with the movement of her head. He much preferred running his hand through her hair than getting whipped in the face by it. Several loud thuds from beyond the closed door made him wince. It deepened into a grimace as he listened.

"Christopher," he mumbled, turning on his heel.

When he opened the door, the hallway appeared empty. But sprawled at either end of the corridor, both Christopher and Xannan were fetching their unsheathed swords. Hands on his hips, Charles swiveled his focus from one to the other, debating which would receive his wrath first. A gentle hand rested on his forearm, firm and persistent.

"It stopped humming." She shrugged. "Same reaction as yours?"

He nodded and smiled at her soft chuckle.

She added, "It's nice to see him knocked to the ground rather than me."

His smile vanished, replaced with simmering anger threatening to boil over uncontrollably.

"We could take him." Charles glared at Xannan as the Lost Prince sheathed his sword and approached. No emotion was easily discernible on the blond-haired man's face. Remembering the ridiculous connection, Charles said, "I could take him. Why did you tell me not to?"

Christopher joined them. All of their weapons were back in their sheaths, though Charles itched to remove his. No one would enjoy killing Xannan more than he would, but Rosealyn's fingers intertwined with those of his favored sword hand, and he made a mental note not to tense his hand.

"We have an idea of what will happen when the connection is broken," Rosealyn said. Her dejected tone made Charles's heart plummet. "Celena said after the weapons were made that one would have to die to break the connection. But then, with Gailin, it was altered. I believe the Gift should have been from the sword itself not through the bloodline."

"You fear the change means that if one dies, you both could die?" His grip tightened involuntarily, grateful she'd saved him from potentially harming her.

"Now that Christopher's and Xannan's weapons have touched, there's only a few combinations left to try," she muttered, squeezing his hand in return. "Though I was hoping for a decent bit of"—she swallowed and gave him a curious glance that made his cheeks warm— "conversation and rest first."

Flanked by guards, Xannan rubbed the back of his neck, wincing.

"Theories, conjectures, limitations, and consequences." Xannan's lack of malice surprised Charles. "Tomorrow?"

"A day of rest might help us think more clearly." Rosealyn squeezed his hand again, and he nodded.

"I imagine your list of combinations will result in much the same as this did." Xannan lowered his arm and tapped a finger against his sword. "Magic dislikes being controlled."

Charles's gaze flicked from guard to guard, hoping the unspoken command was understood.

An obnoxious chuckle—only deemed such because of whom it came from—sounded and Xannan added, "It was I who theorized the possibility of the broken connection resulting in death for both." He folded his arms and canted his head with a smirk. "I won't attack without provocation."

"You bring her harm again"—Charles hoped authority laced his tone rather than anger—"And I will make you wish you were dead."

"The magic of the Twin Blades is its own entity. We are merely its wielders," Xannan retorted, those bright green eyes flashing. "And all this threatening is quite aggravating."

Before either Charles or Rosealyn could say anything more, Xannan returned to his room and slammed the door. Charles turned his focus to Christopher. No physical scars marred his face, and the invisible ones he had endured seemed buried. Brows furrowed in a deep glower, Christopher thinned his lips as he met Charles's condescending glare.

"I'll give you a moment." Rosealyn patted his arm and retreated back to the bed where she resumed her position and pretended to study the ceiling. Charles almost smiled at her lackluster attempt to disguise the eavesdropping, until he remembered why he was standing in the doorway and not sitting beside her. He leaned against the doorframe and crossed his arms.

"Guard him, not fight him." Charles gritted out. "What were you thinking?"

"Go here, do this, don't do that." Christopher tossed his hands in the air. "A compromise? Being told what to do still? Between you and Aunt Marsha, I spend most of my time trying to decide if I can even have a decent thought of my own anymore."

Charles stiffened at the unexpected outburst. His younger brother was right; both he and Marsha had given Christopher one task after another. Since the nobles were familiar with Christopher, it made more sense to ask Christopher to speak with them on his behalf. Charles thought it a way to show his budding trust in his brother, but evidently Christopher had seen it differently.

"Christopher," Charles said, stretching out a hand that Christopher waved away. He clenched his jaw. He'd never been close to Christopher before leaving, not with how close in age he had been to Zane and Silas. He needed to find a way to understand and trust Christopher.

"There is a place for you here, Christopher. We just need to find the proper fit."

"It's not with the soldiers." Christopher scoffed with a disdainful sneer at the posted guards that Charles wasn't sure how to decipher. "And half of the nobles I can barely stand. The half that don't drone on about their impressive mansions go into grotesque detail about . . . other activities." Christopher crossed his arms, digging the toe of his shined black boot into the dark carpet. "I thought you planned to be different."

Christopher shook his head while Charles debated between moving closer or standing as they were. The space separating them felt like an immense canyon that could never be filled. Instead, Charles crossed his arms. The door remained open, and a quick glance inside showed Rosealyn was still doing a terrible job of hiding her eavesdropping.

"How so?" Charles asked his brother softly.

"Well, now I know. You won't ever trust me completely." The cavern between them widened. "I can't be a leader like they tried to make me when all the rest were gone. Guess I'll have to—"

Charles jerked his head up. "They?"

"Father and Aunt Marsha." Christopher looked at Charles with a deep but hollow gaze. It was uncannily like looking into a mirror of a younger version of himself who had let his curls grow long and almost untamed.

Rosealyn's footsteps announced her approach. "You two are glaring at each other like my father and Uncle Theo used to," she said. "What's wrong?"

"Nothing." Christopher walked away, not realizing he'd given Charles a potential clue to their mother's continuous poisoning.

Rosealyn's arm snaked through his, tugging him back inside the room. Though his eyes ached and his head throbbed, he followed the motion, looking down to find a familiar mischievous twinkle. Charles tapped the door closed with his heel, not waiting for it to click shut before he kissed her. Her hands gripped his coat jacket, closing what little space remained between them. Their collective tension eased, lost in the simple joy of sharing something they'd denied each other for far too long. Chests rising and falling almost in unison, Rosealyn pulled away, licked her lips, and devoured him with her gaze. Her breath hitched, and she buried her head in his chest, arms tight around him.

"That was a pleasant conversation," she whispered, voice cracking when she added, "I don't want you to leave."

He hugged her tighter, chin resting atop her head as she melted further into his embrace. The slight shake of sobs he'd expected earlier began. She'd remained stoic throughout his descriptions, reminding him Xannan had told her the details as well. With a gentle nudge, he guided her back to the bed, lowering them both to its edge once more. Side by side they sat, her head resting against his shoulder, hand intertwined with his. Once her sobs subsided and her chest lifted and fell rhythmi-cally, Charles deftly laid her down and stood.

Rosealyn curled her fingers around the blanket he placed atop her, and he tucked a strand of hair away from her face. Before he closed the door, Charles gazed at her, torn between elation and worry that whatever they felt might not last, not when they had their own countries to rule. But Rosealyn, and her father, had saved him. The least he could do was offer her whatever help she needed.

Chapter Nineteen

More trials and threats were all Xannan envisioned awaiting him once they arrived at the field. The number of guards amused him; trapped and feared was a dangerous and wondrous position to hold. The soldier turned king and Rosealyn walked side by side, while the king's younger brother, Christopher, ambled alongside Xannan.

"Our weapons reacted the same as yours and Charles's did?" Christopher asked. The prince looked more lost than Xannan had felt since the fog of Eilon's control had first cleared.

"Similar, yes," Xannan confirmed, gaze roaming to the open fields around them. Per Rosealyn's recommendation, they'd let him keep his sword. Though he refused to let it show, relief had flooded him when Charles reluctantly agreed. The weapon was an extension that, for all he knew, had molded itself to him as some type of life-giving force.

The guards' coats were a deep red, so dark they could have been black if not for the subtle play of light displaying their hue. "There was no heating of the weapon on my end this time."

"My sword was blessed by a younger dragon," Christopher explained.

Silently, Xannan decided Synda had likely grafted a piece of her own magic into Christopher's weapon. Once they reached a patch of grass, Charles motioned the guards into position and approached. One goal stood at the forefront of Xannan's mind, and he could see the same goal etched on Rosealyn's face—dissolve the connection. Not part of a magical bloodline himself, all he knew of magic was what the Twin Blade offered. Without the blade near his person, his ability to relive the past became elusive. Threads formed—memories of his creation that were nothing like the submersion into every minute detail the magic of the Twin Blade let him see. Xannan frowned, wondering what Eilon had changed in the past century.

"This should be more than enough space, and where you two should have let those weapons touch instead of in that hallway," Charles said, hand resting on his sword hilt while the rest of him all but glittered in the rising morning sun. "And if you do anything except what Rose tells you to do. . ." Charles glanced back at the princess. If the blades combined again, it could be she who felt the pain, rather than he. Or so Xannan hoped.

Xannan chuckled at the incomplete subtle threat. "You should know," he told the king of Jearnia as he pulled his weapon from its sheath, relishing the power he felt rolling through it. "I desire the break in this connection just as much, if not more, than either you or she does."

Hand still on the hilt of his sword, Charles approached until little space remained between them. "What will you do if nothing works? Or if it does?" Charles asked too softly for anyone else to hear.

With a simple shrug, Xannan shifted his gaze to the sword which had slowly begun to feel foreign to him. Those stupid black clouds roved within, rolling from point to hilt and back again as though trapped in a stream of unending movement. Trapped, that was all he could think about. Without a break in the connection, he would always be trapped.

As another thought roamed into Xannan's mind, the princess approached and snaked her fingers through Charles's, deftly shifting his hand away from the sword hilt as she did.

Xannan's gaze snagged on their joined hands as he asked, "What would you like to try first?"

"Mine against Charles's at the same time as yours against Christopher's?"

It would fail miserably. Just as every other potential idea to break the connection had. The flames from the dragon had been the most obnoxious and the most useless of all.

"A simple tap," came the king's specific command with a glare toward Xannan and another at his younger brother. Xannan fought the smirk, working to maintain the lackadaisical demeanor he'd donned. He'd have to hunt for answers to later, if he could ever determine what dynamic would suffice here.

The other swords were drawn. Rosealyn counted down, and then a simple tap elicited nothing more than it had before. But the concussion was much less—because of the combination or because they all expected the reaction, he wasn't sure. The princess demanded they try again, with a little more force than the tap Charles had requested.

Not even a concussion this time.

They shared confused looks, and Rosealyn mumbled out another option—the Twin Blades at the same time as the Jearnian royalty's. Nothing.

"Worthless magic," Xannan said as he hefted the sword.

The princess pinned him with that obnoxious knowing glare. He sighed, sheathing the crystal of roiling black and gray clouds. Any information that could change whatever this was should be shared, even if it had nothing to do with breaking the connection. "The weapons might react to the bearer's intention in addition to the magic itself. You." He swiveled to look at the younger prince. "What were your thoughts as our weapons met?"

"Mixed," Christopher admitted, shoulder-length curls blowing in the breeze and hiding whatever emotions the young prince might portray. "Mostly curiosity of what could happen."

"Then we try again, with specific intention," Rosealyn said, that grating tone of hers returning as she motioned with her sword, as if where they stood was of any importance.

"It won't work." Xannan cut off any additional explanation when one of the many guards approached Charles.

"Why?" Rosealyn's question drew his attention away from the Jearnian soldier's motion.

"As we've established, this magic, this connection, is bound to our bloodline." Xannan itched to discover what had been so important for one guard to approach.

"A connection which could be broken through death," she acknowledged with a singular firm nod, her resolve to kill him etched into her posture.

"True, but what happens when there is no heir for this magic to latch on to?"

"Others of our bloodline?" She shrugged, blade shifting in her hand. "My aunt and uncles? My cousin? Your lineage?"

Xannan froze as the question dredged up memories he preferred to keep hidden, memories of his betrothed. "Perhaps." He forced himself to remain stoic. *Our bloodline.*

"And neither of us would be remotely willing to die to test such a theory," she mused aloud and shook her head, pointing with the sword as she spoke, "All four at once."

Chapter Twenty

The land beyond the Jearnian Hills was much the same as the Orda'anian plains, though with more vibrant colors. Fields of flowers, properly blooming flowers, greeted Adela and her small entourage along with thriving trees and abundantly healthy crops. The journey had been almost as quick as her travels from Cantadad to Vandyl. Granted, she had been persistent that Jacin and Moss keep a decent and steady pace. When the large city of Volante came into view at the base of the mountains, Adela thought it might be best to delay their arrival one more day. But she was too close to turn back. And if her niece wasn't there. . . She refused to finish such a thought. One could hide in plenty of places on the continent of Ebios. Such a scenario was unlikely; Rosealyn knew her responsibilities.

Volante's castle was one Adela had only ever heard of in stories. First from her father, then from her brothers. Within these fields or along this path, her father had met his demise. Had it not been for all of her brothers traveling with him, she wasn't sure what would have happened to Phillippe in his sudden weakened state during the Passing. She frowned and swayed with the horse's plodding as Volante's castle came into view. Built into a mountainside, it should have been breathtaking. Stone parapets buttressed against rocky facades, with dirt hills sloping down around them.

A path beckoned to be followed, leading through a uniform city and meeting the gates which blocked the entrance to the sprawling mountain-backed castle. Above the plodding of hooves drifted a familiar sound, one that made her chest clench and her throat tighten. Whatever mesmerizing scent she'd discovered in the surrounding blooms faded until that sound overwhelmed her. Swords clashing. A weapon she'd refused to learn how to wield.

Adela looked askance at Moss with her unspoken question. In answer, he shifted the reins, moving toward the sound rather than away from it.

"We sent a message of cooperation," she whispered, wincing at the smack of weapon against weapon. It was too sporadic to be more than a few soldiers. A second clash sounded in immediate succession after the first. More than a few soldiers.

Jacin shifted closer to her as they neared the ringing of metal. Four figures stood near one another, surrounded by a circle of guards in deep red jackets that blended into the field of flowers. One of the four wore a dress, pointing her sword as though giving specific commands. Adela's jaw slacked while Moss and Jacin chuckled, as though they had expected to find their future queen in a random field in their longtime rival country, telling others what to do. Lips pursed, Adela tugged on the reins to stop her horse's steady movement forward.

"Guess General Moss's hunch was right." Jacin halted his mare next to hers. "I'd always wondered if there was more to that bodyguard of hers. And now. . ."

Jacin bristled at Adela's stare and rolled his shoulders back to sit taller. "A union? Could they reunite the countries into one?"

"They could," Adela said with a curt nod, turning her attention back to the four in the field. She felt hot and cold at the same time, her heart thundering inside her chest while her lungs released a deep breath of relief—Rosealyn was very much alive. And in Jearnia.

"Now what?" Jacin rubbed the blond beard that barely covered his chin. "Insist she return home and become the ruler she was raised to become?"

Adela pressed her lips together. "I doubt it will take much encouragement."

"Something kept her from going straight home," Jacin amended.

The general whose answers continued to be too vague for her liking cleared his throat, looking down when she swiveled her head to stare at him.

"The Twin Blades?" he asked. Adela's eyes narrowed at Moss for a second, but that had also been a part of the king of Jearnia's message.

Taking a deep breath, Adela urged her mare forward. Jacin followed, staying close to her side while Moss did likewise. After riding down the soft slope of the hill, she could make out the group's features. Charles's clenched jaw could portray a wide array of emotions; another Jearnian with obvious kinship to Charles stood near, face blank. Rosealyn's hair swayed in the breeze despite the identical braids along the side of her head. The fourth made Adela's heart stutter when he looked at her. For a second, a brief second, she wondered if Phillippe had returned from the grave.

"Another one to threaten my life, I assume?" the man said in a voice so far from any tone she'd ever heard from her brother. It wasn't quite malicious, but it was certainly not kind.

"Adela, my father's younger sister," Rosealyn said by way of greeting, gesturing toward them. "And Jacin, my older cousin by a few years. Why are you here?"

Adela harrumphed, handing her reins to Moss so she could dismount without worrying about the horse skidding out from beneath her.

"I must ask you the same, Rosealyn," she said, deciding against crossing her arms and patting the horse affectionately instead. But she moved her hand too swiftly, whacking against the pommel and hissing at the sudden pain.

Rosealyn lifted the sword in her hand with a shrug. "I was trying to break the connection of the Twin Blades."

"Celena claimed it was unlikely," the Lost Prince grumbled, holding out his weapon to study it despite Adela's arrival.

Before she could stop herself, Adela stepped away from the weapons and those holding them out with such ease.

"Were there any other combinations left to try?" Charles asked, making Adela feel more neglected. Once Rosealyn shook her head, he turned to Adela. After sheathing his blade, he dipped his head in a slight nod and offered what he likely hoped was a warm smile. "Welcome to Jearnia, Duchess Adela."

His hair was longer than she remembered, and that simple smile was more emotion than she had ever seen from the princess's bodyguard. Adela returned the simple nod, unable to focus on any one person. Based on the sheen of sweat coating each, they'd been in the field for some time. She decided to direct her attention to Rosealyn, though the accompanying burgundy-clad soldiers increased the palpitations of her heart.

"I'm sure you could attempt to do that at home just as well as here," she told her niece, holding her skirts down when a soft wind blew.

Rosealyn grimaced and sheathed her weapon. "Not exactly."

Thankful all of the weapons were now properly stored, Adela's voice cracked as she said, "You are coming home."

"I plan to," Rosealyn said with that air of annoyance she'd always held. With a nod to each she added, "It's good to see you, General Moss. Jacin."

"If there's no other reason for us to be out here"—the younger Jearnian noble rubbed his palms together—"I'd like to return to the warmth of my rooms."

"You are welcome to stay in the castle," Charles said. "I am sure a few days' rest, even a week, would do you all good."

Adela's grip on her skirts tightened as she noted how close Charles stood to Rosealyn.

"He's right, Aunt Adela," Jacin said. He had moved nearer to her as they spoke, almost as though standing guard in front of her. Her chest loosened at his presence, though it refused to relax completely.

"You will be my honored guests." Charles met her gaze with a firmness that made her believe his words. "Guests of the king will be protected. You are all safe here."

"There are—"

"Updates can happen when we get back to the castle, Adela," Rosealyn interrupted as another cool wind whipped through the slit skirts of the girl's dress and she shivered. "Their hallways are as cold as Vandyl's, but the fires burn warm all the same."

"And where will *he* be?" she asked, staring down her nose at the man who looked so similar yet so different from her brother. "He's the one—"

"Xannan, the *Lost Prince*." The man lowered his arms to his side, shoulder-length blond hair swaying as another chill breeze swirled around them. "Get in line if you've your own threats to make."

"He's got a point." Rosealyn tilted her head at the looming castle, her expression distant.

Chapter Twenty-One

As they walked, Rosealyn kept glancing over her shoulder, fearful she'd hallucinated Adela, Jacin, and Moss. Adela shivered with each gust of wind and with each glance at Xannan. Rosealyn grimaced; the woman had always been hard to read but had always been kind.

Swords clanged against belts with each step, and Rosealyn squelched the memories which tried to surface. She itched to intertwine her hand with Charles's. But as often happened, he remained stiff and observant.

"A week?" she asked curiously.

"If possible," he said with that veiled tone Rosealyn believed meant he was hiding something. She arched a brow, prompting him to explain further. "Events are moving forward here, as they are supposed to."

With a half smile, Rosealyn chuckled and reached for his hand. "That's not an explanation."

Charles shrugged, grasped her outstretched hand, and returned her smile with a soft one of his own. It was good to see him smile, to see the tension ease from his shoulders and allow those emotions he had always buried so deep to surface.

"It was a suggestion, not a requirement. Though having Orda'anian nobility present at my coronation will provide proof we are allies."

Her hand almost went limp in his. His coronation. She let the thought be crowded away by the bumping swords and plodding hooves. Once on the path leading directly to the castle gates, the horses' hooves clicked loudly against stone. Before signaling for the gates to open, Charles turned to her with a weaker half smile and said, "It is also a selfish suggestion as I'm not ready for you to be needed elsewhere."

It was hard to decide whether she should smile or frown. One full day was all she'd had with him so far. Charles had spent the day showing her the entire castle, while Xannan paced behind them, scowling. She had inquired about a few of the portraits and about the brothers he had lost, but those questions elicited cryptic responses and sad smiles. And in that time, she had come no closer to understanding what the Gift wanted of her, except to know that what she desired to do differed from what she needed to do.

Several soft murmurs floated as Adela, Jacin, and Moss followed her and Charles through the halls. With a few more tours of the sprawling castle, Rosealyn believed she might finally make sense of its maze of hallways.

"This is the wrong hallway," she said when Charles stopped walking.

"This is the wing for visiting nobility," Charles explained as he released her hand, opened a door, and ushered them in. "There are only the four rooms in the other. Several guests have already arrived for the ceremony but chose rooms at the furthest end of the hall." He nodded at where the hallway disappeared around a bend and then at the opposite side of the corridor. "The room across the hall is empty, so Jacin and Adela can remain close." He tugged on each sleeve, hand lingering above his sword hilt and dropping to his side. "I figured you would want to speak with Adela and Jacin alone?"

Rosealyn realized she was rubbing the fabric of her dress between her fingers and clenched both to make them stop. He was right, as usual. Proper conversation was the only way to understand why Adela had come here, of all places, with the cousin Rosealyn had not seen for years.

"I'll be right out here, keeping an eye on him," Charles said with a slight jerk of his head at Xannan. That man had remained surprisingly quiet since the night before, his barely disguised amusement dissipating. Between the slight downturn of his lips, drooping eyes, and lack of retorts, he'd come to the same conclusion as she. They'd both known. It had just taken longer for her to accept. As far as either of them knew, they had nothing else to try which could potentially break the connection.

"I may not feel what he feels at the moment," she said. "But don't do anything stupid."

Charles crossed his arms, shooting a glare toward Xannan that she wanted never to be on the receiving end of. "I won't if he doesn't."

Sighing, Rosealyn smoothed her skirts, gave Charles one more admonishing glance, and entered the guest rooms. Similar to the others, the bed and dressers were on one side, a small table to the other, with a few plush tall-backed chairs near the crackling fireplace. Rosealyn claimed the chair closest to the fire, savoring its warmth after the cold winds of the fields had chilled her almost to the bones. Jacin took the seat to the other side of the hearth, rubbing his hands together near the flames.

"Aunt Adela I understand, in a way, showing up, but you?" Rosealyn asked her cousin. She considered him kind and cordial but had spent little time with him. His father often sent Jacin elsewhere.

A tense, sidelong glance met her and returned to the warm fire. His cheeks held a slight flush, likely from the sudden transition of the outdoor cold to the heat wafting toward them.

Adela stood between the two chairs, arms crossed with an uncharacteristic frown marring her features. "Jacin agreed to come with me. And, thank the Blazes, disagrees with his father."

"Disagrees about what?" Rosealyn asked as her aunt paced.

A steady beat of three steps, then the swish of padded shoe against stone as Adela turned on the ball of her foot and continued the other way.

"You're alive," Adela announced, as though that in itself was a surprise.

Rosealyn's frown deepened. Those spots of color on her cousin's cheeks were definitely not from the heat, Rosealyn decided.

"Uncle Theo wanted proof and, if none could find me, Jacin would be given the crown?" Rosealyn asked, and Adela's footsteps halted midstride. "It's understandable. Mother disappeared, I fought a . . . a dragon. Sort of. I wanted to come straight home but—"

"You said you need to 'break a connection'?"

Rosealyn grimaced, having no desire to explain how she was irrevocably attached to Xannan. Instead, she gave a simple nod. "Is there any other reason besides Uncle Theo's plans for you to be here? Come to insist I return home soon?"

"Tomorrow," Adela said with a curt sharpness that vaguely reminded Rosealyn of her mother. *Or at least the one I knew.*

"Charles offered us a week *and* invited us to his coronation." Rosealyn straightened in her seat, trying to decide why saying the phrase aloud incited pangs of jealousy. "It would be rude of us not to accept such hospitality or attend."

"We shouldn't be in these lands, in this castle," Adela said, the words coming out in a sharp whisper. She returned to her pacing.

Rosealyn blocked her aunt's path. "I will go where I want to go. What's the harm in staying here?" Rosealyn spread her arms to indicate the spacious room they'd been offered. "An alliance, Aunt Adela. Or do you still hate the Jearnians so much you can't see the kindness Charles has offered?"

Her aunt blanched at the question. "You don't know Charles's true intentions, Rosealyn. What if it's been a part of his plan all along? To make you believe him enough to agree to a mar—"

"Ten years, Adela." Rosealyn held up her hand when her aunt attempted to speak again. "For ten years, I have known Charles. I know he's unreadable to many with his stoicism, but he helped us. Helped Orda'an. Charles risked men who barely saw him as their king in order to protect *our* people." She rounded her shoulders and lifted her chin.

"I'll send Uncle Theo a message myself. But we are staying for the ceremony."

A strange sound escaped from Adela's throat, and the woman grasped Rosealyn into a tight hug. "I'm just . . . this place, these people. . ."

After the initial escape of breath from her lungs, Rosealyn returned the embrace. "Trust me when I say my own shock was much greater than yours the last time I stayed in his castle." Rosealyn backed away from the embrace and almost laughed at her own words. *His castle. How strange.*

She motioned for Adela to sit at the table, and beckoned for Jacin to do the same. Then she opened the door to ask Charles for a proper meal, but the hallway was empty. With a roll of her eyes, she closed the door and sat with her family with a hope that the two men didn't roam too far or try to hurt one another.

Once she was seated with her hands folded atop the table, Jacin finally spoke with a curious twinkle in his eye. "Tell us everything."

CHAPTER TWENTY-TWO

After speaking with her aunt and cousin for most of the day, Rosealyn sought out Charles to let him know they would stay for the offered week. Then, before her uncle launched a coup, she had to return home. It didn't take long to find them, not with the soft buzz indicating the location of the other sword. She found them in the training yards, and their sparring stopped as soon as she came into view. When Charles asked if she would like a round, she agreed.

A true sparring match, without the potential consequence of a solid blade piercing her flesh, would be a comforting activity despite Xannan's presence. He leaned against the wall next to a vibrant colorful bush. She ached for the gardens of her home, hopeful her father's favorite black rose bushes had survived.

Soldiers at every turn were nothing new, but these were not *her* country's soldiers. They were *his*.

Rosealyn studied the array of wooden weapons. "I didn't think you were serious when you said you missed these."

"It would be foolish of me not to make sure your training continues, Princess," he said in a slightly teasing tone.

The light wooden sword was a comforting weight in her hand. When she turned to find him with arms crossed and no weapon in sight, Rosealyn frowned. Every sparring match involved a test, though she wondered if those would continue.

This time would be different. The last time they'd sparred was the day before Synda whisked her away. Rosealyn had intended to disarm him the next time and insist he spill every secret he had ever harbored no matter how it might make her feel.

But as far as she knew, he had no more secrets.

"What weapon will you use?" She squinted at his crossed arms, his sturdy footing, and at the obvious tight grip of his fists. Despite not seeing the weapon, Rosealyn knew he held one. Maybe two.

"Come and find out."

"Daggers?" She stepped closer, but not too close. Daggers gave him the advantage in close combat. Charles shrugged, gaze roaming from her shoulders to her feet and back again. She fought the blush, deciding it was not the time to consider how much she enjoyed kissing Charles. As she circled him, he remained stiff.

She smirked. "Afraid of hurting me?"

That obnoxious stiffness returned. Rigid posture, tight lips, and flushed cheeks.

"Yes," he whispered, shifting his position to keep her in view as she walked around him, wooden sword loose in her hand. He cleared his throat. "And no."

"Afraid I'll hurt you?" Rosealyn asked with a darting glance at Xannan. His featureless expression was made more prominent with his blond hair tied back. She'd done the same to hers, though she wanted to savor the feel of the wind through her auburn tresses.

When she returned her attention to Charles, he was slashing with a dagger in each hand. Rosealyn ducked, sweeping one leg into his ankle with what she thought would be enough force to knock him down. He stumbled to one side, regaining his balance long before falling to the ground.

"Definitely not," he said, though the grimace on his face said otherwise.

Rosealyn lowered the wooden blade. "We don't have to train against each other. There are others—"

One of the small wooden daggers was beneath her chin, the other pressing against her abdomen. Charles kept them there for a few seconds and removed the weapons with a reminder. "Never let your guard down in the middle of a fight."

"This," she said with a wave of her arm between them, "is not a fight in which I might actually die."

A second approach, but she was ready this time. She twisted away from the first strike, though it brought her closer to him. Too close for it not to distract either of them. Her chest against his, sword useless at her side. Not useless. She thrust its hilt into his side and ducked away from the swift strike Charles tried to land.

"Never let your guard down," she recited back to him, shifting away from another slash of the two daggers. When the daggers seemed to gleam in the sunlight, she raced several steps backward, gasping for air. Phantom pain radiated in her thigh, but she pushed it aside. The past was in the past; she could not change what had been done.

Rosealyn took three swift steps, ducked, and landed another blow to Charles's side. Strong enough that he grunted, a hint of concern in those soft blue eyes. But Rosealyn had a point to prove and kept pressing.

She parried each slice of Charles's daggers until striking with enough force to knock the small wooden blades from his hands. A faint trickle of amusement tickled at the back of her mind, strengthening with each movement. The slices and slashes met whispers of air more often than not. She gritted her teeth, inching closer, striking harder, the wooden sword whistling through the air. An immovable force created an abrupt stop. A hand wrapped around her wrist. Xannan's hand.

He applied pressure, and her hand spasmed open, dropping the wooden sword.

"Sorry," she whispered.

The Jearnian soldiers moved closer, pausing at Charles's order.

"I was wondering if bloodlust hid in you, too," Xannan muttered, releasing his hold of her wrist.

"Why did you—"

"He was too shocked to stop your tirade," Xannan said.

That was when Rosealyn realized Charles was on the ground. She'd knocked him down. The memory was there, a brief moment of triumph haunting it. She gave him a weak smile and reached out a hand with another mumbled apology.

"Perhaps training with others would be best." Charles grasped her hand, stood, and straightened his shirt. "I thought you weren't mad—"

"Not at you," Rosealyn released his hand to grip her dress-skirts. "Not anymore, at least. I . . . I was trying to prove a point, and my mind was lost in that one thought."

"Bloodlust," Xannan said with a firm nod. "It got worse after the weapon molded itself to me."

"There has to be something else we can try to break this stupid connection," she grumbled.

Xannan shrugged and walked away.

"I still want to ram a sword through his heart," Charles grumbled at her side.

"Me too."

"I tried to stop you," he whispered, and she felt the heat of his hand hovering above her arm. "I . . . I couldn't get a hold of you. It was like you couldn't hear me. Like you were elsewhere. Until he—"

Rosealyn stared into the surrounding flourishing gardens, smelling the faint scent of rose bushes in their midst. "I wish—" She grunted. "Idiot." Rosealyn glowered in the direction Xannan had walked, rubbing her chest. "Stupid connection, stupid swords, stupid secrets!" Rosealyn hollered, the echo off the stone walls mocking her. She rounded on

Charles. "You swear there isn't anything you haven't told me? Anything you've continued to leave *unsaid?*"

Soft calloused hands rested on each cheek, guiding her gaze up to his. "None of life-shattering importance," he said, eyes the color of the sky searching hers. "Though, there will be dancing after the coronation."

Rosealyn leaned her head to one side. "Dancing?"

Charles nodded with a sheepish grin that made her cheeks flush. "And you better not say no to having the first dance with me."

She narrowed her eyes and pursed her lips, and though she knew Adela would have a few words to say about it, Rosealyn nodded her agreement.

"Good." His gaze flicked down to her lips and back to her eyes, shoulders stiffening.

"Stiff? Again?" she asked with a roll of her eyes which stopped as soon as his lips met hers. A pause, long enough for her to murmur, "That's better."

She held his hands against her cheeks, relishing in the feel of his lips against hers. He tasted like berries and smelled like freshly budded flowers. When he caught her lip with his teeth, she gasped and pressed herself closer to him, demanding more. Soldiers' presence be damned, Rosealyn planned to steal every possible kiss before returning home. His hands remained on her cheeks as he kissed her again.

CHAPTER TWENTY-THREE

Catarina lifted the torch to light the dark, damp tunnel. The long-forgotten dingy cell bars glinted, and she grimaced, mumbling about her idiotic cousin.

"You've been keeping her down here?" Catarina asked the guard again, and the man grunted in response.

"Per Praetor Ramon's request," came the same explanation the guard had given before. It had taken her days to learn her sister was in the building and longer to discover the one person who knew where Roseanne was. This one guard, an inconsequential man of low rank hidden among the many who helped the council building run smoothly from day to day.

Catarina flinched at the scurrying feet of vermin. "At least he didn't kill her, too."

The guard didn't respond, nor did he follow her when she trekked down the tunnel, lifting her skirts to hold them away from the water puddles. A small part of her wanted to laugh at such a move, considering how much water she had seen in recent years. Not just an ocean view, but living on a small island surrounded by water as far as she could see. These puddles were not ocean water. Most of the cells lining the tunnel stood open, though even shut, their metal bars would hide nothing.

Furthest from any hint of light that could reach these depths, Catarina found her sister chained to the wall. Clothed in that deep red Tenoan dress she'd always preferred, Roseanne flinched at the torchlight. Streaks and smudges betrayed the past presence of tears. The woman's dress was soiled, coated with dirt. And blood. Roseanne sniffled, shifting an arm to wipe at it, but the loud chink of the chain halted her hand and she winced.

"You're not the guard," Roseanne said without looking up. "The footsteps are lighter. Which means—"

She drug out the words, eyes growing wider as she looked up to see the sympathetic grimace lining Catarina's face.

"Ramon is dead." Catarina fumbled for the keys and opened the cell door.

Roseanne stared at the ground, chin to her chest, and shoulders slumped in complete defeat.

"'The most beautiful rose may have the worst thorns.'" Catarina's voice echoed through the tunnel. It was Phillippe's most common refrain, spoken like a mantra that always sounded more like a warning. "I never thought he would mean you."

"He always trusted you more." Roseanne shifted to cross her arms despite the loud clinking of the chains connected to her wrists. "He told me my husband would finally be at rest, and like an idiot, I didn't realize what he meant."

Catarina tensed, gripping her dress-skirts with one hand and the torch with the other. Teeth tugging at her lower lip, Catarina buried the words she had dreamed of saying to her sister in the moment of their reunion. Of all the options she'd considered, standing outside a cell with her sister chained inside had definitely not been one.

"What has already happened cannot be changed," Catarina said with an air of finality and determination. "As much as I want to, as much as I know we both want to, the past is already written."

"Any news of Rosealyn?" Roseanne blurted out.

"She attended a summit in Violet Grove," Catarina murmured, biting her tongue before saying the next words. "Jaida killed Ramon."

"Her name is Rosealyn, and good," Roseanne replied as she pushed herself to standing. "I hope she did the same to Xannan."

"I suppose I should get you out of those chains and that cell. Your brothers and sister-in-law may wish to speak with you. And they are looking for Jaida."

Roseanne's eyes flared at Catarina's use of the name she had given her daughter, but Catarina dismissed the thought of arguing. She set the torch on the ground, hoping it wouldn't roll into a puddle of water. Keys jangled against one another, and each failed turn only added to the tension.

"Where have you been?" Roseanne asked at the same moment the lock clicked inside the metal rings. "I looked for you. I thought you were lost to me. Forever."

"The Islands of Izari," Catarina explained, hands shaking and dropping the ring of keys. Like shattering glass, they fell upon another, and Catarina mumbled at her hands to function properly. "Islands in the midst of the Vadamon Sea, where the crystals capable of absorbing magic grow, and where those with natural born magic are sent for safety. Now, with the dragon who would deign to steal their magic gone, those beings can return. I am their representative."

"A representative for magical beings when you have none?"

Catarina smiled with the soft knowing lips of one about to speak words the other already knew but could not admit. Her hands steadied, and she waited for the chains to clatter to the ground before she spoke. "You must remember my fondness for plants, dear sister?"

Roseanne nodded, rubbing at her chafed skin and wincing while Catarina shook her head and tsked. She never understood why one would further irritate the already aggravated skin. From a hidden pocket in her skirt, Catarina pulled a small vial with a concoction made by one of the elves, claiming the liquid could heal simple wounds. The chafing of Roseanne's wrists was red and angry, streaked with the grime of however long these cells had existed below the council building. A few drops fizzled and absorbed into Roseanne's skin, the redness fading and allowing Roseanne's dark brown skin to shine once more.

"I can manipulate plant growth. At first, it manifested when I would touch the leaves of a plant and it would grow to its full potential only to wither and die quickly thereafter." She pocketed the vial inside her simple gray dress. It, too, showed off her dark skin, a near match for her sister's. She held out a hand, and a small flower formed within. "Creating without what nature provides is more difficult, though I have been learning."

"The palace gardens," Roseanne breathed, and even without her sister explaining the exhalation, Catarina knew the man they both cared for had maintained the garden she'd helped grow. Some of those plants were the first she had created.

"I wonder if the pink rosebud tree still stands, or if those rose bushes still bloom with that unexpected black mingled with green. Neither were what I intended, of course."

"That's—" Roseanne cleared her throat. "Amazing."

CHAPTER TWENTY-FOUR

After two full days of tempering her aggravation, it was all Catarina could do not to screech at her sister's despondent demeanor. Bathed and properly dressed, Roseanne did naught but stare into those flames. No matter what Catarina said, all Roseanne did was shrug.

Standing at the door and not knowing how else to reach her sister, Catarina gritted out, "Wallowing in pity will get you nowhere."

She tried not to slam the door behind her, but the motion couldn't be stopped. Resting her back against the wall next to the door, Catarina smacked her palm against the wall. Those words rang true in her ears, words she had learned to live by after leaving all she loved. Not wallowing in pity had allowed her to find new joys, until Naomi sent her away. Until Naomi sent all of them away from Izari. Almost all of them, she reminded herself. Magic harboring crystals grew on the island and were extremely enticing to those with powers they did not want nor could not control.

After a brief tap of her head against the wall and a muttered curse, Catarina moved swiftly down the hallway toward the kitchens. The new ruling council of Tenoa did not want to meet with her, though they'd been kind enough to give them warm rooms. Surprisingly, they had done the same for all those who had returned to Delphi with her. Once empty of all but Ramon's personal requests, Catarina's magical friends now resided throughout the domed building.

When she returned to Roseanne's room with two full plates, the once resolute queen of a kingdom had not moved. She watched the fire as though begging it to engulf her rather than provide warmth.

For a heartbeat, Catarina forgot about the plates in her hands. She attempted to grasp her skirts, but the tipping weight reminded her, and she moved her arm swiftly to avoid the plates clattering to the ground. Even at her sharp inhale of breath, Roseanne didn't shift. Catarina's sister was lost to her emotions.

"I told you," Catarina said, blocking Roseanne's gaze into the fire and offering one of the plates. "Wallowing in pity will get you nowhere."

Roseanne made no move to grasp the plate and stared through Catarina instead. One plate set on the hearth, Catarina resumed her seat at Roseanne's side, wiggling her feet to remove the thin slippers and tuck her legs beneath her. "You should eat," she prodded.

At Roseanne's heavy sigh, Catarina stifled an exasperated exhale and set to nibbling on her food. Sooner or later, she would get Roseanne to talk. Often all it took was aggravating Roseanne and Catarina would receive a berating for her actions. But this was not the older sister she had once known.

Catarina frowned at the grittiness of the water she sipped and asked, "Do you wish to return to Orda'an?"

It was as good a question as any to start, but Roseanne didn't budge other than to shiver.

Catarina tugged at her bottom lip with her teeth, tapping her fork soundlessly in the air. "What will they do? If you return?"

"I'm a traitor," Roseanne whispered no louder than the crackling fire. "I'd rather not know what they will do."

"Ramon was a traitor who led you astray. No one can fault you for trusting your family."

No flicker of a movement or a response; Roseanne had withdrawn deeper inside as far as Catarina could tell.

Catarina chewed on a mouthful of bread as she considered how best to help her sister. "So, what now?" She flicked at the kernels of rice, hoping a dose of tough love was the best path. "Leave Jaida without help?"

"Her name is Rosealyn," Roseanne whispered, though it sounded less fervent than the day before when they'd trudged their way back up from the dungeons to this room.

"To you, yes."

"And to all of Orda'an. She has no need of me." Roseanne lowered her chin to her chest. "No one does."

Catarina chewed on her tongue, thinking as Roseanne watched the soft crackle of the dying flames. So many years separated their last conversation, one filled with such strife. She itched to be in a garden, surrounded by the comfort of plants.

"I need you," Catarina whispered as she set her plate on the hearth. The words were true; she missed her sister. The subtle shift of the blanket tightening around Roseanne's shoulders was her only answer.

"You'll likely fight me every step of the way." Catarina donned her slipper-like shoes and stood. "But you are getting out of this room and coming with me. And no, you don't get to ask where or why. If you don't feel like talking, then I'll do it for the both of us."

She approached her sister, flinging the blanket away from Roseanne's shoulders, grasping both of Roseanne's arms, and pulling her to standing. "Shoes," Catarina mumbled, eyes darting around the room for a pair. Shoes found and forced on to her sister's feet, she hooked her elbow with Roseanne's and tugged.

Roseanne froze, staring down at Catarina's arm linked in hers, mouth agape. After a visible swallow, Roseanne gently removed Catarina's hand and whispered a hoarse, "I'll follow."

The few words were sufficient enough, though nowhere near reassuring. They walked through the rounded darkened hallways of aging stone until the scent of salt from the nearby Vadamon Sea coated Catarina's nostrils, mingling with the refreshing aroma of budding plants. Her sister's steps lingered with a painful slowness, and she considered pulling Roseanne along to where she hoped the beauty of nature would help.

Without thinking, she reached for Roseanne's arm again. Roseanne slapped her hand away, and Catarina froze. At her arched brow, Roseanne looked away. Grimacing, Catarina gripped her skirts and crouched to peer up at her sister. "Sorry," she whispered. "But the sunlight, and the oasis, will be good for you."

She knew Roseanne followed only by the soft footsteps plodding behind her. That and the heavier breathing. Finally at the doorway which would grant the quickest path to the nearby oasis, Catarina turned and gasped. Roseanne had pressed one hand against the wall, while the other was held against her stomach. Breaths became more ragged with each set of inhales and exhales, and Catarina's eyes widened. Her sister. Her resolute, proud, immovable sister was in the throws of panic.

A tentative step forward was as far as she got before Roseanne lashed out as though to slap her again. With raised hands, Catarina stepped back and gestured toward the bright sun-filled sky visible through the doorway. "Please come with me."

Roseanne shook her head, breaths heaving with a rapidness Catarina knew was unsustainable. When she stepped forward, Roseanne held up her hand. Not to strike this time, but as a command to not come closer.

Straightening, Roseanne wiped at her eyes. Her breaths slowed, growing deeper with each rise of the chest. All Catarina could do was stare and wish her sister would let her in, let anyone in. A simple flick of a gesture was all the acknowledgment Roseanne gave that she would continue to follow. With narrowed eyes, Catarina studied her sister. Breaths steady, jaw set, but Roseanne's gaze was too distant. Catarina continued rubbing the fabric of her dress, and one of her nails caught on a loose string. Lips pressed together, Catarina led them to the oasis.

Glorious sunshine washed over her as tall trees reminiscent of the forest coating Izari's island surrounded them. Unlike the ancient growths of Izari, these trees were young. Catarina rested a hand on a nearby sapling, savoring the youthful strength within, urging one of its buds to bloom. Her heart fell at Roseanne's distant withdrawn gaze. Arms crossed and a frown would have been less concerning.

"I'm surprised you don't have magic as well." Catarina patted the ground beside her and sat cross-legged next to the young sapling she'd coaxed into blooming. "I wonder what your ability would have been."

Silence and a glare, so Catarina sighed and continued, "Magic comes in all shapes and sizes. Here, in this oasis, I will thrive. In the middle of the desert, the middle of the ocean, I feel cold and alone. As I'm sure you do right now." She plucked the bloom from the tree and met her sister's gaze. "Ramon broke your trust, broke our trust, broke the trust of everyone he ever knew." Catarina traced the petals. "The council has been reforged, and they've acknowledged we are not responsible for Ramon's actions. So what would you like to do, Roseanne?"

Not a sound came from Roseanne, just a flicker of a reaction at the description of magic. Catarina placed the bloom on the ground. "We could live here. Forget the past and begin anew." She frowned and smoothed her skirts. "That won't work for me, though."

Catarina plucked another bloom, cradling it in one hand as she recreated an identical bloom in the other. "I found a place on Izari, a voice for those who did not speak up for themselves. Between Naomi's request and Ramon's final letter to me, I had to return home. I left an island full of people who relied on me with the belief that Ramon was asking for help. Had I not been delayed by my hesitations and storms on the sea, I'm sure he would have shoved me into a cell, too."

A wince, an almost imperceptible wince. Catarina saw it, took note of it. She hoped she wasn't pushing too hard, too soon. She set the created bloom on the cobblestone, patting the dew-filled grass beside her. When she glanced back at her sister, the woman was standing with arms crossed and a slight frown. Catarina smiled. That was the sister she remembered.

"The LeNoir Gift is another form of magic, an ability latched to them through the magic of the dragons," Catarina said, voice hushing to a whisper as she concentrated on recreating another bloom. This one's leaves wilted as soon as it formed, her distraction too great when forming its image in her mind's eye. "Some wish to take that magic away. Crystals can harbor magic, can leech it from those who no longer wish to have it. Until the months before I left, it was always a mutual agreement. Only those with magic they no longer wanted would have it removed. Those abilities would then be given away, typically to elves of certain lines who are capable of wielding the crystals."

"The Twin Blades." Roseanne breathed, and the distant gaze from her eyes dissipated into worry, maybe even fear. "They were originally made of crystal? And Xannan has one of them."

Catarina dipped her head, concentrating on the empty space in her right palm. She frowned at the wilted petals of the latest flower she had attempted to create. "None but the original bearer of such magic should be able to host it, in my opinion. There is always a reason for the magic with which one is born. It is a part of them that should not be taken, unless they no longer wish to have it."

A green-tinged black rose bloomed in her palm.

Catarina set the fresh bloom from the sapling on the cobblestone beside her, patting the ground again. To her surprise and relief, Rose-anne curled down beside her. She cradled the bloom Catarina had set aside, tracing the outline of each petal. "And when the magic is a gift, not how they were born?"

That question was filled with so much more than simple curiosity. A second green-tinged black rose appeared in her palm. "It's a common saying among the elves that what the dragons gift is not an accident, just misunderstood. I have yet to answer a greater question. Misunderstood by whom? The elves? Magic-bearing humans? The dragons themselves? The other creatures this world believes extinct?"

Catarina frowned at the two black roses resting in either palm. "She offered to take mine too, but it is a part of me."

"Why tell me any of this?" Roseanne snapped at her side. "I am nothing."

Lips pursed in thought for a moment, Catarina set both of the black roses on the ground before them, prodding them enough to keep the petals vibrant and pristine, refusing to let them wilt away. She lifted to rest on her knees and face her sister, grasping Roseanne's hands in each of hers.

"You are angry," Catarina said, staring into the depths of her sister's eyes, knowing her words at that moment would burrow deep. "It's okay to be angry, to be frustrated, to be mad at yourself for what you did or did not do. You are not 'nothing.' Daughter, sister, wife . . . and mother."

Roseanne flinched at the last word. "I may have raised her, but she's as wild and unpredictable as you always were."

All Catarina could do was chuckle under her breath, recalling the many stories of the princess's upbringing that had come to her through those rare and precious letters.

"And she may have magic of her own," Catarina added. "She now has the gift latched to the LeNoir line from the dragons in addition to her own ability."

Roseanne's eyes narrowed at her, and before her sister could ask the question, Catarina explained, "Letters can cross oceans. Phillippe sent at least one each year."

CHAPTER TWENTY-FIVE

Rosealyn's undone auburn hair tumbled over her shoulders, and she lifted it, staring in the mirror resting atop a small desk at one edge of the room. How would she ask to have it done? One long braid like her aunt? The dual braids signaling her position as the princess and heir of Orda'an? Or the braided crown of the queen's station? Better yet, let Viola decide. The maid had been more than kind in the past week. Besides, this ceremony was not for her, and she doubted anyone save herself would care or notice how her hair was done. Except perhaps Adela.

A newfound anxiousness crept in, chilling her insides. After properly full plates, she'd regained strength. And with that strength came a pinch of clarity alongside vortices of emotions. She had no reason to be anxious, not at this precise moment.

"Apologies, my lady," Viola said from the doorway. "I should have knocked, but I assumed you were elsewhere. You often are at this time of day."

Elsewhere meant sparring, which was rare for Jearnian women. Or in her own home, really. Rosealyn ran a hand through her auburn hair and tilted her head, smiling.

"Does it bother you? That I spar with them?"

Viola shook her head of bushy brown hair, light-colored eyes glinting with envy and pride. "Would you be willing to teach others as you've been taught, my lady?"

"Perhaps. But I'm not sure how to teach when I am certainly no master."

"I've watched you," Viola said quietly, approaching with a basket full of items which could transform her hair and face. Viola set the basket on the table and retrieved a hairbrush. "I'm sure you could defeat many of our soldiers in the ring, my lady."

Rosealyn released a clipped laugh, wincing when the brush found a tangle. "Only because most men are too afraid to hurt a woman."

"I'm afraid I haven't found that to be true, my lady," Viola mumbled, holding Rosealyn's hair at a different angle to remove the knot she'd found.

Rosealyn twisted and studied Viola's demeanor. She gripped the back of the chair, and her skin turned as cold as the ice coating the river in the midst of winter. Chills slithered along her neck, down her arms, and culminated in a burst of pain in her core.

"My lady?" Viola questioned, holding Rosealyn's hair to one side with wariness.

"Fear," Rosealyn whispered, grip tightening. "Fear is cold."

Viola's eyes widened. "But you're fearless, my lady. I've heard what you did."

Rosealyn grimaced. "No one is ever fearless, Viola, least of all me."

Viola bit her lower lip, gaze roaming. "The ceremony approaches. Braids again, my lady?"

That dreaded question. It shouldn't matter how she wore her hair. Traditions could be changed. Yet it felt wrong. If she wore it in a different style, did it mean she was stepping away from her responsibility? It was just a hairstyle, nothing more. Heart racing, Rosealyn turned back to the mirror. Her light brown skin and complementary auburn hair were a stark contrast to Viola's white skin tone.

"I trust you to make the decision for my appearance at the ceremony tonight," Rosealyn said. "But I want you to trust me, too. What is it you're afraid of, Viola?"

"The last time someone said anything, they disappeared a week later, my lady," Viola whispered, shifting strands of Rosealyn's hair to-and-fro. It was not a braid she was creating; it was more intricate, more grandiose.

"I'll make sure you're protected."

Viola was silent for a moment. She continued the twists and turns of Rosealyn's hair, creating weaves within weaves. "I know how conflicted you are about the man who arrived with you and how much His Majesty wants to get along with Prince Christopher and how much Prince Christopher wants His Majesty to trust him. And how worried you all are about Queen Nerida."

"These are all things I'm sure are evident in how we speak and interact," Rosealyn said.

Viola huffed. "Your tone and actions have been vague enough for others," Viola explained as she twisted her lips in an almost frown, as though unhappy with Rosealyn's hair. "But loud thoughts ring clear as day for me, my lady."

"You can hear people's thoughts?" Rosealyn gasped, turning in the midst of Viola moving her hair, making the woman lose her hold. Viola chuckled, shifting Rosealyn so she could begin the process anew. Rosealyn's thoughts tumbled like leaves on a strong breeze. So much she'd never learned, despite all of her studies.

Viola nodded, and Rosealyn added, "You may see me as fearless, but you could be invincible."

"Hearing the thoughts of others doesn't mean I'm strong enough to stop them, my lady," Viola muttered, adding the finishing touches to Rosealyn's hair.

"Then starting tomorrow, I'm going to help you fix that," Rosealyn decided as she stood. Her head felt . . . different. Not heavier but certainly not lighter. Viola had done her hair in a way so similar and yet so different from the dual braids she'd spent her life wearing. Rather than braids, Viola had pulled wide swaths of her hair to join at the back of her head with a singular clip. The clip, Rosealyn discovered with a mirror trick Viola shared, was decorated with small flower buds. Looser, freer in some ways.

"No one knows what tomorrow may bring, my lady." Viola spoke quietly as she gathered the items she had used. She pulled out the colored paints which many used to enhance their facial features, but Rosealyn shook her head, chuckling at the shades. None would work well on her skin, so it was better to go without.

"Before the night ends, Charles will be your properly appointed king. We know that much for tomorrow." Rosealyn's heart lurched at the thought while her mouth went dry. He'd been gone for a decade and was receiving the crown he'd won before she received her own. Foolish of her to be jealous, but it reared its ugly head nonetheless.

"I'm aware, my lady." Viola finished packing the items into the basket. "You aren't ready to go home."

Rosealyn tugged at her lower lip, rubbing the fabric of her robe between her fingers and gasped, "I'm still in my robe!"

The realization chased away questions of what tomorrow would bring. Viola smiled and set the basket down to help Rosealyn change. The gray dress shimmered in the late afternoon sunlight streaming through the ceiling windows. No wide skirts, no ribbons of string to cinch her torso inside the dress—this one, she realized with some apprehension, would accentuate her slight curves. Rosealyn traced the translucent lace crisscrossing her chest, debating if she would have chosen the dress herself. The skirts were a smooth silver, with no slit to allow for wider strides. Silver buttons traced her spine and tickled as Viola fastened them. For a final touch, Viola tied a black sash with white fringe around Rosealyn's waist. A representation of Orda'an's colors, Viola explained.

"My work here is done," Viola announced as she hooked the basket on her elbow. "Enjoy the ceremony, my lady."

"My offer remains, Viola." She reached to pat her hair but smoothed her skirts instead, fearful that touching her hair would ruin Viola's work. "Starting tomorrow, I will teach you what I know."

With a small curtsy, Viola smiled. "Thank you, my lady."

CHAPTER TWENTY-SIX

A full plate stared back at Rosealyn, though her stomach ached as though she had already eaten several. Food hadn't been her primary goal in recent weeks, and seeing so much of it at once caused a twinge of frustration for what she'd been unable to provide her people. In addition to the strange, though positively delicious, morsels in front of her, she was surrounded by a vast array of strangers. Charles sat to her right, though it felt more like she sat next to him. His guest, a place of honor at the table with the family of the properly crowned king of Jearnia.

He'd been right about his aunt giving him a much more elaborate crown, encrusted with dozens of jewels that sparkled in the flickering torches lining the vast, gilded room. It sparkled almost as brightly as the throne room had during the ceremony.

To Charles's other side sat his aunt, brother, and Queen Nerida. Seeing them all in one spot made clear the uncanny resemblance between mother and sons, and even Marsha fit right in with the others. To either side of the table were other nobility, families visiting to speak with their new king and offer their notes of approval, or potential disapproval, during the ceremony. And in the far corner, surrounded by four guards, was Xannan. Lackadaisical demeanor rampant, he watched them all with arms crossed. No matter how many soldiers surrounded him, he remained relaxed.

"Eat as much as you'd like," Charles said, gesturing at the full plate in front of her. Once she'd finished the first, another was brought. Laughter sounded nearby, and she turned toward Charles with a smile, resting a hand on her abdomen. Worry flitted across his face.

"The invisible wound is gone," she reminded him, leaning forward to rest her arms on the table and survey the room again. Most wore simple dark colors—deep grays, dark greens, and pleasant browns. Every other noble present seemed to be dressed to make Charles stand out no matter where he was in the room. Between the exorbitant crown and the flame-like coat, he'd be impossible to miss. At times, it was difficult to stifle the laugh at his appearance, but his new outfit had grown on her.

Even her gray dress seemed muted compared to his outfit. The dress was vibrant, shimmering with the lights, while a strange sheer mesh covered what the solid material did not, attaching to the edges of the relatively deep divot along the bodice and stopping in a straight line at her collarbones. It was a gorgeous dress, she could admit that, but it was also extravagant, heavy, and cumbersome. Not to mention, the skirt forced her to walk in strides nearly half their typical length.

"I know," he said, his gaze roaming again. "The dress suits you well."

"I'd much prefer my training dresses," she mumbled, resuming her study of the gathered guests. "A simple beige dress, slit skirts so I can actually take a decent step, loose sleeves so I could move my arms properly, and—"

"You're beautiful," he interrupted, and her cheeks heated while his turned the same color as his coat. "It's the dress, and you, it's…"

"Thank you." Rosealyn smiled and nudged his arm with her elbow. "You said there would be dancing? We, well, I haven't done much of that. Read about it, though."

He smiled and leaned over and whispered into her ear, "It's like sparring, but no hitting and less getting knocked down to the ground."

Before she could respond, he stood. The invisible weight she'd always seen on her father reappeared on Charles, though his tone was both firm and jovial. A king among his people. Not her bodyguard, not a soldier in her army, not her enemy. After thanking those who attended, he announced it was time for the dancing and held out his hand for hers.

Charles gave Rosealyn a reassuring squeeze as she placed her hand in his, her brows furrowed with that mixture of curiosity and annoyance. She could read him probably better than he understood himself, which meant Rosealyn knew the first dance was important. Grip firm, Charles led her into the open space between the three occupied tables, wrapped his arm around her waist and pulled her close. Their joined hands held out to one side, he looked into her eyes and nodded for the music to begin.

"Follow my lead and flow with the music," he murmured in her ear while guiding her steps. Soft whispers floated around them, and her chest heaved when some of the words became clear. Questions arose of his intent, of why the crown princess of Orda'an was there, and why he'd allowed her a place at the table with him. By dancing with her first, Charles was taking the initial step to repairing the ancient rift between their countries.

Rosealyn swayed alongside him, learning as quickly as she had in her earliest training sessions. A quick study with weapons in hand, she'd honed her skills against his. This, however, was not sparring. Every step stole more of his breath, mesmerized by her willingness to follow his lead. The beat of the song slowed, and their steps followed. She laid her head on his chest, one hand intertwined with his while the other wrapped around his back.

Savoring this moment, Charles twirled her and drew her in close again, whispering into her ear, "You have no idea how happy I am you're here." He leaned back to gaze into her eyes. "And alive."

"I'm happy you're alive, too," she whispered back, shifting away as the music faded. He held on, glancing around at those gathered. A few other couples had joined them in the midst of the vast room, holding each other closer than he held Rosealyn. Even Christopher had offered a hand to a young lady Charles vaguely recognized from his week of meetings.

He leaned down, smirking, "The dancing is only beginning."

Rosealyn looked through her lashes, a question in her gaze as she squinted at him. "And now I really wish I was in a different dress. Or had received decent instruction of when, where, and how to move." She forced a frown, betrayed by the mischievous twinkle. "This is nothing like sparring."

He chuckled and guided her through the quicker tempo of the second song. A song of celebration. As Charles flowed with the music, he fought the childhood memories that threatened to rise. His mother sat with that knowing smile she'd had when admonishing him for leaving anything unsaid while his aunt failed to hide the slight frown.

Word would spread throughout Jearnia quickly, especially with all of the nobles in attendance. By dancing with her that night, Charles was showing all present he intended to work with her. Heartbeat quickening at the thought some would now consider targeting her, like someone was targeting his mother, his grip on her outstretched hand tightened. A small simple smile, and she squeezed back.

"Perhaps not exactly like sparring," he agreed, tucking away the worry to concentrate on the present. "Though I can't think of many other activities that bring two people this close together."

"It is nice," Rosealyn murmured with a hint of mischief. "Not to have to worry about you trying to knock me down."

"I wouldn't be so sure about that." Charles guided her through another twirl while she looked at him with tight eyes and an inability to frown. "There are much more complicated dances than this one."

From the silver dress accentuating each slight curve, to the new hairdo holding her long auburn locks so they didn't whip him in the face as they often did when sparring, to the twinkle in her eyes, and to her thin lips parted ever so enticingly, Charles allowed himself to soak in the moment. He never wanted to let go, never wanted this dance to end.

Each small step he guided felt monumental. Dynamics between many would never be the same. Not even with Rosealyn. Over the past week, after Adela's arrival, after exhausting every potential to destroy the connection of the Twin Blades, and while preparing for this night, the stiffness Rose had always berated him for had slithered further away with each kiss they shared. The beat of the song faded, and he tugged her into him until no space remained between them.

Charles lifted her chin, grinning when she clasped her hands behind his neck and tugged him closer.

The music and laughter faded as he lost himself in the kiss. He held her cheeks, longing for more. Rosealyn tasted like fruit and salt, wine and sugar, a combination of all she'd consumed during dinner. Musicians resumed their playing, but Rosealyn didn't pull away. And he wasn't going to stop her.

CHAPTER TWENTY-SEVEN

Long string-like items coated by a pale red liquid covered Adela's plate. She flicked her fork at the noodles, as the servant had called them. Simple chunks of meat, fruit, and vegetables were all one needed. Not whatever this combination happened to be. Out of respect for the kind monarch, she ate. And ate plenty, for it was more delicious than it appeared, and the room was filled with more food than she had seen in years.

Dabbing at her mouth with a napkin, Adela said, "It seems General Moss was wrong."

"About?" Jacin's plate was clean of every morsel, and he sat with the tense posture of a soldier.

Adela stared at her niece, standing in the middle of that wide open space at the end of their second dance, kissing the officially crowned king of Jearnia as though no one else in the room were present.

"It appears those two did admit their feelings for one another," she explained, frowning at her nephew for not realizing the same. "What does this mean for Orda'an?"

"They could reunite the countries." Jacin leaned back in his seat as the third song began. Faster than the last, it didn't seem to draw Rosealyn's or Charles's attention.

"Phillippe had to have known," Adela whispered, stabbing her fork into the noodles and twirling as she'd seen others do. "A type of peace."

"This can only accomplish so much," Jacin said, gesturing toward his cousin. "Hoclia is demanding Pasea be relinquished to them. And before I left, the idiotic young King Nathaniel insisted his armies attack us sooner rather than later. And Orda'an's armies—"

"I know," Adela said, lips tightening. Calm and joy etched Rosealyn's features as she and Charles moved in time with the music. "Rosealyn knows her responsibilities."

"It appears they're more aware of responsibility to each other at the moment." Jacin scratched his short blond beard. "Do you plan on finishing that?"

Adela absentmindedly pushed the plate over. Hands resting in her lap and sitting tall, she surveyed the room. Again and again. Whispered murmurs increased as Rosealyn and Charles shared dance after dance. All she'd ever been taught about Jearnia was to hate them, to dislike them for wanting to take Orda'an as their own. *Cunning of you, dear brother.*

One dance melded into another so quickly Rosealyn lost count of how many times the music changed. As her breaths became shorter, she was grateful this dress did not squeeze her inside. A spin, a sway, another kiss. She could live in this moment forever.

Strong arms drew her to Charles's chest, so close she could feel his muscles tense beneath the irritatingly bright coat. A small part of her hadn't wanted to get this close earlier, not with so many watching, but it was like the gates holding them back had opened, and she refused to let them shut again. All those years of his stiffness, which only dissipated when they trained, dissolved further each time their lips met.

A steady note rang loud and clear, followed by a slower beat than the previous song. Her heart, however, raced faster as she and Charles resumed the proper dancing position. Keeping a grip on his arm allowed her to feel when he tensed and provided a hint of where and when to move. Though she appreciated the small boost of height the shoes gave her, her feet ached. But she was too mesmerized to stop.

With each dance, flowing with the music came more easily. It was little like sparring in the strictly physical sense, especially since neither had tried to knock the other down yet, but that ebb and flow was the same. Forward and back, a step here to a step there, a quick twirl that stole her breath each time his hand guided her into it. Then a tug in close, a gentle lift of her chin, and his lips were on hers. Weightless, that was how this kiss made her feel. It made her forget what—and who—was around them. And what awaited. So she pushed aside the throbbing in her toes and tightened her grip on his arm, encouraging him to hold her closer.

Warmth infused her body. It didn't matter that she probably looked like a foolish awestruck little girl. The secrets and tension between them were gone.

A quick twirl dislodged several strands of her hair, and she blew them off her face, smiling as Charles tucked them behind her ear.

"What happens next?" she asked.

"Moss said the repairs are going well at Vandyl." Charles guided her steps in time to the music, hands firm in their placement. "You should return home before Theo does something rash."

Rosealyn jerked her head at the corner where Xannan stood. "I'd rather not take him with me."

"We tried everything aside from using a different weapon to kill him," Charles reminded her. "An idea you said not to attempt for fear it could kill you both."

With another squeeze of her hand, Charles glanced over her to glare at Xannan. The Lost Prince was well-guarded and rested with one ankle propped over the other and arms crossed. He hadn't even sat down for the meal. Stood there, nonchalant.

"I know." The space between her shoulder blades twinged, a tingle spreading throughout her back and shoulders as though in warning. "I'm surprised you haven't tried anyway."

Charles paused in his gentle sway, and his hands fell to his sides. "I thought about it but . . ."

"But what?" Rosealyn grasped his hands and stepped in close, wincing at the ache in her feet. The shoes would need to come off soon.

Before Charles could explain, a guard marched up and bowed at the waist. Music faded with a stuttering stop, giving way to curious whispers until Charles raised an open palm. All halted their movement, and he addressed the guard, "What's happened?"

Pale cheeks flushed from the violent, winter winds, the guard gave Rosealyn a quick survey, and turned back to his king. "Sire, Alkaan attacked Orda'an."

"Attacked?" Rosealyn asked. A stream of curses flew through her mind, each more aggravated than the last. "Where? When? How many?"

The guard's mouth slacked, gaze sliding back to his king. After Charles's subtle nod, the guard answered. "That is all I was told, Your Majesty."

"Thank you." Charles glanced at her, his jaw tense and lips pressed tight.

Though Rosealyn tried to remind herself to breathe, her chest held the air inside. She vaguely recognized Charles addressing all gathered, heard the whispers continue as shoes clicked against stone, affecting her ability to process the news.

Jacin and Adela approached Rosealyn and Charles and began to speak, but Charles shook his head. Several people lingered outside the doorway, and he indicated the furthest corner of the room, where Xannan maintained his lackadaisical stance.

"I told you," Jacin said. He grumbled out a curse. "Nathaniel was not happy when he returned home last month. I'm surprised it took him this long to attack."

"Where?" Rosealyn reiterated, pinning the guard with the stare that had often worked to get answers from others. "Several border towns are abandoned because of the blighted fields. He may not have known—"

"He knew. Scouts were thorough." Jacin rubbed the short hairs of the dark blond beard that made him look ten years older than he was.

"Blazes." Rosealyn kicked off her shoes and retrieved them, stopping short when the doors opened again. No matter how many times she saw the red-irised eyes of the elves, Rosealyn was taken aback by the sight. Celena's white hair only added to the elf-woman's shocking appearance.

"Swords remain connected, I see." Celena did not wait for permission to approach.

"Why are you here?" Rosealyn asked as she contemplated pacing again despite her sore feet.

"You've had enough time to attempt to annihilate the connection. So now you either wield Futurae and Praeteritum together—on their own—or as Praesidio. Or we use a weapon not dragon blessed to kill one of you."

Xannan guffawed, short and clipped. "Whoever tries to kill me will find themselves dead first."

"As I suspected." Celena's gaze bore into each of them in turn.

Rosealyn ground her teeth, and the tingling across her shoulders coated her entire body.

"Did none of you think about the consequences for killing a dragon? How the land itself might react?"

"It's not like you or Arjun stopped Xannan from killing Eilon." Rosealyn clenched her hands into fists, almost forgetting one hand held her shoes.

Celena turned her attention back to Rosealyn. "In addition to the attack by your northern neighbors—which I already warned you about, if you recall—the droki are returning. Synda has spotted multiple packs. They are finding each other and finding those with magic." The elf blinked, eyes churning a deep red. "They were trapped, not eradicated."

"So we eradicate them this time." Charles wrapped an arm around Rosealyn's shoulders. "And we'll make sure Orda'an is protected."

Air emptied from her lungs, and she ducked out of his embrace to tilt her head back. Shimmering golden plaques decorating the ceiling blurred as the true meaning of the guard's words hit her. "Already attacked, Charles. They've *already* attacked." Rosealyn tried to grip her skirts but flexed her hands at her sides, worried she might tear the pristine material. "It makes sense. If you want a country, you should kick them when they're down, but . . . Blazes. What do I do?"

"Protect Orda'an first." Xannan lifted from his lean against the wall. "Droki are brainless. Makes them dangerous, but it also means they do not organize and work together."

Rosealyn's stomach made a strange flip as she lowered her head to meet Xannan's gaze. His brows lifted, though his arms remained crossed.

A thought surfaced, and she whispered, "I think we'll have to fight the droki before we fight to reclaim Orda'an."

CHAPTER TWENTY-EIGHT

While his mother's hands wrapped around Christopher's arm and emanated worry, Marsha radiated anger and annoyance. Between the two women, Christopher understood why Charles often wore a frown. A too-weak queen, a princess who should have gone home, an ancient Lost Prince stuck where he didn't belong, a meddlesome aunt, and a duchess from an oceanic city with her nephew—each with their own reasons to maintain stoicism. Christopher idly wondered why he even bothered to remain.

"Droki first?" Charles asked the princess.

"The land of Ebios is dying in small pockets," Celena explained. The words were monotone, as though a dying world did not also impact the elf-woman. "Before, it was Eilon's doing since much of his magic came from taking the life-giving force of other elements. People, plants, animals. The only one he could not siphon from was Xannan, prevented by the dragon's magic harbored in that weapon."

Xannan grunted. "Magic I cannot control." Never one to mince words; Christopher appreciated that about him.

"Not when the weapons are separated, no," Celena agreed. "But when it blended back together as Praesidio? You killed Eilon because you wielded his magic against him. Though I am curious if it will always incapacitate the same or alternate—"

"You want them to purposely reunite the weapons?" Charles shifted to stand behind Rosealyn, gripping her shoulders.

Celena nodded. "When properly used, that power can mend wounds."

Those strange red-irised eyes turned to Christopher, and though he tried, he couldn't prevent the flinch.

He didn't dare say a word; only the two of them knew he'd even asked about it. The answer both enticed and frightened him. Not to mention the brief hunger he'd seen in her eyes as she spoke of the trapped power. It had been so brief he'd almost dismissed ever seeing it.

A storm was coming, a whirlwind gaining strength that none could begin to fathom. Except perhaps Xannan and the elf.

"Why?" Christopher stepped forward, ignoring Charles's stern expression. His mother's grip tightened on his forearm, as though he were a tiny child running unabashedly through the castle halls. "Why do you care, *elf*? You are nothing more than a stranger here. You once told me you would not follow my orders, so I see no reason why we should be so willing to follow yours. For all any of us know, you are some filthy manipulator planning to take that dragon's magic as your own and enslave us all!"

Celena didn't flinch. A void. An unreadable void.

"Christopher!" his mother admonished in a heated whisper. "He's scared, as are we—"

"Scared, Mother?" He barked a laugh and turned to her, though he dared not remove his support from her. The inane doctor, another elf, was beyond wrong. Their mother was not recovering. Her condition only fueled the heat of his words. "This is anger. Frustration. Annoyance at everyone who deems me lesser than someone else."

He gestured toward Charles then. Though his face softened in its hardness, his brother, his king, released his hold of the princess's shoulders and straightened. "You are not—"

"I am! I always have been and always will be. Just another piece to be played. Right, Marsha?" He rounded on her. She stood tall, hands held quaintly before her simple gray dress, though her necklace of crystal beads sparkled in the torchlight and her brown hair rippled like waves over stiff shoulders. Christopher scoffed. "So whose scheme will I play out first? Aunt Marsha's? The *elf's*? Rosealyn's?" He turned back to Charles, glowering. "Or yours, *brother*?"

Blood boiled in his ears while his hand grabbed for an absent dagger. They'd not been allowed their weapons for the dance—not even their king or his honored guests. A simple change from their father's dances, a smart move considering many of the visiting nobles' proclivities.

Hands grasped and tugged against his arm, but Christopher shimmied from Marsha's grasp. "You have no reason to be here."

Marsha turned to Charles with a raised brow. The heaving of her chest made Christopher smirk. He didn't dislike his aunt, but she was almost as commanding as his father. That, and he needed Charles's trust. Creating a rift between himself and Marsha could bring him closer to growing that seed of trust into an impressive flower. And this was his chance.

Charles crossed his arms and gave their aunt a cursory glance. A flicker toward Christopher, back to Marsha, and Charles said. "I appreciate your assistance, Aunt Marsha, but I believe your children are likely missing you at home. Return. If I need your assistance again, I will send for you."

The whisper of a shoe twisting against stone was followed by swift clicks and the thud of the door. The seed of trust had peeked through the dirt.

"Which cities?" The duchess's voice was soft and meek. Beside her stood Jacin, who appeared nearly the same age as Charles. The Orda'anian's hand also searched for an absent weapon. Though Christopher was positive weapons would appear if needed; daggers were easier to conceal, and use, than those supposedly magical swords.

"Hoclia claimed the lands of Pasea promised to them." Celena paused when Jacin loosed a low muttered curse. "Alkaan has taken Lobelia and, per last report, advances on Lycene."

"Nathaniel asked for nothing in return." Rosealyn gripped her skirts. "Hoclia does have rights to Pasea, so long as the priests agree to the exchange."

"Our lone priest will not make a firm statement one way or another." The duchess's heels clicked too loudly against the stone. "Both you and your father nearly *died* to protect Pasea last summer. What changed, Rosealyn?"

Rosealyn's chin fell to her chest, and she shrugged. "I thought I did the right thing." She lifted her head and turned back to the elf-woman who always stood so tall, so unyielding. The princess's voice was dangerously low. "Tell us about *all* of the dragon-wrought blades. Where are they, who own them, and what precisely can they do?"

"No other dragon-blessed weapons exist besides your four." Celena paused with her head tilted, squinting as though she was solving a problem she didn't understand. "The Twin Blades latched onto the bloodline of the LeNoirs and to their direct descendants. Without children of your own, if either you or Xannan die or are killed, the magic within those weapons could be used by anyone. Their magic would no longer latch onto one bloodline. Or, at least, that is my understanding after watching their creation. I relived that moment so many times with Magna. The power they threw at each. . ."

A crack in the fortress, portraying more emotion than she'd had when explaining the same to Christopher after Rosealyn had killed the foolish Tenoan in the middle of the night.

"Such power should not be handled lightly." Celena paused again and clasped her hands behind her like one of his instructors. She shook her head and chuckled softly. "The Twin Blades enhance the magic the LeNoir family possesses."

"I have no magic of my own." Xannan grunted and crossed his arms. "Hers did not come from the LeNoir line."

All turned toward the princess. She shuffled her bare feet, the heels of the shoes held in her hand clicking together. "He speaks true."

Not even the elf-woman who liked to make plans for others said anything. Celena's head remained tilted at an odd angle, studying the princess as though Rosealyn were a puzzle to solve.

Charles broke the silence by clearing his throat. "Jacin, you were within the ranks of the Alkaanian army, correct?"

The Orda'anian offered an affirmative nod, befitting a trained soldier who knew when to keep his mouth shut.

"So you know the strategies he may employ? His plans of attack?"

Another firm nod. "Nathaniel plans to send smaller battalions to each large town throughout Orda'an and take it by force. I shared such with Father and Uncle Alan before leaving. I stand by my earlier thought that Moss should have stayed at Vandyl."

"But so few after. . ." Charles's shoulders drooped, but he straightened to his full height again. A king, a commander, a decision maker—all the things Christopher believed he was not. "Christopher, take Jacin to General Ashtar. He will need to know what strategies the Alkaanians employ if we are to send aid."

"If?" Rosealyn gave him a heated glare. "If you think your people don't know you will send aid to mine when asked, then pull them all back in here and dance with me again. With another lengthy kiss, just for good measure."

Christopher noted the surprised blink from Charles and grimaced. Though he thought it foolish to send aid to an already suffering country, Christopher kept his mouth shut. *Trust is not easily won indeed.*

"Tell Ashtar to take as many men as Jacin says may be necessary to fend off whatever Alkaanians the Orda'anian army cannot. It is not our role to engage but to protect. Remember, we are not the instigator, they are. Go now."

"So I'm a messenger now?" Christopher stepped forward, halted by his mother's grip on his arm. "Sent away before the real plans are made?"

A muscle in Charles's jaw twitched, making the scar along his chin more prominent. For a moment, Christopher regretted the words, but he needed to know the answer to his question.

"The mountains blessed me with broody sons indeed," their mother mumbled as she patted Christopher's arm. "Show Jacin the way to Ashtar so plans can be made. And then, tomorrow, you two and I will speak." She grasped the silver winged pendant. "You cannot continue down this path of anger, Christopher. But first, take care of the more pressing matters."

Christopher swallowed, and his muscles tensed. Between his mother's plea and Charles's stern stare, Christopher acquiesced and led Jacin to the hallway. Rumors would abound from this night. Whether in fear or planning would be hard to say. Many of the Jearnian nobles toed a fine line, always looking for the best path into the king's favor. Such thoughts had led many of them to seek out Christopher, and he already dreaded how many more might approach him after this night.

His brother's reign, however, would not be their father's. Christopher had had the thought time and time again. That night, more than ever, Christopher realized the truth of that statement.

Walking by his side as they turned the first corner, Jacin said, "I understand."

The castle was like a maze, and it would be easy to get the Orda'anian lost. Christopher could offer directions rather than show the man, but that would only make the next day's inevitable conversation worse.

"Raised and trained for what would likely never be yours. I understand that frustration."

Christopher paused. "But you're—"

"Her cousin?" Jacin finished with a raised brow. The Orda'anian glanced at the cross section of hallways where they stood, and Christopher flicked his hand to the right. "I am. And the elder cousin by almost three years. Just as my father is the eldest of his siblings. Father believed the crown should have been his regardless of the Passing. When Uncle Phillippe had no other children besides Rosealyn, my father concocted an idea I could one day assume the throne instead of her. So he trained me for such."

Christopher stopped at another crossroad. To reach the general and share the king's commands, they'd have to go right. The general stayed in the castle proper, as did the guards on duty, while the remaining soldiers were housed outside the castle's walls. A first line of defense, a previous king had once said, likely the one who built the sprawling castle. To the left . . . it'd take a few more turns but could allow more conversation.

"That's different." Christopher turned right, and Jacin followed. "I doubt you would understand my situation."

Their boots scuffed against the dark, carpeted hallway. "How so?"

An innocent question, one Christopher refused to react to. In the few years since his first brothers' demise, he'd feigned a belief he wanted them dead.

"There were once five of us Jearnian princes." Christopher rapped his knuckles against the general's door, knowing it gave Jacin little time to process such a statement.

General Ashtar's maid opened the door, and the gray-streaked bearded unarmored soldier looked up. He offered no more than a brief nod as an indication a prince of the kingdom had entered his quarters. "If this is your brother sending our army to protect someone else while leaving us a wide open target," the general drawled, swishing a bottle in one hand as he propped his feet on the table, "be kind enough to tell him no for me, will ya?"

Though he tried not to, Christopher gagged at the stench.

Jacin entered and covered his mouth. After a few seconds, he recovered his composure and explained, "We don't need your entire army. I know your troops are organized in groups of fifty, which will be the perfect size for my plan." Jacin glanced back, smirking. When Christopher arched a brow, Jacin shrugged. "I'll tell you where to send each. Training to be a royal also yields useful skills for spying."

"How many troops?" Ashtar's words slurred in a deep drawl, and Christopher frowned as the general took another swig from the bottle. Christopher remembered his return, how the man had seemed a tinge more obedient. Either this was the drunkenness talking or the man definitely needed to be demoted.

"Ten." Jacin stepped closer to the table and shifted the papers, pulling out a map of Orda'an. He frowned, glancing between Christopher and the general and grabbed a pencil. He added one town after another, circles indicating the ones he said would need protection. "I imagine your brother and my cousin would want us to join the troop protecting either Vandyl or Cantadad. Flip a coin?"

"Vandyl will have Moss and the majority of Orda'an's army. So I'd suggest Cantadad." It was a selfish recommendation; Christopher wanted to see the ocean again.

"We shall see what the monarchs decide."

CHAPTER TWENTY-NINE

As usual, the guards escorted Xannan to his luxurious room across the hall from Rosealyn and the now officially crowned king of Jearnia. But rather than blissful silence, the fancy silver shoes dangling from the princess's hand clacked against each other as she followed him inside. Charles's glower dark as ever, his weapon had found its way to the man's waist, and he was drumming his fingers against the hilt.

"How can our four swords fend off *packs* of droki?" Rosealyn demanded of Xannan.

"By hoping we stab them before they kill us." He shrugged despite the fear boiling inside. If not for Magna's interference, the droki could have overtaken all.

Rosealyn shifted her shoes to her other hand, studying him. "Celena claims you have magic of your own."

"The ability to see the future or the past is a byproduct of the weapons." Xannan leaned against the bedpost with arms crossed and one ankle propped over the other. Her chest heaved, hair clinging to her neck. It was only his insistence to remain amused by her that kept his own anger and dismay at bay. The princess had a lot to learn. Too much.

"That's why my family's gift passed from one generation to the next," Rosealyn acknowledged, and the lack of surprise confirmed his suspicions of what she knew. "I assume the same will happen when . . . no, the weapon is not as attached to your lifeline as it is to mine. Something changed when Gailin asked for Magna to take it back. Or did that change how it worked for you as well?"

"Not as if we can ask Eilon if he ever did anything," Xannan muttered, lips turned between a smile and a grimace. He still mentally searched for the beast, as though a part of his self was missing. "But either way, I have no magic of my own. Without the connection to the sword, I am no more than a man."

Rosealyn released a haughty laugh. "I'm surprised you didn't say prince instead of man."

He resisted the urge to roll his eyes at her incessant distrust of him.

"So no magic of your own, but the droki?" she said, shaking her head emphatically. "Why do you fear them? The one we encountered did nothing."

"Yet. They're poisonous little fiends. Eilon once embedded their venom in my sword." Xannan paused at Charles's shift and tilted his head to the side. "All I remember is our blade's concussion, nothing more."

"I don't believe you," Charles said, fingers still drumming against the sword's hilt. "That venom cost me one of my companions."

"One?" Xannan stepped away from the bedpost and held up a finger. "Just one?"

"During that encounter, yes." Charles seethed. "Let us not forget the havoc you and Eilon wreaked upon Vandyl in your quest to find Rose. Would you have given her the slow death of that poison as well?"

Xannan shook his head, chuckling while he let his hand fall to his side. Though not all of his memories had recovered, the aftermath of the droki attacks had surfaced several times. "I watched thousands of men die from droki poison. Not just soldiers. But farmers, blacksmiths, horse wranglers. And not just men. The droki do not care who or what you are. From what little I remember—" He paused and bit back a curse, wondering if he truly wanted all of his memories to heal. Xannan tilted his head, donning the emotionless mask he'd perfected in the past week. "If you have magic, they consume it until you're gone. Women, children, infants. Eilon and Magna would have known how to destroy them. But without—"

Words halted. He didn't know what he was without Eilon. He was still Xannan, he was still the Lost Prince. The need to destroy anything and everything he could remained, but that sensation had lessened. He retrieved the weapon, which roiled with shades of gray, white, and black, from his bed. Their movement never ceased and the cause of it made his chest ache. His portion of the blade was changing. Not to the extent the other half had, but soon it would never be the same again.

"What?" Rosealyn blurted, forcing him to abandon deciphering what the changing colors meant.

"We can kill them with a dragon-wrought sword, as I told you before." He shrugged. Even if he was different, he had faith in his abilities and his knowledge. Most of it. "But if I go after them, you cannot go to any of the Orda'anian cities currently targeted."

Xannan heard the gulp, understood the princess's concern. As monarch, it was her duty to protect them. It was a consistent tug on them both, on all three of them.

"Jearnia can take care of the droki," Charles said, taking a single step forward to stand next to the princess.

"Can you?" Xannan asked, stepping forward as well. "You saw what a weapon laced with their poison can accomplish. How do you plan to fight against the animal itself?"

"Christopher and I also have dragon-wrought swords," Charles replied, matching Xannan's forward step with another of his own.

"You're a fool. Anyone you send to fight against the droki will not return. Not one. Including you."

"But you've survived them?" Charles asked, arms crossing as he took another step forward. "You've fought them and defeated them? Without Eilon?"

A tilt of his head and another step forward, Xannan was sharing air with the arrogant king. He didn't remember fighting the droki, but he wasn't about to admit that. "And if I haven't?"

"Then we have no need for you to keep talking, *Xannan*." The king spat his name as though it was a curse. And to him, it likely was. They both hated him for Phillippe's death. A fatal wound he did not recall landing. Its memory was too painful for the princess to recount, and Xannan was only vaguely aware of his actions that day.

Rosealyn pushed him and Charles away from each other, with her head swiveling to address Charles first. "Xannan is a connection to the past. As much as I don't want to say this. . ." Rosealyn paused to take a deep breath and looked at Xannan. "We need your help. Right now, I trust you more than I do Celena or any of the elves."

This time he didn't need another push to step back. Her words held truth. It was there, in her gaze, in her features, in her stance. A firmness he had not yet witnessed. Charles grasped her arm, pulling her to him with a heated whisper. "What did you see?"

She glanced back at him, a newfound kindness softening her gaze that Xannan never expected. "It doesn't always have to combine," she whispered. "We can wield it together. Fight together. And we will. Against the droki."

Xannan grunted and leaned against the bedpost again.

"But Rose—"

The princess whipped her head back to Charles, and the man's words halted, lips tightening into a sour grimace. Xannan had heard that tone before. All those years ago when he'd worked alongside his brother.

"No one else need come with us," Rosealyn added, voice unwavering while her gaze remained on the king. "Let me speak to him. Alone. I'll be over in a few minutes. Promise."

She held her hand out to Charles, a simple motion of endearment, while Charles's gaze bore into Xannan's. He didn't flinch, nor did he move. The hardness disappeared when Charles glanced down at her, backing away rather than turning from them. He even left the door open, brows furrowing when Rosealyn closed it.

"Care to share?" Xannan asked from his lounge against the bed frame. "What does our future hold, Princess?"

She put her shoes back on, returning her to his height. It was all he could do not to curse at the pity emanating from her. "Death then?" he asked. "And the blades won't combine this time?"

Rosealyn shook her head, rubbing the folds of the dress-skirt between one hand, the other lingering near her hip where a sword hilt would be if it hadn't been for the dinner. "The magic balances when nearby. But we will each fight. With our own blade. As for death. . ." Rosealyn shrugged, pausing her rubbing of the fabric and meeting his gaze. "I cannot say for sure."

"Where?"

Another all too familiar shrug, just how Gailin used to respond.

"Trust me more than the elves now, you say?" he asked, not bothering with a subtle transition of one topic to the next. If the droki appeared near this castle, he'd fight them. None deserved such a death. He pushed off from the bed frame and away from Rosealyn's studious gaze. It was easy to forget he had given others that death, especially since he had no recollection of it. But meeting his long-distant ancestor's gaze made him feel too guilty and empty.

"I said I trust you more than them, which is true," she amended as she crossed her arms, tapping her finger against her brown-hued skin. "That does not mean I trust you implicitly. The Gift can be trusted, yes. Charles as well." The tapping stopped. "Right now I only trust you will assist so long as it also protects your own life. It's why your first concern was death rather than where. Or when."

Xannan grunted. "And who will protect the cities Alkaan targeted? What if Hoclia gets greedy and seeks more than Pasea?"

"I'll accept what aid Charles offers. And there are more Orda'anian soldiers than those housed at Vandyl."

A huff of a laugh burst from him as he turned to face her again. "What is your priority, Princess? Your people or his? What reason do you have to protect this land instead of fending off the armies attacking yours? His crown rests upon his head, unchallenged, while yours lies unprotected in an empty throne room. Unless your uncle made good on his plan already. I wouldn't blame him. From where I stand, you're not worthy of it."

"He can't," Rosealyn whispered in a singular heavy breath. "That's not how it works."

"He will," Xannan retorted as he lifted his sword to hold it before him. "The magic attached to us through these weapons is not enough to abandon Orda'an's cities."

"I'm not abandoning—"

"You are and you know it," he yelled at her. "Were I able to do so alone, I'd return to Vandyl. But without you, even without this idiotic connection, they'd kill me before I uttered a word."

Her lips thinned into a tight line as her upper body went rigid, and the tapping of her finger against her arm halted.

"Which leads me to one last possibility," he realized, his chuckle surprising him. "Fighting the droki does lead to my death and thus the dissolvement of our connection so you can return home without me."

"That would be preferred." Both of her fists clenched, and she held her chin high. "Sleep. You'll need proper rest to fight the dreadful droki."

As the door slammed shut behind her, Xannan contemplated following. But there was no changing the stubborn woman's mind, and the arrogant king would be of no use. Not even the younger brother could likely speak some sense into either Rosealyn or Charles. Sheathed sword in hand, he gripped it tight enough to make his knuckles ache as the leather grated against his calloused palms.

Without this sword, without that one day in that cave, neither he nor Gailin would have gained the ability to see the future and the past. Without this sword, he would have died long ago. Without this sword, he would not be inexplicably connected to a princess who did not understand what it meant to protect her people. With all the force he could muster, Xannan threw the sword at the door, swallowing the scream that threatened to accompany it.

CHAPTER THIRTY

Rosealyn jumped when a thud came from within but rounded her shoulders and turned to where Charles rested with arms crossed and brows furrowed. Dress-skirts gripped in both hands, she gazed from the extravagant crown resting on Charles's dark brown hair down to his clean-shaven chin to the now-unbuttoned red coat to the trim black pants and the sword wrapped around his waist. All of him was beyond tense, like an animal ready to attack its prey.

"Now who's eavesdropping," she muttered with a slight smirk in a halfhearted attempt to lighten the mood.

"When it involves a new threat that none but the elves and he seem to know anything about, yes," came the heated response.

"You have no need to face the droki," Rosealyn said as she removed the shoes which both made her feet ache and assisted in boosting her height. "Xannan and I can handle them."

"Did you actually see his death?" Charles asked, head twitching toward the wall behind him.

She both appreciated and wanted to dissipate the new fierceness in him.

"I feel a future loss, a type of grief," Rosealyn explained. "It could be his death. Or anyone's."

Charles pushed off the wall, hands flexing at his side. "Battles are coming."

Her vision blurred, and she cursed herself for being so prone to angry tears. Charles's arm wrapped around her shoulders to guide her into his room. Rosealyn had hoped it would give her more clues about his younger self. But the room was void of personality. Slightly larger than the room to its right, Charles's room was just that: a room.

Rosealyn paused at the doorway, thinking. She had followed Charles into his room because she did not want to be alone. Attacks, magic, the elf—she had no idea how to respond to any, especially since two weeks ago she hadn't known she possessed magic of her own other than the LeNoir Gift.

She wondered if her magic combining with that of the LeNoir Gift would allow her to understand the emotions it forced to the surface. Some of Xannan's emotions were clear to her, but she believed that was due to the swords. Was it possible to withhold or fake emotions? Or did she feel whatever they felt regardless of what they wanted to portray? Granted, it was possible her magic had nothing to do with feeling the emotions of others or that it did not exist at all.

While she was lost in thought, Charles paced the room, almost as if he'd forgotten she was there. Flame-like coat hanging loose on each side, sword leaning against his bed, his studious gaze remained on the floor as he walked the length of the table in front of the hearth.

They would have to part. Again. Not a single piece of her wanted to be somewhere he wasn't, yet responsibilities loomed. Responsibilities Rosealyn knew she could no longer ignore. Ruling her kingdom was impossible to do from here.

Hands flexing at her sides again, her chest lurched at the sight of the man in front of her. He'd stopped pacing to sit on the bench with elbows resting on his knees and chin resting on his palms. Though neither had voiced it, she knew he was coming to the same conclusion. By accepting his role as king of Jearnia, he could no longer remain at her side. Nor she at his. Not yet, at least. If she. . .

"You're making that 'I should say this but won't' face."

She jerked at Charles's sudden proclamation, and her gaze swung to find his face set in a tense smirk. She set one hand on her hip and raised a brow. "I don't make a face."

A proper smile blossomed, and the tension oozing from him lessened. He leaned back, shifting so his elbows rested on the wooden planks of the table. "You have many faces; everyone does. What are you thinking?"

She rubbed the fabric of her dress idly between two fingers. A bad habit, so her mother had once said. Fabric gripped tight, she strode over to sit beside Charles. Resting her head on his shoulder, Rosealyn smiled when he hooked his arm around her and hugged her closer to him.

"I never thought I'd say this about Jearnia, but I don't want to leave here," Rosealyn said, glancing up at him. "It's nice being with you. And with Adela and Jacin here it feels like a part of my home has joined yours."

Slight shivers shimmied up and down her arm, following the path of his fingers grazing her bare skin. Rosealyn tugged on her lip, study-ing the floor and mentally admonishing herself for briefly considering holding back. Cautiously, she laid a hand on his leg and pressed the other against his chest, relishing the steady and soothing beat of his heart as he leaned his head against hers.

"I'm glad you feel comfortable here in this castle, in this country." Charles's hand stilled, and he pressed a kiss against her temple. Heat flushed her cheeks as he added, "I'm grateful you are comfortable with me." He cleared his throat and straightened. "I was worried you'd be afraid of me now."

Lower lip sucked between her teeth, she mulled his words over for a moment. "Pretty sure I'll always be a smidge angry with you for one reason or another, but you are the closest I have to a friend. As wonderful as my father was, getting out of the castle was not high on his list of priorities for me."

"I'm well aware."

Whatever story hid in those words would have to wait.

"What do we do now, Charles?" Though she wanted to remain seated, she couldn't, so she paced. "Do I take Xannan to fight the droki and hope he dies in the process? Find a different solution?" Rosealyn gestured at nothing in particular, paused, and turned on her heel. "What about the cities already attacked?" She chewed on her tongue. "Do I lead those charges myself? Return to Vandyl? Cantadad?" Rosealyn unclasped the clip holding back her hair, kneading her temples. "Where do I even start?"

"We agree to work together in whatever ways we are able." He leaned forward, forearms resting on his legs. "You should probably follow the Gift's lead. Phillippe always did, often to Azeiah's frustration."

She froze, thinking of the two men who had lost their lives to the one she was now to work alongside if any of those visions were to be believed. It had taken many questions, but not until she saw Moss accompanying Adela and Jacin had she known the truth. After several quick blinks, she sighed.

"That's the problem." Rosealyn resumed pacing. "I'm not sure what it wants me to do. Everything is a jumble, a tumultuous waterfall. Roaring thunder, a constant noise making it difficult to follow any line of thought. Nor do I know the difference between my natural abilities and those of the Gift. I doubt the Gift is designed to work at will, either." She made extravagant motions with her arms. "I can't think 'Show me the future.' It either happens, or it doesn't."

Rosealyn's pacing took her to Charles's bed, and she perched on the edge, resting her elbows on her knees as he was. The mantle, the burden, the heaviness she always saw in her father—she understood. Others besides her Aunt Adela were reminding her of the necessity of returning home. "I hate it when he's right. And he's right far too often."

"Xannan?" Charles asked. He stood and removed the bright red coat, revealing a plain white shirt. The exuberant crown she knew he did not want had, at some point, been removed, too. The absence of those items made it easier to talk to him.

"Unfortunately." Rosealyn lay back, picking at the shimmery silver dress. Despite the more accommodating attire, it was difficult to stretch her arms above her, so she propped herself up with her elbows.

"The man knows more than he's said." Charles hooked his jacket on the back of a chair and leaned against the wall near the head of the bed, brows furrowed. "You mentioned a feeling of loss?"

Rosealyn stared at the ceiling and rested her hands on her stomach, grateful this dress allowed for proper breathing. The small windows were dark and clouded, and her gaze flitted across the few stars she'd once studied with her father. With his loss, there'd been no warning. She swallowed and unnecessarily smoothed her dress-skirts, wondering if it was better or worse to know a loss was coming. "I'm not sure if it's from the cities I've already lost or something yet to come."

Loss nagged at the edge of every thought, balanced with overwhelming worry. Charles looked down at her. The earlier fierceness had dissipated into a mesmerizing twinkle, and she wondered if her eyes did the same thing when she looked at him, but the sense of losing someone, or something, wafted through her.

"What do you know?" He sat precariously on the edge of the bed.

She stifled a laugh. "You don't have to keep such distance, you know? I like being close to you." Rosealyn rolled to her side, resting her head on her palm, grateful the invisible wound was gone so she could once again move with ease. If the skirts of the dress weren't as constrictive, she'd consider stealing a kiss. But his face was etched with worry. "I'm not entirely sure it's a loss related directly to me."

"And what did you see?"

Rosealyn huffed and pushed herself to an awkward seated position in the middle of the bed, legs bent at the knee to avoid ripping the pristine material. Slits in the skirts would have made it perfect, but she did enjoy how beautiful it made her feel, even if it had become tarnished with the memory of learning the dangers encompassing her home.

"I saw those things approaching from the north, but not at the castle walls. We were beyond Volante, I think." Rosealyn shifted closer to Charles and laid her head on his shoulder.

He stiffened but released a long breath and wrapped his arm around her shoulders again, giving her a reassuring hug. "That's it, isn't it?"

Rosealyn nodded. "This Gift isn't as impressive or as easy to understand as I thought it should be." Resting her head on his shoulder was surprisingly cozy. "Then again, I don't think my ancestors also had any magic of their own."

"Magic of your own," he whispered, tucking a loose strand of hair behind her ear.

Pleasant shivers crawled along her skin, and she wished they could lie in simple, blissful silence and not discuss how her world was crumbling.

"Supposedly," Rosealyn said, smoothing her skirts again.

"What. . ." Charles swallowed, and his hand paused in its movement. "How did you figure it out?"

"Arjun gave me a letter from my birth mother, Catarina. A thorough explanation that gave me more questions than answers, really. As for my ability. . ." Rosealyn shrugged. "I have no idea what it is. I can sense Xannan's emotions, but I'm positive that's the connection of the weapons; otherwise, I would sense others' emotions."

"You know what he's actually feeling?"

"For better or worse, yes. He finds us amusing, but he also fears the droki more than anything."

Rosealyn lay on her back again with one arm over her face and laughed, understanding why Xannan found them so amusing. The walls between them had only partially fallen apart rather than crumble entirely as she wanted them to.

"He was right. I have abandoned my responsibilities."

Charles jerked to standing and gritted out, "He said what?"

Though she tried, Rosealyn failed to maneuver into a seated position with any modicum of grace. "I already hate him enough for the both of us," she muttered, frowning at the tight dress-skirts. "I should change."

She reached out a hand, and Charles pulled her to standing. Lower lip sucked between her teeth, she opened her mind and emotions to what she thought was the Gift, or perhaps her own ability. The sense of loss grew, and her heart skipped a beat at the intensity of it.

"Stay with me tonight?" Rosealyn moved in closer to him, holding tight to his hand. "At least until I fall asleep?"

He lifted her chin, lips gentle and warm as they met hers. The kiss was a whisper of a promise. "Anything you need, Rose, I will give you."

CHAPTER THIRTY-ONE

Charles lay next to Rose for hours after she fell asleep, unable to do so himself and not wanting to leave her side. His mother would admonish him and Christopher for not quite getting along. Christopher was difficult to understand. One moment his younger brother seemed to be open to working together and the next Christopher would give in to an angry tirade that pierced Charles to his core. Not for the first time, Charles wondered if he could have prevented the pain Christopher had experienced, but Charles couldn't change the past.

Eventually, he drifted to sleep but was awoken by a distinct loud clearing of a throat by a person standing near the door. Sunlight streamed through his closed eyelids, and he tensed, realizing his arm was pinned beneath Rosealyn. She had a fistful of his shirt gripped tight, head nestled into his chest. Squinting, Charles saw Viola, the young maid who appeared less afraid with each passing day, failing to hide both her grin and her blush.

"Good morning, Viola." Charles tugged his arm free and pried Rosealyn's hand from his shirt, resituating the blankets as she resumed the steady rhythm of sleep.

"Good morning, Your Majesty," Viola said with a short curtsy. "Would you prefer breakfast here, Sire?"

"Let her rest a while longer," Charles said, glancing down at Rosealyn and tucking the hair away from her face. Peaceful sleep suited her features much better than the glowering anger of discussing if she should retaliate and attack or defend and protect. Their ideas on strategy, he had learned, differed more than he expected. "Are Christopher and Mae awake yet?"

"Prince Christopher is, Your Majesty."

"Thank you, Viola." He sidled off the bed and shook his tingling arm.

The maid curtsied again, and his jaw clenched, reminiscing on the days when he'd followed others' commands.

Before he got to the door, Rosealyn asked, "Leaving so soon?"

"I must speak with Mae and Christopher." Charles paused in the open doorway, smirking at how Rosealyn was a comforting sight even with her hair a tumbled mess. "You should probably speak with Adela. I'll meet you at her room?"

"I'll wait for you to return here when you're ready to go with me to speak with Adela." Rosealyn stretched and stood, lips quirking mischievously. "Besides, Viola and I made plans for this morning, didn't we?"

The maid's blush deepened, gaze darting between the two.

Despite Charles's arched brow, Rosealyn waved a dismissive hand and said, "Meet here in an hour?"

"An hour should be more than enough time for Mae to admonish us."

Charles opened the door to his mother's room and paused. He'd been expecting to speak with his mother first, without his brother, but Christopher sat across from her, and a third chair remained empty between them.

"Have you learned anything more of what transpires beyond the Hills?" His mother patted the seat next to her, but he remained standing. For once, she looked more awake. Perhaps what Eonar had provided was truly beginning to work. That or whatever was causing the poisoning had been removed. He glanced around the room, gaze snagging on the white cloth with red thread, and wished she would use a different color.

"We all know the same as the scout told us last night, in addition to the information Celena provided, of course. Rose must return home, and she will need aid."

"She can take care of herself. As can her country," Christopher mumbled. He leaned back in his chair with arms crossed and unkempt shoulder-length curly hair covering part of his face.

"Orda'an saw the brunt of Eilon's wrath," Charles reminded his brother. "Many of their cities have no way to fend off any invading force. Not anymore. They need aid."

"You cannot be our king here and race off to help every time she asks." Christopher shifted, resting his left ankle on his right knee. "And what are these *droki*? I've never heard or read of such a thing."

Charles grimaced; he'd worry about Rosealyn wanting to fight the droki later. "What do you recommend, Mae?"

"I know you want to go with her because you've spent so long protecting her, but you forget she can protect herself. You've told me the stories of how well she can handle weapons."

His heart flipped in his chest. She was right. But he wanted to make sure the lifeblood of another never covered Rosealyn's hands again and to watch her properly assume the Orda'anian throne. All of which he could help her accomplish. All of which she could do on her own.

When his mother patted the chair beside her again, he obliged. Would Rosealyn welcome his help in retaking her home from the northern countries? And what of his people? The ones he had sworn to protect the previous night? His chest tightened when he recalled how vulnerable Rosealyn had been when the weapons combined the first time.

"I promised to provide her with an ally." He wiped his palms on his knees. "But I can't leave here without losing what little traction I've gained."

He shifted to stand, pausing when his mother's hand rested on his forearm. "There are more options to consider, Charles."

After a cursory glance toward his brother, Charles leaned back and folded his arms, wincing at the stiffness of his flame-like coat. "I'm not sure he's ready to rule in my absence."

"And are you so confident in how to rule yourself? I learn what's discussed at those meetings. You would not have had such success without Christopher's assistance, would you?"

Charles nodded, and a muscle along his chin spasmed. He hadn't wanted to bother her since she needed to recover. But his mother was as meddlesome as anyone.

"I'll leave you both to talk it over, but know Christopher received the same, if not more, instruction on how to rule a kingdom than you did." Their mother rose, gently patting them on a shoulder before leaving the room.

Once the door shut behind them, Christopher leaned forward and chuckled. "The only reason you're contemplating leaving me as steward is because of Rosealyn. You may claim it's because you trust me or you want to compromise, but whatever you tell me to do means I'm not making the choice of what I get to do."

Several heartbeats of silence passed. Charles tilted his head and asked, "What would you like to do?"

Across from him, Christopher's jaw slacked, but he clamped his lips together into a tight line and lowered his foot to the floor.

While Christopher thought, Charles added with a wave of his hand, "You're right. Whatever I ask you to do at this moment means you did not get to make a decision. As my brother, and a prince of this kingdom, your opinion matters. I make the final decisions, but I will value your thoughts."

The tight line of Christopher's lips twisted into a smirk. "I know what you want me to say. You've learned I'm not the most well-traveled, and I'm not exactly fond of weapons. So it would be logical for you to travel while I remain."

"If that's what you'd prefer." Charles offered a subtle nod, though his heart fluttered more intensely than it had when considering staying.

"Ah, but that last wasn't a decision, merely a commentary. Did she tell you about killing her cousin?"

Charles jerked, squinting at his smirking younger brother.

"I'm guessing not the details. Not how she gutted him with her sword."

"What point will this prove, Christopher? I'm aware she can protect herself. I'm the one who taught her to do so."

"So shouldn't she be able to fend off all of her enemies herself?"

"If it was just Hoclia or just Alkaan, perhaps. But it's both, and Tenoa is unstable as well. Factions there disagreed with Phillippe and Roseanne's union. And, as we are well aware, disagreements often lead to bloodshed."

"Bloodshed happens." Christopher shrugged, leaning forward with elbows on knees and hands clasped together. "I'd rather stay. Though I told Jacin I'd go with him to Cantadad since it meant I could see the ocean."

Despite the tension, Charles laughed. "The ocean?"

"I've never seen it before." Christopher shifted his gaze to the floor.

"That's a lie." Charles chuckled again. "That's where you were when it came time to kill Eilon. You ran off to see the ocean?"

"Among other things."

Charles drummed his fingers along his arm, waiting for his brother to say more. When no additional explanation came, Charles stood and tugged at his sleeves. "If you are to remain as steward in my absence, I want you to follow a few rules."

"Logical." Christopher remained with hands clasped before him, curly hair obscuring most of his face despite his looking up. "And these rules are?"

"For starters, no unnecessary killing."

"Unnecessary?"

"If the droki attack here then by all means, kill them. Hopefully they don't." Charles placed both hands on his hips. "Apparently only dragon-wrought swords can kill them, so it'd be up to you to kill any droki which appear."

"Wonderful." Christopher shifted his hair from his face and leaned back in his seat. "And if something besides the droki needs killing?"

Charles glared at him.

"Understood. No unnecessary killing. Is that all?"

"Do not revoke any of the treaties created between the plantation owners in the past week. And no creating any new treaties or plans without me. The rest you should know how to handle, if Mae spoke true about your training."

"She did, though I enjoyed stories more than the actual lessons." Christopher stood and straightened his coat. A similar cut to Charles's, though its red hue was significantly less ornate. "Thank you. You didn't need to trust me, or let me live, not after how I treated you." Heat flushed his cheeks as Christopher rubbed the back of his neck. "I cannot promise there will be absolutely no killings, but I promise to do my best."

Charles held out a hand, the pressure in his chest increasing when his brother grasped it. "Last rule. A message a week with updates. Properly sealed and you must handpick the messengers."

"I thought I'd send those messages by bird, actually." Once Charles pinned him with a stare, Christopher waved a hand dismissively. "No unnecessary killing, weekly updates, and maintain the plans you created, which will mean mediating any disagreements between current owners in the event of potential land and labor disputes."

Any other advice Charles thought to give his brother had been summed up in that statement. Like their mother said, both were more than capable of ruling. Yet knowing Christopher was capable did little to assuage the tightening of his chest.

"One more thing." Charles released his brother's hand and retrieved the white cloth with red thread. He hovered a finger over the design, tracing it without touching the thread. "I think I know how Mae's being poisoned."

CHAPTER THIRTY-TWO

The bed was comfortable, Xannan finally decided while lying with his hands resting beneath his head. Ceiling windows were a nice touch, especially since they allowed the light of the morning sun to illuminate the bare room. The completely empty dressers intrigued him. However, searching the room was merely a distraction. The room served as a type of prison, a place they left him until Rosealyn decided she wanted to go somewhere.

Memories continued to surface. Moments with his brother, both before and after the swords had melded to them. His first kiss with Anna, the woman he would have married had Eilon not killed her. Among pleasant memories were those that helped him understand why he was so hated. He supposed those actions also made the others ignore his presence. Just another byproduct of magic. A tool to be used whenever the true need arose. Nothing more. Not a legendary king as his father had been. Or his brother.

Rather than stare at the ceiling, Xannan relived those moments, entering them as though he were there. He felt the emotions, the movement of his own body, his brother's voice, his beloved's warmth, even his parents' aura. Each time he relived such memories, returning to reality became more difficult. The memories held no aches, no incessant throbbing of his head. Reliving these moments, the moments he chose, were fulfilling.

He glanced where his sword lay after having thrown it at the wall the previous night. Many memories had a black haze, a fuzziness making him wonder if they were real.

Since the sun had risen an hour ago and none had arrived to insist he stay close so Rosealyn could go where she wished, he figured it was a good time to try a new idea. Most times, he would close his eyes to relive such scenes. But the elf claimed this blade enhanced the magic within his family line, and what he thought had been visions from Eilon could be his own.

A faint and indiscernible sound tickled at his ears. When he willed himself to hear the words again, but louder, he was greeted with an obnoxious rapid succession of a fist pounding on his door.

He waited, searching for her emotions—he knew she could feel his—but nothing came. One more knock, and the door opened.

Rosealyn explained, "I need to speak with Adela and Jacin."

Of course she does, but she doesn't think to ask my advice. None of them do.

After retrieving his sword, he followed. Reluctant, but he hated the feeling when they ventured too far away.

The newly crowned king was, as usual, walking alongside her. Guards, ever present and armed, followed close.

"Christopher agreed to stay," Charles said.

Rosealyn gave him a sidelong glance. "We can discuss everything with Adela and Jacin. They should be a part of the decision-making process."

Two paces behind them, Xannan's chest tightened, and his jaw ached. He remembered receiving the same glances they exchanged. And he recalled having his opinion valued. Trained to lead, no different than they had been.

After a quick stop at Adela's room to find it empty, they continued to the chambers Jacin occupied. The door stood open, so Rosealyn entered and announced, "There you are, Adela."

The duchess jolted and blurted, "We need a formal alliance. Otherwise, in the cities Jearnian soldiers will protect, people will attack."

"I know," Charles said. "That's why I'm coming, too."

"We already discussed this. I can protect myself." Rosealyn stepped into the room, allowing both Charles and Xannan to enter. "And Xannan and I stopped trying to kill each other."

Xannan snorted and leaned against the wall near the door, assuming his common lackadaisical posture.

"I don't trust him," Charles said with a glance toward Xannan.

Xannan smirked and crossed his arms.

"Stubborn idiots," Adela grumbled from her place at the table.

Both Rosealyn and Charles turned toward her while Xannan crossed his legs at the ankles.

"Theo believes he should give the crown to another, and now you think you should leave the crown you received last night, so yes, stubborn idiots making rash decisions," Adela said with pointed gestures at both Rosealyn and Charles.

"We've all made rash and idiotic decisions." Rosealyn moved to stand next to Jacin, who sat across the table from Adela and had done nothing but continue eating since they'd arrived.

"I'm not leaving Rose alone with him again." Charles jerked his head back toward Xannan.

Try as he might, Xannan could not withhold another derisive snort.

Rosealyn turned and crossed her arms, glaring at the king. "Like I explained last night," Rosealyn said, "Xannan and I will handle the droki. Moss should return to Vandyl and Adela, with an escort, to Cantadad. That was the end of our discussion. You did not mention Christopher staying or you coming with me."

"Because we fell asleep." Charles straightened and gripped his sword hilt. "I disagree with your plan. And now we have a new one. A better one."

"You know how to protect a country from an assault?" Rosealyn stepped toward Charles, chin lifted as though it would help her become taller than him.

Adela cleared her throat and asked, "Fell asleep?"

Rosealyn blushed, Charles's shoulders stiffened, and Xannan chuckled silently. Though it was frustrating to be ignored, it was also entertaining.

"So my training as a crown heir and as a soldier mean nothing anymore?" Charles took a deep breath. "You valued both those facts last night. You protect from an assault by making sure the enemy never reaches their target."

"Defend, do not attack, that was Father's motto."

"That method won't work anymore, Rose. Trade routes gone, fields upon fields destroyed, because he waited for the enemy to come to him rather than annihilate the threat." Charles ran a hand through his hair and turned away from Rosealyn's glare. "You don't have to live by his—"

"I choose to!" Rosealyn's arms stiffened at her sides. "Father taught me everything I know; I'd be a fool to do something different."

Charles shifted his attention to Adela and Jacin, probably hoping they would help him convince Rosealyn to consider his advice. Neither spoke. So Xannan did.

"Not a fool." Xannan approached the table. His stomach grumbled, and he was worried Jacin would eat everything provided soon. "A wise leader considers all possibilities. All options. There are many paths you have not considered, Rosealyn. Your path has been colored by a desire to get rid of me. You've failed to consider I could also be an asset."

"An asset?" came Rosealyn's haughty question.

Xannan smirked and surveyed the platters. After selecting pieces of fruit, meat, and a decorative roll, he sat beside Jacin and indicated the remaining seats. Rosealyn stared at him as though she could burn a hole through his skull, and he chuckled. Across from him, Adela inhaled sharply as though she was about to speak, but when he glanced her way, she slumped back into her seat.

A slight tilt of his head, Xannan shifted his gaze back to Rosealyn. "Yes. You forget I've fought and survived the droki before any of you were thought about. I also know more about magic."

And now she's pacing again. At least she isn't wearing heels this time.

He waited, savoring the sweetness of the fruit, the slight saltiness of the meat, and the perfect texture of the bread. The others exchanged glances, waiting for Rosealyn's response.

After several long moments, Jacin, whose plate was empty, said, "Other cities are in danger, Rosealyn. I shared with General Ashtar which cities Nathaniel would target first, though their maps of Orda'an are severely outdated." He paused to down a cup of water and shrugged. "Alkaanian troops will reach Lycene before us, even if we left now." Jacin scratched at his short beard, frowning. "Moss says Lycene became a haven for those displaced after Vandyl's destruction. At least one battalion protects them, but Lycene is only two days' ride from Vandyl."

"I'm aware of what Nathaniel and Jordan want." Rosealyn paused in her pacing. Xannan expected her to make some snide comment about Vandyl's destruction again, but she resumed her pacing and added, "It initiated the discussion of what I think we should do versus what Charles thinks we should do."

"And you didn't ask my advice." Xannan tsked.

"Why would your opinion matter?" Adela asked. When Xannan met her gaze again, she flinched.

"The consensus is obvious it doesn't, but it should." Xannan offered a mocking smile and sank his teeth into the decorative roll. Warm and fluffy, he found Jearnian food to be more than appealing.

Rosealyn halted immediately behind him. "What would you do?"

A tug on his chest, so similar to the one which occurred when they ventured too far, made him twist around and study her posture. He remembered that tug. Though he couldn't remember who had caused it before, Xannan knew what it meant. Unlike the other, she needn't look directly at those she wished to persuade.

"Rebuild your army, reclaim your cities, then attack." Xannan plucked another roll, tearing it into pieces and dipping them into the sweet golden liquid, explaining, "Destroy their armies and negotiate a new treaty. From what I've gathered while listening from the sidelines—since no one cared to ask my opinion—you bargained with Alkaan and Hoclia, yes? And both dishonored those agreements?"

"Hoclia, no. Alkaan, yes." Rosealyn's words were clipped and terse.

"You gave Pasea to Hoclia?" Charles asked, reminding Xannan the king hadn't left the room.

"They wanted more, but I convinced them to accept Pasea and no more. So we can send a messenger to them with a formal treaty." She paused and began pacing. Again.

When she approached behind him, he stood and blocked her path. "Attack Alkaan."

Rosealyn stumbled backward and clutched her dress. The motion revealed the slits in the skirts of her usual beige dress. "I must protect Vandyl."

"Leave troops to protect Vandyl, take troops to claim Alkaan's capital."

She bit on her lower lip and faced Charles. "Would you agree?"

Xannan ignored the king's glower by sitting down to resume eating.

"I agree," Jacin said. "But I will do as Rosealyn requests since she is, in all but ceremony, our queen."

When silence lingered, Xannan glanced back and realized Rosealyn and Charles had walked out into the hallway. He turned to Jacin. "Agree with me, do you?"

"I would recommend the same. Nathaniel is young and will take the vast majority of his forces to Orda'an's eastern cities, including Vandyl. It would not require much of our forces to capture his capital."

"And if King Charles agrees to send his troops to protect Orda'anian cities, then she can take Alkaan while reclaiming Orda'an."

"I have agreed." Charles had returned. "Ashtar should have already prepared them."

"If he remembers," Jacin said and, at Charles's arched brow, added, "He was drunk last night."

"Please find Christopher and remind Ashtar of his orders."

"Before you go," Rosealyn said as she approached Charles's side and intertwined her hand with his. "We'd appreciate it if you stayed here, Jacin, to assist Christopher as needed."

"Anything for my queen," Jacin said. He stood and left. A loyal soldier and cousin. Still seated, Xannan tilted his head, studying Rosealyn. He was putting the pieces together, understanding what her magical abilities likely were, but he was surprised by the level of control she already had. *A request, not a forceful demand.*

"Lycene first to assess its condition. We'll send messengers to Vandyl from there. Then, dependent on what we learn, we will decide if we journey north to take Alkaan, or south to reclaim Vandyl. Aunt Adela, please send a message to Theo and Alan with our plan."

"Who, precisely, is we?" Adela asked, leaning forward.

"Me, Charles, Xannan, you, and Moss. Along with however many soldiers Charles and Moss consider absolutely necessary." When Charles made to protest, she held up a finger. "And not a single one more. Most of us are more than capable of protecting ourselves."

"So, not the droki first?" Xannan stood and rubbed his hands together. The slight tension which had appeared after her look of pity the night before eased.

"Not first, though I fear they may find us before we want them to."

He nodded. Magic attracted droki, and Rosealyn was using it without realizing.

CHAPTER THIRTY-THREE

Synda paced the wide cavern, unable to quell the constant motion of her tail as it dragged behind her. Occasionally she had to stamp it against the dirt as frustrations arose again. They'd shut her out. Communicated without speaking to her first. With Magna's death, she should be the matriarch of their race. Yet her fellow dragons ignored her. So she paced, contemplative, while the land opposite the mountain range begged for her assistance.

Tired of wallowing in a cave by herself, Synda pranced to the cavern's edge and dove, snapping her wings out before she struck the ground. The air buffeted her until she could see the lake. In its center was the Dragon's Shield. That wasn't one of the mountains, as some assumed. It was the ever-pulsing flame which resided on the island in the center of a dark lake. No creature resided in those waters, and Synda had never dared touch it herself. She banked lower, circling the Dragon's Shield and beating her wings to propel herself toward the opposite edge of the lands hidden beyond the mountains. This was the land of her kind. No humans, and the only elf any of them tolerated was Celena. But Celena had been asked to withdraw to Andalova and await her fate along with the rest.

Synda landed with a purposeful thud in the center of the ring of dragons. A rainbow of colors surrounded her, most without the characteristic orange glow which indicated they had gained their flame.

Only dragons with inherited magic could also produce flame. Dragons chose, upon their demise, to allow the magic to die with them or to gift it to the one which they believed would honor its power. After the last of Magna's kin had gifted their small store to Synda in her first decade of life, the matriarch had kept her protected lest others find ways to steal her magic. Now, with the bulging stores of Magna's well, Synda felt unstoppable.

Smack within their center, Synda forced all to see a singular image: the resurging droki. Without their aid, without a dragon's flame, the droki would overwhelm the continent. One of those with his flame stepped forward and replaced her image. Their land aflame followed by clouds of ash, the dark lake empty, and the Dragon's Shield snuffed from existence.

She wanted to roar and spout flame at the other but couldn't. His vision was as accurate as hers. So many of them disliked the other races and did not hide their apathy. But Synda shared the image anyway: providing aid to the wielders of Praeteritum and Futurae. Between the power their weapons contained and that of the magic wielding dragons, Synda believed they could change these images.

Naila, whose scales were a bold shimmering purple, stepped forward with her head lowered and shared her intent to join Synda's quest. The movement elicited a flurry of images, claws scuffing against the dirt, and angry growls.

A small voice was heard by all based on their reactions. Celena's voice, reminding them of Magna's final request to remain a united race. Two more dragons, the golden Indil and the burnt-like orange Zuda, stepped forward with heads lowered. Since all three had their flames, the lowered heads would indicate allegiance with only a quick burst of flame to scorch the ground, but none of them moved to do so.

Synda swallowed her flame, waiting and hoping more would step forward. Several shifted, circling around the eldest remaining of their race. Those with flame shared a quick burst, those without lay prostrate. His gaze met hers, and though a tremor ruffled the feathers of her wings, Synda did not lower her head. If she succeeded in ridding Ebios of the droki, she would have to fight to enter these lands again.

The three who had decided to join her vaulted to the sky, and Synda followed. She shared with them caves similar to Magna's where they could reside and glided toward where Celena leaned against the cave's wall with arms crossed and red eyes churning so deep in color they were nearly black.

You were supposed to unite your race, not divide it. Celena followed Synda's flight pattern. The beating of the dragon's wings matched Celena's irritation. *How else can you rid the world of the droki if not with the full force of your race?*

A huff of flame was Celena's answer as Synda beat her wings to hide above the clouds. With no beast to scowl at, Celena began the long trek through the cave and back to her home. The journey would take her just over a day, unless she rested in the mountain cave for the night. The enormous cavern where she'd first gained her ability was homey. And it had been a long day of stretching her ability to its limit. Proximity went a long way when reading a dragon's thoughts.

She meandered through the tunnel, trying to sense where the young white dragon had flown off to, but either Synda was too far or Celena's ability too taxed. In the smaller cavern where she'd first met Rosealyn, Celena paused and sat on a rocky ledge jutting from the cave's wall. From her belt, she tugged out a small pouch of nuts and idly wondered if the princess had taken her advice to heart. While the wielders of Praesidio were unconscious, the country's leaders had made plans.

Lost in a daze, Celena was surprised to find the pouch empty. Tucking it back into her belt, she started down the familiar mountain path.

She knew where the tree roots poked from the dirt, where the branches would smack her face if she didn't duck or push them aside, and where the larger rocks had fallen. New obstacles appeared on occasion, but she'd walked the path often enough to know where to place her feet and hands without much concentration.

Once at the mountain's base, Celena paused. Yesterday, a boulder had rested there. Not a large one, but she noticed its absence. Sounds of a struggle echoed off the stone face of the mountain's side. She tilted her head, listening while her mind searched for Synda's presence. The dragon remained out of reach. Celena homed in on the sound, careful to approach as quietly as possible. One of the shouts had a familiarity to it. As she got closer, the shouts gave way to tired grunts. Darting from tree to tree, Celena peered around each before moving.

"You can't—"

A loud crack preceded a heavy thud. Celena froze, hands pressed against the rough bark of the tree. Arjun wasn't supposed to be near Andalova; he should have been in Violet Grove to resume his duties there. Leaves crunched beside her and a solid arm propelled her head into the trunk. Gasping, Celena tried to focus her vision but a second hit followed.

CHAPTER THIRTY-FOUR

Charles's sword, several possibly beneficial daggers, and changes of clothes were strewn across his bed. It had taken significant effort to find plain-colored coats, but wearing bright red mingled with orange would not bode well for subtlety.

Twisting the silver flame-engraved ring around the first finger on his right hand, Charles mentally recited what he had asked to be completed before the journey. Cooks made food to take, Ashtar—who sobered up after a bucket of cold water—prepared battalions, Rosealyn spoke with Jacin to learn all she could about Nathaniel, Moss prepared the mounts, and he . . . he stood in his room. Charles threaded his fingers through his hair, idly wondering if he should have made time to cut it since the slight curls were beginning to appear. But the sooner they reached Lycene, the better.

Signed papers occupied a corner of the table, all detailing new rules for plantation owners throughout Jearnia. Charles was creating a new era that would make him proud to call Jearnia home. Workers would receive proper care and compensation, and punishments would be more appropriate to the crime. He wrapped the sword around his waist and traced the engraved burst of flame. Methodically, he tucked daggers into his sleeves and boots and folded the first coat.

"You should pack at least one red coat," his mother said.

He turned, his smile fading when he noticed Marsha standing nearby. "I thought I told you to return home, Marsha."

"I will, as soon as everything is ready."

"You can leave this room now." Charles jerked his head toward the door.

Marsha's lips tightened into a thin line. "I've done nothing but support you, and you send me away?" She waved a hand, scoffing. "I'll return when Queen Nerida sends word she needs more thread."

Charles closed the door behind Marsha. Palm pressed against the crack between the door and the wall, he tried to forget the sense of loss Rosealyn had mentioned and how it could connect to his mother's poisoning. Since her skin remained pale and her voice weak, Charles made a mental note to tell Christopher to keep Marsha out of the castle.

"Thread?" he asked, tugging on each sleeve and leaning against the door. "The red thread you use while stitching?"

His mother nodded, taking slow measured steps to the table. Conspicuously, she set a small black box with a gold clasp next to the signed papers. Hand hovering above the box, she explained, "Marsha has always provided the thread. Though I do tire of red sometimes." Nerida lowered to the bench, shifting each leg and adjusting her skirts to remove any wrinkles.

"Perhaps you should request thread from elsewhere." Charles folded the last spare jacket and perched on the edge of the bench, shifting his sword so it didn't hit the tabletop or his side. "It's good to see you outside your room. Eonar's medicines are working well?"

"They are." She nodded toward the bed. "You should take the proper attire for your station. You did the last time you left."

"Because I had little time to find something else. And needed the soldiers to see me as their new king." Charles shrugged and clasped his hands. "The color I wear means little compared to how I treat them."

"Learned much from our neighboring country, I see." His mother gripped her winged pendant necklace with a tight smile. "Respect, as opposed to fear. A new era indeed."

"You let us decide for ourselves, but I'd like to know your opinion." He tapped his fingertips together. "Do you think I should stay, as opposed to traveling with them?"

"Traveling with Rosealyn, and the soldiers, will help them respect you more." She smiled at him, ringlets of curls bouncing as she gently shook her head. "You are also proving to Christopher you do trust him. Changing your mind now would ruin his belief in your words." She released the necklace and gripped the bench beneath her. "I shielded him when able, but there was much I had no control over."

"You don't have to stay here, Mae. Christopher and I can take care of ourselves."

"This is true, but mothers must nudge their children in the right direction."

"Meaning?" Charles glanced askance at the box his mother had brought. He knew what could be hidden within.

"How many women make you feel the way you do when you look at Rosealyn?"

Even with his suspicions, Charles was taken aback by the direct question and was grateful to already be seated. Silently, he cursed his mother's intuition for asking questions he didn't know how to answer. Not yet at least. Shifting, he rested a hand on the table and drummed his fingers along the wood, wondering if the sun had found sanctuary in his room. Her question dredged up memories. Positive and negative.

"When I wasn't training or guarding Rose, I sparred with other soldiers. I had little time for anything else." Charles shrugged.

"You didn't answer the question," Nerida said, poking his shoulder. "Bold move last night. Dancing *only* with her, kissing her. But you, my dear son, are holding back."

Charles rubbed his forearm and looked away, remembering how Rosealyn had kissed him first. He had wanted to kiss her for longer than he cared to admit, almost from the moment they'd met, but he'd forced himself to stop thinking about her in that manner. While he surveyed from all angles, Rosealyn often dove right in. He pressed his lips together, unable to refute his mother's observation.

"So. . ." His mother drew out the word. "How would you handle seeing her with another?"

A quick glance at his mother, he raked a hand through the slight curls of his brown hair, tugging them away from his forehead. Just the possibility of Rosealyn with another created a metaphorical hole in his chest. "Not well."

His mother's knowing smile grew broader. "Do you love her?"

Charles decided the fire must have encased him. He tugged at his shirt collar as the week wondering where Rosealyn was after she'd disappeared from the cliff resurfaced. That had been worry for a friend, not love. Or so he thought. Either way, he had more to consider than his feelings. Or hers. *Mae had to ask it directly, didn't she? But how does one know?*

While searching for an answer, Charles recalled his last conversation with Rosealyn's father and avoided the question by saying, "Phillippe once told me not to resist growing close to her."

"Whether or not you love her is not a question another can answer for you, Charles."

"I know." He studied the box. "But it's hard to ignore a man who could see snippets of the future."

"If I recall correctly, Rosealyn has the same ability. What has she said of your future?"

"Not much." He shifted in his seat, twisting his ring again. "She's mentioned a sense of loss, which is logical considering the battles to come."

Charles loosened the collar of his shirt and, despite his mother's brief protest, grabbed the box and opened it. His heart and thoughts raced faster than they had in any battle he'd ever fought. Inside the box was a delicate ring. Similar to the crystal of the dragonsword, the circular object was coated with white swatches. One brow arched, he held it up. "If I can't answer if I love her, what am I to do with this?"

His mother's smile turned mischievous. "You know the answer. You just aren't ready to admit it." She placed the ring in her palm, tracing the smoothed edge. "Eonar fashioned it by wrapping one of Magna's white scales around a crystal. He's amazing at more than healing with potions."

The perfectly formed circle resting in his mother's palm overwhelmed Charles's vision. A marriage would unite the countries more than their spoken alliance. But marriage, a union of such magnitude, would change them. Not only them, it would tip the scales of power across the continent.

An uncomfortable ache reared deep inside. "Rose doesn't know all of my past, Mae." He looked down, studying a now-familiar striation in the wooden bench. "What if she doesn't accept who I once was?"

"Why should that matter?" She placed the ring in his palm. "She values you for who you are right now. Didn't I already tell you this? Your past does not define your future."

"You did." Charles imagined placing the ring on Rose's finger, visualizing how bold it would be against her darker skin. But the stuttering of his heart because he'd spent so long hiding the true depth of his emotions scared him. "I suppose hiding my past helped me hide my feelings, too."

She curled his fingers over the ring she'd laid in his palm and held his hand with both of hers. "Whatever happens in the years to come, Charles, do not let the true desires of your heart slip from your grasp." She tucked an errant strand of curly hair behind her ear, revealing dangling earrings, and rested her hands in her lap. "I created the design and asked Eonar to craft it for the crowning ceremony. Without the interruptions, we would have had this conversation last night."

Charles arched a brow, and his heart hammered forcefully. "During the ceremony or after?"

"After, but someone was too eager to begin dancing." She poked him in the shoulder, harder than the first time, and his cheeks warmed again. "You have your mother's blessing to marry whom you wish, as all should be able to do."

Charles tightened his grip until he could feel the circular imprint. "Thank you, Mae." He replaced the ring into its protective box. "Rose will appreciate the simplicity while wanting to know exactly how Eonar retrieved one of Magna's scales and fashioned crystal into a ring."

His mother released a contagious laugh. "She is curious, isn't she?" She held a hand to her stomach, silent laughter shaking her shoulders. "I look forward to seeing her wear it."

After adding the box to his packed bag, Charles cinched the bag closed. When the time was right, he wanted the ring near.

He returned to his mother's side and offered a hand to help her stand. "Let's find Christopher and Rose, and have a proper, friendly conversation. Maybe one that doesn't involve swords or dragons or droki or soldiers." At his mother's amused smile, Charles sighed. "May be impossible, but I'd like to try."

CHAPTER THIRTY-FIVE

"You're positive he'll use smaller, multiple attacks on major cities?" Rosealyn asked, shifting the notated maps Jacin had made that covered the table where they sat across from each other. Filled plates atop several maps were growing colder the longer they strategized.

Since the connection insisted on an unreasonable closeness that day, Xannan leaned against a wall. He always stood rather than sit. After the morning interruption, Rosealyn expected Xannan to intervene again, but he looked bored. Or distracted. Either way, with Jacin's advice she created multiple plans of attack.

"Unless he discovered I was spying." Jacin shifted the maps so the easternmost section of Orda'an occupied the center. Lobelia taken, Lycene in danger, and then Nathaniel's largest group would be upon Vandyl. Jacin marked average travel times dependent on battalion sizes. "But this has been his plan since before Eilon."

Rosealyn studied his markings, flipping the map toward her. Creating an offensive plan scared her after being raised with the motto to defend, not attack. These plans soured her appetite. But she worried they would be too late to save those she was meant to protect.

"No wonder you were already there," Rosealyn said, tracing the markings. "Uncle Theo's idea or Father's?"

"Both." After making another small notation, this time near Vandyl, Jacin met her gaze with his golden-brown eyes. "How did you convince Nathaniel and Jordan to send aid?"

Rosealyn shrugged and followed the path her finger was making along the map. "I asked and he agreed. So did Jordan."

"Makes no sense," Jacin murmured while filling his first plate of food. Strategies first, then sustenance. Rosealyn's appetite remained absent.

"This is more than retaliation, though." Rosealyn shifted the papers so the three sections of Orda'an rested side by side and placed her arm across the center. "Split down the middle, they said. Neither Jordan nor Nathaniel expected me to survive fighting Eilon."

Xannan guffawed. "You didn't fight him, remember?"

Rosealyn shot him a glare and rounded her shoulders, grateful for the loose training dress, and asked Jacin, "What compromises would you suggest I offer?"

"Always come back to land and resources." Jacin scratched at his short beard. "Are you willing to relinquish land to Alkaan as you did to Hoclia?"

Rosealyn's cheeks flushed. It had been a desperate move to give Hoclia a portion of what they'd requested and had been done out of guilt. "Hoclia accepted the offered land and has not pressed their luck further, correct?"

Jacin grunted. "They've broken promises in the past."

"Promises are made to be broken." Xannan approached, and Rosealyn stiffened when he sat beside her. "And broken promises lead to seeking revenge."

She shifted away from Xannan. He'd been right the previous day; she needed to consider his advice alongside others. One hand atop the other, she laid her head down on the table and groaned. Auburn hair blocked her view and allowed her to feel like she was alone for a brief moment. In for three counts, out for three. Repeat. It was nice to have options, and she understood why Xannan recommended attacking Alkaan's capital city of Algatha, but that plan wouldn't protect her people.

Head lifted, she shuffled the papers to retrieve the map of Alkaan and tapped its capital city. "We could head here first, true. But I stand by yesterday's decision. And neither of you will change my mind."

Jacin lifted his hands, palms open, while Xannan leaned forward on the table with that ingratiating smirk.

Rosealyn pressed her palms against the table. "What is it with being amused by me?"

Xannan shrugged. "You can figure it out once you pay close enough attention."

Across the table, Jacin paused in eating his midday meal and glanced between them. "Though I would prefer to go with you, I understand why you've asked me to stay. I am honored to remain here not as a spy but as a liaison to our new ally."

"I was worried you'd be upset." Rosealyn folded her arms on top of the table with a sad smile. "You've been gone from home so long."

Jacin lifted his cup with a gentle grin and sipped. "Change is coming." He set the cup down and met her gaze. "Orda'an doesn't need me. It needs you, its rightful queen. I'll keep watch on everyone here. Unlike someone"—Jacin smirked at Xannan, who grunted—"I quite enjoy being a shadow."

At her side, Xannan tapped the table and stood, "You've made up your mind and had your conversation. I'm getting restless with all this sitting and talking."

With one eyebrow arched, Rosealyn shared a glance with her cousin. "He so enjoys trying to tell me what to do."

"Simply returning the favor." Xannan's tone was sharp and the thread of annoyance too strong.

Brows furrowed, Rosealyn collected the notated maps, mouthed an apology to Jacin, and left with an aggravated ancient youth on her heels.

Ten steps from her was as far as Xannan could get. When she hesitated at a cross section, he pointed. "Right."

So simple, yet it earned him a scowl and a harsh "I knew that."

They continued for several more turns. Before opening her door, Rosealyn motioned between them. "Thoughts on why this close today?"

Leaning his shoulders against the opposite wall, Xannan shrugged. No matter how long he mulled over the connection between the swords, he had no answer. At least nothing satisfactory. In some ways, the connection seemed to want them closer the more aggravated they were with one another. Or the more he thought about how to use the connection. Head tilted, he wondered if the swords fed them small amounts of power, similar to when combined into one. Another idea for experimentation. Later.

"You weren't short on words this morning." Rosealyn propped a hand on her hip, papers held loose in the other. "Why so quiet now?"

"How have you not figured it out yet?" Xannan's shoulder-length blond hair shifted into sight as he shook his head.

She squinted at him, papers audibly crinkling. "I hate it when you're vague. You know more than you share."

Her gaze roamed as it always did when her mind was putting pieces together. The interim was his to continue thinking as well. Most days she didn't use her ability. Eventually he decided the lack of continual accidental use was because she trusted most of those surrounding her. Except him.

In the week after their arrival, he'd listened for the slight change in tone and knew she didn't realize when it was happening. The moment with the drokos was unexpected and convenient. He only hoped Volante's closeness to the dragon's home offered some protection from the droki.

"Magic?" Rosealyn whispered the word. Almost like she believed magic was some falsehood in stories despite all she'd seen and done.

"What about magic?" Xannan asked dryly.

"You know what my ability is, and you've been waiting for me to figure it out."

"There's little fun in simply telling you."

She tossed both arms up into the air, almost losing her grip on the stack of maps, and disappeared into her room. Once the door slammed shut, Xannan waited, expecting her to return and demand to know. If she asked in the right way, he'd have little choice.

But she hadn't asked the right question yet.

CHAPTER THIRTY-SIX

Rosealyn crinkled the maps in her hand and counted her steps, grateful when the number extended past ten. Ever changing, that connection. Magical swords and her own magic. She continued pacing and grimaced. Xannan knew. He knew and refused to share.

Rosealyn ransacked her memories for the inkling of an idea. Fire did not blossom from her hands, she could not relive the past, the wind did not obey her wishes, nor did the weather which remained too cold for her preference. Items did not appear out of thin air or float toward her if she thought it. Nothing. Nothing aside from the swirling sense of loss, courtesy of the Gift she couldn't control.

Twelve steps from one edge of the room to the other, no strange tug. Twelve steps back to face the door and she shook her head. He was waiting for her to figure it out; she had no reason to walk over and demand an answer. Since Charles was settling matters before leaving in the morning, Rosealyn supposed packing a bag would be a good idea. After a quick glance around the room, she realized she had nothing to pack. Most of the dresses she had worn over the past week had been gifted, and none would serve well for a week-long journey across a country.

When the door opened, Rosealyn tensed and prepared to demand an answer from Xannan. She wasn't sure if she was relieved or aggravated that Viola entered instead.

"Good afternoon, Viola." Rosealyn studied the pile of dresses draped over the maid's arm. "Are those all for me?"

Viola's bushy dark hair bounced as she nodded and set the stack atop the bed. Free of their burden, Viola shook her arms. "Queen Nerida insists you pick as many as you'd like." The young girl shifted through the pile and retrieved one in a shade of light blue. "This one is my favorite for you, my lady. It complements your complexion, though the simple gray would do the same."

"But the blue would match Charles's eyes." Rosealyn set the maps aside and ran a hand along the smooth material. A smidge thicker than the dress she currently wore, it would help her stay warm while traveling. Then she noticed how each dress had slits. "These were made for me, weren't they?"

"Yes, my lady." Viola arranged the bold red, soft blue, and vibrant gray dresses of similar styles.

"They're gorgeous." Rosealyn laid the bold red across her arm and pursed her lips. "Thoughts on the red?"

"No matter which dress you wear, it will be perfect, my lady."

"You can be honest, Viola. Not all colors work well with my skin tone. I've worn red before, but it wasn't quite so bold. At least this one isn't laced with orange like Charles's coat." She twisted her lips in thought, head tilting, "How do the seamstresses manage that feat?"

Viola chuckled softly and selected a darker gray dress. "You could wear the ugliest dress ever made and His Majesty would consider you beautiful. It's the strongest thought I can hear from him, my lady." Viola glanced over her shoulder toward Rosealyn, smiling.

Blushing, Rosealyn patted the red dress draped over her arm. She'd almost forgotten about Viola's ability to hear others' thoughts.

"As for how the red and orange are mingled together, all I know is the colors of string are woven together, my lady."

Rosealyn tugged at her bottom lip, surveying each dress and making a pile of the soft blues, simple grays, and a deep green. All would be perfect if stealth became necessary. "You can hear thoughts from anyone?"

"Almost anyone, my lady."

"Those should suffice." Rosealyn patted the pile of dresses and sat on the edge of the bed. "What thoughts do you hear from me, Viola?"

Viola's forehead crinkled as she folded the dresses Rosealyn had not picked and placed them in a second pile. After a moment, Viola said, "You're surprised at your own comfort here, you care deeply about His Majesty, and sometimes you want to hurt . . . Xannan is his name, yes?"

Rosealyn nodded and shifted the sword belt around her waist so the hilt would not dig in while she sat. "And what do you hear from Xannan?"

"Nothing." Viola shrugged and folded the dresses Rosealyn had chosen. "And before you ask, no, I cannot read minds. I cannot search for what others think."

The dresses folded, Viola gathered the rejected options and winced while smiling. "Thank you for the lesson this morning, my lady. May the mountains bless your travels."

"My plan was to continue teaching you all I've learned and encourage Charles to continue your training. Along with others. But I was never going to stay here long, though I wish I could."

Dresses draped over her arms, Viola looked down and shifted her feet.

"What is it, Viola? You can speak freely with me."

"It would be wrong of me to suggest it." Viola's bushy hair covered her face. "My apologies, I should not have said that, my lady."

"Tell me what you were going to suggest, Viola. I insist you speak freely with me."

Another twist of her feet, Viola shifted the stack of dresses draped over her arms. "I think I would enjoy traveling with you and His Majesty, but I've never been outside Volante."

"Never?"

Viola shook her head, picking at the material of the dress on top of the pile and smoothing it back out. "My mother was a servant here as well. After she died, I knew nothing except for staying here and doing as I was told. I dared not ask to leave the castle grounds for fear they wouldn't let me back in."

While Viola picked at the material again, Rosealyn gripped the edge of the bed with furrowed brows. Life in Jearnia had not been pleasant under the rule of Charles's father. Most of the traveling group would be soldiers. All save herself and her aunt. When Rosealyn did not speak, Viola murmured something which sounded like an apology and turned toward the door. Rosealyn grasped Viola's arm, but the motion made Viola drop the dresses, and the maid who couldn't be much different in age than Rosealyn trembled. Bushy curls swayed as Viola dropped to her knees to gather the fallen dresses. Rosealyn joined her on the floor, folding the bright red dress she'd chosen to leave behind.

"It will be dangerous." Rosealyn set the dress aside and twisted her belt so it stopped digging into her side while she sat on her knees. "There's no guarantee you'll return here. Not because Charles wouldn't let you back inside the castle, but because there's no guarantee he or I or anyone who travels to Orda'an with me will survive." She sat back on her heels, blinking back the tears which threatened to escape. "My country is already under attack."

Viola paused in her folding of the dresses, face drained of what little color it usually held. She swallowed, wringing her hands, and said, "I can treat injuries and would not be a burden."

Rosealyn considered hugging Viola but stopped herself. Instead, she smiled and picked up a bold yellow dress she would never wear and folded it. "No one should ever be considered a burden. I will not force you into joining us, but I will not stop you either."

Viola retrieved another red dress from the haphazard pile. "His Majesty would—"

"Likely be happy to show you there is more to this world than this sprawling castle. As would I." Rosealyn set the folded yellow dress atop the red. "We leave first thing in the morning. Each tent fits up to four, so Charles claims. Adela and I would welcome additional company amid all those soldiers."

The dresses folded once more, Viola picked up the stack and stood. "I'll return after the evening meal. King Charles wishes to dine with Queen Nerida, Prince Christopher, and you, my lady."

After Viola left, Rosealyn couldn't wipe the smile from her face. A proper dinner with simple conversation would be a welcome reprieve.

CHAPTER THIRTY-SEVEN

Gailin's Journal-Annotated by Rosealyn

One's journey through life is unique, isn't it? I've lived mine to the best of what I know, led not as I was taught by my father, but as I felt to be right. Both Father and Xannan would admonish me for some of the choices I've made. To concede land we claimed as our own? A necessary compromise to save lives, to allow families to thrive, for them to enjoy their days in peace.

Xannan is was the warrior, not I. Swordplay allowed a focus for his simmering anger, until these weapons entered our lives. Called to us, molded to us, latched [*latched to what?*] on to some aspect of our being with a refusal to let go, these swords changed us both. It's been long enough I've resigned myself to believing Xannan is lost. Not lost his life, for I know he lives [*How did he know? The sword's connection?*]. But he does not wish to be found. Or perhaps he does not want me to find him?

Before I visited Magna all those years ago, I swore I could hear the call of the other blade. It must have been wishful thinking because while I have that unceasing urge to search the mountains again, I have not heard anything close to what I did before Magna changed this sword. So many of my court attendants believed I left that crystalline sword buried somewhere for none to ever find it again, not knowing the blade wrapped around my waist is the same, just disguised.

It's funny how easily memories can be manipulated [*Were Gailin's memories changed? Others'? Is that how Xannan became the lost prince?*]. How quick others are to believe one versus another. So many of those who lived during Xannan's time here in Cantadad have passed, and those who have assumed those roles believe my brother is no more than a story. Why correct them when, in some ways, I'm beginning to believe the same myself? But how can I, after all we went through together in our youth?

PERSUASION

CHAPTER THIRTY-EIGHT

"I thought you said it would take less than a week to get to the Cliff of Lycene," Rosealyn said, wishing the ground would stop squelching around her boots. One rainstorm after another had followed them since that first day of travel, but she was grateful no snow had fallen. She shivered, thinking of icy droplets of rain prickling against her shoulders and scalp. Little reprieve awaited between each, as though the constant torrential downpour's sole purpose was to make all wish for the confines of stone walls. Most walked next to their mounts, as she did, reins held in hand, coats tied close around them. Beneath her coat, her sword bounced against her side. Many soldiers had a second scabbard on their saddles, as her father had, but she wanted the sword close. She and Xannan, who walked several spaces ahead of her and Charles, were the only two who kept their swords belted around their waists.

All were drenched, and Rosealyn would peer behind her on occasion, wary of what anger the soldiers might harbor for marching through such dismal weather.

"When not encumbered by storms, it takes around four days to travel from Volante to Vandyl. I estimated Lycene to be two days away, maybe three." Charles tugged his horse's reins and stepped closer to Rosealyn. "And since you brought it up again, you must be anxious?"

"Of course I'm anxious." Rosealyn tugged against the sucking mud, grateful her boot did not stick. "The closer we get to Orda'an, the more I hear—sense—these cries for help." She took several more grueling steps. "I wish the rain would stop."

"These men have weathered storms like these before." Charles offered his hand when her boot sank into the mud, and she grasped it to gain leverage and pull her foot free. "As have I. Though it's been a few years."

Several tenuous steps passed, each making an obnoxious squelching sound Rosealyn decided might be the death of her hearing. Or perhaps that was the faint hollers she both swore were and were not real. One moment, Rosealyn was positive she could recognize the voice. The next, she wondered if she had heard anything at all. She released her hold of Charles's hand and gripped the hilt of her sword. That action quieted both her anxiety and the faint cries. Releasing the hilt, she scanned the landscape around them. Most of it was difficult to make out given the overcast gray skies, though she swore she heard the faint ripple of water.

Within the hour, the rain relaxed to a low drizzle which eventually gave way to a pale blue sky dotted with gray and white clouds. Ahead, she recognized the Guadelaide Lake. Rays of sun peeked through the clouds, glimmering against the tumultuous ripples the wind created in the lake. Arrival at the lake meant they could reach Lycene the next day. Rosealyn expected that thought to quiet her nerves, but they worsened.

Gaze flickering from one gray cloud to the next, Rosealyn said, "I wonder where Synda and Celena are right now. Did you speak with Celena before she left?"

"She departed before we woke the next day. A guard had a message from her, a reminder to prepare for the droki alongside the other threats."

Rosealyn gestured at their swords and at Xannan who walked several paces ahead of them. "We have three dragon-wrought blades, and we have not seen any of these droki since Xannan and I saw that one—"

"You've seen one?" Charles stopped and looked at her, one eyebrow raised. "And you're just now telling me?"

"I—we had other concerns when we arrived at Volante. As I'm sure you remember." She reached for his hand, smiling as his fingers intertwined with hers. Rays of the sun warmed them, beginning the long, slow process of drying their rain-soaked cloaks.

"Any other theories on how to break the connection?"

Rosealyn glanced ahead and lowered her voice in hopes Xannan wouldn't hear. "I've been reading the missing entries, the ones you gave me. I thought Gailin's past would provide the answer, but so far I haven't learned more than what Magna showed me. Or what I already knew from Gailin's journals. Speaking of—"

"Some of the library survived the attack." Charles squeezed her hand. "I did not think to check which books survived, though."

She chuckled and grimaced. "I've memorized most of what Gailin wrote. Chronicles of treaties, skirmishes, wars, the disagreement which led to him conceding the land to Lord Edmund to create Jearnia. All of that history is there." Rosealyn moved as though to dig her boot into the ground, frowning when it sank into the mud instead. "What we need to know about the swords is, unfortunately, absent. I've only had time to read two of the entries." She winced at the squishing sounds. "So cryptic. The pair of them."

"So he has yet to confirm your natural magic ability? And Gailin provided no specifics, I presume? The man did enjoy writing down all of his questions and neglecting to provide any answers he may have found." Charles squinted at the surrounding land and glanced up at the sky. "We should stop here for the evening. If the skies remain clear, we'll reach Lycene by midday tomorrow. I would recommend—"

"Forward scouts to determine Lycene's condition?" Rosealyn interjected. After a gentle squeeze of Charles's hand, she released her hold and handed over the reins. "I'll find Moss."

Charles nodded and led the horses away, signaling for his men to make camp. Rosealyn watched him, appreciating his familiar and simple black coat. Footsteps approached and stopped at her side as she watched Charles weave through the soldiers. He spoke with each briefly, as he had every evening since they'd left. Soon he would help them set up tents and build fires and would make sure each ate, including her, before he dared sit down and take care of himself.

"My hearing is better than you give me credit for," Xannan said at her side. "You should tell me what Gailin wrote. I could provide insight you would never have."

Gripping the hilt of her sword, she continued watching Charles's motions. She had considered sharing the journals. But if Xannan realized something she had not, it would bother her. After all those years studying Gailin's writings, learning about her country's past through his words, she was determined to figure out these puzzles on her own.

"It's not weak to ask for advice." Frustration laced Xannan's words. "The best rulers use the resources available to them. I would have. From what little I've overheard, Gailin did not."

Soldiers sectioned off into small groups of three to four. Her gaze snagged on Moss assisting Adela and Viola. "Help set up camp. We'll speak later." Rosealyn met Xannan's stare then, distracted momentarily by his singular raised brow.

"He left clues but no answers?"

"We'll speak later," Rosealyn repeated and approached Moss, who was showing Adela and Viola how to put a tent together. Again. She paused a few steps away and smiled. Moss had assumed the role of leadership well, better than she would have anticipated given his time as one of her bodyguards. He explained each step in great detail, his light-skinned hands guiding both Adela and Viola through the process. He saved most of his examples for Viola, despite her continuously shying away from him.

Rosealyn frowned at Viola's hesitations and surveyed each group preparing their space. Though she was supposed to sleep in the same tent as Adela and Viola, Rosealyn often drifted to sleep while lying next to Charles instead. Each night she promised to return to Adela and Viola, only for Charles to nudge her awake after the sun surpassed the horizon the following morning.

Every few minutes, Moss glanced her way, but Rosealyn gestured for him to continue. Whenever Moss reached to guide Viola's hands, she withdrew them quickly. Could it be the scars marring half of Moss's face which gave her pause? A thought too strong which made Viola flinch? Or, as Viola had once hinted, perhaps past experiences made her too distrusting of his kindness. Rosealyn glanced at the clearing skies, at the deepening red of the lowering sun, and then west, toward her home she prayed to the Blaze of her ancestors was not beyond recovery.

Once Adela and Viola took their belongings into the tent, Moss approached with a frown. The skin on the left side of his face was wrinkled and dotted with faded purples from the burns he'd endured. His solid black coat was buttoned to the collar, and his once-cropped brown hair had grown to his temples, making him look slightly older. He stopped in front of her, one hand grasping the hilt of his sword, the other in a fist above his heart.

"I'm not used to you frowning," Rosealyn said, shivering as the faint screams echoing in her mind surged.

"The journey took longer than expected. I worry what we will find at Lycene tomorrow, Your Majesty." Moss lowered the hand resting on his chest and moved to stand beside her.

She grimaced, wishing he would not use a title she had not yet claimed. "Assess Lycene's condition and report back. We need to be prepared for what to expect."

He nodded and rubbed his chin. "By myself, Your Majesty?"

Rosealyn tugged at her bottom lip. If she sent Moss alone and Nathaniel's men were already there, Moss could be caught. Or killed. They would have no way to know what awaited them. At the same time, she wasn't sure any of the Jearnian soldiers would listen to Moss as a leader without Charles nearby. Even if she trusted Xannan, the connection made sending him a foolhardy decision. Rosealyn turned toward Moss. "I would come with you, but I know that's not ideal. Not yet."

A brief hint of a smile appeared, and Moss stood taller. "I would agree, Your Majesty. This is not a queen's task." He tilted his head at a tent to their right. "I've made friends among the Jearnian soldiers. Four would be best. Small enough to be discreet, large enough to render aid to one another if needed. If both you and King Charles agree."

Her gaze roamed. She looked for the bright flame-like jacket, only to recall Charles also wore simple unadorned black. Eventually she found him, aiding others in setting up their tents. The men had shown stiff awkwardness the first night he assisted, and the protests continued, but Charles ignored them.

"I encourage you to ask others to accompany you, General Moss." Rosealyn gestured toward Charles. "Please do your best to return by sunrise. And may the Orda'anian Blaze protect you."

Moss placed his hand above his heart, inclining in a slight bow, and jogged off to speak with the three attempting to create a fire. When they repositioned their weapons, Rosealyn searched the camp for Xannan. Since he was busy—surprisingly being helpful—Rosealyn decided to sit with Adela and Viola. With clear skies, Rosealyn could offer the young maid more fighting lessons.

CHAPTER THIRTY-NINE

Rosealyn held her hands above the fledgling fire Moss had created, grinned at Viola, and said, "Moss enjoys helping, doesn't he?"

Bushy brown tendrils of hair swirled around Viola's face with a wind that threatened to snuff the fire but couldn't hide the maid's blush. Viola tucked her coat around her, head gliding to glance over her shoulder at Moss and jerking forward again. Smirking, Rosealyn peered around Viola and noted Moss and three others soldiers speaking with Charles.

Adela prodded the burning logs with a stick. "How much longer to Lycene?"

"Less than a day. I told Moss to return by sunrise. I'm hopeful all is well, but if not—" Rosealyn prodded the fire with a stick and lifted her gaze to Viola. "Time for more training."

The maid blanched and shifted her shoulders. For the first time, Rosealyn understood her father's unceasing worry. Even with proper training, they had no guarantee of survival. Any of them might never see their home again. Resting clenched fists on her knees, Rosealyn studied her stoic aunt. "I know you don't like weapons, Aunt Adela, but you should join us."

Mud squelched behind Rosealyn, and Adela's gaze flickered between her, Viola, and whoever stood behind her.

"I'd rather stay away from *him*." Adela jerked her chin up, shifted her cloak, and set to mending a pile of arrows too wet to utilize. "I have no desire to participate in any training."

Rosealyn clenched her jaw, unclasped her coat, and placed it along the log where she'd been sitting. With luck, the garment would be dry by morning. She resisted the childish urge to roll her eyes at Xannan. Blond hair tied back, he stood with arms crossed, wearing the same ridiculous sleeveless brown leather vest. It bothered her, especially since the brown didn't match the engraved black hilt of his sword.

"You can talk and train at the same time, correct?"

A sly smile spread across Rosealyn's face. "Viola, how do you feel about sparring against Xannan?" Viola visibly swallowed, and Rosealyn looked back at Xannan. "And you will let Viola hit you."

Standing this close, she could hear his teeth grinding together, and the muscles of his arm bulged when he flexed. He nodded and motioned at the empty space encompassing the middle of the camp.

As they walked, Rosealyn whispered to Viola, "Do not hold back. He can take a punch. I know that to be true myself."

"I can't hit someone!"

Xannan laughed. Loudly. His laugh quieted at Rosealyn's glare.

With both hands on her hips, she told him more forcefully than she intended, "Give me your sword."

Glowering, he slowly undid the belt and handed over the weapon, saying, "Careful what commands you give."

Holding his sword, Rosealyn squinted at him. That wasn't the first time Xannan had said something similar. After working with Viola for a while, she would revisit that thought. Rosealyn set Xannan's sheathed blade on the sodden grass and laid hers next to it.

When Rosealyn straightened, she had to fight a laugh of her own. Xannan stood with his arms crossed, brows crinkled together while Viola cowered like the smallest of ants. Rosealyn opened her mouth to speak but snapped her jaw shut, frowning. Every time she and Charles sparred, it seemed so simple. Avoid getting hit; try to hit him. His first lesson had been to hold the sword and gain the necessary strength to swing the weapon through the air at her opponent. But when one had naught but their own body to protect themselves? She sifted through the memories, through the repetitive phrases she'd often tuned out. All she could remember was to watch her opponent's shoulders and feet.

Before she could stop the motion, she located Charles helping others start their fires. Moss's group had already left. She'd told Charles about her promise to help Viola learn. Standing here, surrounded by soldiers, was different from training at the castle. As the world around her blurred out of focus, Rosealyn wondered how Charles had managed to hit her so often despite caring for her. Memories flooded again. Those first training sessions were not amicable. And lack of friendliness made it easy to attack Xannan, especially after waking in that Blazing cave.

Xannan cleared his throat, asking in a monotone voice, "Are you training her or studying the grass?"

His question jolted Rosealyn from her thoughts, and she winced as she stepped closer. "No weapons tonight, but I'm going to demonstrate how to disorient an opponent and provide more time for you to get away."

"Smart, yet predictable. Is she going to shove me to the ground like you did?" Xannan tossed a forced smile her way and stepped closer to Viola. She flinched and rounded her shoulders. Xannan thumped his chest. "Hit hard enough there and you'll make anyone stumble backward. Rosealyn did."

Viola shook her hands, formed fists, and curled in on herself.

Pressing her lips together, Rosealyn adjusted Viola's elbows and mimed the move, explaining, "Uncurl yours fists as you step closer. Focus on hitting his chest with the heels of your palms and pushing as though you are opening the castle's heaviest set of doors."

Viola's arms trembled slightly, and she kept glancing over at Rosealyn as though to receive confirmation she was doing it right.

"Perfect." Rosealyn mimed the motion again. "Always keep your hands in fists in case you need to lash out with a punch or block one."

Hands in position, Viola moved through the motion, halting and withdrawing her hands before they landed on Xannan's chest. Viola swallowed and whispered, "It was different when it was just us."

"Tell her to hit me." Xannan held his hands to either side, waiting. Even when Viola's hands were about to land, he hadn't tried to block her move. He stood there, waiting, arms tensed at his sides.

"Careful what commands I give?" Chin lifted, Rosealyn narrowed her eyes at him. Between his sharp tone and tense stature, she knew Xannan was goading her.

Xannan curled his hands into fists. "You told me to let her hit me."

Rosealyn mulled over his words, tilted her head, and placed her hands on her hips. "That doesn't mean you would."

"Perhaps." Xannan grimaced, arms trembling slightly. "I will only continue helping with this lackluster training if you start telling me what my brother wrote in his journals."

"I don't have to tell you anything."

"Yet you enjoy telling me what to do." He tapped his chest again. "I've been hit plenty of times before, so hit me as hard as you can."

Viola hesitated, glancing between Rosealyn and Xannan. When Viola made no move toward him, he mumbled something beneath his breath and turned to Rosealyn. "Figure it out yet?"

Rosealyn listened to the ripples of water formed by the whip-like breeze, thinking. Muffled conversations sounded around them. Occasional laughter. The scent of cooked fish mixed with the occasional aroma of salted meats and toasted nuts.

"Why would I stand here and let someone hit me?" His volume increased with each word, dripping with aggravation.

She clenched her fists, stepping backward and waving away those who approached. Pieces were forming a new image. Moments when conversations went her way.

"You wouldn't. Unless you had no choice." Rosealyn forced herself to meet his fierce green-eyed glare, and sweat prickled along her brow. "But I don't know when I'm doing it, when I'm forcing another rather than simply requesting. Do I?"

A subtle shake of his head and Rosealyn frowned. Persuasion? That was it? That was her natural magic?

She gasped and covered her mouth with both hands, only to lower them a second later. "The drokos?"

"It sensed your magic, but something you did prevented the drokos from attacking."

"I—" Rosealyn swallowed. *Mere thoughts kept the drokos in its place?*

"Thoughts are powerful, my lady," Viola said.

Rosealyn almost jumped at the sound of her voice. Dress-skirts clenched in each hand, she chewed on her lower lip. "You know when I'm using it on you?"

"And others," Xannan said.

"How often?"

Xannan laughed, low and soft. "Once on Charles, but all the other times I've noticed you've done it to me."

"Blazes!" She twisted the material of her dress between the fingers of each hand. Her shoulders fell. "Jordan and Nathaniel. I must've used it with them as well."

"'It' has a name." Xannan crossed his arms, glaring. "Arjun can do something similar, but his only works on humans and elves. Since your patha vita worked on the drokos, it will work on any creature. Possibly anything living."

"Wait, once on Charles?"

Xannan smirked. "When we first arrived in Volante. He wanted to ram his sword through me, and you told him not to. And he didn't. Never even tried."

Moisture disappeared from her mouth, air evaporated from her lungs, and she pressed a hand to her stomach. People had choices, should decide for themselves. If she was truly so persuasive, why had it never worked on her father? The sword? No, because it worked on Xannan. That thought was overtaken by others. Jacin, her birth mother, Viola. . .

"I came because I chose to, my lady," Viola said.

Silently, Rosealyn cursed herself for forgetting the woman could hear loud thoughts.

Viola chuckled. "Moss has been kind enough to offer instruction on more than how to set up a tent each night. I may not have the experience, but I have an idea of what to do."

"So why not hit me?" Xannan asked with a raised brow and obvious genuine curiosity, though his arms still trembled.

Both of Viola's cheeks drained of color. "I was afraid I might hurt my hands."

Despite the frustration of knowing she had taken others' choices from them at times, Rosealyn laughed. "She's right," Rosealyn said, clutching her side. "It does hurt to hit you."

A muscle in Xannan's jaw twitched. "Time for an intentional attempt. Reverse your order for me to let Viola hit me."

"I, um, release you from the command?"

Xannan buried his face in his hands and scrubbed. "Try again."

Smoothing her skirts and chewing on her tongue, Rosealyn straightened and spoke with her strongest, most commanding voice. "I no longer require that you allow Viola to hit you."

He lowered his hands and tugged on the hem of his vest. With a brief shift of his neck and shoulders, Xannan asked, "Can we discuss Gailin's journals now?"

Rosealyn sighed and addressed Viola. "Moss is a better trainer than I. And a storm with a staff in hand." She sighed. "Xannan and I must, unfortunately, speak alone now."

Viola curtsied and retreated to the fire, curtsying again and sitting across from Adela and sidelong to Charles, who had bundles of food. When Charles began to stand, Rosealyn shook her head once and retrieved both blades. The prickle of sweat from earlier returned when she recognized the swords' faint hum.

Offering Xannan his sword, Rosealyn explained, "Gailin saw how to break the connection but didn't write it down. At least not anywhere I've looked yet. He claimed, 'It will not occur in my lifetime, which makes little sense based on what I saw.' He believed the future, no matter how many times he saw it, could be changed."

"The key we need is hidden in memories I cannot relive. Gailin enjoyed being cryptic." Xannan frowned at their weapons and lifted his gaze to hers. "You remember the last time they hummed like this?"

Rosealyn buckled the sword around her waist. "Does magic exist which could allow you to relive Gailin's memories?"

"I have yet to annihilate the wall Eilon apparently built around my memories." After buckling his sword belt, he glanced at the expansive greenery around them and sniffed. "What were you thinking when we saw that drokos?"

"That I never wanted to hear them again and hoped it would stay far, far away."

He drew his sword, motioning for her to do the same. "Try those thoughts again. And please, be careful how you speak."

CHAPTER FORTY

Charles dropped his plate beside the fire and marched toward Rosealyn and Xannan, shouting, "Why are your swords out?"

Both appeared enraptured by their blades, and the weapons drifted closer. Rosealyn's sword faded from its average silver into a bold glowing white while the tendrils of gray in Xannan's swirled with a fury akin to the recently endured storm winds. The glow of both swords pulsed in unison. Slow, cautious, Rosealyn and Xannan moved their blades until the two weapons almost met. Charles's mouth went dry, and he gripped Rosealyn's arm at the same moment the Twin Blades met.

His grip tightened, but the weapons did not combine. A brighter pulse emanated from both wielders.

Rosealyn laid a hand on his arm. "Remind your men the droki poison is deadly."

"Droki? How many? How do you know they're coming?" Charles's grip tightened, and he pulled Rosealyn closer, fearful she would, once again, be in excruciating pain at the expense of Xannan's carelessness.

But they weren't combined. Rosealyn pried his hand from her arm and held it for a moment. An unspoken request. She didn't need his protection, even if he wanted to do everything he could to prevent her from being hurt.

"No dragonsword?" She breathed deeply and lifted the sword, angling it to study the glowing crystalline blade. "A common goal?"

"Possibly." Xannan scanned the skies and wrinkled his nose. "I can smell the droki. A scent of death coating every sense." He scowled at the northern sky. "Plus, the swords were humming."

Charles followed Xannan's line of sight. "From the north?"

At Xannan's singular nod, Charles turned to his soldiers, covering his ears when a loud keening cry pierced the sky. As he lowered his hands, he glanced back at Rosealyn and frowned. Her face was scrunched while she held the sword with its tip resting on the ground once more. "Rose?"

"I'm concentrating," she snapped, closing her eyes and breathing deeply. When another ear-splitting cry sounded, she grumbled and rounded her shoulders.

Charles searched the skies and drew his sword. He needed to communicate with his men but . . . glowing swords, her posture, the droki. "Rose, what are you doing?"

Rosealyn opened one eye and glared at him. "I'm trying to convince the droki to go away. To return to the north. To anywhere else that isn't populated."

"Convince?"

"Charles, not the time." She closed her eyes and shifted her shoulders. "Quiet, please. Concentrating."

He opened and closed his mouth, unable to speak. How could silence help her convince the droki to go away? She had figured out *something*, they both had. Since he couldn't ask, Charles clenched his jaw.

"She's learning." Xannan patted Charles's shoulder, chuckling. "Feels good for her to command someone besides me."

Scowling, Charles returned his attention to the skies. A distant dark cloud became three separate clouds as they neared. His heart fell. The spots had wings. The droki were too similar to dragons. Smaller, yes, but too large nonetheless.

Charles swallowed and glanced at his gathering soldiers. Many had their swords out. Their weapons would be useless. He tried to shout at them, but no sound came out. Frantic, he waved at them, motioning for the soldiers to return to their tents, but they came closer.

"Blazes." Rosealyn stepped between Charles and Xannan, a frown wrinkling her forehead. "They're not leaving. Why didn't they find us at Volante? If I've been using my magic inadvertently this whole time?"

"My guess is these found others along the way." Xannan lifted his glowing weapon. Tendrils of gray intermingled with black swirled within. "This magic is too enticing for them to turn away."

Charles cleared his throat.

Rosealyn's eyes widened. "Sorry, you have questions, I'm sure. Um, talk to me?"

She asked the question in a way that made Charles want to laugh, but the droki were clearly visible. Frail wings ribbed with spikes, skin wrinkled, and spindly necks that never ceased their movement. In all the ways a dragon appeared magnificent, the droki appeared like anyone's worst nightmare. At least their ear-spitting cries had stopped when Rosealyn had asked for quiet.

"Your magic?"

"Is confusing and frustrating at the moment." Rosealyn glanced from the skies to the gathering soldiers. She pulled him closer. "Their weapons won't work; the soldiers can't fight them."

"And you can?"

Her brown eyes flashed with anger, and Charles berated himself for the retort. Her hand was clammy. Another shrill cry pierced the night sky.

Rosealyn winced, grip tightening. "They'll come straight for Xannan and me. There's too much power brewing in these swords for them to leave despite how much I really want them to simply wink out of existence."

Charles stepped closer, and before he could say anything, her lips were on his, kissing him. When she pulled back, her words were timid.

"You should—um. Please—Blazes. I don't want to say the wrong thing." She paused, glancing at the sky and back at him.

He squeezed her hand. "I'll do my best to not die. You do the same."

Rosealyn smiled, released his hand, and grumbled. "I really hope these droki are the only ones who die."

"Agreed." He turned to Xannan, drawing his sword as he said, "If she dies—"

The ground shook beneath his feet. Once. Twice. Three times. The droki surrounded them.

Shrill screams around them made Charles's brain rattle inside his skull. Xannan plunged his sword into the nearest drokos, in the middle of the thing's chest. As he withdrew his blade, the beast's wings stretched and shrank while its neck convulsed with a piercing ululation.

Swords lifted and ready to strike, Charles's men approached. His shout cut off as a cry sounded behind him. Charles ducked, cursing as the drokos's wing whipped through the air above his head. Black-tipped spikes coated the ridges of the creature's wings, and his throat constricted. Crouching, he followed the drokos's sinuous movement. He had to take it out before it hurt him or any of his men.

The drokos lifted onto its hind legs, wings flapping. Its chest was too high of a target, so Charles slashed along the beast's belly. The drokos screamed and collapsed onto all fours. With each gnashing of its black-tipped teeth, Charles sidestepped and swiped.

"In the heart or cut off its head." Xannan's shout came from somewhere behind him.

Charles pressed his lips together and hefted his blade. He tried to shout at his men again, slashing at the drokos's wing. The limb spasmed, almost catching Charles's forearm.

The first one Xannan had hit continued lashing out at any who approached. To his right, Rosealyn and Xannan faced off against the third. Largest of the three, it continued to snap its jaws despite black blood oozing from a multitude of wounds.

Charles's chest clenched. Its wing approached, and Rosealyn slashed her sword through it, shredding the leather-like skin. Chest heaving, she turned and lifted her sword, eyes widening and narrowing.

Charles tried to duck, but the wing tapped his shoulder, and he grunted. Spinning away, he heaved his sword into the drokos's chest. He tugged the weapon free and brushed his arm. Breaths steadied. None of the spikes had pierced his skin. Just a bruise.

The drokos snapped its head forward. Charles swung his sword with as much strength as he could muster to slice through the drokos's neck. His sword stuck halfway, and he shouted at the approaching soldiers to stay back. Its cry halted. Charles tugged on the blade, lifted it, and swung again, hacking until the beast's head was no longer attached to its neck.

Charles pointed the sword down, fearful that merely touching the dark liquid might be deadly. He focused on his soldiers, and a muscle in his jaw feathered rapidly. Three of his soldiers were wounded. He forced himself to breathe, remembering what Xannan had said of the droki's poison.

A small bit of tension eased when Rosealyn and Xannan struck the last standing drokos in the chest simultaneously. When that one fell, Xannan sliced off its head. The last twitched and spasmed, riddled with wounds Charles's soldiers had given it. First to be hit, yet the last one alive. Did stabbing them in the heart actually kill them? Or had Xannan missed that organ? Many more wounds than the one Xannan had given it riddled its body, enough Charles was sure the drokos couldn't move if it tried. Nevertheless, he hacked through the drokos's twitching neck.

His soldiers cleaned darkened blades on wet grass, and he scrutinized each. None but the three were injured. That was three too many.

Before speaking with his men, he looked for Rosealyn. Chest heaving, the sword's glow dissipating, she looked unharmed. So why did she look so distraught? The injured soldiers? Something else?

"There's nothing to combat their poison," Xannan whispered.

Though Charles had assumed as much, the confirmation made his insides twist. Three droki dead in exchange for three of his men about to die. In some ways, it was a small price to pay. But it was a price he didn't want them to pay.

He offered an absentminded nod. "Swords didn't combine this time."

"True. I believe she tried to draw on their power."

"I was trying to use that patha vita you claim I have." Rosealyn sheathed her cleaned sword and gave Charles a scrutinizing gaze. "Even with all that power, I could barely convince them to slow their attacks, much less stop attacking entirely."

"Patha vita?" Charles raised a brow. His sword continued to drip droki blood, creating a black puddle in the grass.

"Apparently I can persuade anything living."

"And it works best when she's aggravated with me." Xannan cleaned his blade on the grass and sheathed it. "Three is a small pack. Very small. I doubt we will be this lucky next time."

"Unless I can properly persuade them." Rosealyn bit her bottom lip. "We have to tell those who've been injured."

Charles retrieved a cloth to clean his sword, glancing up between strokes at his soldiers inspecting the droki. All so curious. The three who were injured pointed and questioned, either considering the best ways to attack or guessing what had caused their injuries. Discarding the soiled cloth, he sheathed his sword and rubbed his shoulder where the drokos wing had almost pierced his skin.

"You controlled the drokos, didn't you? When its wing hit me?" Charles studied their wings, wondering how one of those spikes had not hit him.

"It was one of two thoughts they listened to." Rosealyn tilted her head back and crossed her arms. "I wanted them to stop making those awful sounds, and when I saw it coming toward you, I—I can't remember what I thought. Better its wing than teeth or claws, though."

"All soldiers know and understand danger. But as far as I know, all poisons have an antidote." Charles ran a hand through his hair and steeled himself for the coming conversation. He'd come to know these men by name.

Black webbing oozed along one's upper arm, visible through the gash in the soldier's sleeve. That was Daekin, a soldier younger than Charles who'd been hopeful to meet a girl at the next Harvest Feast. Teeth grinding, Charles wondered how to tell the injured men they would likely be dead before sunrise. Or sooner. This time the poison came straight from the source, not Xannan's sword.

CHAPTER FORTY-ONE

Christopher shifted in the throne, trying and often failing to concentrate on the two elderly men standing before him. If he leaned back, the immovable stone dug into his shoulders and held his neck at an awkward angle. If he leaned to the side, his elbow went numb from its position on the armrest. If he leaned forward, his lower back ached. So he sat tall, drumming his fingers against the armrests, and refocused on the current conversation.

Each request was a more ridiculous dispute to settle than the last. Several had been too frustrating to deal with, and rather than react rashly, Christopher had sent them away to revisit said complaints another day when, perhaps, he had more patience to muster. Who knew people in the valley cared so much about who farmed what land? The food all eventually went to market anyway, right? Was the profit between grain and corn that prominent? Or fruits and vegetables? The arguments over livestock had been not only the most annoying but the most confusing. Apparently, animals strayed between pens. Some farmers claimed a stray animal was theirs after one night while others had tagged their own as proof the beast's profit should go to them.

In response, Christopher doled out the appropriate punishments. Nothing as severe as his father would have given, but as outlined by his brother, punishments befitting the crime. An animal stolen meant returning it. Overcharging another for grain meant paying back the difference. Many disputes were resolved with simple solutions. Except for these two, who were to be his last meeting of the day.

They had been arguing for over half of the afternoon, claiming each had rights to a tiny portion of land located at the edges of their plantations. Any time he thought they'd come to an agreement, one would bring up a new demand.

"You have no right to do anything to *my* lands," one said, verbatim to the dozen other times already. "My lands, my choice."

The other harrumphed. "I don't understand why you're upset. I'm caring for a portion of your lands you've neglected for years."

Me neither. Christopher had almost said that aloud several times. Most of this conversation helped him understand why his father was so quick to slash necks. Perhaps it was the only way to get these men to stop talking. Christopher paused the drumming of his fingers against the silver-painted throne whose shine reflected the surrounding torches, giving it an orange glow. He clenched his hand into a fist, mentally reciting Charles's request for no unnecessary deaths.

"Intentionally neglected, Henry," the first said, folding his arms across his chest.

Finally, a name—should he have made the two plantation owners introduce themselves first? They were from the far north and had only stayed after the coronation ceremony to have this dispute settled. If they hadn't had the proper proof, he wouldn't have believed they owned anything. Both wore stained undershirts barely hidden by their aged brown leather coats. Their purpose-driven outfits made Christopher feel almost too well dressed in his pristine muted red coat and straight black pants. His finger traced the gold thread running along the cuff of his sleeve, and he bit back the retorts he'd been concocting while they spoke.

"For ten years?" Henry exclaimed. "That's more than enough time for the land to recover and produce fertile goods."

Ten years? Despite not being comfortable on the throne he'd always envied, Christopher leaned back, pensive. Either the neglect was intentional or the famine from beyond the hills was encroaching on Jearnian lands.

"But has it been?" The other tugged at his aged coat with a brief wary glance at Christopher and stepped toward Henry. "How fares the produce you are growing on *my* land?"

Henry glared at the other and shouted, repeating how the crops he'd grown there were, supposedly, worthless. They'd followed this line of questioning several times, circling back to the demand that Henry stop utilizing the once-fertile land.

When Christopher stood, both men fell silent. Hands on his hips, Christopher stared at each for a long moment. "If the land produces nothing worth eating, why are we arguing about it?"

Silent blinks answered him, and he massaged his temples. "Return home." Christopher gave a dismissive wave of his hand. "If Henry wishes to continue wasting time and resources on land which fails to produce, then so be it."

"But it's my—"

The unnamed man stopped mid-speech when Christopher raised an open palm. "Both of you must return to your homes now." Christopher assumed a precarious position on the throne. This time he sat on the precipice and contemplated where best to place his hands to indicate he was tired of their pointless bickering. He couldn't say anything about the land's decay, not to them. That was another detail he would have to add to his first message to Charles.

Neither man moved, so Christopher waved a hand in what he thought was a dismissive motion. The two plantation owners shared a quizzical glance.

Henry asked, "Are you telling me I may continue to use his lands?"

"You already are, and it's gotten you nothing but rotten produce." Christopher shrugged. "Sounds like a waste of everyone's time to argue about it."

If these men didn't go away soon, he was going to leave them alone in the throne room. Christopher was beyond done with this conversation and had no desire to continue it, but neither farmer looked appeased. He rubbed one hand along the back of his neck and glanced at the doors to the throne room. "My final ruling on this matter is that neither of you should continue farming this land. It is to be rested for five years, and then, should it prove to appear recovered, we can reopen this discussion."

He didn't wait for their responses, nodding at the guard by the doors. A quick tug on his coat sleeves and Christopher left the two farmers standing in the middle of the throne room.

CHAPTER FORTY-TWO

Christopher rubbed the back of his neck as he walked. Mindless roaming helped. A meandering stroll through winding hallways allowed him to calm his thoughts, to appreciate the level of trust Charles offered. His brother, he thought with a smile, would be proud. Yes, annoyances abounded, but no one was dead. No screaming messengers had been dragged from the throne room. No blood needed wiped off the marble floors. No musky scent of wine permeated the throne room. A new era. What Charles had promised. What their country needed. What *he* needed.

"There you are." Jacin jogged to catch up from the opposite end of the hallway. "You left two extremely confused men in the throne room."

"I needed to clear my head."

Jacin laughed. "In these stuffy old hallways?"

"They are a far cry from the gaudy throne room." Christopher pursed his lips. "I wonder if Charles will change it."

"Perhaps." Jacin shrugged and matched Christopher's pace. "I honestly don't know him well enough to say more." Metal jangled as Jacin shifted his belt. "I worry what they'll find at Lycene or Vandyl."

"We should hear from them soon," Christopher said, wondering if the once spy knew something but wasn't sharing it. One message so far. Storms delayed the progress, and last Christopher knew, Charles and Rosealyn had yet to reach Lycene.

"Dinner?" Jacin questioned.

Christopher couldn't help the chuckle. In the past week, the Orda'anian had not once turned down a meal. Where all that food went, Christopher guessed, had something to do with Jacin spending multiple hours each day with Jearnian soldiers. Training, sparring, the man was a constant whirl of motion.

"Later." Christopher tilted his head at the door beside them. "You're welcome to visit Mother with me if you like."

Jacin shrugged. He'd stayed as a show of support for those in Jearnia to know they were no longer rivals with Orda'an. For the most part, it was working. Unless Jacin continued besting every soldier he faced while sparring. Eventually, the king's protection wouldn't be enough; Christopher was sure of that.

Christopher lifted a hand to knock but paused at the low murmur of angry voices. He listened, eyes widening and mouth going dry as the words seeped in.

"I tire of doing the dirty work for you."

When had Lukas arrived? Or had he ever left? All the fears of his youth resurfaced. Surely the loud voice would wake his mother. His entire body went as cold as ice. If his mother had taken a sleeping draught as she had for the past several evenings, not even the loudest crack of thunder would wake her.

He swallowed. His mother was still the queen of Jearnia, so it would be normal for her to have visitors. But his hand remained frozen above the door. And his mother's voice didn't drift to him.

Perhaps the words came from a frustrated servant whose voice was reminiscent of Lukas's. That had to be it. Besides, neither his uncle nor his aunt would harm his mother. Christopher swallowed again, throat raw. *They wouldn't . . . would they?*

"We should probably go in before this dirty work is done?" Jacin asked, one brow lifted.

After Jacin nudged the door open, Christopher nearly stumbled over his own feet. His body felt clunky and unresponsive as his mind digested the scene.

Torchlight glinted off metal to his left. Christopher reached out as though his arm could grow the length of the room. But it didn't. He couldn't stop the dagger's motion. Not in time. Not when his body stopped responding. Not when the dagger buried itself in his mother's chest.

Her body jolted and a strangled sound came from Christopher when the blade twisted inside her. A whimper, a scream, a plea.

Christopher couldn't move. A dream. It was all a dream. The afternoon in the throne room had exhausted him. Any moment, he'd wake slumped over in the hard and smoothed edges of that silver lacquered seat.

His throat felt like shards of glass as he gulped down air. Blood dripped from the tip of the dagger as its owner tugged it free of his mother's chest. Well-crafted metal limned with blood led Christopher's gaze to the weapon's hilt. A hilt with a bold flame before a dragon's snout. Jearnia's crest. Only those of royal blood were allowed to display it.

Holding the dagger was a man's hand. A stiff cuff, outlined in red, trimmed in gold, and a solid black for the remainder of the sleeve confirmed Christopher's suspicion. Lukas harrumphed and snapped at someone else nearby, retrieving a cloth from his pocket.

Enraged, vision blurring, Christopher barreled toward his uncle. He shoved the older man into the wall, unsheathed his dagger, his Delrich, and pressed it against his uncle's throat.

He dared not look at his mother. She could recover from an injury. She had before. Lukas wasn't the most adept with a blade. It was a warning wound. Christopher's mother had to be alive. Because without her honest bluntness, Christopher wasn't sure he himself would survive. She was kind, yet ferocious. Christopher would try to be the same.

Pain pricked his side, and Christopher swiped, cursing when a dagger cut the side of his hand. He glanced at the weapon as it clattered to the floor. Lukas shifted, stilling when Christopher pressed his dagger deeper into his uncle's neck, drawing a line of blood.

Lukas lifted his chin, hands pressed against the walls. "You'll thank me when the country is yours. Not hers. Not your *brother's*. Your—"

Christopher sank his blade into Lukas's neck and slashed. Blood spurted on his face, on his clothes, on his pants. He stepped back, mouth agape. It was messier than he remembered. Lukas grasped at his neck, blood streaming through his fingers. Christopher's heart raced. The man tried to croak out words as he collapsed to his knees. Blood covered Lukas's dark coat and created a puddle that reflected the lone torch.

Rash, dangerous, unfeeling, uncaring. Christopher's grip on Delrich tightened. The one gift from his father was the tool for his first kill. Fitting.

Reality set in as Marsha approached with raised hands. Christopher growled low, steps quick and intentional.

They would both pay for harming his mother. She deserved so much more, was so much more than . . . his thoughts and movement paused. He looked down at his mother. Ashen skin, no rise and fall of her chest, no faint kind knowing smile, no twinkle in her bold blue eyes all her sons inherited. Gone. Lost to him forever.

"You will—"

Christopher didn't understand how or why he was flat on his back, staring at the ceiling, the air knocked from his lungs. A hand on his chest kept him pinned.

"The true culprit has met his due end," Jacin said. "Think before you act."

"They killed her!" Christopher shouted, struggling against Jacin's immovable hand. Everything shook. Muscles, his vision, even the floor beneath him. Perhaps at his effort to stand, to attack and rid his home of those who would harm him. For good.

Jacin's forearm pressed against Christopher's chest. "You kill her and it makes you no better than him." Jacin jerked his head toward Lukas. "You are better than that, and I know it."

"I didn't kill her," Marsha said in a honey-like voice, too calm for having watched her sister-in-law's unjust death. "I would have stopped him."

Christopher shoved against Jacin's arm with vigor, knocking the Orda'anian backward. He pinned Marsha against the wall. A hand on his elbow stopped Christopher from lifting his arm.

"Think before you act," Jacin repeated.

Fingers dug into Christopher's arm, but the wells blurring his vision were not from the pain of Jacin's grip. A shaky inhale didn't stop his vision from clouding further. It made it worse, so much worse.

"I can't let Marsha leave," Christopher said, his free hand gesturing toward the ghastly scene in the room. "She must pay for this act of treason."

"With immediate death?" Jacin's grip on Christopher's arm tightened. "There are punishments besides losing one's life."

"Why should I let Marsha live after she—after she—"

The words lodged in his throat alongside the growing wells of tears. He tore his arm free and pressed Delrich against Marsha's neck. The blade dripped with his uncle's blood and mingled with the first drops of blood he would gladly drain from his aunt's body.

"I didn't kill her," Marsha repeated, holding her hands out to each side. "Lukas did."

His arm trembled. "'I tire of doing your dirty work for you.' That is what Lukas said before I entered the room." Christopher leaned closer. "*For you.*"

"It could mean any number of things." Marsha shrugged, actually shrugged, with a dagger against her neck. "Place me in the dungeons if it makes you feel better, but punishment has already been given to her murderer." She met his gaze with an icy stare. "The youngest is as rash as his father."

Had Jacin not flung him backward, Christopher would have dug the blade deeper.

CHAPTER FORTY-THREE

Christopher paced the hallway outside the dungeon's entrance. Jacin stood in front of the door, immovable, repeating the same obnoxiously frustrating phrase again and again. *Think before you act.* As if Christopher didn't know that. But something had to be done. He couldn't return to his room. He couldn't speak with his last living brother. All he could do was pace and seethe. Anger was better than sorrow, so he let it consume every fiber of his being.

"What do your laws say about treason?" Jacin asked when Christopher paused in his pacing at the far end of the hallway.

"Any unprovoked attack of or potential threat toward a member of the royal Jearnian family, outside an acknowledged challenge for the throne, is an act of treason," Christopher recited and resumed pacing. That law had been his father's favorite. Treason equaled death, and in Jearnia it was often a quick one.

"And the punishment, as outlined by the laws?" Jacin prompted.

Christopher paused, this time standing directly in front of Jacin. Fists clenched at his side, Christopher muttered, "Death. What else?"

Jacin tilted his head but said nothing.

Christopher couldn't stand still. So the pacing began anew. "Death has always followed my family." Christopher gestured with his hands as though waving his arms about could change what happened. "All of my brothers, now both parents?"

In his periphery, Christopher saw Jacin frown, but the Orda'anian was wise not to correct him. Christopher knew the error he had made, but it still felt true to him.

He stopped and whispered a curse. "My cousins," he mumbled. "What do I do about them?"

"What do you think you should do?"

"I—" Christopher's mouth hung open as he surveyed the dark hallway lit by flickering torches. He wasn't supposed to be in charge. He wasn't supposed to make decisions. What others asked him to do, he did. "We should not hold children responsible for the actions of their parents."

"Agreed." Jacin scratched his short blond beard. "But either way, all of your cousins have lost one parent tonight."

The reality of the statement hit Christopher as if the entirety of the mountain range had fallen on top of him. With his head and back pressed against the wall, Christopher slumped to the floor. His arms hung loose at his sides, and he stared at his feet. "And I have none."

Jacin sat beside Christopher. Though he fought the tears, they streamed down his cheeks. His beautiful, kind, sometimes overbearing mother was gone.

When Christopher's tears subsided, he glanced up at the door Jacin had conspicuously been guarding.

"I should speak with her," Christopher said, though he made no move to stand. "Should I?"

He looked over at Jacin, hoping the Orda'anian's facial expressions would provide a hint of an answer. But, as usual, it didn't.

Instead, the expressionless soldier calmly said, "Only you can decide what to do now. It is your responsibility."

Christopher laughed, shocked by how raw and fake it sounded to his ears, and leaned his head back against the wall and stared at the shadowed ceiling. "Responsibility is the one thing they always kept from me."

"Are any of your cousins of age for the throne?"

The question gave Christopher pause. It was a way out, the same way he had avoided the mantle of monarch when he brought Charles home. But he had done that because his father requested it of him, not because he wanted to. Christopher shook his head, wincing when the rough stone snagged a few of his curls. "There's ten of them, so I'm sure one probably is by now."

"You don't know?" Jacin asked.

Christopher shook his head again, already forgetting how it had snagged his hair the first time. "I'm not sure I know all their names, to be honest," Christopher mumbled, cursing his own inadequacy. He was no different from his single-minded father. Worse, maybe. For all he knew, his father had known all the members of their family.

"What would you say to her?"

Christopher peeked through one eye, annoyed by how quickly Jacin switched topics and how the man asked questions Christopher needed to answer. For a moment, he stared straight ahead. Contemplative. The flickering torches created strange images on his shined boots. Boots so black they almost blended into his dark pants, especially with the dreariness of this hallway, deep in the abyss of Volante's castle. Two soldiers guarded each end of the extremely long hallway, and others stood inside the dungeon's entrance.

He didn't remember following them to the dungeons, nor did he remember if he had said anything to his aunt after they'd left his mother's rooms. A lump caught in his throat, and he swallowed it down. It would be his responsibility to care for her body. Despite being the reason their father was dead, Charles had honored the man with a proper burial. But this time, Christopher would be alone. Custom dictated burial occur within a day of one's demise.

The lump escaped, and Christopher bit his lip, hoping pain would chase away his grief. He studied the small gash on his palm. Lukas's body he would toss to the wolves. And after he got his answers from Marsha. . . Christopher grimaced. No matter what the woman said, it wouldn't breathe life back into his mother. Thoughts of entering his aunt's cell where they had her chained to the wall floated in his mind. Jearnian dungeons were unforgiving. It would be easy to slice her neck.

But where will that get me? Feared? Revered?

"I need to know why," Christopher decided aloud.

Jacin stood and held out a hand. Christopher grasped it, pulling himself to standing.

Jacin held out his other hand. "Give me your dagger."

Christopher tensed. "No."

"How do you feel knowing you are responsible for making your cousins feel as your uncle made you feel? Do you wish to cause more of that heartache to your family?" Jacin lifted his open palm. "You've got the desire to rip her into pieces written all over your face."

Cursed man, why must he be right?

Christopher laid Delrich in Jacin's palm, teeth grinding together as he did. With an imperceptible motion, Jacin pocketed the dagger and gestured to the dungeon's entrance. Though Christopher wanted to move, he found his feet riveted in place. Immovable.

One moment passed.

Then another.

And another.

Is this what it feels like to be crushed? To be smothered?

"You don't have to," Jacin said.

Christopher decided such words were prompted because the man was tired of standing watch over him.

"I need to," Christopher said, hands clenching into fists with a fleeting wish he had not relinquished his weapon. The sooner he spoke with Marsha, the sooner Jacin would stop scrutinizing him, so he turned. His steps felt rigid and unnatural.

Chains looser than he expected circled Marsha's wrists. No blood trailed down her arms, and Christopher clenched his jaw. Logical for the soldiers to be kind to their recently deceased monarch's sister by not using the spiked chains. He supposed he should be glad they'd still chained her.

Marsha's gray dress was so clean it made his anger spike. He hadn't wanted to believe the poisoned thread came from her, but she had done nothing as Lukas's dagger plunged.

When Christopher reached for the lock, Jacin made a dismissive sound. So Christopher stood with arms crossed, glowering at his smug aunt sitting on a thin mattress. She acted like the chains didn't exist. Marsha sat tall, inspecting her nails as though waiting for the next dance to begin.

"I didn't harm her." Marsha continued peering at each nail, rubbing at one without looking up toward him.

"You were poisoning her." Christopher gritted out the words. All the years of trusting his aunt surfaced. He clenched his fists, hidden beneath each arm. Everything she once claimed was a lie: his aunt had never truly cared about him.

Marsha halted her inspection of her fingernails, grimacing when she looked through the bars. "You have no proof," she scoffed. She jangled the chains pointedly and gestured around the small cell. "All of this is unnecessary."

Christopher stepped closer. "Charles learned the red thread was coated with violet seed. Though you did not deliver the final blow, you are guilty of treason."

His aunt's smug facade faltered, marred with the subtle hint of a frown. "But how will you prove it was I who mixed this so-called poison into the threads?"

"I will share what I have learned and seen with my cousins. Together we will decide what is to be done." Christopher knew it wasn't an answer to her question. He didn't have an answer to that. Yet.

Marsha barked a laugh that echoed through the dungeons. "And how will you explain to my dear brother Lukas's children what happened to him?" she asked in her too-honeyed tone, the one that always convinced him to respond to her question with honesty.

In his anger and grief, Christopher hadn't considered what they could do to him. It had been logical to take care of the man responsible for his mother's murder. He glanced over his shoulder at Jacin, extremely grateful the Orda'anian had been there as well.

"I'll tell them the truth," Christopher decided, meeting his aunt's icy stare. "As will you."

"Interesting," Marsha murmured, gaze flickering from Christopher's to look over his shoulder. "More influence from the outside."

He had no more to say, not when she had given Christopher the answer without him having to ask. Influence. Control. She made a game out of people's lives to continue swaying him. One step closer to controlling him. One step closer to the crown. One step closer to power. If Jacin hadn't taken Christopher's dagger, it might have found its way into his aunt's chest at that moment.

Back outside the dungeons, Christopher stopped in the middle of the hallway and held out his hand for his weapon.

Jacin set it in his palm and said quietly, "Your brother gave you the ability to make decisions in his absence." The Orda'anian's tone emanated pity. "Use such power wisely."

Christopher stared at the dagger with blurred vision. He gripped the hilt, glancing back toward the dungeons. What had already happened would be difficult enough to explain. He needed to write a letter to Charles. But he stood in the hallway until his feet ached and he had lost feeling in the fingers curled around his dagger.

CHAPTER FORTY-FOUR

"Careful." At Charles's voice, his soldiers turned to him with weary salutes. He hoped his fear remained absent from his voice and face. "They're poisonous, and I don't know how death affects their venom."

"Poisonous, Sire?" The soldier with the gashed sleeve, Daekin, asked, and Charles nodded.

Threads of black laced down Daekin's arm, far too similar to the webbing Charles had watched wrap around Rake's leg before that poison claimed his friend's life. Owen, who had a singular scratch along his thigh, and Liam, who had three parallel gashes across his upper back, joined them. Distracting himself by tugging on each sleeve, Charles wondered if the poison would differ based on the type of wound received. All three soldiers had received gashes by claws. No bites.

But lines of black were spreading around each wound.

Charles tried to relax his jaw. "You three were injured. Anyone else?"

A successive murmur of negations accompanied by subtle shakes of their heads answered him. None of the three injured could be much older than Christopher. They looked a bit like his younger brother, too, but with close-cropped hair. Most of the soldiers were hardly into adulthood unless they were higher ranking. If Charles had given in to Ashtar's initial plan, all of the soldiers of this battalion would have been seasoned veterans. But Charles hadn't wanted the special treatment and insisted each battalion be formatted the same: two commanders, four colonels, four captains, and forty soldiers.

These three soldiers were of lower ranks, likely expecting promotions once they all returned home.

"Sire?" Daekin's voice was timid, soft. His fear-filled gaze met Charles's but darted to the side when Rosealyn approached. "Deadly poison?"

"As far as I'm aware." Charles noticed Rosealyn's slight affirmative nod in his periphery. His jaw tensed while his soldiers whispered among each other. He motioned for Colonels Omar and Levi to follow him aside.

"Check each soldier for puncture wounds. And question them all on what experience they have with poisons. Keep them in their groups and away from the droki. I want frequent updates on those three."

Both colonels nodded and bowed their heads, jogging off to follow orders.

After raking a hand through his hair, Charles turned to Rosealyn and scanned her from head to toe again. When his gaze made it back to her face, she offered a forced smile. "You promise none of those things injured you?"

"Promise. And I have no plans to let them attack again." Rosealyn held out a hand, palm up, but Charles hugged her to his chest tight enough to make her grunt with the sudden pressure.

"It's one thing to know you might be in danger. It's different to see you in danger." After another squeeze, he released the tight hug. Palm resting against her cheek, Charles lowered his forehead to hers.

"That must have been difficult to be honest with them." She pressed his palm into her cheek. "And it is a different type of fear to see rather than know."

Charles grimaced and tensed as Rosealyn placed her hand on his chest. Her eyes glowed with the setting sun, searching his. "I know you want to be strong for them, but you do not have to hold all of it in when it's just us."

"Sorry." A shudder worked its way from his shoulders and down his back. "There must be *some* way to counteract any poison. Mae was poisoned and is healing. Slowly, but she was no longer bedridden when we left." Charles bit back a curse. "I didn't ask Eonar for potions to combat poison." He twisted his lips into a frown. "Or anything actually."

She leaned back, looking up into his eyes. "You embarked on a journey, knowing we would encounter enemy soldiers at some point, and maybe more, and didn't think to speak with the doctor now under your charge?"

Heat found its way to his ears and cheeks. He had meant to speak with Eonar before leaving, but a certain conversation with his mother had distracted him. It was not the time to think of that conversation, though. "Have you asked him about counteracting the droki's poison?"

"No." With her hand pressing into his chest, Rosealyn lifted to the tips of her toes to look over his shoulder. Settling back onto her heels, she said, "But we can ask in a minute."

His muscles tensed as he traced one of her braids. Rosealyn gripped his shirt and moved in closer, lifting to her toes to press her lips against his.

Soft, gentle, and comforting, but he pulled away. "Feels selfish to share a kiss with you when those boys may never get another chance to."

"You said yourself. All soldiers know the danger." Rosealyn threaded her fingers through his. "I understand, though. Let me know what I can do to help."

A singular nod, he rounded his shoulders and listened to the rising sounds of the camp as most settled back into their nightly routines. The death of three soldiers would not have phased his father. He doubted Xannan cared much either. The man was alive, which seemed to be the only life the man cared about. Mud squelched nearby, and Charles turned to find Xannan's pale-skinned emotionless void.

"How long do they have?" Charles asked.

Arms crossed, Xannan shrugged. "Depends."

"On?"

"Type of wound, health, amount of poison. The stages may be the same. At first they'll feel weak, like they're tired. Then it becomes difficult to move, and most fall asleep, never to wake again."

Rosealyn gave Charles's hand a gentle squeeze and asked Xannan, "You don't remember how to combat their poison?"

Another shrug. "No memory of that. I barely remember fighting them before."

"So you were either wrong about the heart or you missed?"

Xannan scowled. "At least we know slicing their heads off is effective. Would be a cruel twist of fate if that hadn't worked."

Charles's brows crinkled, and he quickly dismissed the idea of any creature's head regrowing after decapitation. "Vague recollections of fighting them, but you remember the stages of the poison's effect?"

A tilt of his head, Xannan asked, "You remember every kill you've made?"

"So far, yes. And I doubt I'll be able to forget fighting these. Especially if it happens again." Charles crossed his arms. "Methods for stopping the poison? Applications to the wounds themselves? Liquid medicines for the infected to consume?"

"Salves to the wound, medicines if they became feverish." Xannan's tone remained flat. "I'd recommend a liquid to end their suffering before it begins."

Rosealyn wrapped her arms around Charles's arm, halting his forward movement.

"I will not resign myself to the idea that there is no hope for healing." Charles tempered his voice. "Arjun tried a dozen different medicines on Rake, and nothing worked, even what he applied directly to the wound."

Rosealyn gasped and raced off toward the tent she was supposed to share with Viola and Adela. He supposed some might misconstrue her remaining in his tent every night, but he hated to wake her once she had drifted to sleep. Since they had not yet settled for the night, her belongings were still with Viola and Adela.

"Even if you save these three, it will not save you from the pain of losing those you lead." Xannan's words were a simple, emotionless cadence.

"Doesn't mean I shouldn't try."

"You care too much."

"You care too little."

Another nonchalant shrug, but Xannan didn't deny the statement. That left them to stand in silence and wait for Rosealyn to return with whatever she sought. Several minutes passed in that manner, until Rosealyn raced back with something gripped in her hand.

Breathless, her words were rushed. "From Celena. After Ramon stabbed me in the thigh." She held the bottle out to Charles. "Arjun gave her this to drop in the wound. It eliminated the pain. Perhaps it can do more?"

"It's not much, but it offers hope." Charles grasped the bottle.

"Fool's hope," Xannan mumbled.

"Why did you come over here?" Charles asked, crossing his arms to hide clenched fists.

"An idea occurred to me when the swords connected that the magic of the weapons may have interfered with her natural magic and that's why she struggled to use it."

"Or." Rosealyn stopped short and winced. "It wasn't the swords working together because this patha vita did work when the thought was strong enough. Hard to focus when danger lurks."

Xannan tapped a finger against his bare arm, frowned, and walked away. Confused and aggravated, Charles watched the man stalk away, wondering what other ideas he might convince Rosealyn to try when it came to the swords' connection.

"Thank you for this." Charles lifted the bottle in his hand, peering through its clear exterior. "Perhaps it will keep the poison at bay long enough for them to return to Volante, and then maybe Eonar can help them recover as he helped Mae."

"Lead the way." Rosealyn gestured with an arm, and Charles raised a brow. "They're here on my behalf. I'm coming with you."

He nodded and approached a larger group of soldiers, assuming the three injured resided there. As he and Rosealyn approached, the group dispersed. Colonel Levi approached and whispered low in Charles's ear, "Liam passed out. Daekin and Owen are weak but conscious and coherent. The rest are worried about another attack, Sire."

Swallow, nod, Charles told himself. His throat clenched, voice hoarse. "Shift Liam so I can reach the wounds on his back."

Two nearby soldiers obliged, and Charles dropped the liquid into the first gash. Liam spasmed and moaned, eyes fluttering without opening. Grimacing, Charles waited for others to hold Liam down as he dropped more of the liquid.

After doing the same to Daekin's and Owen's wounds, Charles looked up at Rosealyn. "This is all you have, isn't it?"

Rosealyn nodded. "They can take the bottle with them. In case more is needed on the journey back."

"The journey back, Sire?" Colonel Levi questioned.

"Select four to escort the injured home. Perhaps Eonar can create an antidote." Charles handed the half-empty bottle to Levi. "They leave once their bags are packed. I've seen similar poison before, and that companion did not wake with the sun the next day."

"Yes, Sire." Levi bowed to Charles and gestured at several soldiers who each ran off to do as asked. "I have to ask, Sire, do you think there is any way to prevent death after a wound from one of those things?"

"For all our futures, I have to."

CHAPTER FORTY-FIVE

Rosealyn studied the injured yet conscious soldiers sitting on the grass across the fire from her. Blank stares accompanied paling skin and dejected postures. She wondered what thoughts roamed through their minds as they processed the possibility these wounds might kill them. That thought gave way to another: her own death. The Gift showed each LeNoir their death, and she had yet to see hers. Once, she'd thought the flash of a white blade signified her demise. But the white blade was the sword at her hip.

When Charles returned with three soldiers dragging cots, Rosealyn murmured her country's benediction to each of those leaving. These men needed all the hope she could provide. Perhaps it was a fool's hope as Xannan had claimed. After he'd walked far enough for the connection to tug on her chest—and his, Rosealyn assumed—he'd found an abandoned campfire to sit at. Alone.

As the moon rose higher in the night sky, Rosealyn wondered if any of those accompanying Moss had unknown magic a rogue drokos might scent out. That thought led to others. Xannan spoke of them as though one could encounter hordes of the beasts. Chills ran down her arms. Three were more than enough to deal with at once. Another set of chills culminated in the back of her neck, and she whipped her head from side to side, positive something unwanted was watching them.

No one. Nothing. No hum from the blade. But Rosealyn couldn't shake the feeling of unease. Without thinking how the motion might be perceived, she gripped the hilt of her sword. It was the only thing that quieted the Gift when it chose to play her emotions against her. At the moment, however, it was not helping and only served to make the gray-clad Jearnian soldiers shift and tense.

She forced herself to release her hold as several questions raced through her mind. Danger in Volante? Or Vandyl? Awaiting them in Lycene? Did the Gift not know how to warn of the droki?

More droki could arrive at any time, especially if she didn't learn how to control her ability. Or was she a constant source of magic? The Gift was always there. Prodding, pushing, overwhelming her senses with foreboding. *Dire situations await.*

Charles sat beside her and offered a plate of salted meat. She chewed slowly and thoughtfully, barely registering the conversation Charles was having with his men. If she could persuade anything living, could she command one to remain alive?

A tap on her arm jolted her from the depths of wonder, and she jerked her head up to find Charles holding out his hand. It was a short walk to his tent. A fire already blazed in front of it.

"Daekin, Liam, and Owen set up my tent tonight." Charles lifted his brown hair to reveal the lines of worry creasing his forehead. "Was I foolish to give them hope?"

Rosealyn removed her sword belt and sat cross-legged on a damp blanket one of the young soldiers had been kind enough to set on the ground. "When there is hope, you keep trying. With hope, they will hold to life longer. Does it mean they'll survive?" After resting the sword across both thighs, she rubbed her hands together above the fire's warmth. "But why else would Xannan fear the droki more than anything, even Eilon?"

Several beats of silence passed, and Charles sat next to her. "What would you have told your soldiers if they had been hurt?"

She traced the Orda'anian crest on her sword and tugged at her lower lip. "My soldiers? I—I haven't thought about that."

"You're smart and compassionate." Charles nudged her with his shoulder. "You would say the right thing."

The comment made her smile appreciatively at first, only for a frown to take its place. "What if I say it in the wrong way, though? I could *persuade* soldiers to run into a fight I know they will not win without necessarily intending to." Rosealyn studied her palms. "Whatever this patha vita is, it's going to be as frustrating, if not more so, than the Gift."

"You used the patha vita today with good intentions, probably saved my life."

Face buried in her hands, Rosealyn mumbled, "I also told you to be quiet, and you couldn't speak until I told you to. Remember?"

"An hour ago you didn't realize what your ability was, so I think it's normal not to understand how to use it the second you know it exists." Charles shifted closer, resting a hand on her back. "I asked them to send word back to me about those three the second they get to Volante."

"And where did you tell them to take the message?" Rosealyn lifted her head and motioned with her hands. "What if Lycene isn't safe? What if we don't recover Lycene? What if—"

Charles reached for her, but she shrugged away from him. "Wait for Moss's report. There are ways to succeed, even in dire situations."

Hearing the same phrase she'd thought earlier, Rosealyn's insides chilled and her mouth turned dry. "I know dire situations are coming. I'm not sure where or when, but they are." Rosealyn worked moisture back into her mouth. "Much worse than tonight."

Though she didn't look over at him, she could visualize Charles's pensive expression. "No indication of direction?"

Rosealyn rubbed her face and rested her chin in both hands with her elbows digging into her legs. "All directions. Everywhere is in danger."

Charles nodded, brows furrowed in thought. "You mentioned cries for help earlier today. Any idea whose cries they are?"

The points of her elbows dug into her thighs, and the flickering flame consuming her vision blurred. When she concentrated, she could hear those cries. Faint shouts desperate for aid. Protection and help. One seemed louder and most distant before its sound cut short.

Each time, they sounded more familiar, as though voices she had heard before. Not only heard before but knew well.

"Maybe. Not definitively." Sighing, she lifted her head to look over the fire. "I'm afraid to concentrate on using any magic. Not when the droki can hunt it."

Charles wrapped his arm around her shoulders and pulled her into his side. She flowed with the movement until her head rested on his shoulder, smiling when his hand trailed up and down her arm. A hitch came in his steady breathing, and the movement of his hand stilled. "What happened with the swords?"

Rosealyn picked at her dress-skirts. The swords. Magical entities that changed the second she thought she understood how they worked.

"There is an impressive amount of power inside those two weapons. How to use or access it, I have no idea. One moment they hummed, the next we tapped the blades, and then—well, my vision was clearer."

"Their glow pulsed in unison, too." Charles's fingers created pleasant shivers as they trailed up and down her arm again.

Rosealyn continued picking the material of her dress, lips twisted in a frown. "I should talk to Xannan about it."

His hand stopped its slow movement. "Can you trust anything he says? Everything he does is to protect himself and no one else."

"I'm not so sure anymore." Rosealyn gripped her dress-skirts with both hands and glanced to where Xannan sat before a fire, alone. "He fought the droki with us and has offered advice. I may disagree with his suggestions, but they have been . . . helpful ideas."

"He has his own agenda," Charles grumbled.

Rosealyn looked at him. The earlier worry etched across his features had only deepened. A muscle in his jaw ticked, drawing her attention to the jagged scar along his chin.

Rosealyn smiled and placed her hand on his cheek, running a finger along the scar. "We all have our own agenda, Charles. Besides, the more I know, the better."

He returned her soft smile, gently lowering her hand. "Information is power."

"I'm sorry about the injured. If I'd known—"

Charles rested a finger on her lips. "Do *not* apologize for what you cannot control." He lowered his hand to hold hers. "You did what you could, and that is what matters."

"You are aggravatingly logical at times, you know that?" Rosealyn released a long breath, stood, and brushed her hands against her skirts.

Before she could retrieve her sword, Charles grasped it and stood as well. "You won't like to hear this, but your father did not always remain on the defensive." Charles studied the emblem engraved on the sword's hilt. "He did with Hoclia, but when Phillippe fought with Jearnia ten years ago, he came to us."

Us? The thought made Rosealyn blink at the sudden reminder of the past.

"Father taught me to defend those in my care, not be an instigator." Rosealyn held out a hand for her sword, and he gave it to her. As she grasped the sheathed weapon, Rosealyn shook her head, scanning the length of the leather scabbard. She had changed nothing about this weapon, but the weapon itself had changed so much about her.

"Sometimes the best way to defend is to become the instigator, Rose." Charles surveyed the camp with his hands resting on each hip.

Low murmurs of voices combined with the mouthwatering scent of cooked meats. Fires flickered, replacing the light of the sun as its rays descended into darkness. "I know you wish to honor your father's memory. And it is worth preserving. So are the people of your—of our countries."

Rosealyn's grip on the sheathed sword tightened. "Our countries. Two nations at odds now working together. Because of us." Rosealyn buckled on the sword and tied her hair back with a string. "I don't trust Xannan, but I believe he wants the truth about these swords as much as I do."

"I'll come—"

"No." Rosealyn smoothed her dress-skirts only for them to fling about her legs with the breeze as she stood tall, folded her arms, and glared at Charles. "I can handle a conversation."

"I know." Charles tucked stray strands of her hair the wind had blown awry behind her ear. "But it's hard not to worry about the safety of the woman I love."

Whatever words she knew disappeared, and her lips parted while she forced herself to take a quiet breath. Already tense shoulders shook, and she gripped her arms so tightly she was sure the imprint of her fingers would be left behind. The muscles of her legs trembled.

Riveted to her place in the rain-soaked grass, Rosealyn looked everywhere except at Charles. Love? Attraction was there, otherwise she wouldn't enjoy kissing him so much. Even before the kissing, hand-holding, and overall comforting closeness, she cared for him. More than cared about him. Did that equal love?

All the questions she had formed about the swords disappeared, overwhelmed by that singular word. Did she know what it looked like to be in love? From her birth mother's letter, it was obvious Catarina had loved her father, but Rosealyn had no recollection of their interactions.

Parched, she scanned the dirt around the fire, desperate to find a container of water nearby. Nothing. Her heartbeat quickened, and her palms turned clammy. Though she had trained with him multiple days a week for years, Rosealyn berated her body for sweating. Her attempt at swallowing felt like a handful of leaves coated her throat.

Frustrated at the lack of nearby drinking water, her gaze made its way back to Charles's. Not knowing what else to do, she nodded, smiled, reminded herself to breathe, and whispered, "I—I won't be long. Promise."

CHAPTER FORTY-SIX

Rosealyn's thoughts were too scattered to pay attention to which direction she walked. "Focus," she whispered to herself while fighting the urge to look over her shoulder. Frozen in place with her hands clenched at her sides, she closed her eyes and mumbled, "Idiot."

Feeling positively foolish, Rosealyn looked over her shoulder and was momentarily surprised Charles hadn't followed her. Instead, he had resumed his seat by the fire and appeared to be rifling through a bag at his side. When she turned forward to survey her surroundings, she jolted at seeing Xannan standing directly in front of her.

"I don't want—"

"To talk to me."

"Or anybody at this precise moment. I need to . . . to think."

"But we need to talk." Xannan gestured at the fire where he'd been sitting.

Rosealyn laughed once, gritted her teeth, and flexed her hands at her sides. "No."

As she turned, Xannan gripped her arm. "Don't walk away from me."

"You walked away first." Rosealyn shoved his hand away and rubbed her arm, glaring at him.

"Because I know when I'm not wanted nearby." At her sharp inhale, he held up a hand. "The swords connected but didn't combine."

"Obviously."

"And we both used them. At the same time." Xannan placed his hands on his hips and tapped his belt. "I thought when they touched while in danger, they would always combine into one."

"Well I'm glad I wasn't useless when danger surrounded us." Rosealyn made a sharp gesture toward the dead droki in the middle of the camp. "Would you have protected me if the dragonsword chose you again?"

"If needed." Emotionless tone, emotionless stare. "But why the change?" Xannan paused, though he looked ready to spring after her if she tried to walk away again. When she shrugged, he said, "I was hoping after combining into the dragonsword, the connection would be broken when it split into two again."

Rosealyn ground her teeth, especially since Xannan was proving he continued to hold to his own agenda. Despite having planned to converse with Xannan about the swords, her mind was elsewhere. At least he was asking logical questions. Granted, they were questions she should be asking rather than him. It wasn't like she had witnessed the sword's creation. "So relive a previous experience and find out?"

Xannan tapped his temple. "Only works when I lived the experience myself. I have no recollection of Gailin and me using these swords in the same manner we used them tonight."

"Glad to hear you know your limitations. Explains why you have questions."

Cooked meat from a nearby campfire filled her nostrils, and Rosealyn's stomach took that moment to remind her she should eat more. One chunk of salted meat per day would not allow her to maintain her strength. The mouthwatering scents mixed with the deathly scent of beheaded beasts and Rosealyn winced. At some point, more food would become a necessity. Perhaps after they'd figured out what to do with the dead droki and she couldn't smell them anymore.

Xannan shrugged. "The droki sense magic, so perhaps the swords' additional connection used less?"

"Then why were they glowing?"

"A defense mechanism?"

"You relived the moment of the sword's creation. Do that again and find the answer?" Rosealyn glanced behind her, heart rate spiking when she found the campfire in front of Charles's tent empty. It didn't slow when Charles exited the tent with what had to be bags of food his cooks had provided and approached her and Xannan.

"Hasn't worked again. Not that well, at least."

At first she fought the urge to roll her eyes, until she noted how Xannan's gaze grew distant, as though recalling a memory. "You're lying. Tell me the truth."

He froze and glared at her. Rosealyn clenched her fists, nails biting into her palms. Heightened emotions made it easier to use her ability. Or maybe it was simply easier to use it on Xannan since, according to him, she had done so often. "That was unintentional, but I would like to know the truth."

"It's been unintentional for weeks." Xannan raised his hands when she stepped forward. "Voices from my past. Anna's."

"Anna?"

"Not a line of questioning that will explain what is happening with these swords." His green eyes flashed in a way that made Rosealyn decide it was best not to challenge his statement. Xannan crossed his arms. "We remain connected, but Gailin saw how to break the connection. Tell me what he wrote. Anything he mentioned about the swords, the dragons." Xannan dropped his arms to his sides and added a dejected "me."

Rosealyn glanced behind her at Charles, whose path had been interrupted by one of his colonels. A snap of Xannan's fingers brought her attention back to him and made her wonder if the pain of punching him would be worth it.

Gentle winds shifted strands of her hair and her skirts, though one side remained held fast by her sword. Nose wrinkling, Rosealyn wondered who should be claiming the sword. It was a part of her and a part of him. Much of what she'd read in Gailin's journals over the years seemed a lie. Even the additional journal entries her father had hidden from her didn't appear to help do anything more than add to her frustrations.

"About the swords?" Rosealyn nudged a clump of mud with her boot. "Not much. Gailin mentions how the swords called to you both, molded to you, and latched on to some aspect of your being with a refusal to let go." She paused and tugged at her lower lip. Something about Gailin's comment of the swords "latching" she needed to decipher for herself.

With a slight grunt, Xannan said, "How helpful. Did he mention how the weapons call to each other?"

"Briefly." Rosealyn shrugged and glanced at Charles again. This was no longer the conversation she needed to be having. Nor was it a conversation she wished to have. Why repeat what they both already knew?

"The dragons? Me?" Xannan folded his arms.

"Later." Rosealyn looked back at Charles, frowning when Charles's hand moved to the hilt of his sword. More droki? No, Xannan and the swords would have notified her of them. One of the injured dead? Perhaps, but they had been instructed to continue to Volante and send word upon arrival rather than spare one of their party before arriving. Those two options dismissed, she came upon another. If Nathaniel had left Alkaanian soldiers to maintain Lycene, it would be logical some would scout the surrounding area. Given that possibility, could her simple instructions for Moss to scout the city have gotten him hurt?

"Rosealyn." The tone with which Xannan said her name made her grind her teeth together and wish he would go away. "We need to understand how the swords work."

"Right now? Not—"

"Yes, now. More droki could attack."

"And if they do, we'll kill them."

"Next time it might be ten, fifteen, a hundred. We need to understand how to access the sword's magic and use it against the droki." Xannan's blond hair whipped across his face with the wind, and his green eyes burned with obvious frustration.

When Rosealyn stepped away from him, she ran into another person behind her whose hands rested on her shoulders and caught her before she might stumble and fall.

"Rose?" Charles's voice whispered in her ear with a tone belying far too much concern.

"I'm—I'm fine." Rosealyn cleared her throat and placed her hand atop Charles's. She looked back at Xannan. "Intentions . . . When it became one sword, my goal was to kill you while yours was to kill Eilon?"

"No, my initial goal was to kill you first. Until those images filtered from the weapons and I learned Eilon had manipulated me." Xannan shrugged. "Then I wanted retribution. Revenge."

Rosealyn nodded and felt Charles's hands grip her shoulders a smidge tighter. "Tonight my goal was to eliminate the drokos. You?"

"Same."

"Then we can agree having the same goal allowed us to use the swords at the time?" Rosealyn waited for Xannan's affirmative nod. "Do you think it can do more than ease our pain and improve our senses when connected?"

"Perhaps." Xannan chuckled. "Damn cryptic brother. I need to read all of Gailin's journals. The answer to breaking the connection is in them. I'm positive."

She squeezed Charles's hand and sighed. "We have to return to Vandyl and hope they survived Eilon's flame."

Charles leaned close enough his breath tickled her neck as he whispered, "Moss sent one of the scouts back."

Rosealyn rounded on him, eyes widening. "So soon? If he's already back, they weren't able to get close enough to the city or—"

Rapid blinks helped stay angry tears. It would be silly to promise no one else would die because a young foolish king sought her country for himself, but Rosealyn let the thought form. If she could tell others to use hope, then she could hold onto the same herself.

"Surrounded. Moss was afraid to get closer because it appears an entire Alkaanian battalion now resides there. He is getting as much information as he can but wanted to send us an update."

She tipped her head back and soaked in the starry night sky. A facade of calm greeted her vision. "Which means two options: reclaim Lycene or head straight to Vandyl and take our chances at the capital."

"Or—" Xannan's voice stopped when her gaze bore into him.

"Let's get one thing straight right now." Rosealyn lifted her chin, and the wind shifted her hair so it streamed across her vision. "*I* choose *my* country's path. Me. It is *my* decision where to send aid and whether or not to attack. It is *my* choice what to do for *my* people." She motioned with an arm to indicate each of them. "We three were all raised and taught to be leaders, to be royalty. I know you think we should march to Alkaan and take their capital. But my home and my people are in danger now."

A singular deep breath, Rosealyn wondered if a late night sparring session would soothe her emotions. While Xannan shook his head and walked away, Rosealyn tugged at her lower lip.

"Nathaniel will go straight for Vandyl. He knows it's the capital and where I should be." Rosealyn turned back to Charles. Lines would become permanent on his forehead if he didn't stop scrunching his brows in worry, though his soft blue eyes held the faintest hint of admiration. "Which would you choose?"

"It's your decision, Rose."

Warmth filled her chest at Charles's words, making the cold anger of her conversation with Xannan melt away.

CHAPTER FORTY-SEVEN

Roseanne wondered how long it had been since she'd moved from the bed. Hours? Days? Weeks? She didn't know, nor did she care. What did matter was how her sister, who'd apparently been alive for the past twenty years, knew more about this continent than she did. Based on their conversation in the oasis, Phillippe had communicated better with Catarina when the two were on different continents. Roseanne knew letters could cross oceans. She wished Catarina had not said such an obvious statement. All it did was stoke the seeds of discontent growing in her aching gut.

When the door to her room opened, Roseanne closed her eyes and feigned sleep. It was the best way to avoid talking. Talking caused frustration. At herself, at the world, at Phillippe, at Catarina. Even at Rosealyn.

"I know you're not asleep," Catarina said in that veiled tone of annoyance.

Family Roseanne had not seen in years had tried to speak with her. When she still had the strength, Roseanne had shoved them out of the bare lightless room with its lonesome fireplace. It was as much a prison as the dungeon cell. At least here, in this room, the rats wouldn't find her body first.

Everyone reminded Roseanne she wasn't responsible for Ramon's actions. Roseanne shivered. Fear had allowed her to trust when she should not have.

"Your breathing is uneven, Roseanne," her sister said with an obvious mouthful of food that garbled the words. "So sit up and eat while it's warm."

Roseanne concentrated on attaining the facade of sleep.

"You've been sleeping, or pretending to sleep, for almost eight days now." In a voice somewhat louder than before, and kinder, Catarina asked, "When was the last time you ate?"

A few more breaths and she'd have it right. Would it help to count her breaths? Worth a try, Roseanne decided.

"And now your face is all scrunched up because you're trying to focus." Catarina sat close enough for Roseanne to feel her sister's warmth along with the divot she created in the mattress. "Sit up, eat. We have things to discuss."

"Lovely," Roseanne mumbled without opening her eyes. She dug her head into the soft pillow. "I'd rather not do any of that. Please leave."

"Not until you eat."

"I'm not hungry."

"Then I'll stay until you are."

Roseanne opened one eye to glare at her sister and was greeted with Catarina's disapproving frown. It was useless for Catarina to demand anything of her; all Roseanne wanted was to be left alone.

"You'll be waiting awhile, then." Roseanne rolled over to stare at the opposite wall, away from Catarina. "I'm not eating."

"Are you trying to waste away to nothing, then?"

"I am nothing, might as well look the part." Roseanne moved one arm beneath her head, legs scrunched up to ease the cramping of her stomach. She had no idea when she had last eaten and had no plans of doing so this morning. Evening? Afternoon? Her plain room had no windows, and she'd lost track of who came and went while she lay on the bed.

Catarina shifted on the mattress, mumbling words laced with a deepening tone of frustration as she gripped Roseanne's arm. "I did not return to this continent to watch you wither to nothing, Roseanne."

"Then go back to your island." Roseanne tucked her knees in closer. "In case you haven't noticed, no one has thought to look for me."

A heartbeat of silence passed, and Catarina whispered, "I looked for you. And I've found you. Now let me help you."

Roseanne shrugged off Catarina's hand. "Please go away."

A muffled screech made Roseanne turn enough to watch as Catarina tugged at her loose auburn hair. Same shade as Rosealyn's, almost the same length, too. Once others at the castle met Catarina, there would be no doubt.

"I'm not leaving until you know exactly what you've missed over the past week."

"I thought you said it'd been eight days?" Roseanne turned all the way back to her sister, one brow raised. Though she didn't want to, her gaze flickered to the plate of food on a nearby table. Close enough to see. And smell. Roseanne wrapped her arm around her abdomen, clutching her side.

"I knew you weren't asleep when I walked in." Catarina stood with an outstretched hand.

Roseanne shook her head. The bed was comfortable; she had no desire to leave it.

Somberness colored Catarina's smooth dark skin, and she lowered her hand. "Jaida is in Jearnia."

Roseanne tried to sit up, but pain spasmed through her stomach and she gasped. Shifting to her back, Roseanne asked, "Captured? Hurt? Why is Rosealyn there?"

Catarina chuckled.

Roseanne scrunched her face. None of those questions were funny.

"Jaida is well. Though Duchess Adela's message was written with quite the slanted hand."

"What else did Adela say? When did you get the message?"

"Oh, good, you do wish to know?" Catarina raised a brow, and Roseanne pushed herself to sit up while nodding. "Adela's message arrived this morning. I came when I got it, but you actually were asleep then, so I let you rest. Before I tell you more, though—"

Catarina grabbed the plate of food, walked back to Roseanne's bedside, and set the plate atop her lap. "Eat. It's been almost two full days since I've seen you eat a bite. Nothing more until half that plate is gone."

A glance down at the plate and back at her sister, and Roseanne knew she had no room for argument. She could toss the plate aside, let the morsels of sustenance be wasted across the cold stone floor the fire could barely warm. Or she could wait out Catarina's patience.

"Hmm." Catarina tsked. "I know you care. Your earlier reaction to hearing Jaida is in Jearnia proves as much. So what is it?"

When Roseanne swallowed, she wondered if it was fear or lack of drink that parched her throat. How long had it been since she'd taken a drink? As Roseanne sank back into the bed, Catarina grasped the plate. Uncontrollable shivers racked her body, making her arms shake as she dragged the blanket up to her neck.

"Well?" Catarina prompted and sat on the mattress again.

Silent tears pooled, streaming down Roseanne's cheeks. "If I help, I'll only get someone else killed."

"Oh, Roseanne." Catarina's hand hovered over Roseanne's shoulder for a heartbeat and made contact. "You can't believe that."

"It's true." She wiped her tears with the blanket. "I tried to help Phillippe, and he died. As did servants. And soldiers." Roseanne swallowed and squeezed her eyes shut, pressing out more tears. "Azeiah." She gripped the blanket, hoping its width hid her shivering. "Any death at Vandyl was because I tried to help. Vandyl was attacked because I trusted the wrong people." Words caught behind the lump of sobs in her throat as she remembered the blurred bloody path before Xannan had forced her into that magical cloud of darkness only to be met with more death surrounding her.

"You weren't there, Catarina. You didn't see soldiers screaming as their skin fell from their bones." More silent tears streamed down Roseanne's cheeks, and she curled in on herself to stop the shaking. "You didn't see as the man Ramon told me to trust"—Roseanne couldn't hold back the sob, and her voice cracked—"as Xannan killed Azeiah and then held the same bloodied black sword to my chest."

Catarina's breathing quickened. Quieter, Roseanne added, "Nor did you see how Ramon butchered the council members. If that is where helping others gets me, I want no part in it."

CHAPTER FORTY-EIGHT

Catarina squeezed her sister's arm, frowning when the woman flinched. "But you survived, Roseanne."

"I shouldn't have!" Roseanne shoved Catarina's arm away and curled back into herself. "I told you. I am—"

"You are *not* nothing." Catarina contemplated moving closer again. Each time she believed she had broken through whatever wall her sister had created, she met another layer of stone. One after another. No end in sight. The message from Adela had helped less than Catarina had hoped. "I refuse to believe you are nothing."

"What can I do, Catarina? Hmm?" Roseanne tucked herself tighter, almost as if she were trying to become as small as possible.

"You could—" Catarina winced and fumbled to find an answer.

"See?"

Another wall. An impenetrable void.

"It's been twenty years, Roseanne. Your skills have certainly changed in that time."

Roseanne harrumphed. "I became a caretaker for *your* daughter."

There was no use denying the statement. Catarina's gaze bounced between the two chairs, the fire, the table, and Roseanne's bed. "A caretaker!" Catarina almost clapped triumphantly, until she noticed her sister's incredulous stare. Softer, Catarina tried to phrase the words as a statement. "You could be a caretaker not for Jaida, but for the people."

No reaction. Catarina knew the woman wasn't actually looking at anything in front of her.

"I didn't say I liked being a caretaker, only that I was."

"True." Catarina sighed and grabbed the plate of food, sitting back down on the bed. She held out a piece of fruit, trying to control her reaction lest she scare Roseanne out of accepting the food. And then, mercifully, it was in Roseanne's hand, which was the closest to inside Roseanne's mouth any food had been for the past two days.

Roseanne merely stared at the piece with those blank, emotionless eyes. Setting the plate down between them, Catarina shifted her wavy auburn hair to rest on one shoulder and ran her fingers through it.

"From what I know—and correct me if I'm wrong—cities across Orda'an are suffering."

Roseanne grimaced. "There was nothing we could do for their crops, so I don't know where this is going."

"Leave the crops to me." Catarina chewed on a grape. "You can help the people."

"Help the people?" Roseanne repeated the words slowly and inspected the chunk of melon. "Why?"

Catarina watched, hopeful Roseanne would eat at least one solitary bite. "Is it not a queen's role to aid the people?"

"I'm no longer their queen." Roseanne dropped the morsel back onto the plate. "Rosealyn doesn't need me around to screw up again."

Rather than travel down that path, Catarina silently ate several pieces of cheese. The rest she would leave for Roseanne, especially considering her later meeting with the newly elected Tenoan council. She had hoped Roseanne would attend as well, but her sister couldn't remain upright. Catarina swallowed the last of the cheese and studied the unadorned white tapestries lining each wall. There had to be something more she could do for her sister. Roseanne had given up *everything* so Catarina and Phillippe's mistake would never be discovered.

But everything Catarina had thought would work had no effect on her frail, malnourished older sister.

Unable to hide the plea in her tone, Catarina asked, "Why won't you eat?"

"Why won't you leave me alone?"

"Because you aren't eating, Roseanne." Catarina tugged at her hair and wiped the brimming tears from her eyes. She needed Roseanne to come back to the surface, to crack the wall on one side while Catarina did the same. Shouts and screams would only add another layer of stone. Catarina stood and faced her sister, speaking as levelly as her emotions would allow. "All you do is sleep or lie here. You haven't walked the halls or taken a step outside to breathe in the fresh air."

"I'm fine where I am." Somehow, Roseanne managed to curl tighter into herself.

"Where you are is slowly dying, Roseanne!" All the frustration Catarina had withheld for the past several days burst. "Do you want to die, too? Or do you want to change the story some may tell?"

She waited, chest heaving, while Roseanne's eyes fluttered closed. Stifling a scream crawling its way up her throat, Catarina stalked to the door and opened it enough to request additional food and drink and a second bed. She refused to leave her sister alone. Not in this state.

Catarina tugged a blanket from one of the chairs near the fire and laid it over Roseanne. The land tugging at her would have to wait longer for her assistance.

CHAPTER FORTY-NINE

After raking his hand through his hair, Charles wished he had cut it at some point in the past month. From watching Rosealyn while sparring, he knew longer hair was more a nuisance than anything else. And at the moment the wind was shifting her hair while she stared at him with an immovable determination. She wanted to head straight to Vandyl, a decision that meant abandoning Lycene to the Alkaanian battalion which surrounded it.

"Rose." Charles gripped both of her arms. "Please think this through."

"I did." She folded her arms and lifted her chin. "Once we are near Vandyl, I want to see for myself what condition it's in. Not just what Eilon and Xannan did, but what Nathaniel is currently doing. And then I'm going to rip his plan to shreds and take back my home."

"Jacin told you Nathaniel's plan. Smaller attacks on each city until the entirety of the nation is under his control." Charles threaded one hand through his hair again. "We're at Lycene now. More scouting and preparation, then we can take back that city. Same as what my other battalions plan to do."

She winced and turned away. "I have to take back my home, Charles."

"And once you're home? What then? What happens after you reclaim Vandyl and Nathaniel's soldiers hold several smaller cities?"

Her chest heaved, and she blinked rapidly, as she always did when angry. "Then we take them back."

Charles gestured west and gripped the hilt of his sword. "And if your people in Lycene die because you waited to help?"

She whipped her head back to him. "The same could happen in Vandyl. Or Cantadad or Lobelia. Demir. Asyir. Verbera." She blinked rapidly, eyes filling with tears.

He pressed his lips together, reminding himself she needed to make her choice.

Rosealyn straightened, swiping at each cheek and resting a hand on her sword hilt. "I know the names of *my* country's cities, Charles. Just like I learned the names of the servants and soldiers, I learned all I could about my country. Vandyl is the most heavily populated. That is why I'm reclaiming it first."

"But it's not." Charles forced himself to meet her gaze. "Not anymore. Most of Vandyl's citizens relocated to Lycene."

She opened her mouth but snapped it shut and assumed a posture much like his own. One hand gripped her sword's hilt while the other gripped her dress-skirt. She made no effort to wipe away the tears rolling down her cheeks. Several strands of hair stuck to her face, and Charles wished they could have more quiet moments like they'd had while eating dinner with his mother and brother. Moments when they shared stories of their younger days, before they knew each other, until one or both of them drifted off to sleep. These moments, the ones discussing impending danger, turned him back into her protector. It wasn't his job anymore, but he wanted to protect her. He refused to let any thought of her hurt or dead fester. Both of them would survive. Both of them could fight. She had a powerful sword and magic to help. Yet, even with all they had, his brows remained furrowed.

"Now you've got a face." Rosealyn wiped at her cheeks and redid the string pulling her hair away from her face. Her halfhearted attempt at light laughter died with the wind. "You're going to give yourself wrinkles. At least, that's what Lori always said when I worried. 'Frowning gives you unhappy wrinkles, smiles give you happy lines.'"

Charles chuckled and tried to smile in response but found it too easy to frown. "I'm worried."

"I know." Rosealyn reached for his hand.

Holding her hand in his assuaged some of his worry. Not much. In the moonlight, Charles couldn't make out much more than the glossiness of her eyes. Where once had been an abundant mischievous light of always planning or plotting some trick against him, now her face held her own version of worry.

After a gentle squeeze of his hand, Rosealyn said, "I worry about you, too, Charles."

The hollowness from before reopened and his hand went limp, releasing hers. Had he said the wrong thing? She couldn't have forgotten what he'd said, not with how she'd been riveted in place for so long. Why had she gone from being so forward with him to whatever this was? Was it how she handled worry and stress? Or was she angry with him for arguing about the plans she made? Unless this was confusion? He frowned. Rosealyn wouldn't leave something alone until she had it solved. *Which means she hasn't solved it?*

Rosealyn reached out for his hand again and gestured toward his tent's campfire withering in the waning night. "I think we should talk where we're less likely to be interrupted."

All he could do was nod and grasp her hand. As they walked in silence, Charles mulled over the same set of questions, wondering what tomorrow would bring. Or the next day. Or the day after. In many ways, the continent was close to full-out war. No news on Tenoa's position despite its entire council's eradication. Hoclia had claimed Pasea, but he worried the Honorable Jordan would thirst for more than one slice of Orda'anian land. If Nathaniel continued to successfully take Orda'anian cities, Jordan might do the same.

Rosealyn ducked in first and released his hand so she could undo her sword belt and set it aside. Close enough to grab but far enough to be out of the way—as a sword should be when danger could swoop down from the sky. Rather than lie down on the cot as she usually did, Rosealyn sat with her feet tucked beneath her and patted the ground in front of her. After removing his sword and resting it next to Rosealyn's, he was lowering himself when she blurted out, "The woman you love?"

He fell to a seated position and grunted, massaging his hand where it had hit the ground. "I hate it when that happens."

At her arched brow and amused grin, Charles sighed. "Mae did something similar. Wait until I'm halfway seated to say something to catch me off-balance."

"That makes two of us."

"Oh?"

"To hate it when someone says something to catch you off guard."

"Right." Charles shifted each leg and glanced around the tent. Wind whispered through, so Charles stood and tied the tent flaps to prevent them from whipping with the breeze. He could feel Rosealyn watching him. When he turned around, the mischievous fire in her gaze had returned.

"So you recommend Lycene first?"

"Yes." Charles folded his arms and looked down at her. The way she tugged at her lip to stop herself from laughing almost made him laugh as well. "What do you think changing the subject will accomplish?"

She shrugged. "Is it working?"

"Are you hungry?"

"Now who's changing the subject?"

"What do you want me to say, Rose?" Charles brushed hair from his forehead and hoped his cheeks weren't as flushed as the rest of him felt. "I do worry about the safety of the woman I love. And right now, I'm frustrated with her."

"I imagine it's normal to feel other emotions aside from love when in a relationship, yes?" Rosealyn tilted her head up at him and bent her legs to one side, tapping the ground again.

"Probably." Charles removed the black coat and placed it beside their swords. The tent was too warm to wear that coat plus the white shirt beneath it. "Wait." He cleared his throat and sat cross-legged in front of her. "A relationship?"

She nodded and untied the string holding her hair. "I'd like to say I've been thinking about us, about a relationship, but what does that look like? Father was forced to marry—" Rosealyn paused and frowned at the ground. "But he was in love with someone else."

Idleness did not suit Rosealyn. Charles knew her desire to be in constant motion mixed with nerves often led to toying with the dress's material as she did in that moment.

"And now you question what love is?" The hollowness in his chest filled somewhat when she nodded, along with the realization that she'd led him back here. His words hadn't made her run away.

"Your parent's marriage was also arranged, wasn't it?" She didn't look up from her incessant twisting of the material.

"It was. My cousins would form the council if my decisions are questioned, but whom I choose to spend the rest of my days with will not be in their hands."

"I wish I could have seen them together. My father and birth mother." Rosealyn paused and took a shaky inhale of breath followed by a quick exhale. Face buried her hands, she mumbled, "I don't know what to say right now. Or do."

Rosealyn peered through her fingers at him, and he blanched at recognizing fear in her features. While he contemplated what to say, she buried her face back in her hands. With a silent admonishment of himself, Charles shifted closer and gently pried her hands away from her face. He brushed his thumb over her knuckles, briefly thinking of the ring his mother had given him to give to Rosealyn. He cleared his throat and lifted his gaze to hers.

"I understand. We've been through a lot in the past two months." Charles paused when Rosealyn withdrew her hands. So he twirled his signet ring, thinking. This was new territory for them both.

Face buried in her hands again, Rosealyn whispered, "I'm worried I'll say the wrong thing."

"Since when have you worried about that?"

"Since learning how much power my words can have." Rosealyn lowered her hands to wring the fabric of her dress-skirts and added with a slight crack in her voice, "I'm scared."

"Of?" Charles shifted strands of her hair and smiled softly when her breathing hitched at the motion.

"Losing," she whispered and swallowed. "Losing—losing my country. No, more than that." Her gaze found his again, and Charles recognized a myriad of warring emotions. "I'm scared of losing you."

"I have no plans of dying, Rose."

"No one does." Rosealyn returned to picking at her dress-skirts. "And that's not what I meant."

His brows lifted at the indirect admission, and he gathered both her hands in his to stop the wringing of her dress. "I don't want you to say anything you're not ready to say."

One slow blink was followed with a soft smile and a whispered "thank you." Rosealyn looked around and winced. "I'm pretty sure that continuing to sleep here will cause Aunt Adela to lecture me. Again."

"Sleep where you're comfortable."

Rosealyn stood and brushed her skirts. "There's no way I'll be sleeping tonight, anyway. I should discuss my options with Adela and see if Moss has returned. And then—" Another quick glance around the tent. Rosealyn shrugged and retrieved her sword. "We could spar?

Could help ease my nerves." She tugged at her lower lip, blushing. "Some of them, at least."

"It might help," Charles said and cleared his throat. Observing her as a guard for several years allowed him to know most of her moods, but this one was unlike any he had witnessed before. "With my battalion here we could practice fighting multiple opponents." Charles frowned at the shadowed silhouette of an approaching man. He gritted his teeth when he recognized Xannan's gait and broad shoulders.

"Moss returned," Xannan said as he poked his head through the tent flaps, as if delivering the message soured his appetite. "Would you like me to share his report or hear it from him?"

"Tell me," Rosealyn instructed while buckling her sword with swift sure motions.

"The citizens of Lycene are alive. And imprisoned."

The movement of her hands halted with the buckle halfway clasped, fingers shaking. She remained petrified until Xannan snapped in front of her face, and she jerked back with a deep glower. "We are going to rescue them. And capture the soldiers responsible."

Rosealyn ducked around Xannan and out of the tent before Charles or Xannan could argue with her.

Face pinched tight, Xannan turned to Charles. "Did you instruct her in strategy?"

Charles didn't deign to give the man a response and focused on donning his solid black coat and buttoning it to his collarbone. He tried to duck around Xannan as Rosealyn had.

But the Lost Prince of Orda'an gripped Charles's arm and lowered his voice. "We don't have the resources to rescue the people. This endeavor will kill more than it saves."

Ripping his arm free of Xannan's firm grip, Charles tugged at each sleeve and swallowed. "I'm aware. Would you not try to rescue your people?"

"These are my people. Or at least they should have been." Xannan moved aside, pale skin glowing in the meager light of the campfire. "The worst lesson I remember being told but never truly learned, that I can recall at least, is that sometimes you must forgo certain battles to win the war." He shoved a stick closer to the fire. "So who's going to tell the proud almost queen that she's making a mistake?"

Charles stiffened. He hated being the bearer of bad news for Rosealyn. But if anyone could help her see reason, he probably had the best chance.

CHAPTER FIFTY

Such a contrast. Dark hallways after the brightness of the Jearnian castle's throne room. While his ten cousins debated what happened next, Christopher stood outside the heavy wooden doors. All that gold plating blinded him when he was forced to stand in the center of the throne room, especially with the sun at its peak as it had been when their conversation began. It made entering these dark hallways quite jarring.

Christopher alternated between standing tall, slouching against the wall, or letting his shoulders slump as he waited. Same as he had while his cousins asked him one question after another. Only the youngest appeared upset about Lukas's death, and none seemed surprised at Christopher's decision to put Marsha in the dungeons. They'd barely blinked when he admitted to attempting to kill Marsha as well.

The eldest of Marsha's children, and the eldest of his cousins, slipped through the throne room doors. So young, all of them. The most awkward part of that day's discussion had been his asking their names. This one was Maya, which he only remembered because the others referred to her by name on multiple occasions. Maya couldn't be more than fifteen, and the rest of his cousins had submitted to her as their voice. She remained silent while he wondered if he was right about her age.

The girl was the spitting image of her mother, which made it more difficult for Christopher to look at Maya. Her hair was straighter but the same shade of brown. Honey-colored eyes hid behind dark lashes, vibrant against the girl's pale skin, though the tight dress showed she had not fully grown into womanhood. That didn't stop her from standing tall and making Christopher wish he could transform into a bug and scurry away from her scrutiny.

"Well?" Christopher spat out the word and winced at the anger lacing his tone. Though he knew none of his cousins were responsible for the actions of their parents, it didn't help.

"We appreciate you are not holding any of us responsible for what happened," Maya said with a face that emanated an unfortunate amount of pity.

"But?"

His cousin clasped her hands behind her back and stood taller, tilting her head up to look into his eyes. "But you are only the steward of our nation, and you took matters into your own hands too soon."

"We discussed that." Christopher's shoulders tensed. "What I did to Lukas is no different from the punishment he would have received, simply more immediate."

"True." Maya's gaze roamed him up and down as though deciphering him. Eventually, she whispered, "You regret killing Uncle Lukas."

Christopher grimaced and wondered when carpet had been placed in the hallways or if it had always been there. Black on dark stone was hard to notice. All he could see for the past few days when he tried to sleep was dragging his dagger across his uncle's neck without hesitation. The action sickened him, yet he was enthralled by it, with knowing he was capable of taking another's life. That image alternated with the last he had of his mother, her face ashen and sickly as he covered it with her favorite shawl. Others had offered to finish the burial and fill in her grave. He didn't let them. Every shovelful of dirt he dropped on top of her was a reminder that he had failed to protect her.

His cousin's face invaded his unfocused line of sight. "You regret it because you know how it feels to lose those you love."

No words came to mind, not when Maya had so accurately described his emotions. Hours of conversation had led her to understanding him, but Christopher was more surprised by her kindness than he cared to admit.

Maya offered a half smile. "The evidence is sufficient for Mother to be tried for treason, but it will be left to the richest nobles to decide. As steward, it is your choice when that trial should be held."

"I'm aware," Christopher said before the entirety of her statement settled. "You are not recommending I be replaced by another until Charles's return?"

Hands still clasped behind her back, Maya tilted her head and chuckled. "I asked the others what they would do had you attacked one of us and we witnessed the act. Since all of us would do the same as you did to Uncle Lukas, we see no reason for a change of stewardship. Besides, none of us desire that responsibility. This conversation was more than most of us ever wish to have in the throne room."

Christopher grunted and folded his arms. "And if I make a habit of killing as quickly as my father once did?"

Maya lifted a shoulder. "I doubt you will."

"So that's it? We spent all morning discussing what happened for you all to agree I did the same as any would have done?"

She nodded, too slow for his liking.

"What else?"

"We want accommodations in the castle so we can be closer in case something else happens."

"But you just said you didn't like having that discussion in the throne room."

Maya patted at her hair that seemed frozen in place and spoke in a way that made him cringe. Her voice was so similar to her mother's.

"No, but we also don't like being a part of the royal family while also being clueless. I had to ask Father about the laws of treason before leaving home."

At the mention of Marsha's husband, Christopher flinched. He should have sent word to the man, said something to him. Maybe. Maybe not. *Maya's right. Stewardship is a lot of responsibility.*

"Father's fine." Maya smiled and clasped her hands behind her again. "Not surprised in the slightest, actually." She pursed her lips and shook her head. "Well, that's not true. Father was surprised it took this long before Mother was accused of anything. For all I know, Mother's been worming her way into power since I was born. Earlier probably."

Christopher acknowledged his cousin's statement with a softer grunt and gripped his arms tighter. "The castle has plenty of empty rooms." He gestured, but his arm froze when Jacin approached with a look on his face. Soldiers knew how to hide their worry; Jacin was not.

Christopher lowered his arm and debated telling Maya to leave. His cousin didn't ask if she could stay either, she simply did.

"Soldiers from King Charles's battalion returned moments ago. Two injured, one dead. Poisoned by droki."

So much for mincing words and breaking the news easily. Christopher's chest tightened as though someone's hand gripped his heart and squeezed. They'd been gone barely more than a week. If they'd returned so soon, did it mean Charles was injured? Or worse? The burden of stewardship already seemed so heavy, and Christopher was positive the mantle of king would be worse. Power was not as pleasant as Christopher had once dreamed.

"Charles?" he croaked out, anxious for the answer. If he'd failed so soon as steward, Christopher was positive he wouldn't last more than a month as Jearnia's proper king.

"Alive and unharmed. They continue toward Orda'an, according to those who returned." Jacin looked askance at Maya, frowned, and asked Christopher, "What did your cousins decide?"

"Christopher remains as steward, and all of us cousins are moving in." Maya smoothed her skirts and patted her hair again as she met Christopher's gaze. "Why did Charles leave? Mother nor Father mentioned anything. Mother refused to allow us to attend the coronation."

Christopher smoothed his features, wondering if his aunt had had plans that had gone awry at the coronation, and offered a brief explanation to Maya. "King Nathaniel of Alkaan claimed several Orda'anian cities. Charles, unsurprisingly, offered aid to Rosealyn." He tugged at his coat and pulled his collar away from his neck. "Why did the wounded return here?"

"To discover a way to remove the droki poison before they kill all those they attack."

Christopher barked a laugh but muttered a curse when Jacin's worrisome facade did not change. "You're serious? I thought those things were a death sentence."

"I suppose it's a good thing this man prevented you from killing Mother." Maya's voice was laced with amusement. When Christopher arched his brow, his cousin explained, "Who else to create an antidote to poison than one who created her own?"

"I'm not speaking with her again. I can't. Not knowing she tried to kill my mother."

"Understood." Maya smoothed her skirts again, the subtle clench of her jaw portraying the most emotion she'd shown about her mother's current predicament. "I'll speak with her, and then you will speak with me."

Jacin pulled Christopher aside, whispering with a jerk of his head in Maya's direction. "This one is Marsha's eldest?" After Christopher's affirmative nod, Jacin's grip on his arm tightened. "Then I would not trust her."

"Wasn't planning on it. Apparently there's no one in this castle I can trust." The moment the words left his lips, Christopher wanted to take them back.

But Jacin's lighter-colored eyes didn't narrow at the comment. Perhaps a life as a spy could make one suspicious enough to never trust anyone. Though, from what Christopher could recall, Jacin did trust his own people. And Jacin's queen trusted Jearnia's king. Did that mean Christopher could trust all of them as well?

"So." Maya rolled to her toes and back onto her heels, hands clasped behind her. "Where is Mother?"

CHAPTER FIFTY-ONE

From her seat near the hearth, Catarina warmed her hands with a cup of tea while watching her sister. It was impossible to know how much time had passed. Why they'd given Roseanne a room with no window, Catarina didn't understand. A little sunlight might have helped her sister. If anything could help Roseanne anymore. Visits with family were pointless, conversations went nowhere, and even sharing the dangers Jaida was in didn't wake Roseanne from her despondency.

While Catarina spent the time deciding what else to try, Roseanne slept. Sometimes Roseanne's entire body trembled. Other times she lay still enough to make Catarina worry, until a shaky inhale announced air continued to reach Roseanne's lungs.

Out of desperation, Catarina sent a message to Izari. To Naomi. Of all the people she knew, the elf-woman was one of the few who might be able to help Roseanne recover. Even asking for the message to be delivered with haste, Catarina worried about the journey. The Vadamon Sea boasted unforgiving storms. But it was the only seed of hope she had. A seed she should have fostered the moment she'd found her sister chained to a wall.

Too frail. Roseanne lay in the same position on the bed she'd been hours ago. Catarina watched for the slow rise and fall of Roseanne's frame, grip tightening on her tea cup at the pause between each movement. Those slow painful breaths had made Catarina desperate enough to force-feed her sister at one point, which was as useless as setting the plate near the woman.

Catarina set the full cup aside and knocked her head against the back of the chair, hoping to release a new idea. She didn't want to lose her sister, not after she'd finally made the choice to return.

"In here?"

Catarina tensed. It couldn't be possible. The journey took too long. Perhaps it was a mere trick of her ears. Since she was thinking about Naomi, the voice sounded like hers. It probably belonged to a servant bringing more medicine and food.

When the door opened, Catarina whipped her head toward the newcomer and her jaw dropped. She could have mistaken the voice, but there was no mistaking the woman in the flesh. Stark white hair brushed Naomi's shoulders, allowing the elf-woman's red-irised eyes to shine bright. High cheekbones and an angular chin matched Naomi's deceptively small frame. Those bones held strength, a strength Catarina would not believe possible had she not witnessed it herself. All Catarina could do was stare. Clad in a tight dark green dress, Naomi crossed her arms, and the pouch hanging off her wrist made a myriad of clinking and jangling sounds. Potions. Medicines. The reasons Catarina had requested Naomi's aid.

"I arrived at port the day your messenger meant to leave."

"I sent the message this morning, Naomi." She gripped her dress-skirts and shook her head. "I wasn't expecting you for two more weeks. If at all."

"I'm here now." Naomi's gaze flickered over the room, resting on the withering Roseanne. "Without aid, she will not be alive in two weeks."

Catarina swallowed and blinked back tears. The elf-woman couldn't know for sure. "That's why I sent the message. I've tried everything I can think to do." She looked at her sister and wiped her cheeks, wishing she had tried harder to help Roseanne recover. "She won't eat. She won't even speak."

"I can cure physical ailments, Catarina." Naomi frowned, her red-irised eyes deepening in color, and pulled the bag of glass bottles from her wrist. "I doubt any of these will help in the way you hope."

"We have to try," Catarina whispered and walked toward Roseanne. Cold stone tingled against her bare feet, interrupted by the occasional dark squares of carpet, one of which Catarina had moved near the head of the bed. She knelt atop it and reached out for her sister, pausing and wondering if it was already too late.

While Catarina's hand remained poised above her sister, Naomi knelt beside her and tsked. "I will look more thoroughly, but you said this is your sister?"

Catarina nodded and grasped Roseanne's hand. Cold. Clammy. Tears rolled down her cheeks. She never should have left her sister's side. She never should have left her daughter. She never should have left her family. Catarina swallowed and shoved aside those useless lines of thought. All she could do was focus on the present and pray to whatever forces cared that her sister would live.

"Similar color to your skin or lighter?"

"A tinge darker, actually," Catarina mumbled, which elicited a faint grunt from Naomi. Though she heard the chinks of glass, Catarina focused on her sister. She shifted Roseanne's hair from her eyes, fingertips brushing her sister's too cold skin. She'd been at others' bedsides as they breathed their last. But most of those had been late in their years. Except those who chose to allow Naomi to remove their magic. Some entered states similar to Roseanne's, but with the right assistance, they recovered and returned home to their families.

Naomi's arm moved above Roseanne's diminutive frame, and Catarina gasped. "Crystals?"

Naomi murmured a phrase Catarina recognized as a portion of elven magic and held the crystal above Roseanne, explaining, "I have learned some of how the human body works. Organs inside provide life. Most of hers are failing."

"So heal them?"

"The person's ability contained in this crystal not only allowed her to heal others but also helped her know how long a person could live in their current condition." Naomi paused, but Catarina refused to witness sympathy from Naomi. "Catarina, she has hours. Not weeks, not days. Hours. Maybe less. This is the first time I've used this crystal, so it's hard to say with any certainty."

"You said that crystal contains the ability to heal. Use it." Catarina's grip on her sister's hand tightened, and she leaned in close to whisper. "Let me help you change your story. Come back to me, Roseanne. Please."

Catarina sensed Naomi's motion at her side, but she focused on her sister's face, willing Roseanne's eyes to open as she stroked her sister's hair. She wanted to make more memories with Roseanne. And this elf-woman who aided magic-bearers by removing magic from those who didn't want the burden was Catarina's last hope. Naomi murmured elvish phrases while working, but Catarina didn't process the words. Murmurs, perhaps a question. Nodding seemed the appropriate reaction, so Catarina did.

At some point, Catarina realized Naomi's movement had stopped. Roseanne's eyes didn't flutter open. Her chest no longer lifted and fell. And the hand Catarina grasped was limp. She tried to speak, but her voice had no sound so she cleared her throat and tried again. "She's gone, isn't she?"

Naomi laid her hand atop Catarina's. "I'm sorry. Magic can only do so much."

CHAPTER FIFTY-TWO

The sparse clump of trees at Lycene's edge offered a modicum of concealment. Xannan recalled appreciating this aspect of the town while housing a group of mercenaries there. Not much around the city to allow an ambush. Few trees and only one major street. No mazes of corridors nor any buildings close together.

From his position behind Rosealyn and Charles, Xannan studied the lackluster town. If Moss's assessment was accurate, the citizens were in the largest building in the center. He vaguely recalled commanding his mercenary army to build it—barracks, dining space, meeting house. Whatever purpose one needed, that building with its exceptionally large room could provide.

Xannan wished he had a choice to sit this out. Let the woman see reality since she refused to consider his advice beyond listening. Even Charles had failed to change Rosealyn's mind. Xannan shifted his shoulders, wishing others hadn't been so logical in their argument about wearing a darker colored coat rather than his vest. Sleeves were atrocious and obnoxious.

Dusk neared. Perfect time to attempt a rescue. Despite Xannan's warning that not annihilating enemy soldiers would cause more problems, Rosealyn stood firm in her decision on taking prisoners.

"They changed their posts," Charles whispered loud enough for all of them to hear. "Moss said no more than two soldiers were guarding each building. Now there's at least five, if not more. Looks like a commander of some sort is in each group now, too."

Xannan analyzed the soldiers' uniforms. At least one of the soldiers in each group had a silver bar on their shoulder that glinted with the setting sun, almost blending into their golden coats. Others wore what appeared to be animal furs. *Odd clothing for soldiers. Must be their colder climate.*

His hand itched to draw his sword and eliminate the threats, but he dug his nails into his palms lest the woman force him not to do anything. "How close do you think the swords will make us stay?"

Rosealyn shrugged. "Should we see if they connect as they did when we fought the droki?"

"I'd prefer not to fight two enemies simultaneously, so I'd recommend avoiding using magic." Xannan glanced askance at Rosealyn, who pressed her lips together but nodded. "Nor do we have the manpower or resources to take these soldiers prisoner."

She scowled at him. "I'm not going to condemn men to death for being soldiers."

He'd expected that response. The woman didn't understand the unfortunate consequences of war. "Soldiers are trained to kill. Either we kill them, or they will kill us."

"There's always another option."

"Not in war."

Xannan tugged at the hem of the strange-fitting coat as he stalked forward, smirking when he heard Rosealyn's muttered curse. The darker clothes and impending night helped him blend in against the darkened wood of the closest building to the city's edge. He listened to the lone soldier's footsteps.

Try not to kill was what she'd said. Not with that frustrating ability of hers, but a simple compassionate request. For a woman attempting to reclaim her country, Rosealyn was too benevolent. Dagger loosened from its sheath opposite his sword, Xannan waited until he could see the soldier's silhouette.

Xannan wrapped his arm tight around the soldier's neck, cutting off his air supply, and sank his dagger into the man's chest. He caught the limp frame, lowering it until the man looked like he'd simply curled up and fell asleep. Some men made this too easy. Unfortunately, the golden coat didn't hide the blood. A quick wipe of his blade on the dead man's coat, Xannan sheathed his dagger and continued into the town.

Every building was guarded, but the group of at least ten in front of the largest building drew his attention. Xannan snaked through the shadows. Behind him, he sensed the closeness of the other blade and motioned over his shoulder for her to return to the cover of trees. He could almost blend in, she would definitely not. Charles's grip on her arm didn't stop her.

She spoke in a heated whisper. "I asked you not to kill anyone."

"Which building first?"

An angry flash of her eyes and she grabbed the hilt of her blade while scanning their surroundings. Occasional voices murmured to one another. No bustle of activity. No screams of terror. Eerie silence that made the hairs of his neck bristle.

While Rosealyn thought, Xannan glanced at Charles, recalling their brief moment of agreement. They both knew how much could go wrong with Rosealyn's plan. Xannan agreed it was noble to free the people and understood that desire, but he anticipated more than one death that night.

"All of them," Rosealyn whispered in a dejected tone and pointed to a building with a mere five guards. One in furs, the others in golden coats, one of whom had a gleam of silver showing along one shoulder. "There. To ask what's going on."

Xannan grunted. "To kill them and see what they're guarding."

"I told you—"

"Rose," Charles whispered, interrupting her. "I hate to admit this, but if we are to have any success in liberating Lycene, it will not be by taking prisoners."

Rosealyn rounded on Charles, and Xannan withheld his chuckle. Whatever the look on her face or whatever she decided to say, Xannan continued moving rather than participate in another useless debate.

Annoyed she'd ignored his advice, again, Xannan decided to prove his point with actions. Besides, it was his country, too. He had no desire to allow enemy soldiers to occupy this land. The best way to solve that problem was to kill them. Quick and efficient.

Approaching a lightly guarded building would allow them to learn what might await in the other buildings. It was also a gamble. By taking out these soldiers in addition to the first, it could alert the others. Though Charles's soldiers were instructed to wait for sunrise and only encroach upon the town if none returned, the enemy soldiers outnumbered them. Not by much, but enough for Xannan to notice.

He paused and glanced at the largest building in the center of the town guarded by ten men. If he had ever taken out ten at once, Xannan didn't remember. Five would be fun. Ten would be plausible but frustrating.

This time he chose against stealth. The other buildings were far enough away. An advantage to the sparsely built town. No matter if that was his fault, it was useful now.

He ranked the five in order of difficulty to annihilate based on stature and movement. Fur, silver-bar, lanky arms, then the two youths.

Xannan drew his sword, appreciative of its comforting weight. Steps purposefully loud, he approached the group, grinning as the fur-cloaked soldier drew his weapon. Slight curve, darkened barbed edges. Poison. Xannan drew his dagger, threw, and winced. He'd missed the heart, but the fur-clad man dropped his sword.

One of the youths retrieved the fallen weapon and attacked wildly with a sword in each hand. Gritting his teeth, Xannan knocked one sword from the youth's hand, then the other, and shoved the boy backward. The soldier lost his balance, fell, and scrambled away. Shouting.

Faint shimmers of gold under moonlight glinted in his periphery. Xannan blocked silver-bar's weapon from meeting his flesh, scanning the pristine metal quickly. A simple, thin blade with no curve or darkened edges. Xannan pressed silver-bar's sword higher, kneed him in the gut, and slashed down, tearing through cloth and flesh alike. Blood splattered the silver bar and shiny gold coat.

One soldier dead, Xannan almost made a motion with his hand. Shaking the confusion from his mind, he returned his attention to the fur-clad man holding his dagger. "That belongs to me."

The aging man's shrug sent another trickle of blood oozing from the wounded shoulder and made the fur cloak fall to the ground. Arm shaking from blood loss and his too tight grip on Xannan's dagger, the gray haired soldier crouched.

Sword held loose at his side, Xannan slashed low, blade slicing along the soldier's abdomen below the thick fur coat. The man gasped and dropped the dagger, pressing against the wound and staring in horror as blood seeped through his fingers. Shock etched across his wrinkled features.

Xannan watched the man fall, head tilted. Different features. Different clothing. A detail had changed since Moss's report.

The elderly soldier's gaze flickered toward the dropped dagger and then at where the younger man who had attacked with two swords had fallen. Empty space. Footprints. When the elderly soldier reached out with his blood-soaked hand for the dagger, Xannan pressed his heel against the man's wrist. Angry eyes met his, and Xannan offered a mocking smile, applying pressure as he retrieved his dagger. No use to wipe them clean. Not yet. He had several dozen soldiers to kill. One at a time.

A grunt sounded behind Xannan, and he turned, surprised to find Charles had gutted one of the three golden-clad soldiers. After removing his sword, Charles said, "You shouldn't have gone off by yourself."

Beside Charles stood a glowering Rosealyn, sword sheathed and arms crossed. "I can't question the dead. And apparently you *both* need to be reminded of that request."

"Too late." Xannan shrugged and resumed his search for the soldier who'd fallen without injury. Nowhere in sight. Three down. Dozens more to go.

Shouts of alarm sounded. Xannan turned to Charles, grimacing. "We both knew what would happen."

At the acknowledgment of their momentary earlier agreement, Charles's jaw clenched tight enough for the muscle near that curious scraggly scar to pulse. "Anticipated, not knew."

Xannan hovered over the once fur-clad soldier whose breathing was labored and sporadic. "If you're so desperate to ask questions, ask this one. Those who can breathe can talk."

Both hands gripping her skirts, Rosealyn appeared as though she wished she could help the man. She lowered halfway to the ground, and the older soldier spat a mouthful of blood in her face. She rocked back on her heels. For a moment, she didn't move. Then with painful slowness she stood and wiped the bloodied spit. "Who's in the building?"

The dying soldier spat again, this time coating her boots. "People."

Xannan twisted, scanning around them. No more shouts. No bustle of movement. No low murmur of conversation. They were forming a united front. It was a waiting game. A tactic he had used himself. If the enemy wants something bad enough, they'll come to you. And Rosealyn was desperate to save these people.

"Useful time for your ability," Xannan murmured, only to receive an icy glare in return. "But remember. Magic brings droki."

CHAPTER FIFTY-THREE

Rosealyn clenched her fists as she processed the dying man. Flashes of a past which seemed so long ago and yet like it had happened yesterday surfaced. She'd never forget how the Hoclian's frame had gone limp. The same features as the man lying below her. Scars across his face like broken glass. Skin paling as blood spilled from his wounds.

Taking in a deep breath, Rosealyn gripped the hilt of her sword and stared down at the already dying man's chest. She didn't want to admit the others were right, that killing the soldiers would be necessary.

Something was amiss in this town. Either Moss hadn't known or he hadn't shared. Her nails dug into her palms, wondering if she had misplaced her trust. No, Moss was loyal. Always had been and Rosealyn believed he always would be. Not knowing wasn't his fault if he hadn't been here to see the new arrivals.

Avoid magic. No need to attract those nasty beasts. She steadied her voice and peered down at the elderly soldier. "Whose people?"

His only response was a sputtering cough.

Teeth gritted, she turned to the two men behind her. One had an ingratiating smirk on his face and held two bloodied blades while the other wore his ever-present facade of worry and had sheathed his weapon. Shoulders rounded, Rosealyn said, "Since he won't tell us, let's go and find out."

"I'm all for killing as many as possible, but this won't work." Xannan gestured at the town with his bloodied dagger. Anger dripped through his usual emotionless tone. "Not the way you hope. Not when they've all gathered in one place to wait for us."

Rosealyn turned to Charles, one brow raised. "Coming?"

Brows furrowed, Charles glanced quickly at Xannan and returned those concerned blue eyes to her. "We should return to the battalion. Regroup." He cleared his throat, the stiffness she'd known for a decade returning. "The dynamic here has changed."

Rosealyn waved an arm at each building as she spoke. "My people are stuck inside these buildings. Trapped by soldiers whose intentions are unknown. I need to know why Hoclians are here. Return to your men if you want. I'm going to rescue my people."

Charles gripped his sword hilt. "Then I'll come with you."

"You said you want to return to your men. Do so." Rosealyn shrugged with a small gesture toward Xannan. "If we allow the blades to connect, I think we could take out the rest of the enemy soldiers on our own."

Charles grasped both of her shoulders. "We can come back in an hour—"

"They could all be dead in an hour!"

"As could we if we don't think this through!"

"Give Xannan and me an hour."

"No." Charles shook his head. "I don't trust him, and I'm worried you'll get yourself killed!"

"And if it were your people trapped in these buildings?" Rosealyn lifted both brows and leveled the fiercest glower she could muster. She wouldn't abandon them when they were in trouble. "Would you let someone talk you into leaving them?"

His jaw tensed, and Charles stepped back, releasing his hold of her, grimacing. That struck a chord. The same as his question had for her after the droki injured several of his men.

Xannan cleared his throat. "They know we're here." He paused as if waiting for an answer and sighed. "No more surprise. If you wish to rescue these people, do so. But it will come at a cost. I recommend proceeding to Vandyl. Or better yet, to Algatha."

Rosealyn resisted the urge to lash out and followed the trail of the now dead soldier's blood through the dirt. She'd trained for this. Studied it. A future queen. A leader. Decisions needed to be made. War was well documented. Who went where, who killed whom, how long or quickly battles could be won. And lost.

They were outnumbered. The idea was to infiltrate without incident. Sneak in and then fight their way out.

"Regroup with the battalion and divide into small groups." Rosealyn reminded herself not to tense. Just because one plan of hers went awry didn't mean the next one would. "They've formed into one large group so let's use that to our advantage and attack from as many sides as possible." Her resolve deepened as she told Charles, "Staggered attacks from all directions. Throw them off. Surprise them. While the soldiers do that, I'll get into the building and free the people. Or whoever is being guarded inside."

"Could work." Charles raked a hand through his hair. He'd let it continue growing, long enough to show the hint of curls Rosealyn recalled mocking. Lowering his hand to his sword hilt, Charles said, "Risky, but possible."

Rosealyn reached her hand out for Charles's, squeezing it as she explained, "I'll wait near the building with Xannan. Last thing I need is for that stupid connection to prevent me from going anywhere."

With her hand in his, Charles faced Xannan, likely pinning the man with a glare.

Before Charles could speak, Xannan held up both hands and rolled his eyes. "I know. She dies. I die. Same threat. Different day." Xannan's gaze flickered toward the Hoclian lying dead on the ground and back to Rosealyn. "Will you continue to be angry if I kill them?"

Rosealyn gritted her teeth and tightened her grip on Charles's hand. He returned the squeeze and blocked her view of Xannan, head bent low to whisper in her ear, "Be careful."

She tilted her head up, lips dangerously close to his as she whispered back, "Always so worried about me?"

One hand resting on the back of her neck, he kissed her. Quick, but passion-filled. Though his hand remained, he pulled his head back just enough to look her in the eyes. "No plan is perfect. Look before you leap and stay observant. Wait for us before you do anything."

Rosealyn smiled. A tense smile she guessed didn't reach her eyes. "Unless there is a reasonable safe option to do so, we will wait for your arrival to enter the building. And then we can refocus our efforts on kicking Nathaniel out of Vandyl."

Charles nodded, looking away as he asked, "If there is no one inside or if those inside are also the enemy . . . what then?"

CHAPTER FIFTY-FOUR

Rosealyn peeked around the building's corner and hoped the shadows kept her well hidden. Behind her, sitting on the ground, was a nonchalant Xannan. Alongside each leg lay his bloodied weapons. While it aggravated her he had to remain close, his presence held an odd soothing aura. A flick of his wrist and trained soldiers died. Rosealyn's heart skipped a beat. He'd wanted to kill her once. Yet here he was, helping.

Back flat against the smoothed wooden side of a house, Rosealyn opened her mouth to speak, but Xannan held a finger to his lips and shook his head. Curling her hands into fists, Rosealyn mentally recited the information they knew.

A strange mix of fur cloaks and golden coats, Hoclians and Alkaanians, all guarded the largest building in the city's center. The buttons of the Alkaanian garb lined the men's sides, easily covered by their arms. Some of the Hoclians wore additional clothing beneath their fur, while others did not. Neither wore armor. Except for bracers on their arms. Rosealyn rubbed her arms, cognizant of her own lack of protection.

No one else roamed the streets. No smoke drifted up from chimneys. No noise beyond the occasional clack of metal against metal when a soldier shifted. As Xannan said, they were waiting for her to move first.

Of all the times she'd waited for something to happen, this had to be the worst. She had time to think about Charles's question. Time to consider if she'd made the right decision, what she might do. Time to worry about her captured people. Time to berate herself for potential mishaps. Most of all, she wondered what was taking Charles so Blazing long.

Rosealyn tied her hair back and turned to Xannan, who shook his head again. No talking. She almost loosened her sword in its sheath, settling for gripping it tightly instead. Any noise out of the ordinary sounds of night would alert them. She pressed her lips together to avoid biting at her lower lip. Simple and direct: rescue the people, take the soldiers captive.

She stole another glance at the gathered group. One hundred to their less than fifty. But strategy could be as effective as brute force. Even Gailin once used the tactic, though she wondered if the ancient king's ideas had actually been Xannan's.

As the wait continued, Rosealyn's mind drifted to the clarity and strength she'd experienced when the swords had worked in unison. Such a wealth of power. Despite having felt it course through her, Rosealyn struggled to understand it. She glanced down at Xannan's blade. Crystal muddied with those mingling and ever-moving clouds of gray, barely visible through the dried blood.

Curiosity, her father once told her, might be the death of her. And she supposed using the weapons together could, especially since magic attracted droki. She wanted to try, though. Not to create that ridiculous dragonsword, but to use them as the weapons Celena had named Futurae and Praeteritum. Rosealyn wondered what could be accomplished by harnessing that power, should it happen again.

Shouts sounded on the far side of the gathered group. Xannan grasped both weapons and stood with a heated whisper. "Finally."

Rosealyn leaned around the building, holding out an arm to stop Xannan from walking around her. Though many of the soldiers had taken the bait, ten remained facing their direction.

"Around the back?" Rosealyn asked, keeping her voice soft and low.

"Or through them."

Rosealyn continued to block Xannan with an arm. "Wait for a clear path."

"Create one." Xannan pressed against Rosealyn's arm and grunted, pointing with his blood-streaked dagger. "We have to fight them. Either on our way in or on the way out. If they're—"

"I hate it when you're right." Rosealyn dropped her arm and took a deep breath. "How long does it take for droki to sense magic?"

Xannan blanched, appraising her. "Minutes, hours. Your guess is as good as mine. Why?"

"Our swords—"

"Are swords. Use yours as such." Xannan surveyed the men. "And please don't die. I don't want to deal with Charles trying to kill me."

Xannan stalked forward, leaving Rosealyn to process his words. Those two would never get along. It was a miracle she was fighting alongside him tonight.

Chaotic shouts overwhelmed Rosealyn, mingled with metallic rings meeting again. And again. Sick thuds as men fell. Cries of terror. Of pain. Of command. Smoke invaded her vision when soldiers tossed torches into buildings that were, hopefully, unoccupied.

Riveted in place, Rosealyn's world blurred. She gulped down air. Then coughed on the smoke. The drawing of her sword seemed to last an eternity and no time at all. *Breathe. Think. Look. Find a path.*

Except she need not find a path because Xannan was creating one. His sword and dagger were as much of a flurry as Moss's quarterstaff. Rosealyn coughed on a mouthful of smoke, eyes burning as she reminded herself to move. She skirted the edge of the unspoken fighting circle. Occasional ducks beneath swinging weapons. A few quick parries to knock her opponent aside. Forward. To free her people from whatever imprisonment these soldiers had given them.

A weapon grazed along her back, followed by a gurgle. Rosealyn whipped around in time to watch Xannan pull his dagger from an Al-kaanian's neck. He shoved his boot into the back of the soldier's knees, moving on before the man thudded to the dirt.

"Almost there." Xannan nodded for her to continue and moved forward, claiming a Hoclian's life by piercing his side and another Al-kaanian by stabbing that soldier's heart.

Rosealyn couldn't respond. Blood soiled dirt, clothing, its scent permeating the air and mingling with the sweat.

Her sword with its divots and scratches remained clean. All she had to do was move forward. Take one step. Then another. She swiveled her head from side to side. Cautious. Tense.

So far, all was working as planned. Minus the death. She'd known there would be a cost. Once again, Xannan was right.

An arrow grazed her scalp, and she gasped, hunting for Xannan as she walked backward up the few stairs leading to the main doors. He was occupied with several soldiers and appeared to be toying with them. Desperate to locate Charles, or Moss, Rosealyn scanned the fighters for familiar faces until the tip of a sword invaded her vision.

"It's uncommon for Jearnian women to fight." A Hoclian, by the accent. Gruff, deep, slurred. "But you don't look like one of them."

Rosealyn faced the Hoclian, forcing her breaths to remain controlled. "I am here for the people of Lycene. Allow me to escort—"

The Hoclian's low, deep laugh made his sword waver and shook his entire body. Rosealyn knocked his sword aside, planted her foot in the center of his chest, and shoved. The motion worked. His sword clattered down the stairs, and he stumbled, cursing when he landed awkwardly and followed the sword's path until he, too, sat on the ground below her. Rosealyn ran to the building's entrance and shouldered the doors open.

She gagged and held the back of her hand to her mouth. Too shocked to speak, she realized why the first Hoclian hadn't given a direct answer.

Even if she had used her ability, the man wouldn't have labeled them as people. Because they were dead. Her people lay in pools of blood, fear-stricken lifeless faces accusing her one after the other.

Fur-clad men and women surrounded the bodies. Rosealyn's chest heaved, stomach churning at the overwhelming scent of death. She whispered a benediction for her fallen people.

"Good evening, Princess."

Rosealyn tensed. She recognized that gruff Hoclian slur. Chills ran down her spine, and sweat beaded along her hairline. A swirling gust of wind loosened several strands of hair from its string, causing them to drift across her vision. She straightened and swallowed down the creeping bile.

"Why are you here, Jordan?" Rosealyn gritted out. Her resolve not to kill those who opposed her faltered with each prone figure she added to her mental tally. "You have Pasea. What more could you want?"

CHAPTER FIFTY-FIVE

Rosealyn kept her sword lowered. Words before swords. Her father's words had been somewhat effective with the Honorable Jordan. Perhaps hers would work better, with or without using magic.

Jordan approached, a smirk on her unmarred face. The soldiers held their weapons. With a shift of the woman's shoulders, the fur coat fell to the floor. The thought of finding more enemies had crossed Rosealyn's mind, especially when Charles had asked her the question, but faced with the problem she had no idea what to do next.

"The usual reasons are land and resources, yes?" Jordan lifted one bare shoulder, and her arms bulged with muscle as she spread her hands. "This is about more."

"I gave you land and what resources I could." Rosealyn watched Jordan's slow movement warily, clenching her teeth together when Jordan chuckled.

Small, almost dainty despite her thickness, Jordan flicked her hand, and the surrounding Hoclians sheathed their blades. "You gave me land which no longer produces." Jordan's voice deepened into a thicker drawl. "And you knew that."

Rosealyn failed to hide her wince and tried to relax her arms. "So you massacred a city for what? Payment?"

"You got my people killed, so I killed some of yours," Jordan said, tone more emotionless than Xannan's. "I brought several hundred to that cliff less than a day's ride from this decaying little town." Jordan shook her head, beaded necklace clacking together at the movement, and sneered. "Do you know how many I brought home?"

Rosealyn's throat went dry, tongue numb to any words. Her grip tightened and loosened on her sword as Jordan took one slow step after another. Through the open doors behind her, clashes and desperate shouts continued. Rosealyn swore she could hear Charles's voice rise above the others, giving orders.

Jordan pulled her sword free. Slow. Painstakingly slow. With an appreciative gaze, Jordan eyed the weapon, displaying more malice than Rosealyn would have guessed from their prior interactions.

"Go on. Give me an answer." Jordan leveled her sword at Rosealyn's chest.

Rosealyn swallowed, gaze flickering from one soldier to the next. Four, five, six, ten. More.

"One." Jordan's sword didn't waver nor did her arm tremble. "Even that devilish little King Nathaniel went home with around a hundred of his men wounded but alive." She lifted her chin, fury glowing in pale eyes that matched her hair. "Me? I alone survived that beast's attack. I offered my aid, lost two troops of men, and my reward is blighted fields?"

"I'm sorry about that. I am." Rosealyn resisted the urge to step away from Jordan. "I did not think a dragon's flame so deadly."

Jordan grunted, a scoffing sound that made Rosealyn flinch. "Nathaniel is thriving on this idea of war, of taking. It was his idea to annihilate this town. I chose to be his weapon. We were both right, too. Believed you would check on Lycene before heading to Vandyl."

Her breath was becoming harder to control, her sword harder to grip, and Rosealyn's thoughts tumbled. She needed to find a way out. And learn how either Jordan or Nathaniel had learned of her whereabouts.

Rosealyn assumed a regal posture and used a voice she hoped sounded like a queen and not a desperate naïve princess. "You have committed an act of war against Orda'an, which I speak for. To prevent—"

"Do you?" Jordan rested the sword on her shoulder. A thin layer of liquid glistened on its edge. Poison. The poison Rosealyn had avoided in her first fight with a Hoclian. "Speak for Orda'an, that is?"

"I am its rightful heir." Rosealyn nodded, reminding herself of the fact. "Do not hold the people of Orda'an's cities responsible for my choices."

Jordan's eyes twinkled with strange curiosity. The change gave Rosealyn the sinking feeling she didn't know all the details, that other cities had also been massacred. She resumed her mental tally of the dead, heartbeat pounding faster with each addition.

When she reached twenty, Jordan spoke again. "Tell me, rightful heir of Orda'an, do you like to create treaties as your father did?"

Rosealyn's gaze fell on a child whose neck had been slashed with a ragged blade. Blood covered his fingers and the sides of his mouth. Her heartbeat became erratic, and though she wanted to lift the sword, she sheathed the weapon and whispered, "Discussion is a preferable first method of resolving conflict, yes."

The twinkle of Jordan's eyes increased with her smirk. "Provide me with more land and a guarantee it will properly produce. In exchange, I will kill only up to the same number of men I lost in the battle with Eilon. Not a soul more." She snapped her fingers, and a soldier approached with a rolled parchment. "I've already drafted the document."

Rosealyn gasped and stepped backward. "I— You—" Her fists clenched. Unclenched. Clenched again. She could force Jordan's hand. One sentence, and she could force this Hoclian leader who was far from honorable despite her official title to return home and never return. A deep inhale, so deep she felt her stomach press against her sword belt. She held the hilt, ready to draw the weapon, "No."

"No?" Jordan raised a brow, mouthing the word again with a shake of her head. "Interesting choice."

Rosealyn's arms trembled from the effort not to attack. "Return home, Jordan."

"I seek payment for my losses along with retribution for a faulty offering." Jordan flicked away the soldier holding the parchment and chuckled.

The call from the weapons indicated Xannan was behind her. If anyone else was there, they didn't speak. Rosealyn focused on Jordan's sword and the soldiers standing watch around the room filled with too many dead. Those screams from the Gift, the ones which had sounded all too familiar, were her people suffering. And she hadn't been able to assist. She wanted to identify the wounded, but Rosealyn's focus had to remain on Jordan.

"I cannot guarantee what land will thrive, Jordan. None of us can." Rosealyn's grip on her sword tightened, the raised LeNoir crest pressing into the tender skin of her palm. "I will not condemn innocent people to death."

Rosealyn knew the words were wrong. She couldn't take them back, not as Jordan's sword arced through the air. She blocked the Hoclian's poison-lined blade from sinking into her shoulder. Barely. Rosealyn shoved and sidestepped. Rage emanated from Jordan's scrunched visage. Growling, Jordan used the momentum to swing with increasing force.

"It's her fight. Do *not* interfere," Xannan said, momentarily distracting Rosealyn from Jordan's flurry of movement.

Arm rattling from Jordan's last strike, Rosealyn recited the lifelong mantra she'd learned from her father. *Defend. Don't attack.*

Her father's motto seemed useless as her chest tingled. She had another way.

Jordan lunged, and her poison-lined blade was a silver blur. Rosealyn struggled to keep it from slicing the exposed skin of her arms. Slit sleeves ending at the elbow were great for ease of movement. Not so great against the Hoclian leader's weapon.

Rosealyn twisted away from Jordan's rush of slashing strikes and swung her sword from high above, hard enough to make her opponent drop the sword. Jordan didn't. The flurry of movement began anew. Up and down, Rosealyn watched Jordan's shoulders and feet until she shoved against Jordan's blade with enough force for them to stand several feet apart again.

Chest heaving, Rosealyn mumbled a curse and uttered a single firm word. "Stop."

With a tilt of the head, Jordan attempted to take a step. Face scrunched in pain, she grunted and attempted to push her sword forward only to emit an annoyed harrumph.

"That's different." Jordan gave Rosealyn a slight appreciative nod and sat cross-legged on the ground with her sword resting across both of her knees. "Only death is forever. I shall wait." She gestured to the soldiers lining the room, the men and women likely responsible for the death of Rosealyn's people. Jordan smiled smugly. "You will not leave here alive."

The Hoclian soldiers at the edges of the room moved forward. The singular command to Jordan had been a gamble, and Rosealyn worried it would not work on so many at once. Glancing to the side, Rosealyn found that Charles had joined Xannan. Why the man had told Charles not to interfere, she wasn't sure.

"Is it over outside?" Rosealyn asked Charles, keeping a wary watch of the advancing Hoclian soldiers.

Dark spots dotted his face, and he grimaced. "Almost. But it's not good. We need to end this. Before more are lost."

Rosealyn's heart skipped a beat, and she faced Jordan. "That's what you want, isn't it? The more we kill of your people, the more you will kill of mine?"

Jordan shrugged, and Rosealyn almost screamed. At least the command was working. No movement from Jordan. Only the Hoclian soldiers had moved. Hands ready to draw weapons, they encroached on the small space where Rosealyn, Charles, and Xannan stood. One movement, and they'd attack.

"Sometimes defending also means you need to attack, Rose." Charles's words were clipped. "If you leave Jordan alive, she will kill again. Look at what she's already done."

Her gaze found Charles's again. Found the pity, the understanding, the weight of the decision she needed to make. Loud clanging to her right pulled her away from Charles's sorrowful expression to witness Xannan gut one soldier and throw his dagger into another's chest. A line formed to block his path. Toward Jordan. He wouldn't leave the Hoclian alive.

"Stop," Rosealyn whispered. Too soft, without proper conviction. Three more soldiers surrounded Xannan, and he took them out, too. Six soldiers left, not including Jordan. Xannan didn't stop. His strikes aimed to kill. Perhaps Xannan was as angry about these deaths as she, considering he had once mentioned his own claim to her throne. Soldiers were one thing, civilians another.

Transfixed, Rosealyn couldn't peel her focus away as Xannan plowed through the soldiers. The Hoclian leader stayed seated cross-legged on the floor, hands resting loosely atop the sword balanced on each knee, face blank as Xannan struck down each of her remaining soldiers.

Rosealyn took two long strides forward, blocking Xannan's downward strike before he took Jordan out permanently. The moment their swords met, the glow began, and the silver facade of her blade turned a bold white. She wrenched her weapon away before the magic could continue its work, fearful it would merge and render her unconscious. Or bring the brainless droki.

Swallow. Inhale. Rosealyn said, "Do not kill Jordan."

He glared over his shoulder at her with almost as much anger as Jordan had. Holding his gaze, Rosealyn repeated, "Do not kill Jordan."

"Funny." Jordan rose in one fluid motion, sword resuming its position on her shoulder. "Your country is no longer yours. Those who maintained it in your absence have been killed."

"My uncles—" Rosealyn dared not finish the thought.

The Hoclian leader smirked. "Nathaniel didn't flinch at the blood, surprisingly. He's been enjoying his time in Vandyl. And now it appears I'll be adding at least another fifty to my tally."

"Soldiers know—"

"Save the speech." Jordan sheathed her sword and settled her fur coat back on her shoulders, reveling in the carnage. "You are fighting a war you've already lost."

Rosealyn screeched, drew her sword, and pressed it against the base of the Hoclian's neck. She ground her teeth and hefted her sword to her opposite hand to swing her stronger arm at Jordan's jaw. Jordan stumbled to the side and rubbed her jaw, regaining her balance and glaring at Rosealyn, whose sword rested on Jordan's chest.

Rosealyn pressed harder, drawing a thin line of blood. "The only thing I've lost is the people you and Nathaniel killed."

Jordan shrugged. "You will accomplish nothing by killing me."

"I know." Rosealyn applied more pressure. "I want to kill you for what you've done to these people, but I won't." Her chest heaved with the effort not to shove her sword through Jordan's chest. The woman had information she could use. "You will tell your soldiers to stand down, and you will answer for your actions here. And you will share what you know."

Jordan flicked a finger against the glowing white crystalline blade. "Always thought those swords were a myth. Until Eilon."

A rush of footsteps accompanied by heavy breathing preceded Moss's announcement. "All enemy soldiers are neutralized."

Rosealyn smiled faintly at the words, not letting her sword stray from Jordan's chest. "Lay your sword on the ground."

Lips pursed, Jordan obliged. For someone surrounded with a sword pointed at her, Jordan was far too much at ease.

"Where is the rest of your army?"

"Waiting." Jordan smirked, hands raised.

"Waiting where?" Rosealyn asked, wondering how to know the difference between the successful earlier command and a simple series of questions.

No response.

Rosealyn turned so both Jordan and Moss were visible and said, "Bind her." She lowered her sword after Moss tied the woman's hands behind her. "We keep her alive, learn what we can before approaching Vandyl."

After the earlier exchange of blows, it surprised Rosealyn that Jordan didn't fight back. She had details Rosealyn didn't. Starting with her uncles and how many other cities had met this same fate.

While Moss led Jordan from the building, Charles wrapped his hand around hers and took the sword, whose blade remained a glowing white crystalline, from her hand. Another detail Rosealyn needed to process.

"How are you doing?" An edge of despair tainted Charles's gentle tone.

She moved to survey the room, but Charles gently guided her gaze back to him. Words seemed impossible. Nothing she could think to say would encompass how it felt to see this sight.

"We should check—" Rosealyn paused as the emotions she'd subdued during her confrontation with Jordan swelled in the form of a lump climbing a quick path up her throat. A thick swallow, she whispered, "I should check for survivors."

"Rose—"

She pulled away, shaking her head, ignoring the blurring of her vision as she approached the first prone figure. A woman, probably close in age to herself. At twenty-four, perhaps this woman was preparing for a wedding or eager to begin a family, only to be stabbed in the chest because she was Orda'anian. One after another, Rosealyn knelt at their side, heart sinking and tears falling as the number of dead climbed until she no longer had the will to continue counting. Many were faces she remembered darting through the castle hallways.

Eventually, Rosealyn lost the desire to move while kneeling beside an older child. Tall, lanky, he should be visiting trade masters and choosing an apprenticeship.

"Sacrifices." Charles's voice made her look up, wiping at her cheeks as she did. He lowered to his knees and set the glowing white sword between them. The dark spots covering his face earlier were gone. "All monarchs make sacrifices."

She etched the young boy's face into memory, a reminder of whom she was meant to protect. "Our people should not bear the weight of our decisions."

"They always will, Rose." He released a lengthy exhale and sounded as confused as she felt. "Our people will reap the benefits of our good choices and suffer the consequences of our mistakes. You cannot blame yourself for Jordan's actions. There's no way you could have known the 'Honorable Jordan' would seek this type of revenge."

"And if Jordan's right? What if I'm asking you to help me fight a war I've already lost?"

Charles gripped her shoulder. "I can't recall a time I've seen you admit defeat. Not until every possibility has been explored and tried."

Rosealyn rested her head on Charles's shoulder and sniffled. "Your men?"

"Ten wounded." He hesitated, whispering, "Twenty of my battalion are . . . dead." Charles shifted to cross his legs, raking a hand through his hair once he settled.

The earlier edge to his tone, Rosealyn realized as she watched his jolting movements, had to have been him fighting to keep his emotions from showing. "The rest are tired but alive. Omar and Levi organized groups to check the other buildings, care for the wounded, and watch over the prisoners."

"I thought the only prisoner we had was Jordan?"

Charles wrapped his arm around her and kissed the top of her head, speaking into her hair. "I know how much you hate the idea of killing without reason. And I agree with that, when it's possible."

She patted his hand and nestled her head deeper into his shoulder. Silent sobs racked her body, held steady by Charles's tense arm. For a time, Rosealyn soaked in his comforting presence. His arm didn't move from her shoulders.

"Proper burials for *all* those who died is our first priority." Rosealyn stood, wiping her tear-streaked palms on her dress. She sheathed her sword, grimacing when she met Charles's red-rimmed eyes. A massacre like this would not happen again, not while she was alive to prevent it. "Then I'm questioning Jordan."

CHAPTER FIFTY-SIX

Silence surrounded Rosealyn, broken by the occasional footsteps of those standing watch outside the vacated buildings of Lycene. She had two options. Stay and continue arguing about what to do next. Or leave and reclaim Vandyl on her own. Almost on her own. Xannan would have to come, she reminded herself as she shoved more food from one of the food storage closets they'd found into a pouch.

After shouldering the pouch, Rosealyn pulled her sword far enough from its sheath to confirm the blade remained white. With a small sigh, she shifted the belt around her waist, wishing Gailin were alive so she could ask him about the blades. Or she could force Celena to answer more questions, but who knew when the elf-woman would randomly appear again. Rosealyn exited the building and tugged on each strap, wishing they were shorter.

Xannan leaned against the wooden frame of the building, one ankle crossed over the other in his common lackadaisical pose. "Leaving without telling anyone, are we?"

She descended the porch steps in quick succession. "Glad I don't have to wake you."

"Obnoxious, that tug of the connection." Xannan pushed away from the building and pulled on the straps to stop her. Moonlight glinted off the too-pale skin of his bare arms. No more long sleeves for him despite the chilly pre-dawn air. She doubted he would be convinced to change again. Not that it had made a difference. "Why are we leaving before dawn?"

"Charles would try to stop me by saying I should wait for reinforcements. Adela wants to come with me and probably get herself killed." Rosealyn shifted the pouch on her shoulder, surveying the surrounding area. Two days was not nearly enough time for the injured to recover. Nor was it enough time for the blood staining the dirt to dissipate. "So, yes, leaving before dawn without telling anyone."

Xannan frowned. "That's a bad idea."

Rosealyn glared and motioned for an explanation.

He studied her, visage too analytical for Rosealyn's liking. He walked back toward where she was supposed to be sleeping. Rosealyn gritted her teeth and followed. This venture would only mean more arguments. What came next was her choice alone.

Chills crawled down her arms as they passed the mass of dirt mounds. She'd insisted on separate burial sites for each person, soldier or citizen. That simple honorable act had led several Alkaanians to inform her that both her country and Jearnia had been infiltrated by spies. Logical, given their leaders' desperation to claim her land. Despite the recent famine, Orda'an continued to boast the best produce. After Jearnia, but few traded with the Jearnians.

Xannan paused near the building she had shared for the past two nights with a restless Adela and an exhausted Viola. The young maid had proved useful in aiding the injured while Adela demanded to speak with Jordan. Rosealyn refused the request since it would only increase Adela's frustration as it had her own.

Shoulder-length blond hair drifting across his face, Xannan appeared contemplative and curious. "So the plan now is to infiltrate your own castle and, what, kill Nathaniel?"

"At the very least kick him out of my home."

Xannan chuckled softly. "You are good at kicking people. Removing Nathaniel from Vandyl will not solve the greater problem."

"We've been down this line of discussion. My first instinct is not to kill my opponent."

Xannan shrugged. "Killing eliminates the threat. Permanently."

"Does it, though?" Rosealyn asked, grimacing at the few rays of sun setting the horizon aglow. Dawn was closer than she'd assumed. She gestured at the burial sites and the singed buildings. "More than one can hold the same aspirations. As evidenced by Jordan joining Nathaniel."

"True." Xannan jerked his head toward the building. "Charles went inside a few minutes ago. Looking for you, I presume."

"I don't need to speak with Charles. I need to go to Vandyl. If I could go without you, I would."

"You don't *want* to speak with Charles. You should—"

"Are you giving me relationship advice?" Rosealyn's brows climbed, incredulous. "You? Of all people?"

"What do you know of me, Rosealyn?"

She opened her mouth but closed it when Xannan flinched and muttered, "Don't answer that."

Rosealyn squinted at him and pressed her lips together. More winds brought the fresh scent of morning dew though it barely coated the lingering stench of death. She rubbed her tingling skin to warm it, thinking. Some nights she fell asleep wondering if she had, in some ways, forgiven Xannan for killing her father. He had claimed, on multiple occasions, that act wasn't his choice. Other nights the ferocious anger she harbored for him resurfaced. Yet after a month of the ridiculous connection, Rosealyn realized she pitied him. Before Eilon had stolen Xannan away and lied to him for generations, he'd had a life. A life he could never reclaim.

"You mentioned a name once." Rosealyn waited for his retort, but he flattened a mound of dirt with the toe of his boot. "Who was Anna?"

Xannan shoved both hands in his pockets, which appeared awkward with his sword on one side and dagger on the other. His shoulders fell, and he didn't lift his head. "She died a week before we were to be wed." The words were quiet and reverent. "A week before Father changed his mind about the succession—mostly because of my actions after Anna's . . . and my mother's death. Anna was everything to me. And Eilon killed her to get to me." Xannan tilted his head back to the sky. "That was the truth I saw when the blades combined. Why I killed him."

Rosealyn waited, wondering if he wished to say more. When the silence lingered too long, she whispered, "I'm sorry for your loss."

Pulling both hands from his pockets, Xannan nodded and flicked a hand toward the building. "I'm an observant, albeit often frustrated, shadow. Talk to him. And if he wants to come with you, let him." His green eyes met hers with a fierceness she'd not yet witnessed. "If I could have protected Anna and prevented her death, even if it meant my own . . . Do not deny him that choice."

Rosealyn gripped the straps of her pouch, murmuring, "It's odd when you're nice like this."

Face hidden by his blond locks, the smirk in Xannan's voice was clear. "Perhaps I am not the man you first encountered."

"Well, you do prefer to kill first and ask questions later."

That elicited a chuckle. "True." He tilted his head, and for once his smirk didn't make her want to punch him. "Go. I won't be far." Xannan patted the hilt of his sword as an unneeded reminder.

Rosealyn sighed, lowered the pouch of supplies to the ground, and climbed the stairs into the building, steeling her nerves for the impending arguments. Like Xannan said, if Charles wished to join their journey, she shouldn't stop him. In fact, she probably should have asked him to come with her. But Adela and Viola would most definitely be staying here.

Before she'd stepped through the door, Adela blurted, "I'm coming with you. I need—"

"No, Aunt Adela. You're not coming with me. Stay here where there will be at least some protection for you." Rosealyn let the door swing closed behind her. Her aunt must have been pacing the length of the small room. Viola sat on one of the beds, appearing as though she would fall asleep while sitting upright.

Next to the door, Charles stood with arms crossed. Scowling. Rosealyn shifted her shoulders, unused to viewing anger marring Charles's kind features.

Adela invaded Rosealyn's line of sight, seething, "That Hoclian claims Nathaniel killed my brothers!"

"I'm aware." Rosealyn noted her aunt's rigid shoulders and haggard appearance. A haphazard once-pristine sandy-blond braid rested over Adela's shoulder, its color seeming too dull next to her sallow skin.

Adela flipped the braid off her shoulder. "I'd like to see for myself."

"And do what, Aunt Adela?" Rosealyn tensed and stood taller. This wasn't the first time they'd had this discussion. "If Jordan is to be believed, Nathaniel already occupies Vandyl. That means I'll have to fight my way in." When Rosealyn gripped her sword hilt, Adela flinched. "You're not a fighter, Aunt Adela."

Adela bristled. "I know enough."

"My answer remains the same." Rosealyn didn't shift her gaze from her aunt's. This was an interesting aspect of life, learning to give orders to those who had once taught her. "Stay here, Aunt Adela. If I've not returned in a week, then you may do as you see fit."

"Fine." Adela plopped onto her bed, pulled the braid back over her shoulder, and tugged. "One week. And in that time, I *will* be speaking with Jordan."

CHAPTER FIFTY-SEVEN

"I'm sure the Hoclian will remain silent. As she has for the past two days." Charles adjusted his lean against the wall, stiffening. He recognized the look on Rosealyn's face. No matter what he or Adela said, Rosealyn had chosen her path. The last remaining strength he had for arguing with her decision fled. Charles could handle staying behind. He'd take his men back to Volante and make preparations to protect that home by rooting out whatever spies Hoclia and Alkaan had planted. He almost placed his hands in his pockets but kept his arms crossed to hide his clenched fists. If he stayed, he would break his promise to himself and to Phillippe. Offer aid and protection. Charles forced his fists to unclench, unable to look at Rosealyn. "Are you leaving now?"

A pause preceded Rosealyn's whisper. "I am. Well, we are. Xannan's waiting outside."

Charles tugged his collar away from his neck. Somehow, his anger toward Xannan had dissipated. Three weeks earlier he'd feared Xannan would kill Rosealyn the moment the connection between the swords was broken. Though Xannan preferred to kill first, Charles believed the man no longer saw Rosealyn as an enemy. This rash Nathaniel, however, was an adversary all of them wished to destroy in different ways. While Xannan wanted to destroy the boy's castle, Charles had recommended a conversation. Rosealyn had listened and made her own decision.

Wood striations made for excellent studying when Charles didn't want to know Rosealyn's answer before hearing it. "Were you trying to leave without telling anyone?"

"I thought it would be easier." Rosealyn ventured closer, stopping when her brown boots blocked his study of the floor. Charles looked up to find her smooth dark skin creased in a myriad of emotions. Confusion. Sadness. Worry. Resolve. All emotions evident in the words she spoke, too. "I didn't want to argue again. But here I am. Having another conversation that will lead to the same conclusion. I am going to take Vandyl back from Nathaniel."

A part of him swelled at seeing this level of resolve from her, especially that she had not raced off on her own. That showed she understood the importance of the help being offered. Not that it was much anymore. Ten capable fighters with an additional ten injured would be of little use in reclaiming Vandyl. Those numbers would not be enough if Jordan's army arrived at Lycene, as Charles worried it would considering the Hoclian leader's smug confidence despite being tied up inside a building.

Charles's shoulders fell, torn between wanting to travel with her and to stay with his men. "You don't want me to come with you. Do you?"

Eyes closed, Rosealyn tilted her face up to his, eyes darting as they searched his.

"I don't." Rosealyn uncrossed his arms, taking each of his hands in hers. "And I do."

Brows raised, Charles couldn't stop the smallest hint of a smile. "Someone's starting to worry about me as much as I worry about her."

"Possibly," she whispered as she squeezed both of his hands. The woman searching his eyes was not the princess from six months earlier who had raced off on her own to help protect a town she'd never visited. Rosealyn's face softened into a small smile. "The choice is yours, Charles. You've done more than enough already. Lost soldiers. And with no contact from Christopher since we left, I wouldn't blame you for wanting to return home once everyone can travel."

Had he not been standing hand in hand with her, he might have taken a step back. A choice. Not an argument that the fewer who traveled with her, the better. The mention of no news from Christopher made the muscles of his jaw tighten. Silence from his brother meant either no news to share or the messenger had gotten lost. Worse, Christopher could have gotten himself killed. Charles doubted that last, though he wondered if something terrible had happened that his brother couldn't write down.

"I promised Christopher I would trust him to do his best. If I race home after two weeks of no news, I would be betraying my own words." A deep breath, he was prevented from moving his hands when Rosealyn tightened her grip. The pressure made him smile. Though she had not voiced it in the same manner, he knew those feelings were there. Even knowing she was capable of sneaking into her own castle, the long ingrained command, and subsequent desire, to protect her never seemed to leave him. "I'm sure you would appreciate more pleasant company than that one waiting outside. Besides, Omar and Levi can handle things here."

"So he can go, but I can't?"

At Adela's words, Rosealyn tensed. "You agreed to stay, Aunt Adela." Rosealyn glanced over her shoulder, voice hardening. "I need you to fight for Orda'an if anything happens to me."

That made Charles's grip on Rosealyn's hands tighten. She would be a better leader than he and deserved the chance to prove it. He followed her gaze to Viola, the young maid who had been a wonderful asset to their group. Rosealyn released his hands and sat by Viola.

"I can hear your worry, my lady," Viola whispered, stealing a glance toward him. At his small nod, Viola added. "His Majesty asked me to escort those too injured to fight back home. I'm to find other maids with similar skills and travel with a new battalion to Vandyl."

Rosealyn's head snapped toward him, and he swallowed as she said, "You didn't tell me that."

At least she isn't telling me not to. Charles tugged at both of his sleeves and, out of habit, settled into the common stance of a soldier. "Hard to tell you anything when you've been avoiding me for the past day."

Her lips tightened, but she didn't deny it.

"Viola's skills saved several men's lives these past two days by caring for wounds in ways I never knew existed. My men need to recover." He drummed his fingers against the sword hilt. "Even if you succeed in gaining access to the castle and speaking with Nathaniel directly, you'll need soldiers to tip the scales in your favor." Charles expected her to argue against the idea. Though it had been his choice to command his army to aid her, he knew she felt responsible for the lives lost. But he had yet to think of a way to win any war without taking lives. "Removing an enemy's leader is only a small part of winning the war."

"True." Rosealyn smiled at Viola and embraced the maid who seemed to be more a friend than a servant. "Keep practicing so you can protect yourself. Got it?"

"I will, my lady. Sire." Viola gave a brief nod to each.

After another quick embrace, Rosealyn stood and gave her aunt the same treatment. Her farewells complete, Rosealyn led them outside, pausing beyond the door. Before them, Xannan was speaking with a Jearnian, laughing about something. Xannan was obviously at home around soldiers, and after witnessing Xannan's prowess in battle when they'd attacked Lycene, the Jearnian soldiers accepted him.

Rosealyn nudged Charles's arm with her elbow, pulling his attention toward her as she asked with a slight smirk, "Are you going to threaten him once an hour? Or once per day?"

"Only as necessary." Charles gently elbowed her back, grateful she'd not disappeared in the middle of the night. "Thank you for not leaving without telling me."

"Thank him." Rosealyn gestured toward Xannan and chuckled when Charles raised a brow. "It is not my story to tell."

CHAPTER FIFTY-EIGHT

Occasional light from the full moon pierced through the gathering storm clouds, casting the empty plains with an eerie glow. Rosealyn scanned the land and wished she knew how to cultivate the crops properly. Most of the fields they'd passed during their four-day trek back to her home were empty. Dark clouds lining the northern sky threatened a torrent of rain. Rosealyn shivered. Or snow. Perhaps a wetter winter would equal a more prosperous spring. If Eilon's magic had died with him. She rubbed her palms together, cupped them, and breathed into them to warm her numb fingers.

She leaned against a tree, the first of many bordering the space where they'd set up their tents at sunset. Despite the empty roadways, Rosealyn insisted on setting a watch. Charles kept watch first and woke her after a few hours. After her turn, Xannan would take the final watch. With the rise of the sun, they'd continue their slow trek to Vandyl.

Rosealyn rubbed her arms, visualizing the last moments she'd spent in Vandyl. One moment she had been reading her father's final words, and the next her cheek had been buried in the mud of a cave after she was magically transported by the young Synda. Rosealyn frowned, wondering where Synda might be. The dragon's ability to appear somewhere else in an instant would have proved quite useful. Rosealyn dismissed the thought. None of her silent pleas had worked.

Perhaps Synda or another dragon hadn't listened because Celena had concocted other plans.

Jaw aching as she yawned, Rosealyn tipped her head back against the tree. Unbraided hair snagged on the bark when she jolted at a wolf's howl. Her scalp tingled where the braids usually lay. Unbound, her wavy auburn hair spilled across her shoulders and swayed with the breeze, tickling her nose and cheeks. She gathered the straying locks and held them to one side while listening to the rustling leaves and soft whistle of wind. Rain lingered on the air, bringing a somber heaviness.

Through the threatening storm clouds and surrounded by a smattering of pulsing stars, the moon reached its zenith. Before the moon reached the center of the night sky once more, she would reclaim her home. Or die trying.

A comforting quiet enveloped her. They'd considered all possibilities. The repairs to the castle, Nathaniel's resources, the supplies Jordan had sent to the younger king, and how to gain access to the Orda'anian soldiers. Each plan had its contingencies. But all ensured she and Xannan got inside the castle to confront Nathaniel. Charles offered the possibility of a secondary infiltration if she and Xannan hadn't returned by nightfall.

Covering her mouth as she yawned, Rosealyn traced the cold metal engraving of the LeNoir crest on her sword hilt. Two swords between two dragons, separated by a cloud of smoke. Two halves of a whole. As the wind shifted her hair across her face again, she wrinkled her nose. She hadn't realized how well those two braids held her hair out of the way.

Storm winds whipped around her, lifting her skirts and making her skin prickle. Rosealyn rubbed her arms and surveyed the surrounding plains with a calculating gaze that snagged on Charles exiting the tent they'd ended up sharing. From the other, Rosealyn could hear the sometimes too loud snores from Xannan as he slept.

Clad in a simple white shirt, black pants, and the ever-present sword wrapped around his waist, Charles approached with his lips twisted between a smile and a grimace.

"Trouble sleeping?" Rosealyn lifted away from the tree and tugged her hair free of its bark, wincing.

Charles rubbed his eyes and sighed. "He's snoring again."

She chuckled. "If I recall correctly, you once slept in the same barracks as how many other soldiers?"

"Too many." He rubbed the back of his neck, scanning the plains as she had been, likely out of habit. "Minus the snoring, it's peaceful here."

An overwhelming coldness bubbled inside her. It mixed with a clawing desperation that she couldn't ignore. "Only if you forget how many are in danger of dying." Rosealyn sank to the ground and clutched her legs in front of her, resting her chin atop her knees. "Or already dead."

Charles tilted his sword and joined her on the ground. "Don't do that." He nudged her shoulder with his. "Don't berate yourself for what you cannot change."

"Sounds like something you need to remember as well." Chin digging into her bony knee, Rosealyn searched the plains again. Empty save a small cottage far enough away she could cover it with her thumb. She kept expecting to see an army of fur-clad men appear out of nowhere.

Charles sidled closer and rested his back against the tree trunk. "True, it is a good reminder."

She turned to him, shifting her swirling hair to study him. "There's more than his snoring keeping you awake, isn't there?"

Charles nodded and picked at tufts of grass as he spoke. "Did your feeling of loss go away?" He pulled a blade of grass free, twirling it between his fingers. "You stopped mentioning it, but I'm not sure that means it's gone."

He was right. She didn't like sharing what the Gift forced upon her. Or even thinking about it. Reality was hard enough without worrying what future pain was in store. Despite its earlier surge, nothing surfaced when she searched for whatever the Gift wished to share. All she could hear were the faint chirps of the bugs in the night blending in with the snoring. She almost laughed at herself, wondering if she could use her magic to make the snoring stop. That, however, would probably be a waste of magic.

"The screams stopped with Lycene." She crossed her legs at the ankle and rearranged her dress-skirts. "The feeling of loss dissipated around the same time, but I'm not sure it was connected." Rosealyn rubbed her arms, her worry that Jordan had spoken true about her uncles' fates resurfacing. But there were many things either of them could have lost since leaving Volante. She watched Charles twirl the singular blade of grass. "Is this because of Christopher's silence?"

"It is." Charles squinted at the star-lit cloud-filled sky, and she followed his gaze. A dull, miserable horizon would greet them with a soaked terrain. Any moment, the clouds would loosen their hold and release thousands of raindrops. Charles kept his focus on the sky. "You said you weren't sure it was a loss related to you. And not only has Christopher not sent word, no one in Volante has. Unless you heard from Jacin and didn't tell me?"

"I wish I could say I had." Rosealyn rubbed her arms again, though it didn't warm the sudden chill running down her spine. "Would someone try to hurt Christopher?"

A clipped laugh sounded strange coming from Charles. "Try? Possibly." He let the wrinkled blade of grass float away on the wind. "Jearnia thrives on challenges. Always has. Succeed in hurting Christopher?" A softer chuckle sounded as Charles rubbed both hands along his outstretched legs. "He survived Father's wrath, so I'm sure he'll be fine."

Both arms hooked around one of his, Rosealyn leaned her head on his shoulder and breathed deeply. "Viola is smarter than others gave her credit for. She'll do as you asked and will hopefully be able to deliver the messages your brother either couldn't or refused to send."

Charles tugged another blade of grass free and broke it into small pieces. Each floated away from them, whisked away by the increasing intensity of a storm almost directly above them. He continued until no grass was left in their immediate vicinity to occupy his hands.

It was difficult to create quiet moments. She envied those who lived in the tiny towns they passed. The ones whose populations deemed them too small to place on any map. In those towns, the main concern of families was how to keep food on their tables when the crops continued to struggle. Those families visited larger towns to barter and trade. At one point in her youth, she'd asked to visit one of these family-run farms. The visit had never happened because Hoclia had attacked.

Charles rubbed his palms together. "We should arrive at Vandyl before midday tomorrow."

"I know." Rosealyn lifted her head, chest warming as she faced Charles. Lines of worry creased his forehead, and his frown made the scraggly scar along his chin less prominent, as did the shadow of stubble from a week without shaving. Heat flushed her cheeks and chest as she contemplated tracing his jaw with her fingers. Voice a hoarse whisper, she said, "I'd rather not talk about that right now."

At Charles's arched brow, she offered a mischievous smile. They didn't need to run through their plan again. All three of them knew what to do. But if it didn't work, Rosealyn wanted to make this last night before their arrival worth remembering.

"I need to apologize." Charles jolted, and she held up a finger. "I know. You'll tell me I don't need to apologize for things I can't control. This is me apologizing for a reaction I did not expect to have and for avoiding you for an entire day."

She contemplated moving into a more comfortable position, distracted by Charles's arm tensing. "That would be something to not apologize for, Rose. If anything, I should apologize."

"You? For being honest about how you feel?" Rosealyn shook her head and smiled while chuckling. "Now this seems silly."

"Agreed." He twisted the silver ring he wore on his right hand for several long breaths and looked over at her. Those soft blue eyes, his warmth, his care, she could get lost in it. "I am in love with you, Rose. Even if you do frustrate me sometimes, it would destroy me to lose you." He smirked, laughing. "I doubt either the being in love or being frustrated will change anytime soon."

Rosealyn stared into his eyes and placed a hand against his cheek. The stubble along his chin and jaw tickled her palm, and she wondered if a short beard would make him more or less handsome. "I should have said this already, considering we're supposed to leave nothing unsaid." She hesitated and mentally berated herself for it. "I want you with me. Not two steps behind me, but at my side." Rosealyn ran her thumb along the scar marring his chin and rushed through her next words. "Because I'm in love with you, too. At least, I think—"

His lips pressed against hers, stealing her voice. Despite the chilly air, his palms were warm against her cheeks. All of her pulsed with heat at the intensity of this kiss, more authentic than any other kiss they had shared. Charles's hands roamed. Down her neck, fingers briefly tangling in her hair. Down her arms, to her sword belt, which he removed and set aside faster than Rosealyn believed possible. Grip firm on her hips, Charles pulled her closer until she was sitting on his legs.

Wind whipped her hair into a flurry, and she leaned back, chest heaving. Disentangling herself from the wayward strands, Rosealyn licked her lips as she tied her hair with string. "You've been holding back." She smirked, grabbed a fistful of his shirt, and let her voice drip with mock accusation. "Don't coddle me now, Captain."

"Wouldn't dream of it," Charles said, a sly smile spreading across his face as his gaze flickered toward their unoccupied tent. "Princess."

Rosealyn flattened her palm on his chest, leaning closer until their chests pressed together. Their lips locked again. Each breath brought them closer. Her body pressed against his, Rosealyn inhaled that scent of ever-present mountain snow. She wished this moment would never end. A tingling warmth followed the trail Charles's hands made from her hips to her waist, back up her arms, then once more holding her head. His lips continued their gentle caress.

Hesitant, cautious, and curious, Rosealyn's hands strayed from his muscled chest to his strong shoulders. Breath hitching, he pulled away, though both of his hands remained on her cheeks. For a moment, he gazed into her eyes with love, adoration, and desire. Another quick kiss, and he whispered, "I really like it when we leave nothing unsaid."

"Same." She leaned in to kiss him, and a drop of rain hit the tip of her nose. Rosealyn wiped it off. "But never call me princess again."

"Only if you never call me captain again."

Several more raindrops hit her scalp, and she crossed her arms, tapping a finger against her chin. "I will reserve the use of calling you captain for . . . special occasions."

Charles laughed. Deep and hearty in a way that made Rosealyn's heart swell. Sporadic raindrops became a steady drip. His blue eyes twinkled. "As you wish, Princess."

Head tipped back, Rosealyn laughed. The few drops turned into a torrent of rain, soaking them both. Her dress clung to her the longer the rain fell. Charles joined her in laughing as he glanced at the sky. Rain slicked his slightly curled hair against his forehead and drenched his clothing, reminding her of the times they'd sparred while he wore no shirt.

The canopy of leaves offered no protection, but the consistent beat of drops against her skin became distant as their lips met again.

Tender, thoughtful, a perfect moment even with the intensity of the storm pouring down upon them. Time slowed as the patter of rain transitioned to a drizzle and Rosealyn memorized how safe and warm she felt in his arms.

He paused and she followed his gaze to the sky where a break in the storm clouds revealed the bold full moon halfway through its descent. Charles grasped her hand and brushed his lips across her knuckles. "Do you—" His gaze flicked up to hers, searching. "Would you. . ."

Rosealyn shifted a lock of his hair off his forehead, hand lingering as she processed his unspoken question. His face constricted, smoothing when she whispered "yes" and kissed him again.

CHAPTER FIFTY-NINE

Rosealyn peered beneath the rim of her hood, throat clenching at the sight of Vandyl's castle. Her home. Seeing the damage hurt her soul. No more dark dragonstone glinted with the sunlight. Simple gray blocks stacked one atop the other. Between two thick pillars, where the metal gate should be, two large wooden doors were held shut by a heavy beam.

The three of them lingered on a street corner, observing. For their plan to work, they needed the proper timing. Soldiers guarded the castle gates in rotation but left the broken walls briefly unguarded with each change. Rosealyn shifted her shoulders, back tingling where it met the leather sheath of her sword strapped to her back beneath her cloak.

Mud from passing carts soiled the hem of her last clean dress. Sodden clothes were difficult to remove and, apparently, more prone to tearing when one wasn't focusing on clothing. Rosealyn tugged at her hood to hide her blush as she remembered the early morning hours she'd spent with Charles. Awkward yet sweet.

She jumped back from a cart passing too close to them, scowling at the larger splotches of mud. Balance regained, she muttered, "This feels the same as that day we fed the children. But with more mud." Rosealyn frowned. "And fewer children."

Charles grunted in response, remaining focused on the hushed conversation of a nearby group of golden jacketed Alkaanian soldiers.

Clad in simple black, Charles stood out amid the drab colors of the city. Xannan would have blended in if his brown-toned vest had sleeves.

After several painfully long moments, during which Xannan joked about the weather with a man selling a cart of cabbages, Charles tapped her on the shoulder, and they wove through the city street. He continued until the bustle of Vandyl's market street no longer rattled in her ears.

Rosealyn dug her boot into the ground. "It's the same as you described."

"It's like they let Nathaniel walk in." Charles frowned. "I didn't see any new damage."

"Neither Uncle Alan or Uncle Theo would let him do that."

"This time we should go around back," Xannan said. The last hints of the smirk he'd been wearing while watching them pack their belongings and stow them away that morning had faded.

"As we planned." Rosealyn reached behind her to make sure her sword's hilt was within reach. She wasn't sure which was more awkward, wearing a sword around her waist or on her back. Neither would ever be truly comfortable, but at least the weapon would be within reach when—if—she needed it.

"Remember the map I drew for you?" Charles asked, and she nodded. Lips pressed into a thin line, his gaze flickered around them as though making sure no one else was present.

With a soft laugh, Rosealyn wrapped her arms around him. "You made me draw it for you how many times?"

"True." He hugged her into his chest, gave her a much too short kiss, and whispered, "Be safe."

"You too."

As Charles walked back into the city, she and Xannan waited. A few well-placed mishaps with produce and other citizens, and soon the somber city was bustling with action. Soldiers trained to rush toward danger left their posts. Their curiosity and duty to assist allowed her and Xannan to climb over a shorter section of the castle's outer walls, landing behind the barracks.

The appearance of the castle grounds jarred her. Hallways where she'd run as a child and had walked many a sleepless night awaiting her father's safe return were gone. It was like someone had taken a heated knife and sliced off a portion of the castle. Each tapestry displaying monarchs she vaguely recognized and the unguarded corridors made Rosealyn's heart beat faster. She tempered her footsteps, mentally reciting their plan as they neared the throne room doors.

Since that room was in the center of the castle, it had remained unscathed by Eilon's flame. They paused at the end of the corridor and exchanged a glance. No soldiers stood outside the throne room doors. Without waiting for her, Xannan cracked the doors open and slid through them. A moment later, he leaned around the door and motioned for her. She approached, muscles tensing with each step. This was too easy. No monarch would leave themselves unguarded, especially not while residing in a claimed castle.

Rosealyn scanned the room as she entered while Xannan remained by the door. Naught had changed here. A throne of solid white stood beside a throne of solid black with a banner of the LeNoir colors hanging from the ceiling. "Empty?"

"Empty," Xannan confirmed. "And so few soldiers."

Rosealyn sighed and chewed on her lower lip. "So do we wait for Nathaniel or look for him? Or search for my uncles?"

CHAPTER SIXTY

Distractions sufficiently caused, Charles approached the same broken section of the wall he'd told Rosealyn and Xannan about after scouting the day before. A gold-clad man with sandy-brown hair blocked his path, and Charles tensed.

"Pardon, sir." Charles stepped to the side, but the man followed his movement.

"I recognize you." The stranger spoke in a slow, careful monotone while appraising Charles too closely.

"Must be the uniform."

"No. It's more than that." Recognition lit up his eyes.

Charles paused in his attempt to walk around the man. The stranger performed another uncomfortable survey, halting at the scar on Charles's chin.

"I have places to be. So if you'll excuse me, sir."

As Charles stepped past, the man grabbed Charles's arm and lowered his voice. "Where is she?"

After shoving off the man's hand, Charles straightened his jacket. "Where is who?"

"Don't play me." He reached for Charles's arm, muttering a curse when Charles shoved it away again. "Where is my niece? Where is Rosealyn?"

Charles clenched his jaw to keep it from dropping, wondering if Jordan had lied. One of Rosealyn's uncles lived. Supposedly. While he tried to remember which uncle was which and to recall a mental image of either, the man walked away from the castle proper and motioned for Charles to follow. Wary and worried, he obliged, gaze darting about as they went. The few golden-clad soldiers glanced their way on occasion, but none made a move toward them. He looked over his shoulder and sent a silent wish for Rosealyn to stay safe and not do anything other than what they had discussed.

As they walked, the man whispered, "I'm Alan. Since you're here, Rosealyn must be close. Perhaps inside the castle already, yes?" He glanced at Charles.

Charles offered no more than a slight nod. He needed to know if this man was telling the truth.

"She came back without an army?"

"Not intentionally." Charles grimaced. Too many of the battalion accompanying him were dead.

Alan grunted and continued walking, head swiveling about as he did. "If she's expecting to find Nathaniel inside that castle, she won't."

Charles halted mid-step. "Then what will she find?"

"A trap. What else?"

Before Charles could ask more, Alan continued walking. The constant movement made it difficult for Charles to determine whether this man was the Alan he remembered meeting over the years. Neither of Phillippe's brothers had spent much time in Vandyl, visiting only when absolutely necessary. A precaution, according to Phillippe, as it would be foolhardy for an entire family to remain in one place. Muttering a silent curse, Charles followed and asked, "A trap?"

"My brother," Alan grumbled. "Gave up the second Nathaniel arrived. We could have taken them." He muttered a curse as his boot landed in a puddle, coating his pants-leg in mud. "Nathaniel didn't arrive with his whole army. But he told us where the rest were. Claimed he'd burn a city to the ground for every day we didn't give him the country. So Theo struck a deal. I tried to convince him not to."

Alan entered one of the many narrow alleyways off the main street. After several paces of silence during which Charles's hand itched to grasp the hilt of his sword, Alan shook his head and mumbled, "I'm not sure Rosealyn can do anything to change this."

"Where is Nathaniel?"

"Probably in Cantadad by now." Alan muttered another curse and sighed. "Maybe. I'm not sure."

"Wait." Charles stopped walking and gripped his sword's hilt. Neither of Rosealyn's uncles would be so quick to relinquish control, even with Nathaniel's supposed threat. Two golden-clad soldiers approached from the opposite end of the alleyway with hands on hilts, and Charles's heartbeat quickened. He listened closely to the footsteps behind him as the realization settled. "You would know. Even if Theo forced you out, you'd do more than roam around the city and wait for us to show up."

The sandy-brown haired man who claimed to be Alan smirked and rested both hands on his hips. "Figured my ruse wouldn't work long. Nathaniel's been waiting for her to arrive. Thought there'd be a bit more fanfare, though." He held up a hand, signaling the other two soldiers to halt in their approach. "I've heard many stories about you from our spies in the Orda'anian army."

Charles tensed while the other man waved a dismissive hand and his smirk deepened. "Oh, come now. You had spies in our army, we had spies in yours. You had to know Orda'an was falling apart from the inside out; otherwise, you wouldn't have started spying on them ten years ago."

He could hear the rustle of clothes directly behind him. The man standing in front of him was as nonchalant and smug as Jordan had been while they questioned her. Charles flexed his hand. "Where is Nathaniel?"

The Alkaanian drew a small knife and flipped it end over end. "Where is Rosealyn?"

Charles shrugged. "What makes you think I would know?"

"Spies can be quite thorough in their reports." The Alkaanian stepped closer and pressed the knife against Charles's chest. "Think she'll come out of her hiding place if I drag you back to the castle and threaten to harm you?"

"Where are Alan and Theo?"

The Alkaanian looked over Charles's shoulder. "Are prisoners supposed to ask questions or answer them?"

Charles pinned the Alkaanian's arm against the narrow alleyway's wall, and ducked. A sword sparked against the stone above his hand. Charles relieved the first Alkaanian of the knife and plunged it into the man's heart. The false Alan stumbled backward into the main street, clutching at his chest. He pulled the blade free and gasped as blood spurted from the wound in time with his beating heart.

Charles drew his sword and turned to face the other two soldiers. One knelt with his hands raised, sword on the ground. The other ran. Charles muttered a curse and kicked the sword away from the kneeling man. Shouts neared.

"Where's Nathaniel?" Charles asked the one who had laid down his weapon.

"In the castle." The soldier squeezed his eyes shut. "I'm sorry I don't know about Dukes Alan or Theo."

"Don't be." Charles peered down the alleyway and down at the sword whose hilt felt too warm. "What about the Hoclian and Alkaanian armies?"

"Split amongst the cities to maintain control."

"Logical." He turned in the direction of Vandyl's main street. Blocked by a sea of gold and flashing metal. Charles grimaced. *Where is the man who actually enjoys killing when you need him?*

Not wide enough for more than two men side by side, the alley made it difficult for Charles to maneuver his longer blade against the Alkaanians' shorter ones. His gaze flickered to the weapon the soldier had forfeited. Charles gripped his sword with both hands, mentally calculating the likelihood of leaving this alley uninjured.

The first Alkaanian shuffled forward and swiped. Missed. He stepped closer, and Charles pressed his blade against the Alkaanian's, pivoted, and elbowed the man in the nose. Bone crunched, and the man's gold coat splattered with dark splotches. The Alkaanian dropped his sword and clutched his nose. Reminding himself it was between his life and theirs, Charles stabbed his sword into the man's abdomen.

Charles pulled his sword free, and the Alkaanian fell to his knees. As the wounded soldier tipped sideways, another took his place. Charles ducked below the swing, grabbed the shorter blade, and sliced his next opponent's shins. Screams echoed down the alleyway, silenced when Charles shoved the short blade through the man's chest, stopping his heart.

He stood, curling his fingers around the hilts of both his Jearnian dragon-blessed sword and the shorter blade he'd claimed. More shouts. Commanders giving orders. Charles grimaced. It was going to be a long, bloody path back to the castle.

CHAPTER SIXTY-ONE

A hand that was both too gentle and too firm—and in the way of grasping her sword—stopped Rosealyn from turning back toward the entrance to the throne room. "Took you long enough to come home, Rosealyn."

She mouthed her uncle Theo's name. This wasn't what she'd expected. When an enemy claimed another's capital city for themselves, they often remained in the throne room. Xannan claimed to have done that when he took Vandyl. Even Charles agreed that was likely where she would find Nathaniel.

"I was told Nathaniel killed you," she whispered. "You and Uncle Alan."

"He didn't." As Theo spoke, Xannan moved into her periphery only to be halted by her uncle's hand grasping Xannan's shoulder.

Xannan squinted at her, but she shook her head.

Her uncle's voice remained monotone. "Adela mentioned you two were working together now. That's a surprise."

"Is Nathaniel gone?" Rosealyn twisted away from Theo's hand, but his grip on her tightened and she frowned. He might have disagreed with the laws of succession, but this wasn't the uncle she knew. "Uncle Theo? What's going on?"

Theo guided them to the center of the throne room, stopping only when they faced the two thrones. She glanced at Xannan, who held a finger to his lips and shook his head, and she lifted a brow. Why would he tell her not to speak?

"Rosealyn, good to see you again," came a jovial voice from the doorway. "I see you've met my new friend."

She blinked in surprise and tried to turn, but Theo didn't loosen his hold. "Friend?"

"Mmm, yes, friend." Nathaniel's booted steps echoed throughout the empty throne room. "He's done so well at doing what I ask, too." As he walked past, Nathaniel patted Theo on the cheek, and her uncle didn't flinch.

Torches lining the walls made the young Alkaanian king's annoyingly bright and fanciful armor of golden metal gleam. Rosealyn saw their reflection on Nathaniel's armored chest. Stiff between them, Theo's face was blank, hers confused, and Xannan's annoyed.

She mouthed the word "magic" at Xannan.

"Oh, no." Nathaniel's exclamation brought her attention to him. "No secret communications while we all stand in the same room."

Two loud chinks sounded as Nathaniel placed his hands on each hip. "Now, where to begin?"

"I've returned to reclaim—"

"I know, I know. You want your country back." Nathaniel sighed and tipped his head back, lips twisting with what appeared to be concern. "Did I ask for wine?"

"You did." Theo's monotone made Rosealyn's heart sink. Magic had to be involved.

"Good. Then we can talk with proper sustenance." He climbed the few steps up the dais and sat on the white throne she had only ever seen occupied by her father.

Rosealyn shoved Theo's hand off her shoulder, unclasped the cloak, and approached Nathaniel while pulling her sword free from its scabbard tied to her back.

She leveled the blade at Nathaniel, as close as she could to his neck without piercing his skin. "You need to leave. And never return."

"Point your sword down, Rosealyn." Nathaniel spoke calmly, light brown eyes twinkling as they stared into hers.

Rosealyn swallowed her gasp, searching his eyes. "You have magic, too?"

Try as she might, Rosealyn couldn't resist his request, and despite the confusion and danger, she regretted how often she had likely forced others to do something. But Nathaniel's command was far from unintentional. He knew what he was doing.

"I've met several friends in the past month." Nathaniel drummed clunky metal-covered fingers against stone armrests. "Interesting things. Crystals. Capable of storing unfathomable abilities."

"That explains how you got in without fighting." She rested the tip of her sword on the marbled floor. If this dragon-blessed blade could change how another's magic worked on her, it would be the perfect time for it to do so. But if that was the case, her ability wouldn't have worked so well on Xannan. With a slight shake of her head, she asked, "You told them to let you in."

"Mmm." Nathaniel's brows lifted until they almost blended into his cropped blond hair. He stood and clapped his hands once. Rosealyn winced at the sound of metal clinking together. "Ah, the wine!"

While Nathaniel selected a specific cup of wine from the tray a servant set between the two thrones, Rosealyn glanced at Xannan again, a brow raised. Ever the best at communicating, Xannan shrugged and tapped the hilt of his sword. In all of their planning, not one of them had considered Nathaniel would come to possess any type of magic. Or know how to use it. *Is it stronger than mine? Theo appears completely brainwashed.*

She approached the tray herself, lifting a pitcher to pour a glass with one hand, and attempted to discreetly lift the sword with the other.

Nothing. Yet. Perhaps the more she did as Nathaniel requested, the less magic he would use. "Where's my Uncle Alan?"

Nathaniel swirled the wine in the glass and sipped, smacking his lips after swallowing. He wiped a trail of wine from his chin with a gauntlet thumb, sucking the liquid with an ingratiating smirk. "I told Theo here to kill him." He leaned back and peered through the clear glass. "She claimed I could make *anyone* do *anything* with this crystal. What better way to test that theory than to force one to kill someone they love?" Another sip and Nathaniel rested his arm on the side of her father's throne, making his metal armor creak. "It worked so well. I forced Theo to stop crying, too." The Alkaanian king's grin turned wicked. "Fascinating how that worked."

Rosealyn fought to maintain her composure as she replaced the pitcher of wine. Her throat tightened and her sword arm trembled as she glanced over to where Theo maintained a firm grip on Xannan's shoulder. Her uncle's face remained blank. Xannan's twisted in disgust.

She stamped down the rising fury. "What have you done about the droki attacks?"

"Droki?"

"Similar to dragons, they are creatures that hunt magic," Rosealyn said slowly while she picked up the glass she had poured.

"Haven't seen anything like that." He smiled in a way that made her believe he was lying, but she returned the fake smile and lifted the glass to her lips. Right before she tipped the liquid back, Nathaniel spoke again while holding her gaze. "Don't drink it."

Her arm trembled as she lowered it. Nathaniel laughed and smacked a gauntleted hand against his armored thigh. "Oh isn't that fun?"

Rosealyn threw the wine in Nathaniel's face. His laughter subsided, and he tilted his head, features growing sinister as red liquid dripped from his cheeks and onto the bright gold armor. After a long slow sip, Nathaniel's gaze shifted to her uncle.

"Theo." The rash Alkaanian king waited for her uncle's gaze to meet his. "Kill Rosealyn."

Her uncle went rigid. Before Theo's blade cleared its scabbard, the hilt of Xannan's sword met the back of Theo's head. She gasped as her uncle crumpled to the ground.

"You." She approached Xannan, wondering if Nathaniel's command to point the sword down would apply if she tried to attack someone else.

CHAPTER SIXTY-TWO

Xannan sheathed his sword and held his ground, waiting until Rosealyn could hear him whisper, "He has to look you in the eye for it to work."

She froze, glancing at Theo, and a rush of air left her while Xannan hoped he wouldn't regret not annihilating the potential threat. But the man obviously wasn't himself, and Xannan knew how that felt. When Rosealyn looked back at him, squinting like she was trying to ask him a question without speaking, Xannan fought the urge to roll his eyes. Instead, he arched a brow.

"Draw your sword," she said.

"Remember, magic—"

"Pretty sure droki are already coming." She gestured for his sword, a small enough movement he doubted Nathaniel noticed. "Combine them? Maybe that will reverse his command to not lift mine?"

Xannan glanced over her shoulder at the now-observant Nathaniel. Rosealyn had a point. Droki were coming in greater numbers than before. The group of three had been child's play. What approached. . . He shook his head. The swords combining. That thought gave him pause. He had no desire to relinquish control and saw no need to do so.

"Let's kill this pompous brat." Xannan pulled his sword free, noting the clouds of lighter gray roving within. Nowhere near as white as the weapon Rosealyn held. Confirmation, Xannan supposed, that they currently sought a common goal. Threads of anger surfaced. As strong, if not stronger, than those he'd once felt before.

"Oh good." Nathaniel's gauntleted hands caused a ringing reverberation as the young king clapped. Hands clasped together, Nathaniel looked directly at Xannan. With effort, Xannan averted his gaze to the floor. The young king laughed. "This will be quite the fight to watch, won't it? The legendary Lost Prince, now the dragonslayer, and the well-trained princess of Orda'an."

More creaking of armor sounded as Nathaniel descended from the raised dais. Rosealyn ground her teeth loudly enough Xannan winced at the pain she was causing herself. All Xannan could hear was the Alkaanian king's clunky movements as he kept his gaze on the marbled floor.

"I should have asked for more wine. Maybe fruit or cheese. Food is so hard to come by these days, though." An audible slurp, meaning the idiotic youth still had a glass of wine in his hand. "Fight until . . . hmm, until you both drop dead? Yes, that!"

Rosealyn moved into his periphery, pausing when Xannan tapped his sword against hers. "Careful—"

Nostrils flaring, she held out her hand.

"I told you to fight," Nathaniel growled.

Xannan almost lifted his head to the Alkaanian king. *Odd, I thought the little brat knew he had to make eye contact.*

Rosealyn snapped her fingers and gritted out, "Sword, please."

The slow clomp of Nathaniel's steps stopped. In the corner of his vision, Xannan could see the youth turning his head from one to the other. Metal chinked against metal. A proper warrior would move silently in armor. Not that the armor appeared useful for anything other than appearance. Bulky, shiny. It was impressive. And annoying. The front and back panels didn't meet at the sides. Nor did it cover the king's neck.

A gleam of gold metal invaded Xannan's vision as the young king's hand approached his face. Xannan's crystalline blade of light gray clouds met golden armor with a clang, the wine cup shattered, and Xannan ducked beneath Nathaniel's opposite arm. Under normal circumstances, Xannan would stare his opponent down. But he had no desire to become anyone else's puppet. Least of all this fool's.

"That hurt." Nathaniel's voice cracked as he shook his arm and walked away. "Attack *her*, not *me*."

Between the hum of the swords, the changing colors, and the anger seeping from her, Xannan didn't want to acknowledge what could happen. Theo stirred and blinked groggily. Xannan looked up at Rosealyn. She had noticed Theo stirring as well. Her gaze slid back to his, and she took a deep breath, and with that frustrating ability of hers that he wondered if he should have explained more, she whispered, "Give me your sword."

He slowly lifted his sword and squinted at her.

"How boring," Nathaniel intoned from across the room. He had removed his gauntlets, flexing the fist that had blocked Xannan's sword. "Parry, thrust, block, repeat. Or do Orda'anians fight by staring instead?"

"Now, please." Rosealyn gave him a poignant glance at where her sword's tip rested on the marbled stone. Solid glowing white, pulsing in time with the hum of the blade in his hand.

Xannan clenched his jaw and held the hilt of his sword toward her outstretched hand as he shook his head. The boy's command had been strong enough she still couldn't do anything with her sword except point it at the ground. Nathaniel's screeched command for her to stop did nothing.

CHAPTER SIXTY-THREE

Rosealyn released her glowing white blade as she grasped the hilt of Xannan's sword. At first, she blanched at the strangeness of it. It felt heavier. Perhaps more of the blade's power resided in Xannan's sword. Either way, Rosealyn was grateful to be able to lift the sword and hold it in the proper stance. Xannan caught her sword before it tumbled to the ground, holding it with the same curious look she was positive she had given his.

Her curiosity was short-lived as Nathaniel's obnoxious clearing of his throat sounded like a clap of thunder. She should have realized both he and Jordan would seek retribution for whatever had befallen their people.

"Look in my eyes." His voice was like congealed honey, dripping with animosity. All she could see were his hands propped on his hips, fingers tapping impatiently.

She glanced behind her as Theo sidled away and made no attempt to retrieve his weapon. That was a small relief, a realization that whatever commands Nathaniel had given had been broken. Beside her, Xannan tilted his head from side to side and pulled his dagger free. His restraint wouldn't last much longer.

Rather than give Nathaniel the satisfaction of looking at him, or speaking to him, Rosealyn swung the sword. A blind warning. Not close enough to harm him but close enough to make the younger king jump back with a muttered curse.

"She said I could make *anyone* do *anything*." Distraught and distracted, Nathaniel paced.

She followed the motion of his boots with her eyes, remaining stationary, and asked, "Who is this she?"

A pause, a mumbled curse, and Rosealyn fought between a smile and a frown. It was becoming too easy to rely on her ability.

"She never gave me a name." The tip of Nathaniel's boots touched hers. Even his boots were a gleaming gold. Rosealyn sighed. This young man was no more than a nuisance of an obstacle. He had been corrupted by a power he was never meant to have, a power Rosealyn wished did not weigh so heavy on her soul.

"If you attack me, I will kill you." Rosealyn glanced up at Nathaniel long enough to see his eyes widen. Her gaze trailed down his arm to the dagger he gripped in his hand.

"Not if I kill you first."

Rosealyn spun away from Nathaniel's swing, anticipating each of his movements by the sound of his armor. When she knocked the dagger from his hand, he cursed and backed away.

"Then again," Nathaniel said as what sounded like hundreds of footsteps rang out behind her. "It is so much more fun to watch others do the killing."

"Excellent leadership skills." Rosealyn scoffed and settled into a proper stance. Feet wide enough for good balance, gaze darting between Nathaniel's shoulder and feet. A quick glance over her shoulder revealed more Alkaanian soldiers. "Letting others do the work for you?" Though she didn't look, Rosealyn envisioned the fierce look on Nathaniel's face.

Anger poignant in his voice, Nathaniel gritted out, "I dislike getting dirty." A heartbeat of silence passed. "Kill her."

"Stay where you are," Rosealyn countered. Xannan's sword hummed in her hand, warming until it was almost uncomfortable to hold. "All of you soldiers, stay where you are."

"You are so going to hate what comes after all this magic use," Xannan mumbled. He gestured at Nathaniel with Rosealyn's sword. "May I?"

"You defer to her?" Nathaniel guffawed, dagger clinking against the rounded metal over his abdomen as he held his hand there, as if doing so could subdue the laughter racking his frame. But the laughter was short-lived as Xannan attacked. With each of his steps forward, Nathaniel backpedaled. Xannan was faster. The flickering flames of the torches danced along Nathaniel's armor and the glowing white sword as both became a flurry of movement.

Nathaniel's strikes were wild, crazed, and fearful. Xannan's were steady and purposeful, pressing Nathaniel backward until the boy was flush against the wall. The younger man tried to form words, but Xannan covered the boy's mouth with his hand.

Rosealyn watched, frozen in place, waiting for the final strike she knew Xannan would happily deliver. In a strange sensation, she wished her hand held the weapon poised to strike. In that split second of waiting, Nathaniel pressed back. Light glinted off metal daggers and gold armor in a flurry of brightness, interrupted by the glowing white sword Rosealyn wanted back in her hands.

As Xannan made quick work of pinning Nathaniel against the wall again, Theo approached her side. Her chest tightened as she watched several tears stream down Theo's cheeks. He looked so similar to her father, even incredibly similar to Xannan. A clatter of metal against stone tore Rosealyn from her thoughts. Xannan had dropped her sword and drawn his dagger. He pressed the slender blade against Nathaniel's unprotected neck while his other hand resumed its position covering the disarmed youth's mouth. When Nathaniel lifted a hand, Xannan pressed the dagger deeper, and the young king halted his movement.

"Hold him there." Theo's expression turned callous. "Nathaniel's mine."

Xannan exchanged a glance with her while Theo walked toward them. She nodded, lips pressed together. Though Nathaniel struggled and his eyes widened with true fear, Xannan held him against the wall, dagger pressed against the young Alkaanian's throat.

"Didn't you say it was poetic?" Theo's voice was too calm and too low as he paused and collected one of Nathaniel's daggers. Her uncle studied the dagger, turning it so the flames danced along the clean metal. "So incredibly poetic for one to die at the end of their own blade."

Rosealyn shivered at the haunting statement, and Nathaniel tried to speak. His words were muffled and incoherent, almost blubbering as he attempted to break free of Xannan's hold again.

The second Xannan lowered his blade, Theo struck. Rosealyn only knew the dagger had pierced skin when streams of blood marred the shiny golden armor. Theo remained riveted in place, staring as the Alkaanian king slumped to the floor. He dropped the bloodied dagger on Nathaniel, not flinching at the ring of metal or the clatter of steel on stone.

A shudder racked through Theo. "One brother avenged." He sighed, lifted his sword, and faced Xannan.

Brows rising, Xannan exchanged another quick glance with her and backed away from Theo.

"Blazes," she muttered under her breath as she approached her uncle. "Stay—"

"Don't attack." Rosealyn continued her quick steps until she stood between the two men. Theo frowned, holding his sword as though he could harm Xannan without hurting her. Every movement he made, she blocked.

"Rosealyn." Theo's words belied his emotionless visage. "Move."

"You will not attack Xannan." She gritted out the words, momentarily surprised she wasn't allowing another to attack Xannan as she had contemplated so many times.

Theo flinched. "You too?"

She pointed at the dead king whose dark pool of blood reflected his fanciful armor. "I am not him." Rosealyn's arm shook. "And, Blazes, I hate magic sometimes. Right now, I—"

"But he—"

"I'm really tired of the reminders," Xannan interrupted from behind her. He held the hilt of her sword toward her, and she grasped it, handing his back to him. The hum, the heat were both too strong. "The droki are almost here."

She bristled and looked back at Theo, who appeared to be at a loss for words. "I'll explain later. Right now, Xannan is helping me. Right?"

"I've had little choice," Xannan murmured as he hefted his sword. "But it was once my home as well."

Another shudder racked through Theo. With a deep inhalation, he sheathed his sword. When he inclined his head, Rosealyn's chest tightened. Her uncle's voice was tense but respectful. "What would you have me do, Your Majesty?"

Rosealyn offered a tight smile in response and turned around. Arms half-raised, several with blades half-drawn, the Alkaanian soldiers appeared unable to move. "Blazes," she murmured. "They—"

"I've told you," Xannan said. "Careful what commands you give."

She nodded absently, surveying the group of Alkaanian soldiers. While contemplating what to do with them, she turned to Theo. "Get the people of the city to safety. Do not let anyone but the three of us fight the droki. Understood?"

Theo nodded. "Three?"

"Blazes." Rosealyn tensed as her gaze darted about. There was no way Charles would see the droki approach and *not* head toward them rather than away. *And he has the audacity to remind me not to jump into things unprepared!*

"Lay down your weapons." Rosealyn waited until each Alkaanian soldier set their swords, daggers, staffs, and any other manner of weapon on the floor. When the clatter of metal against stone dissipated, Rosealyn rounded her shoulders and stared at each of the Alkaanian soldiers in turn. "You will be given a choice. Surrender or face the consequences for destroying towns and killing Orda'anian citizens." She gripped the sword tighter, focusing on the intention of her words. "Remain in this room and do *not* touch any weapon."

To her left, Theo stood with arms crossed, a muscle in his jaw pulsing. To her right, Xannan raised a brow but didn't speak. Instead, he glanced at his sword. Clouds of gray continued to grow lighter, closer to the bold white of her sword, and swirled with ferocious intensity.

None of the soldiers spoke, or moved, making Rosealyn believe her command had worked. She lifted her solid white, glowing weapon, wishing magic were not so quick to wreak havoc on people's lives. Once the droki were annihilated, she'd return to this group and dole out the necessary punishments for their actions.

Theo murmured, "Some here might be Orda'anian. Not all. It was one of his first *orders* for our—your soldiers to wear his colors."

She nodded and assumed the tone she was beginning to recognize as her ability coloring her words. "If you are Orda'anian, you may leave this room." Two extricated themselves from the group, relief etched across their features. Rosealyn turned to her uncle. "Take them and look for other Orda'anian soldiers. I believe his death breaks whatever commands he gave."

After a slight bow, Theo moved toward the throne room doors, pausing next to an Alkaanian soldier who wore a silver bar on each shoulder. Before Rosealyn could register Theo's intentions, the soldier collapsed to the floor, oozing blood from a gash that ran across him from hip to opposite shoulder. As the injured Alkaanian convulsed, Theo turned away from the sight. "That one laughed. When Nathaniel forced . . . and he. . ." Theo snapped his jaw shut, turned on his heel, and left the room.

"At least he gets it," Xannan said, surprisingly appreciative considering how recently Theo had threatened him. "Kill your enemy and then they cannot rise against you again."

"But there is never just one enemy, is there?" Rosealyn murmured, fixated on the gutted and dying Alkaanian soldier. "How long do you think my commands work on others?"

"Considering Charles hasn't attempted to outright kill me over the past two weeks, a while." Xannan crouched over Nathaniel's body, lifting the man's arms more quietly than the young king had ever moved them himself. As Xannan searched, her sword flared with heat, distracting her with thoughts of what awaited once they left this room.

"No crystal?" Rosealyn asked as Xannan stood.

He grimaced but didn't answer.

"Let me—"

"You have plenty and are becoming quite well versed at utilizing it." Xannan strode through the open door. "Best get moving before there are no people left in this city either."

CHAPTER SIXTY-FOUR

Christopher's elbows dug into his thighs, hands clasped together. On the other side of the bed on which the lone survivor of the droki lay, Eonar mixed yet another concoction. Eonar applied the thick substance to the now-smaller scratch along the boy's thigh. Despite the diminishing wound, the boy remained unconscious.

"No change." Eonar murmured words Christopher didn't understand and set the medicine aside.

Long hours had turned into even longer days. Another week had passed, and Christopher refused to send any message to his brother. Not when all he could send was one sentence of bad news after another. Something would have to work soon. He hoped.

More questions, more discussions of liquid elements which caused a variety of reactions. While Maya pulled information out of Marsha, Christopher insisted both Eonar and Jacin join those discussions. The more involved in finding a possible antidote to the droki's poison, the better. That, and it was extremely difficult to be in the same room as his aunt without wanting to kill her. A proper trial, Christopher had decided, would not occur until Charles returned home.

Eonar picked up a second medicine, a liquid-like substance, and poured it into the boy's mouth. Christopher rubbed his face. According to both Maya and Eonar, Marsha had shared all she knew. It hadn't been enough to save the other who had survived the journey.

Christopher suspected the first mixture they'd applied to the soldier's arm had made the wound worse. A webbing of sickening black had encompassed the arm and claimed his life less than a day after they'd arrived. This last appeared to have the smallest amount of the beast's poison in him. A singular darkened scratch on the soldier's thigh. But he looked too frail to survive.

"New mixtures or same as yesterday?" Christopher watched Eonar flip through a small book. Though the doctor's skin was shriveled, his movements were sure. Tawny hair pulled back made the elf's red-irised eyes prominent as they churned with a deeper color. That changing color, Christopher decided, meant the elf was worried.

"The application to the wound was the same. It is the only one that actually helped the injury heal." Eonar snapped the book shut, pocketing it inside his loose robe. "Slight changes to the ratios of elements in the liquid. I fear Marsha may be right that we can only make a proper antidote with a fresh supply of the initial poison."

Christopher pressed against his legs and stood. "Find me if anything changes."

Without looking over at him, Eonar nodded and opened the notebook to make a quick scratching notation while frowning. A slight shake of his head and a sigh, Christopher left the room. An infirmary, Eonar called it. Apparently it had always been there.

Several steps down the dark hallway, he encountered a stoic Jacin. Neither of them had heard from Charles or Rosealyn. Perhaps if there was no reason to send word, there was no reason to worry. A foolish hope when the last message received had been the arrival of wounded soldiers.

"Based on that expression, he's not dead but he's not awake?"

Christopher nodded. "The wound is healing, though. Hopefully that's a good sign?"

"Hopefully." Jacin rubbed his bearded chin. "More waiting."

"I wish I could see what they're up to right now." Christopher walked. To where, he wasn't sure, but he didn't want to stand still.

Jacin grunted. "That makes two of us."

Outside, Christopher decided. Fresh air would clear his mind. Rain, snow, sunshine, anything would be preferable to these stuffy hallways. "Seen Maya today?"

"You can talk to her yourself, you know. Same goes for all of your cousins, whose names you should probably stop forgetting."

Christopher glared.

Jacin chuckled. "No, I have not spoken with her today because it's the middle of the night, Christopher."

Christopher halted in the midst of the dreary hallway. "Middle of the night?"

"You fell asleep in the infirmary. We let you rest."

"Thanks," Christopher mumbled. "I think."

He began walking again, thinking. No proper antidote for the poison. No new messages or sudden arrivals from either Charles or Rosealyn. And no idea what he could or should be doing other than listen to citizens whine.

"You know"—Jacin matched Christopher's pace—"the theory behind think before you act does not mean you spend all of your time thinking and no time acting."

"I'm aware." Christopher glanced askance at the Orda'anian, noting the man's sallow skin and disheveled blond hair. "But that doesn't mean I know what I *should* do."

"We each have different opinions of what one should do." Jacin stifled a yawn with the back of his hand. "I stayed here because Rosealyn specifically asked me to. So you're stuck with me until she requests otherwise. Which I can only guess means she believes you needed someone nearby. Either to keep watch on you or help you. Or both."

Christopher frowned, wishing he didn't feel like a young child again. As Jacin stifled another yawn, Christopher said, "Go rest, Jacin. I'll have someone wake you if anything happens with Owen. Or a messenger arrives with news."

They rounded the next corner together and almost walked into the bushy-haired servant Christopher had half-expected not to survive the journey with Charles. Standing tall, Viola looked at him directly. She wasn't shrinking into herself, or keeping her head lowered, but looking at him.

After a slight curtsy to them both, she said, "Prince Christopher, I'm glad we found you so quickly."

So distracted by seeing Viola meet his gaze without hesitation, Christopher hadn't noticed another accompanied her. The other embraced Jacin.

"Good to see you again, Moss. Viola." Jacin nodded to each in turn, almost as if he was using their names to remind Christopher who these people were.

He'd never admit it aloud, but he was grateful for the reminder of the other Orda'anian's name. Though he supposed he should have remembered given the amount of scarring that marred half of Moss's face.

Christopher clasped his hand behind his back and pinched his fingers together. "More wounded by droki?"

The tension in Christopher's shoulders loosened as Viola shook her head. "But wounded nonetheless."

He squinted at her. Barely two weeks away from the castle and her demeanor had changed. When he'd first returned home with Charles, the young maid would shake almost uncontrollably in his presence.

"And Charles?"

"His Majesty is well last we were aware." Viola's gaze flickered between his and the floor while Christopher's squint transitioned into furrowed brows.

Viola continued more softly, but she looked between him and Jacin more often than she did at the floor. "His Majesty, Queen Rosealyn, and Xannan left for Vandyl the morning we began our journey here from Lycene. His Majesty requested we form a new battalion, gather additional men and women who can assist the injured, and journey to Vandyl."

Before Christopher could overcome his slight confusion, Jacin asked, "How fares Lycene?"

Viola and Moss shared a glance, and the Orda'anian soldier's face turned ashen as he whispered, "Massacred."

Jacin muttered a stream of curses, and Christopher's eyes widened. *Massacred? What kind of tyrant kills complete innocents?*

When the answer to his internal question formulated, Christopher shoved the thought aside and cleared his throat.

"The culprits got their due end, yes?" Jacin sounded angrier than Christopher believed possible for the ever-calm and constantly hungry Orda'anian.

The scarred soldier bristled. "Most of them, yes. The 'Honorable Jordan' and her surviving soldiers are with us. At our queen's request, Duchess Adela agreed not to go with them to Vandyl. I recommended she stay in Lycene but. . ." He let out a long breath. "Wherever Duchess Adela is, she is not with us."

For a moment, Jacin stared into the dark hallway. Anger sharpened the Orda'anian's features, chasing away the earlier exhaustion. "Rosealyn insisted on Jordan's survival?"

The other Orda'anian cleared his throat and whispered, "On anyone's survival if possible."

Jacin nodded once, though his jaw clenched, and Christopher frowned. He tried to imagine what was going through Jacin's mind, hearing that an entire town of his home country had been annihilated. And to know the culprit of such destruction lived. He shook his head, unbound curls briefly invading his vision. Christopher remembered meeting both Nathaniel and Jordan and knew they would attempt to take sections of Orda'an for themselves. They'd taken it further than land and resources.

"Time to form a new battalion, then." Christopher took one step forward and stopped. "I should go with them this time."

Jacin who arched a brow and asked, "Should you?"

"Would you stay?"

Jacin shrugged, prevented from responding by Eonar, whose countenance had drastically changed. The elderly elf appeared almost happy as he announced, "Oh good, you didn't stray far. Owen's awake."

Christopher looked from the bright red-irised eyes of the elf to a shocked yet tired Jacin to a suddenly confident Viola, and . . . the scarred Orda'anian. He turned back to Eonar, feeling heavier and lighter at the same time. Though he had no confirmation others were injured, Christopher believed it would be necessary to create more of the antidote. "How much antidote could you create before morning?"

"Before morning?" Eonar retorted. "None. We used the last of the nacea for Owen, and it will take time to cultivate more."

"Then you best get started, Eonar." Christopher turned to Viola as Eonar walked away, frowning at how the scarred Orda'anian angled himself as if to protect the maid. "Viola, go wake—"

"His Majesty was quite specific in what I am to do," Viola interrupted.

Christopher fought to keep his jaw from dropping while the other Orda'anian smirked.

"I need to speak with the other maids to see who is willing to travel with us and aid in healing the wounded."

She turned away, paused, and curtsied with a murmured, "Apologies, Your Highness. I've meant no disrespect and want to ensure my given task is completed in a timely manner."

"Sure, yes," Christopher stammered while she and the other Orda'anian walked away, leaving him once again alone with Jacin. "You should definitely get some rest now. The battalion will leave as soon as there is enough antidote worth taking."

"A suggestion then," Jacin murmured as the soldier and Viola continued down the hallway. "Wake Maya so she can help Eonar cultivate the necessary materials."

CHAPTER SIXTY-FIVE

Before long, Charles lost count of how many men he'd stabbed. A miserable gruesome path trailed behind him. He stabbed and ducked, parried and thrusted, grimaced and cursed. Even though he tried to keep to the shadows, Alkaanian soldiers noticed him. Granted, anyone walking through a city street with a bloodied sword drawn and ready to use would be cause for concern. Whenever Charles considered sheathing the weapon, more soldiers approached.

Those with faces he recognized laid down their swords and knelt with hands raised, same as the one in the alleyway. The flurry of Alkaanians attacking prevented Charles from questioning those who capitulated. He wanted to understand why Orda'anians wore their enemy's colors.

Charles hissed when a dagger grazed his arm. Berating himself for losing focus, he sidestepped the next toss and searched the street for a reasonable escape route. Citizens cowered behind carts. Children peered through windows. Fewer soldiers now.

His aching arm was a reminder he hadn't properly maintained his strength. Were it less likely he would face multiple opponents, Charles would have considered switching hands. Instead, he pulled the dagger he so rarely used.

Four soldiers approached. Charles blocked the first strike, teeth jarring at the impact. He turned to land a blow with his dagger to the next opponent's chest, twisted away from a third's swing, and ducked to slash his sword along one stomach, then another. His lungs and muscles burned, but he gritted his teeth and threw the dagger at an approaching Alkaanian.

He pressed forward, reminding himself to ease the tension in his sword arm despite the hilt growing hotter. Not hot enough to burn, but hot enough to know the heat was not from holding the weapon.

The warmth of his blade's hilt made his jaw clench. They'd agreed. Discussed it multiple times. Convince Nathaniel to stand down *without* using magic. Yet Charles feared Rosealyn had done the opposite.

Covered in more blood than he would have preferred, some of it his own from the stray knives and daggers that had managed to nick his arms, Charles rounded his shoulders as another Alkaanian attempted to block his path. One swipe, and the Alkaanian fell, gasping and clutching the gaping wound in his thigh.

Piercing cries sounded long before Charles saw the droki, and all those around him froze to study the sky. Skinny, lengthy black bodies streaked across a pale blue sky, easily visible without storm clouds to disguise them. Charles used their distraction to gain ground toward the castle, hoping the beasts' approach meant Rosealyn had succeeded in reclaiming Vandyl.

Several thuds were followed by fearsome shrieks, and Charles turned around as he mumbled to himself, "Droki scent magic but attack any-thing in their path first?"

An Alkaanian soldier approached him, weapon raised, but the boy was too distracted by the beasts landing in the street. Their outstretched wings grazed buildings, knocking over the men and women who didn't scramble away. Charles's heart sank at the sight. Droki lashed out, snap-ping their snake-like necks and biting off arms, wounding shoulders. He hefted his sword, grimacing when the nearest droki swiveled its head to him. Magic, he'd been warned, came with a cost. At least a dozen droki remained in the sky, circling.

"You're worried about me with those things arriving?" Charles pointed his sword at the nearest drokos. The undulating cries from the droki circling above created a melancholic harmony to the people's sorrowful desperate pleas.

The younger soldier followed the motion, swallowed, and shuffled toward Charles. Eyes wide, the younger man halted when another drokos landed between them. It screeched, head lifting and neck twisting. Charles hefted his sword and plunged it into the beast's chest where he hoped the thing's heart resided. When he pulled his weapon free, the drokos fell to the side, pinning the Alkaanian soldier's foot.

The Alkaanian grasped for his weapon, but it had tumbled too far out of reach. With a shake of his head, Charles offered a hand and pulled the boy free. "You should be more afraid of the droki than me."

"But . . . you . . . we. . ." The Alkaanian limped two steps toward his fallen sword, fainting when a drokos screeched above.

So much for meeting them inside the castle. No magic, that was the plan.

Charles surveyed the streets. Emptier now, though too many writhed on the ground. Several golden-clad soldiers stood petrified, almost as if they didn't recognize their surroundings. One removed the gold coat and tossed it to the ground when another drokos landed nearby. Then another. And another. Not surrounding him, but close enough for Charles to wish he could send the droki away with no more than a thought. They each sniffed the air, necks craning to-and-fro like slithering snakes.

"A few more dragon-wrought swords could prove useful." Charles's murmured wish was lost amid ear-splitting cries, and he glanced toward the castle, sending a silent plea that help was on the way.

Arms tired, muscles weary, Charles wasn't sure how long he could last against one drokos, much less three. Or more. Combine their presence with the arrival of properly clad Alkaanian soldiers, and Charles wished he had ignored the one claiming to be Alan.

The soldiers wearing simple white shirts exchanged glances with those in sparkling gold. A few of the Alkaanians glanced at him askance, and he realized he must quite the sight to behold. Clad all in black, holding a sword dripping with the mingled blood of human and droki.

The next screech of the droki was like a battle cry. Weapons clashed. White-clad unarmored soldiers attacked with abandon. Blood-curdling cries reverberated around him. Recognition surfaced as he placed their shouts. Men he'd trained and fought alongside lashed out, annihilating enemy after enemy.

Charles stared at the sight, grateful for the reprieve of being the sole focus. Until those creatures made the sound that turned his insides to ice. After sheathing his dagger, Charles rubbed his neck, massaged his shoulder, and flexed his arm. Proper dragons would be a welcome sight, but they had stayed sparse for long enough Charles figured they had no interest in aiding others anymore. Based on his understanding, dragons used humans when it benefited them and abandoned them when help was most needed.

"How do we kill those?" came a youthful voice at Charles's side as he strode toward the droki.

Charles appraised the young man. White shirt, sword drawn, eager expression. Charles grunted. "*You* don't."

"You're a fool to face them alone!"

"You can't kill them without one of these." Charles lifted his bloodied blade. "Perhaps cutting off the head would work without a dragon-wrought blade, but I don't want to risk learning that the hard way." Charles grasped the boy's arm. "Do *not* approach the droki. If it approaches you, avoid bites and claws. Their poison will kill you. Understood?"

"I don't take orders from a stranger." The young soldier sneered and tugged his arm free. "I became a soldier in the Orda'anian army to help where needed." He glowered at Charles. "You need help."

"Your comrades, who once took orders from me, need it more. I can take care of myself." Charles walked in the direction of the droki again, wondering why the creatures seemed to be waiting. Their necks continued to move in that strange slithering motion, but it was as if they were stuck. *I really hope she used magic for a good reason.*

The thought halted his forward movement for a split second as Charles considered others there might have magic, but he shook the thought from his head and focused on the task at hand. Kill the droki before they harmed anyone else.

Though his heart seemed to beat inside his throat, Charles forced himself to take one step after another toward the droki. He flexed his hand on his sword hilt, shoving aside the aches of overworked muscles. Black liquid dripped from the closest drokos's teeth, and it snapped its jaw toward him, then sniffed and huffed. Its wing scraped a building, spikes catching in the wood, and the droki screeched. Charles shuffled closer, following the movement of the beast's neck. The drokos lowered its neck, and breath putrid enough to sour any meal wafted over Charles. Jaw clenched, Charles hacked at the drokos's neck until the head was severed from the body.

Once the drokos's body fell, Charles retrieved a discarded gold coat and carefully wiped his blade free of the poisonous blood while scanning his surroundings. Grunts and screams mingled with the ringing clash of metal. Even if Rosealyn had defeated Nathaniel, the fight for the city was only beginning.

Charles muttered a curse when he noticed the boy from earlier marching up to a drokos at the furthest end of the street. Swords and daggers flashed toward Charles as he wove through the fighting. He elbowed one in the face, drew his dagger, and flung it at another's chest, all while trying to keep the foolish boy in his periphery.

The drokos's slashing claws sliced through the boy's arm. Then it lowered, sniffing. A low rumble emanated from the drokos and as it inhaled, the boy fainted.

Another sword streaked into Charles's line of sight, and he knocked the weapon aside with furtive glances toward the unconscious youth. The attacking soldier wore no golden coat, but his ferocious attacks increased. Back pressed against a building, Charles swung at the soldier's blade hard enough to disarm him. The Orda'anian snarled and lashed out with a fist. Charles ducked and rammed his shoulder into the man. Sprawled on the ground, the Orda'anian lifted his hands, jaw dropping as Charles offered the man his sword back. "Tell the Orda'anian soldiers I'm here to help and that their true monarch, Rosealyn, may need help in the castle."

Recognition lit in the Orda'anian's eyes. He nodded, grasped his sword, and sprinted toward the castle. Sighing, Charles jogged to where he'd last seen the younger soldier, tensing as three droki landed nearby and inhaled with that unusual deep rumble, making him wonder if the young boy had magic.

Charles slowed his approach and studied the droki's movements. Unsure if he had the strength left to cleave through their necks, Charles focused on how to pierce their hearts without their teeth or claws finding purchase in his skin. Others approached—citizens and soldiers alike. Charles waved them away. None of their blades could harm these dragonesque fiends.

He ducked and pivoted, trying to shuffle closer, but the creature's neck kept invading his path. One's wings lashed out and Charles jumped back, nearly stumbling over a discarded weapon lying in the street. It belonged to the boy whose form was already too pale.

Four droki surrounded the youth, distracted with inhaling his scent. Charles used their distraction to weave through bodies twice his height, cursing when the closest one almost crushed his foot with a clawed paw.

Air was difficult to gulp down. He was too close to the creatures. Too close to the dripping poison. Too close to their teeth and claws.

No speed remained in Charles's legs, but he pulled from the depths of his strength and thrust his sword up with quick stabs at the nearest drokos and jumped away from the beast before it collapsed into a writhing, screeching mass.

Chest heaving, mouth dry, Charles stumbled back several steps and focused on the next two droki. His fingers ached and his arm trembled as he lifted the dripping sword. No one else would receive a gash from the droki, not if he could help it.

CHAPTER SIXTY-SIX

Xannan rounded the first corner out of the throne room and was attacked. By the time Rosealyn approached—with her sword unsheathed—Xannan had killed the soldier. She scowled and stepped between him and the next approaching soldier, announcing Nathaniel's death as if it would stop the Alkaanian from attacking. It didn't. After fewer moves than Xannan expected, her blade struck true.

Brows raised, Xannan muttered a curse at the stomping of boots echoing through the hallways. "The quicker we get—"

"I know," she snapped at him. Rosealyn sighed, closed her eyes, and clenched her dress-skirts.

Xannan thought about the crystal he'd pocketed, wondering what it would feel like to use it, to wield such power over another's will as she was attempting to do to the droki.

Grunting, she opened her eyes and asked, "How many droki?"

Xannan chose not to respond because the swords' hum was almost as strong as it had been before they combined, and the deathly scent of the droki overwhelmed his senses as they fought their way through the castle. This had to be a full pack. Not a small group of three. Or a lone drokos by a mountainside. An entire group of creatures only they could kill.

He twirled his sword and frowned at the Alkaanians' hesitant strikes. It would be useful if Eilon and Magna would return from the dead so they could destroy the droki. Not that such was possible. Rosealyn shouted in frustration, and he turned to see her pinned against a wall. A heartbeat later, her attacker slumped to the ground with Xannan's dagger protruding from his back. Xannan peered down at the body. Death was permanent. The two great dragons were dead; neither could help rid the world of droki now.

Xannan retrieved his dagger and followed Rosealyn through dilapidated hallways. A myriad of thoughts nagged at him as he used simple moves to incapacitate one soldier after another. Many of his past memories were vague, difficult to determine truth from reality.

A large group blocked their path, and Rosealyn resorted to commanding they relinquish their weapons and remain in place. As in the throne room, she released Orda'anians from her control. Several recognized Xannan and kept their distance.

By the time they reached the city streets, ten Orda'anian soldiers had joined them. They paused at the bend in the main street. Chaos ensued. Citizens and children cowered by buildings or in alleyways while men in white or gold attacked one another with whatever weapons they had nearby, including their own fists. Produce trampled by booted feet, coated with mud and blood, littered the street.

Shadows drifted as droki flew above, their skinny necks slithering to-and-fro. Xannan patted the pocket of his brown vest containing the crystal. He needed to speak with Arjun to learn how an ability so similar to the elf's had made its way into Nathaniel's hands.

"How much magic can one crystal store?" Rosealyn whispered, appearing as though she was trying to assess each individual fight at once. "If Nathaniel could cause this much sway—"

"I know of their existence but little of how the magic is stored." Xannan sheathed his dagger and pointed with his sword to where several droki had gathered. "Shall we?"

Rosealyn lifted her glowing white sword, holding it almost as if it were a foreign object in her hand rather than a weapon she had obviously trained to use. She met his gaze with a fierceness reminiscent of when she'd finally awoken in Magna's cave. "Don't hold back."

He smirked and twirled his sword; the roving gray clouds had turned almost completely white. "Glad to hear you've finally learned that lesson."

"No one attacks my home, my people, my country, without paying for their actions." Each step purposeful, the glow of her sword pulsing in time with his, she met the first Alkaanian who raised a sword against her by ducking beneath his swing and thrusting her weapon forward. She glanced over her shoulder and pulled her sword free. "I'm done talking."

Sword lifted to meet hers, Xannan's smirk turned into a full grin. Rosealyn's jaw set with determination as she touched the tip of her sword to his. The world became clearer, brighter. He listened, homing in on the rhythm of battle and eager to add his melody.

Rosealyn spun away from an encroaching quarterstaff, slicing the wooden stick in two and planting her foot on the man's chest to send him reeling into the gathering group. Xannan chuckled and rubbed at his chest, brows climbing as Rosealyn cleaved a path through the city street. He caught those who escaped her flurry of strikes, ending them as quickly as Rosealyn ended those in her way. One after another, the Alkaanians fell, fatally wounded by her glowing white sword.

As she'd said, she was done talking.

Wind buffeted beneath Synda's wings. Heat swelled in her neck, the orb of flame eager for its release. A pack of droki circled the city. Neck shimmying, Synda swallowed back a small bit of flame. Those beasts could hunt magic. But magic could control them in return.

All of it—from her birth to finding her flame—came back to magic. How it was used and by whom. Magic, no matter how large the well, no matter how vast the store, always had a cost. Harmony. Peace. That was the intention of the sword. Instead, what should have created unity had caused more strife. And now they had to contend with the inane droki.

Synda snorted steam and shimmied her head, sharing a singular image with the three dragons accompanying her. These three were the only ones with their flame who had chosen to listen, who had agreed to aid Rosealyn. Synda's ability was not like Magna's. She did not know how to offer the same level of protection. Though the power was there, the knowledge remained buried. Other, useful and necessary, knowledge surfaced.

Flame of a dragon destroyed droki more thoroughly than anything else, even the magic-imbued dragon-wrought swords. Three blades hummed in her vicinity. One amid several droki. The others. . . Synda scanned the scene below. She couldn't locate Rosealyn or Xannan, but she felt the pulse of the blades harboring Magna's and Eilon's magic. The fourth, which Synda believed should be with them, was a vague sensation at the corner of her mind, too far away to be of any use for the city far below.

A small voice sounded, almost a whisper. Similar to Celena's. Synda beat her wings languidly to hold herself in place. The whisper asked about Praesidio, the name both the dragons and elves had given the original blade before it split into two. As quick as it had sounded, it was gone. Most times when Celena communicated with her, Synda could at least determine in which direction her elven friend could be found. But the voice was too faint.

Molten flame coated her throat with heat. The droki swarmed the city. Synda held the heat at the base of her neck; she would need to conserve the flame to destroy the droki.

CHAPTER SIXTY-SEVEN

Jaw clenched, Rosealyn pulled her sword free of an Alkaanian and continued through the fray of gold-clad men attacking her soldiers, pressing toward the droki. Though she couldn't see him, Rosealyn imagined Charles was there, fighting alone against creatures which could cause death with a single scratch.

She grunted as her sword met another blade, slashing it to the side as she spun in close enough to elbow the man in the face. Bones cracked and his nose spurted blood. Rosealyn grimaced as she caught the dagger he'd dropped to hold his nose and used his weapon to stab him in the heart.

A roar sounded as another rushed at her, sword and dagger a flurry of motion. Rosealyn gritted her teeth, reminding herself to anticipate her opponent's moves. His slashing dagger split the skin of her forearm. Rosealyn hissed. The wound stung and pulsed with her racing heart. Overhead, flickering shadows blocked the sun's light. More Blazing droki.

Rosealyn acknowledged her fear of the beasts and forced her breaths to remain even. Fear, along with her coalescing anger, would make her careless. She needed to focus and defend. Gripping her sword tighter, Rosealyn became a whirlwind of movement, pressing her opponent back until he tripped on one of the many bodies covering the dirt street. She swiped her sword across his neck, forcing herself to watch as his lifeforce darkened the obnoxiously bright gold of the Alkaanian livery.

Men in simple white shirts approached, hands raised to indicate they meant no harm. Her gaze flickered from one to the next, recognizing soldiers she'd once sparred against.

"Take out the Alkaanians." Rosealyn pointed her glowing white sword at the Banner-Captain she remembered, Adrian. Words disappeared as she watched droplets of blood fall from her sword's edge. Swallowing, she lowered the sword to address the group. "Preston, take command of this group. Spread the news that Nathaniel is dead and the order that no one but me or Xannan"—Rosealyn jerked her head at Xannan who was retrieving his dagger from an Alkaanian's neck—"fight the droki. The dragon-like creatures. Go, and may the Blaze of our ancestors protect us."

The Orda'anians offered proper bows, and she quickened her pace toward the droki. Xannan remained close, which was comforting since he had a dragon-wrought blade, but also frustrating because her tenuous trust of him was faltering. She knew he had the crystal, and though he hadn't necessarily lied about it, Rosealyn worried what he might attempt to do with such an ability.

An overwhelming number of shouts sounded behind them. A quick glance back found more of her soldiers had arrived with Theo leading them. Soon, the Alkaanians occupying Vandyl would be no more than a memory. But that didn't solve the greater problem.

Their forward movement was halted when a drokos covered in flames fell in front of them. The creature writhed and screeched until Xannan decapitated it. Rosealyn's heart soared as she recognized the feathered and scaled white dragon swoop and twist in the sky.

"Synda's here," she breathed, watching Synda coat another drokos in her flame. Three more dragons—one a bold shimmering purple, another as bright as the obnoxious gold of the Alkaanian's armor, and the last reminiscent of the deepening orange as the sun set each night—weaved through the droki. Blasts of orange spewed from the dragons' mouths in quick succession.

Rosealyn returned her focus to the three droki they'd been approaching. One lay still while the other two craned their necks to-and-fro, snapping their jaws. Her chest clenched when she recognized Charles ducking and slashing amid those dripping maws. Rosealyn ran. Dark liquid streaked his sword, and his coat was a tattered mess. She swallowed, hoping his wounds were not from the droki.

A second drokos fell from the sky and landed atop a building. Rosealyn skidded to a halt, grateful Xannan remained nearby. "We have to get them away from the city. Before every building gets burned to the ground."

"So persuade them," Xannan grumbled at her side as he watched the sky above. Droki versus several dragons was a sight to behold.

Beads of sweat formed along Rosealyn's forehead as she focused on where Charles fought the beasts. His movements were languid, slower than she was accustomed to him moving with sword in hand. A young boy lay nearby, dead, with a blackened gash on one arm.

Rosealyn gulped down air. Think. Focus. Persuade them. She'd done so before. Not with the level of success she'd desired, but she knew it was possible.

Thoughts had worked with the droki, so she willed them to leave. To enter the air and flee the city. One obliged while the other swiped a clawed wing at Charles, coming much too close for comfort. Rosealyn grimaced and whispered through gritted teeth, "Get away from him."

Both droki lifted into the sky, but the release of building tension in her muscles was short-lived as several other droki surrounded her and Xannan. They'd scented her magic.

Xannan plunged his clouded sword into the nearest drokos's chest. Its wings spasmed once, and it collapsed—striking the heart did kill the beasts. Rosealyn turned to do the same only to encounter a pair of dark beady eyes as the drokos sniffed her. Dark liquid dripped from its sharp teeth, marring her simple blue dress. Rosealyn licked her lips and lifted her sword, but her arms froze. The drokos inhaled, and an odd hum entranced her. She felt dizzy, as though she were being pulled up by invisible strings. A weak thought formed, a desire for it to simply go away, which was granted when someone sliced through the drokos's neck.

"Rose?" That was Charles. Tired, a bit breathless, but he was upright and looking at her with those soft blue eyes that always looked so worried for her. "What's wrong?"

A shake of her head, Rosealyn worked to regain her bearings. More droki landed. Dragons attacked them overhead. The sword in her hand hummed, still warm with a pulsing glow. Clashes of weapons reverberated. Screams sounded as droki fell from the sky, smoldering and dying by the dragons' flame.

"Away from the city," she whispered, hoping that voicing the thoughts would help. "Follow me."

Rosealyn sprinted through the city streets, avoiding the dissipating fighting as best she could. Once outside the city proper, she continued until she was halfway to where they had camped the night before. Chest heaving, Rosealyn faced Vandyl. Charles and Xannan slowed as they came closer, but she concentrated on the sky.

Synda and the other dragons spewed bursts of orange flame that lit up a cloudless sky. Rosealyn willed the droki toward her. Breaths deep and even despite her racing heart, she flexed the hand gripping her sword. Its pulsing hum kept time with her heartbeat, matching the ebb and flow of Xannan's sword.

She counted as the beasts approached, shoulders tensing. Twelve. Twelve droki versus three dragon-wrought swords. And four dragons, Rosealyn reminded herself as Synda and her companions followed the droki.

Almost as one, the four dragons released swaths of flame and took out four of the droki. The beasts screeched their ear-splitting cries, and Rosealyn wondered if she should wish for them to be quiet. But she focused on pulling them away from the city. Vandyl had suffered too much.

"How did Nathaniel avoid these while using so much magic?" she murmured aloud as the remaining eight droki approached. Rosealyn's gaze flickered from dragon to dragon, pausing on Synda as the ever-present orange orb grew in intensity at the base of the white dragon's neck.

"We need to find the woman who gave him the crystal is my guess," Xannan said.

Rosealyn resisted the urge to turn away from the droki.

"Nathaniel had a magical crystal?" Charles's breaths were ragged, and he clutched his side. "That explains a bit."

Languid movements in combination with a weary voice made Rosealyn wonder what had prevented him from following through with their plan. Not that making said plan had mattered.

Synda's flame rekindled, taking out one more drokos as the remaining seven swooped down at Rosealyn. They sniffed the air, homing in on her as they slashed with clawed wings and snapped with dripping teeth. Rosealyn swiped back, slicing through dark, splotchy wings. She couldn't reach high enough to ram her sword through their hearts or slice their necks. One after another dove, sniffing at her before she could will them away.

The deep orange dragon regained its flame, spreading the swath so it hit two droki at once. Down to five. For a moment, Rosealyn considered persuading the droki to leave. But that would only allow them to return once the command wore off.

A flurry of claws and wings met three swords. Rosealyn stabbed the nearest drokos's chest with all her strength. Its dying screech was echoed by two others.

"Down to two," Rosealyn whispered and willed the creatures closer.

Heat from a dragon's flame emanated from above, close enough she swore it singed some of her hair. One left.

Fog encroached on the edges of her vision at the drokos's low emanating rumble. Rosealyn tried to blink or move. None of her limbs responded to her thoughts. Nor did her voice. Frozen in place, she tried to shout, but Charles pushed her aside. Sharp claws sliced into his flesh as Xannan hacked off the last drokos's head.

Rosealyn counted the dead drokos. Twelve corpses. Her throat clenched as she stared Charles's torn sleeve. Erratic breaths made her feel dizzy again, and she whipped her head about, fearful another drokos was scenting her. None were there. The droki which had attacked her home were all dead. She tried to lift her gaze to Charles's but was fixated on the broken, darkened skin of his arm visible through his gashed sleeve.

"You . . . you knocked me out of the way," Rosealyn said, heart rate spiking as Charles's sword tumbled out of his grip. He blinked and looked down at the blade.

"You weren't moving." Charles twisted his arm to study the wound, frowning. "It doesn't hurt."

"Yet." Rosealyn dropped her sword and grasped Charles's arm to inspect the wound. Several nicks marred his arms. Almost all were an angry red. Except one. Black lines spread from the cut. She froze, holding his hand in hers, gaze roaming up and down.

Breathe. She needed to breathe. And think. She could find a solution. Problems could be solved. Including this one. Her heart skipped a beat. They didn't know the fate of the three poisoned Jearnian soldiers.

Charles pulled her closer and her heart sank. His grip was weak. "I couldn't let them hurt you."

Throat dry, Rosealyn tried to swallow. "No," she whispered, placing her hand on Charles's chest. His heart beat rhythmically beneath her palm. "It's not too late." Vision blurring, she looked in his eyes and whispered, "I won't let you die."

"Not sure even your ability can counter that," Xannan said.

All she could do was glare at him and fight the urge to hit him for his nonchalant attitude. He held out her cleaned sword, and she snatched it from him and slammed it into the sheath at her side. Xannan picked up Charles's sword, cleaning it as he squinted at the city they'd prevented from being burned. "Think the fighting is over yet?"

"Hopefully." Rosealyn returned to inspecting Charles's wounds. Simple scratches should not create such fear.

He nudged her chin with his hand, lifting her gaze to his tense and tired smile. "You saved your home."

She grimaced in return. "It wasn't supposed to happen this way."

A soft thump on the ground made her shoulders tense, relaxing only once she'd realized Synda approached. The white dragon's companions maintained their flight path, orange orbs pulsating at the base of each dragon's neck. The swooshing sound of Synda's wings shrinking into her sides brought Rosealyn's attention to where the young white dragon sat on her haunches.

When Rosealyn's gaze met Synda's solid white eyes, she saw what Synda wanted to share. Two women.

"Celena and—" Rosealyn gasped, recognizing the woman she'd seen in a vision once before. She'd asked about her mother's safety and had seen this woman in response. Dark skin reminiscent of the woman who'd raised her. Hair the same auburn color as her own. Rosealyn's grip on Charles's hand tightened, but he offered no reassuring squeeze in return. After a wary glance at him, she turned back to Synda. "My . . . my birth mother?"

The vision dissipated into a blurred image of Christopher, Jacin, Moss, and Viola packing supplies. *But no Adela?*

"Help is coming?"

Synda sent a third image. Cities overrun, taken. Rosealyn clenched her jaw, head pulsating with pain the more cities Synda showed her.

"And needed." Rosealyn rested her hand on Synda's snout. "Thank you."

An appreciative rumble emanated from Synda as the dragon pressed her snout into Rosealyn's hand. "How soon?"

The rumble deepened into an almost growl, and Synda huffed a smoky breath. Rosealyn bit her lip, blinking away the brimming tears. "How far away is Christopher? Has he left Volante already? Did he actually create an antidote? Or is something else wrong? Can you not help Charles?"

The slew of questions elicited another growl, accompanied by a quick snapping of Synda's wings. Rosealyn frowned, wishing she could speak with the dragon as with another person. But such a wish would require magic. And magic, Rosealyn decided, brought chaos and despair. It was not beautiful, as her birth mother claimed in that letter. No, magic was destructive.

A rush of warm air coating Rosealyn's head and shoulders was followed by another image. A visualization of Vandyl from above. Droki approached but couldn't come closer than where they currently stood.

"Protection?" Rosealyn whispered. "You can block them from entering certain spaces?"

A flurry of wind was Rosealyn's answer as Synda joined the three dragons in the sky. Rosealyn followed Synda's pristine white form and watched the four circle the city once. Then, with a blink, they disappeared.

Rosealyn turned back to Charles. He wavered but remained standing. As she wrapped an arm around his waist, she whispered, "We'll find a solution. We have to."

His head lolled in what she thought was a nod. When he leaned into her grip, Rosealyn grimaced. It would be a long trek back to the castle, where she hoped the castle physician could keep Charles alive until Christopher arrived.

CHAPTER SIXTY-EIGHT

Rosealyn's heart beat faster with each step. Too soon, she had to insist on Xannan's help to support Charles. Weak and weary. Movements too slow. Sweat beaded her brow, both from the effort and the nerves. A nagging thought floated to the surface, wondering what life would be like without him. Rosealyn swallowed, pushing the thought aside. Help was coming. That had to be why Synda had shown her an image of Christopher preparing to travel.

By the time they reached the city streets, the fighting was over. Rosealyn recognized the voices barking commands. Adrian, Preston, Theo. A slew of bodies lined their path to the castle, making it more difficult to maneuver. Even knowing these soldiers had tried to claim her home, Rosealyn felt a pang of guilt. She wasn't sure how many had met their end by her hand. *Protect. Not harm. Why does it seem impossible to do both at the same time?*

When they arrived at the gates, Theo bowed and moved as though to replace her in supporting Charles. Rosealyn shook her head, loose hair lashing her cheeks. She refused to let him go.

"Tell Doctor Alvin to bring anything he has which can provide an antidote to poison."

"Poison?" Theo's brows lifted. "Alkaanians do not poison their weapons as Hoclians do, Rosealyn."

"I know that." She shifted her grip on Charles's waist and risked a glance up. If it weren't for how much of his weight he had relinquished to others, Rosealyn would have thought he was simply tired. "He was wounded by a drokos. Because he pushed me out of the way."

"There was a young soldier." Charles's words were slurred. "He had a . . . a gash down his arm. You should—" Charles swayed. "Others were—"

"Charles, stop." Rosealyn waited for him to look at her, wincing as his head drooped. "Worry about yourself for once. Understood?"

Charles tipped forward, stopped by Xannan's firm grip.

"Uncle Theo, which of the priests survived to confirm me as queen?"

Theo grimaced and shook his head.

"No argument then," Rosealyn said. "Clean the city streets, take care of the wounded. Proper burials for the dead. And then we regroup and take back each city Nathaniel tried to claim."

"Don't forget about Jordan." Charles tried to stand to his full height and step forward on his own, only for her and Xannan to have to catch Charles before he collapsed.

"I know it's not a deep gash, but he's about to pass out, and I don't want to be tasked with carrying him," Xannan said. It looked so odd, seeing him help and not seeing Charles glare at the man.

Theo glanced between each of them again. "Infirmary or private rooms?"

"My—" She frowned. The rooms she had grown up in had been lost to Eilon's flames. "Whatever room has a bed and is close."

One hand on her knee, the other flat on the ground, Catarina infused the land with life. Browned blades of grass transitioned into green, spreading from where her hand rested. Nearby, Naomi held the reins to their horses. Once the growth took hold and spread as far as

Catarina could provide, she pressed against her knee and stood. Each attempt wore on her more than the last. She had been using her ability more than ever in the past. Before, its use was less purposeful. More for enjoyment. An outlet, really.

Catarina watched the land revitalize. No matter how many times she encouraged plants to grow anew, the process fascinated her. Pesky dandelions sprouted amid the field of grass, growing until their bold yellow matched that of the sun high above. After brushing the dirt from her palms, Catarina mounted and nudged the mare into a slow clopping walk. Thankfully with no squelching mud today.

Stops only occurred when the land cried out for aid. Many areas appeared to be healing on their own, utilizing the consistent barrage of rain. The multiple pauses made their journey to Vandyl slow and arduous. Rainstorms provided the perfect opportunity to encourage the land in its rebirth. With the wet season, Catarina didn't have to lend as much of her magic. In general, encouraging plants to live invigorated her.

But a haze lingered. She'd failed her sister. Roseanne should be traveling at her side. Not Naomi. Though it was thanks to Naomi's council she'd made the decision to head to Vandyl. Despite the last message Catarina had received claiming her daughter was in Jearnia, Naomi had offered a logical response: better to wait for Jaida than go traipsing around the continent.

A part of her wanted to roam the land. To forget about the past and lose herself in healing the one thing she could. The emptiness inside her couldn't be healed. All of her family, except for Jaida, was gone. Her throat constricted, wondering if Jaida would welcome her presence or shun it.

Naomi's sudden transition to a trot pulled Catarina from her daze. The elf-woman waved for Catarina to follow suit. Based on the maps she'd studied, and her memory, they should be able to see Vandyl soon.

When they crested the next small hill, Catarina almost halted her mare. The dragonstone Phillippe had adored was gone, replaced with simple gray brick. Buildings sprawled from either side of the castle, blending together with monotonous colors. The vibrant city she remembered strolling through each time Phillippe wanted to escape the confines of the castle was no more.

A strange stench made her cough, and her glaze flickered over what should have been a meadow. Black scraggly creatures littered the ground, heads sliced from their necks. Catarina's mare pranced, huffing and snorting. She tugged against the reins and blocked her nose with her arm.

"What are those?" Catarina asked.

"I thought droki went extinct." Words short and clipped, Naomi's eyes churned the deepest shade of red Catarina had ever seen. "They hunt magic and can only be permanently killed by a dragon-wrought sword or a dragon's flame. But their blood is poisonous. As is any skin-piercing wound they deliver. So keep your distance." Naomi clucked her tongue and flowed with her mare's movements.

Catarina searched blindly for her flask of water, taking a long and slow drink. Even with the water, her mouth was dry. Based on the smell, Catarina imagined they'd been dead for at least a day. Maybe longer. The closer they came to the city streets, the more Catarina's stomach tumbled over itself. Bodies lay in pools of blood. Her brows furrowed, and she held a fist to her mouth, wondering if she'd find Jaida's lifeless body as well.

CHAPTER SIXTY-NINE

The room's colors were wrong. Gone were the alternating black and white tapestries which once graced each room. Same with the running lengths of carpet. All had been replaced with that obnoxious gold Rosealyn would forever despise. Three days had passed since she'd let Theo kill Nathaniel and since Charles had been wounded.

Rosealyn leaned forward in her seat and rested a hand on his chest. Slow breaths. Slow heartbeat. He appeared peaceful in sleep, minus the paling of his already light skin. Alvin had applied every antidote in his possession. None kept Charles awake, but at least they had kept him from dying.

She brushed a lock of brown hair from his forehead, smiling softly at the slight curl, evidence he hadn't cut it. She wished his eyes would open. Then silently cursed herself for the thought. She'd tried that already. Tried to will him to stay awake. To live. But Xannan was right. Her patha vita had limitations.

Persuasion. Forcing others against their will. That was all her magic could do. Perhaps there was more. Maybe she could have aided those wounded by simple swords and daggers. All the Gift shared was that clawing desperation, an unfillable ache spreading through her core.

As far as she knew, when it came to whether one would live or die, she had no sway. Rosealyn leaned closer and, with all the conviction and strength she could muster, said, "Don't you dare die." Then softer, "Please wake up."

Same as the previous hour. And the hour before that. No reaction.

Rosealyn stared at the gray stone, blinking quickly in hope her vision would stop blurring. She didn't look away when the door opened.

"No change?"

She flinched and sat back in her seat. "I'm not in the talking mood, Xannan."

"I figured that much." No footsteps meant he stayed near the door while she kept her focus on Charles. "As requested, I'm informing you that Theo and the Banner-Captains are waiting. Still."

A slow inhale, an even slower exhale. "I'm aware." Rosealyn dug her elbows into her knees, pressing the heels of her palms against her forehead. She turned to Xannan, whispering, "I don't want to leave Charles alone."

"But you are needed." Xannan nodded at the door. "I could stay here. Depending on how far you choose to go today."

Rosealyn huffed a soft grunt. "Not happening."

Xannan shrugged. "I'm not so cruel I'd kill someone who is already dying."

A muscle in her jaw ticked in an annoying rhythm. "I'll find the proper antidote."

"Perhaps."

Rosealyn ground her teeth and stood. "Just because one wasn't found to aid your comrades doesn't mean I won't find one in time for Charles." She reached down to squeeze Charles's too limp hand, desperate for him to return the action. Nothing. No flutter of his eyelids nor a hitch in his breath.

"Demetri," she called and waited for the young soldier to enter. His youthful innocence reminded her of simpler days until he bowed low with fist to heart. "No one but me or Doctor Alvin comes into this room. Understood?"

"Yes, Your Majesty." A fluid motion brought Demetri back to standing, and he resumed his post outside the door.

Arms crossed, Rosealyn took in Charles's appearance, wishing she could lose herself in his caring blue eyes. She took a deep shuddering breath. She wanted to say something important and memorable but couldn't. Not when the giant lump threatened to form again.

Rosealyn peeked beneath the bandage covering the damning wound, lips tightening at how far the black webbing had spread along his arm. She replaced the bandage and resituated the blanket lying on top of him. She could do no more for him now. Not until Christopher arrived, if he was truly coming. Or, she supposed, her birth mother. Or anyone who could help someone recover from the deadly poison given by a simple scratch.

Since Charles had remained hopeful when his men faced the same fate, she could do the same. Another shaky breath, she reminded herself to be the strong leader Charles had shown her how to be.

After adding a log to the fire, she approached the door and asked, "Council room?"

Xannan nodded, and she took one more look at Charles and passed through the door Xannan held open. As they walked through unfamiliar hallways, she shoved down the worry, the despair, and allowed her anger to coalesce. Anger at Jordan for massacring an entire city. Anger at Nathaniel for thinking he could ever take what was hers. Anger on behalf of all those who had lost their lives because of another's personal vendetta.

Brimming like a pot about to boil over the edges, Rosealyn entered the council room where Banner-Captains Preston and Adrian studied a series of maps. They offered the proper bow when she entered and spread out the dozens of maps until the large table which consumed most of the room was barely visible. The vast majority were city maps, with one of Orda'an in its entirety and another of the continent as a whole.

Rosealyn surveyed the names of the city maps. Demir, Verbera, Asyir, Lobelia, even Pasea and Cantadad. On the map of Orda'an, an X had been drawn through Lycene, and Rosealyn's heart sank at two more Xs through the cities of Alimar and Rumaya. She rifled through the maps. "Where's Uncle Theo?"

"Two women who aided the injured have asked to speak with you, my Queen." Banner-Captain Preston set his cup down with a tense sigh. "Duke Theo thought it best he spoke with them first."

"Logical," Rosealyn murmured as she shifted the maps around, as though moving the simple pieces of paper would have any impact. "These are the cities which remain under siege?"

Adrian tapped the maps of Demir and Asyir. "These two fought back according to last reports. We've had no word from any other city. Not all are labeled on the maps, and based on conversations with the imprisoned Alkaanians, Nathaniel's orders for his soldiers were to take any city large enough to house a hundred of their men. We can send more scouts to determine who needs aid, Your Majesty."

"The longer we wait, the more likely there is to be death and destruction." Rosealyn's gaze flickered from one map to the next, wondering how to decide which should receive aid first, especially considering what little remained of the Orda'anian army at Vandyl. Her vision stilled on the markings blotting out three cities. "If we were to create ten battalions, how many men could we spare for each and not leave Vandyl defenseless?"

"Maximum of twenty," Preston said. "That would leave at least fifty men here, Your Majesty."

"That will have to suffice." Rosealyn traced lines from Vandyl's marker on the map, explaining the paths each battalion should take. A brief argument arose when she mentioned traveling with half rations.

The few wares being sold in Vandyl's streets had been destroyed. With a reminder that each battalion could hunt game during their travels, Preston agreed, only to start a second argument about financing each battalion. A stream of curses flew through her mind. Her mother had given the money away to. . .

"Where did you put the money my mother gave you, Xannan?"

He assumed that frustrating lackadaisical stance. "With the rest. Wonder if it melted."

Rosealyn scowled at him and motioned for Adrian and Preston to put her plans into action.

"A simple yet hopefully effective plan." Xannan pulled a small knife to dig the caked blood from underneath his nails. "What about the issue of who succeeds Nathaniel? Does Jordan remain tied up in Lycene? You have more to do than liberate Orda'anian cities."

"One problem at a time." Rosealyn shifted the maps, chewing on her bottom lip, sparing no more than a quick glance up when the door opened, wishing she could make Charles wake. She crossed her arms, tapping a finger against her elbow. Even though they hadn't agreed on strategy, Rosealyn wanted to discuss what to do next with Charles. By presenting his thoughts, he could help her approach events from a different angle.

When the newest arrivals didn't speak, Rosealyn sighed and lifted her head only for her breath to catch in her throat. She couldn't stop staring at the woman she'd once seen in a vision. As her uncle said something that didn't register, Rosealyn scrutinized the woman, wondering if she'd dozed off. It had been days since she'd had proper rest, so Rosealyn scrubbed her eyes and blinked. Nothing changed. The woman with skin a few shades darker than her own gripped her dress-skirts, glancing between Rosealyn and her uncle.

"They healed many who would otherwise have died." Theo cleared his throat.

Rosealyn barely acknowledged the presence of the one she assumed to be Celena, as that was the only elf-woman who would have an interest in coming to see her.

Rosealyn couldn't keep staring at the woman who had to be her birth mother, so she met Theo's apologetic green-eyed gaze as he explained, "I didn't think it was possible when I first noticed her. Years can change one's appearance, but this is Catarina, younger sister to Queen Roseanne."

Theo paused, brows furrowing when Rosealyn made no movement except to remind her lungs to gulp air. He scratched at the trimmed blond beard which covered only his chin. "Phillippe's decisions make more sense now."

Since Rosealyn didn't want to seem like she'd forgotten how to breathe, she nodded and held Theo's gaze.

He tilted his head and raised a brow. "It is your choice if you wish to speak—"

"Why now?" Rosealyn blurted out. "You had no interest in being around twenty years ago, so what changed?"

Catarina stepped back, visibly blanching. "I—" She lowered her chin and smoothed her skirts with trembling hands, shoulders falling.

"Why are you here?" Rosealyn gathered the maps strewn about the table and brandished them. "In case you didn't know, I have a few problems to solve." She tossed the maps back on the table and gripped the edge. "Most of them are my own fault."

Behind her, Xannan grunted in agreement, and she shot him a glare. He shrugged. "Much is your fault, you're right."

Rosealyn clenched her jaw. "And yours."

He sighed and nodded at Catarina. "Your mother?"

"Birth mother," Rosealyn amended. "I have a letter and a vision Magna shared when I asked her if my mother was alive." She lifted from the table and crossed her arms.

Theo's head shifted back and forth. "I'll see if Preston or Adrian need help."

Rosealyn gave him a curt nod and turned her attention to Catarina. Her birth mother hesitated but stood taller and stepped closer.

Rosealyn raised her hand. "You didn't answer my question."

"Based on what I've heard, Roseanne would be proud of you." Catarina wiped a tear away with her knuckle.

"Doubtful," Rosealyn scoffed. She motioned at the empty table, wondering if sitting would help calm the jumble of angry jitters bouncing over her skin. While Catarina and the elf sat, Rosealyn remained standing and gripped the back of a chair. "Moth— She hates when I'm determined to see something through. For as long as I can remember, she has fought my every decision."

When Catarina looked her in the eye, Rosealyn looked away. Anger had seemed the most appropriate response at first, but she wasn't sure how she wanted to feel in this moment. A part of her wanted to be elated she was reuniting with her birth mother while another challenged Catarina's intentions. Rosealyn had thought of so many questions to ask in this moment, so many answers she desperately wanted. Faced with the woman who could provide them, however, Rosealyn feared what truths might come to light.

Awkward silence lingered and grew, broken when Xannan pulled out a chair and plopped down. "How did you heal the injured? Salves? Potions?" He glanced at Rosealyn and back at her birth mother. "Magic?"

Rosealyn spoke through clenched teeth. "Didn't I ask you to leave, Xannan?"

He titled his head and smirked. "No."

"Well, leave. Now." Rosealyn jerked her head at the door.

"If they have magic—"

"I would prefer to speak with my birth mother alone." Rosealyn craned her head toward the door again. "Go."

"Naomi, I believe that means you should leave as well," came Catarina's soft voice.

Rosealyn scrunched her face as more questions piled on top of the dozens she already had. The name sounded vaguely familiar, but Rosealyn couldn't quite place it and assumed Celena must have mentioned it in passing. This elf shared Celena's red-irised eyes and short white hair, but Naomi looked like a twig about to break compared to Celena's solid stature.

"I'll return to the infirmary." Naomi turned to Rosealyn and dipped her chin. "A pleasure to meet you."

Rosealyn's lips tightened as she watched Naomi glide out of the room. Xannan followed, and she hoped the man didn't venture too far away. She focused on the door handle, settling on what would be the least shocking question. "Did you see Moth— my, um, Blazes." She tugged on her lower lip and gripped the chair until the grain of wood rubbed against her palms. "Sorry. I'm not sure how to address you or her now."

Her birth mother offered an apologetic smile and whispered, "It will feel odd, I suppose, but call me Catarina."

Rosealyn forced herself to release the chair and contemplated pacing. Since she didn't have enough space, she settled with sifting through the maps as a distraction. "Did you see Mother?"

The pause lasted long enough that Rosealyn eventually lifted her focus from the maps to her birth mother. Catarina sniffled and wiped at her cheeks, whispering, "She's gone."

Rosealyn's hand froze in its trailing of a line through the Orda'anian fields, feeling like she'd been stabbed again. That question should have been safe. A simple acknowledgment that her mother was alive and well, resting in Tenoa far away from the dangers encroaching upon Orda'an.

"Gone?" Rosealyn squeezed her eyes shut and recalled what Ramon had said at the summit. "Ramon killed her?"

"No," Catarina said in a dejected tone that made Rosealyn open her eyes to appraise her birth mother's countenance. "Roseanne died because—" She shook her head, sniffling. "I tried to help her. Convince her that one's story could be changed. But Roseanne gave up on living. She refused to eat." Catarina swallowed and held a hand against her chest. "Roseanne believed she was nothing."

Rosealyn slumped into the chair. Her shoulders slouched, her chest hollowed, and her mouth went dry. "How could—" She tried to wet her lips. Had this been the cause of that feeling of loss nagging at her? "I— Blazes. I don't know what to say." Rosealyn buried her face in her hands, elbows crinkling the maps. "I'm not sure what I'm supposed to think right now."

Rosealyn folded her arms on the table. The nearest map of Orda'an showed the northernmost tip of Tenoa, a thick black dot marking its capital of Delphi. She traced the marker. "Where did you bury her?"

"By our parents." Catarina reached across the table, withdrawing her arm when Rosealyn leaned away. "I'm sorry I do not bring better tidings."

Rosealyn nodded and awkward silence consumed the room. Minutes passed. As soon as one thought formed, another crashed into it. She wanted Charles to wake and to know her citizens were safe. Add to those overwhelming thoughts the uncertainty of how Hoclia and Alkaan would react to their monarchs being absent for so long, and Rosealyn wasn't sure she had the capacity for any new information.

"I'll understand if you ask me to leave," Catarina said, head slumping forward.

Rosealyn inhaled, pulled her shoulders back, and rested her clasped hands atop the crinkled maps. "I want answers." She squeezed her fingers together, pushing down the anger which threatened a torrent of tears. "Ever since I read the letter you left with Arjun, I've debated which questions to ask and which to leave to my imagination." Rosealyn pressed her lips together and mentally recited one of the letter's last lines. Reminding herself to maintain an even-tempered tone, Rosealyn lifted her chin. "It certainly wasn't safe to look for me, which means you believe it was necessary." She paused and contemplated if she should use her ability to ensure she got the answers she so desperately craved but dismissed the idea. "Why?"

Catarina's jaw tensed. "I could no longer resist the land calling for aid." She frowned, intertwined her hands, and spoke to the table. "And for selfish reasons. I wanted to meet you." Catarina lowered her hands to her lap. "Naomi insisted as well. It's thanks to the magic stored in crystals that many of your wounded soldiers live."

Rosealyn shifted, wincing when her sword's hilt dug into her side. "Healing magic?"

Catarina nodded, and Rosealyn's heartbeat quickened at the thought that this elf whose name tickled her memory could heal Charles. If Rosealyn's ability could work to cure him of the poison and allow him to wake, it would have already. But this was magic designed specifically to heal. The once shriveling sliver of hope grew.

CHAPTER SEVENTY

Xannan nodded at a pair of servants who whispered cautiously to one another after he passed. Sighing, he continued toward his room. He wasn't sure which made him feel more accomplished: defeating Eilon or reclaiming their country. He paused in the middle of a barren stone hallway and frowned. Their country? Or her country?

He had been no more than a tool, a weapon for her to use and bring her victory. An ache in his chest increased alongside the roaring in his ears. His family, his life, no longer existed. Others might consider his longevity through Eilon a blessing. He did not.

His room wasn't much further, close to where Rosealyn had barely moved from Charles's side. Fancy trick from the elf-woman, halting the spread of the poison until the younger Jearnian prince arrived. Veins of black had been crawling up and down Charles's arm. Each new line of that web-like pattern had made Rosealyn more desperate, more persistent that she would find a way to keep the man alive. It was illogical that an elf holding a crystal could stop that spread. If he hadn't seen it himself, Xannan might not have believed it possible.

Xannan shrugged each shoulder, wishing the elves had been able to halt that poison during his own past. Vague memories surfaced of the deaths he'd witnessed. Perhaps, since Naomi knew how to properly use the magic in the crystals, she could make sense of their swords. But she hadn't been there when the blade was cleaved in two. Those who were had provided what they knew. However the connection could be broken had to remain in Gailin's journals. After rifling through the first of Gailin's journals, Xannan was more annoyed and frustrated than anything. Simple retellings of his brother's daily life. Nothing more.

Xannan wished he could get away from the castle and its stares and whispers. Leave and never return would be better. He had little reason to remain. Aside from that cursed connection. Though the swords allowed them to venture further away the more they used the magic together, sometimes that tug reappeared. Or maybe he noticed the sensation more when exhausted. Often the aftermath of battle was more tiresome than the fighting itself.

He tapped the door closed with his boot and conducted a quick yet thorough search. His room had the simplest necessities. Bed, dressers, bathing chambers, closet, sitting area with a simmering fire. A change of clothes—proper current Orda'anian fashion he had no desire to wear—rested on the bed. He set his sword near the headboard and lay on the bed.

Hands beneath his head, ankles crossed, he stared at the ceiling with nothing to do but think about Rosealyn's first major win. In a strange way, he was proud of the young queen. Many Alkaanian soldiers now resided in the dungeons. The remainder lay dead in the streets, soon to be gathered for a proper burial. That was her decision. Recognition that soldiers followed orders. Soon, she claimed, she would speak with those who lived. He hated to admit it, but even without her patha vita, Rosealyn could use words to achieve her goals. Xannan maintained his belief in taking what he wished by force. When he could, at least.

He shifted, wondering if Orda'an would have fallen to others had he assumed the throne instead of Gailin. A disagreement between Gailin and Edmund, one of his brother's friends, had led to civil war before Jearnia's creation. According to the histories he'd managed to read, at least. But Xannan couldn't stop himself from wondering how the world would be different if he hadn't been trapped by Eilon. What would have become of the relationships between Orda'an and the other countries of Ebios? Or with countries across those tumultuous seas he missed traveling?

Or did it matter anymore? He supposed it initially came as a shock, but he did care. As much as he wished his life had been different, he remained a part of the LeNoir legacy. No reason he shouldn't. Even delegated to the shadows, to the outskirts of most conversations until he butted in, he had a role in both the country's future and its past. His desire to be rid of the responsibility that came with leadership warred with the inclination to make sure Orda'an thrived.

His role in his country's future, Xannan realized, would need to balance his role in its past. Jaw clenched, he mentally berated himself. Not his country. He rested an arm over his head, blocking out what little light entered the room through two small windows.

Any moments Xannan had alone, he searched for the truth of his past. Many memories made him cringe, reminding him how being forced to forget was sometimes a welcome reprieve. Each time he allowed himself to revisit the past, he wished it were possible for time to reverse. One more real moment, not a recreation in his mind. Real. Something he could reach out and touch.

A new nightly routine developed once the days of watching Rosealyn and Charles grow closer began to be too much. Every night, the process became easier to begin while becoming more difficult to slip away into proper dreams. That night would be no different. Besides, he needed the reminder. Words spoken by the woman he loved to calm him.

Prone on the bed, all it took was a single breath, and Anna lay on her side next to him. She wore a tense smile, the one which had always graced her features after he returned home from winning a skirmish.

One hand propped her head up while the other rested on his chest. He knew it wasn't really there, but he relished the simple weight of it.

Delicate, perfect in more ways than he had ever told her. Black hair spilled over her shoulder, matching the dark nightgown that perfectly contrasted with her pale skin.

"Another victory," she murmured as her hand trailed along his chest. He nodded, meeting her somewhat accusatory gaze.

"More dead to protect our young country?" Her hand paused and pressed against him. Pressure. He could feel that pressure. Or was that mere memory?

"That is typical to achieve victory." Xannan wrapped his hand around hers. He couldn't feel her, though he couldn't close his hand all the way. It hurt him how real she looked, knowing soon he would have to return to his reality.

"Not even a scratch on you. This time." She whispered the last and brushed his cheek with a soft kiss.

His skin tingled while his grip on her hand tightened. He dared not close his eyes, for when he opened them, he was positive Anna would once again disappear. He remembered this conversation all too well. It was the last time he'd seen her alive, and the thought only opened the widening cavern inside.

"I learned my lesson. None will ever get that close to cutting me with a weapon again."

"Because soon these battles will be over. Orda'an will stand on its own. We have the elves on our side. And, if your mother and I can find it, we'll have another bargaining chip to convince everyone to get along. A way to help those understand magic better."

"I wonder how Gailin feels about this trip."

She sighed and traced the muscles of his abdomen. "Either positive or negative, he's always so cautious. Makes him annoying to be around sometimes. Born the same day, yet you two are less alike than the sun and the moon."

Xannan laughed at the accurate comparison. "And am I the sun or the moon?"

Anna's lips twisted into something that was neither a smile nor a frown, and she became pensive for a moment. "The sun." She shifted a strand of his blond hair. The twist of her lips turned into a perfect smile. "Bold, sometimes brazen, but never afraid to let your light shine for all to see."

In reality, he'd kissed her after she'd said that. Long and soft until words were a distant memory. Now? He wished he hadn't heard that because his light would always be dull without her.

Anna's figure shimmered. This evening, she'd been more real than ever before. A knock sounded somewhere in reality. He sighed, wondering what Rosealyn might want. No one else would seek him out, so he decided to ignore it.

Pressure increased on his chest. The imprint of Anna's hand. That obnoxious knock again. Short and crisp. Not quite the same as Rosealyn. Her style was more knock once and barge in without waiting for an answer. Whoever this was had knocked twice, but he had no desire to relinquish hold of this moment. All of him ached for one more second of Anna by his side, of her hand in his, of her lips on his.

Xannan turned toward Anna, ignoring the sound of a third knock, and reached for her. Another shimmer, like the flickering of a torch amid darkness, and Anna faded away. It made no sense. How could he feel the pressure of her touching him but not be able to do the same himself?

Agonizing emptiness. At the fourth knock, he pounded his fist on the bed and prowled to the door, flinging it open.

"I had a feeling it was you using that magic." Naomi entered the room, scanning it rapturously. "Where are they?"

"Where are what?" Xannan crossed his arms and leaned against the door frame.

"Your creations. Or did you not just breathe life into something no longer living?"

CHAPTER SEVENTY-ONE

Gailin's Journal-Annotated by Rosealyn

The future is curious. Uncertain and yet I have a sense of conclusion. An ending, if you will. I shared with my son what I have seen and have encouraged him to do the same before he passes on [*Did no one tell Father? Or does Uncle Theo know?*]. The images pressed upon me, a potential future I dare not write down lest it become a reality.

Instead, I will leave the world with this final message. Magic surrounds us. It has been within me and around me even before we met in Magna's cave. Such a blessing, really, that none of my children seem to have inherited any type of magical ability. While I wish my own Gift would leave this land with me, I know it will not. Attached to my bloodline is this Gift and this sword. I imagine the same will occur with Xannan's bloodline. Perhaps he found a place to call home and live a quiet life. But a simple abode would not suffice for him. No, he ~~is~~ was always a man of action.

Wherever Xannan may be, I have no inclination. No sense. No wonderment of direction. It's not the same as how I feel for those I've lost [*Eilon disguised him that well?*]. When I think of Xannan, there is an emptiness. Not sadness, not curiosity. Empty. I can only come to the conclusion that magic is to blame. Why someone would hide him with magic, I dare not guess. But I fear what it means to believe Xannan isn't dead. I fear what it means that my sword has not hummed in search of its other half. I fear what the future holds when Xannan realizes the power he possesses. Not only in his sword but in his own ability. [*So what can he do, and why should I fear it?*]

ACKNOWLEDGMENTS

I'm not sure which is harder, writing the book or writing the acknowledgments. A lot goes into the creation of the book. Family supporting you, friends encouraging you, sharing your writing with other writers in order to gain feedback and make the story the best it can be. Eventually, all of those pieces collide into, what every author hopes, is a cohesive product their reader will enjoy.

All that to say, I am forever grateful to all of those who have made it this far in my writing journey with me.

To my family and friends, thank you for being supportive of this process and for not giving me strange looks and walking away when I'd ask random questions about my characters or potential events in the story.

To my alpha and beta readers, thank you for helping me make A Fractured Legacy what it is now. Several scenes would not exist if not for your encouragment and suggestions.

To my readers, thank you for reading. If you haven't already, I encourage you to leave a review on your website of choice. Not only for my book, but for every book you read. It helps other potential readers decide if this will be the book for them!

Next to all those who work behind the scenes of more than just my book. To my editor, Karen Robinson, who truly captures the heart of my story and makes it the best it can be. To my cover design artist, Stefanie Saw, thank you for these amazing designs. I'm stoked to share the naked hardbacks you created as well and am eager to see all three of this trilogy's covers side by side.

Lastly, to my fellow writers, don't be afraid to keep creating. You never know who is waiting for your story!

About the Author

Cristen J. Faulkenberry is a fantasy author, avid reader, and high school English teacher. She's spent many evenings with her nose stuck in a book, and almost as many at the computer. Cristen currently lives in Northwest Missouri with her husband and young son.

Find her on Instagram or Facebook with the username @dragonheartbookworm. You can also check out her website where you can be the first to learn about her newest release. http://www.dragonnookpublishingllc.com.